BLACK HEART RETALIATION

KRISTY MORGAN

To order additional copies of this book, contact:
Bookwhip
1-855-339-3589
https://www.bookwhip.com

DEDICATION

This book is dedicated to my mother, Judy Threlkeld. Thank you so much for all of the times that you have believed in me; for the times that you have refused to let me give up. Thank you for being a willing ear. Your strength has always been a source of beauty. The way that you persevere when others would have stopped and said no more. So many people owe you for doing what they could not do... you stepped up, and took care of those who could not take care of themselves; caring not the cost to you: mentally, physically, or otherwise. You are a hero. you are set apart. You have a special place in Heaven my beautiful mother, best friend, and champion. I will love you always, and forever.

ACKNOWLEDGEMENTS

I would like to thank God, my heavenly Father for all of the sacrifices He has made in order to give me life more abundant. I thank Him for my accomplishments, for without Him there would be none. I thank Him, not only for what He has done, but what He does every day, and for the things that are on the horizon of my future.

I would like to thank my wonderful husband, and best friend, James Morgan. I could not have handpicked someone that would have fit me better than you. You are always there, working hard to ensure my dreams come true. Thank you my darling for listening, for guiding me and for pushing me to be my best. I will love you forever and beyond.

I would like to thank my amazing mother, who doubles as my very best friend, Judy Threlkeld. You have pushed me to move forward no matter how many times I felt I could not. I am so thankful that God lines us up perfectly, with those who can both nurture us, and keep us on the path, He has set before us. You are an editor, confidant and mentor. I love you sweet lady.

I would like to thank my children for understanding all that goes into bringing one's vision to life. Thank you for your patience. Thank you for moving forward in life, putting one foot in front of the other and finding the people that God has so obviously prepared for you all. I love you Jesse, James, Jessica, and Rebecca. . . I will love you always. You are all now and will forever be my precious babies.

I would like to thank my marvelous editing team, Mellissa Royster, my very best friend and Paris Ruddock, my niece. Without their wonderful works, "The dream team girls" and their wonderful incite, as to where the comma goes and where it doesn't go, I would have been thoroughly, lost. The pages full of red ink; the question marks that meant huh, what exactly do you mean? It all came together to make this book a possibility. I love you both. You have meant, as much or more, to this endeavor as anyone, but God, Himself! I am so thankful for you both. I will hold on to you both like life itself depends on it!

I would like to thank my co-worker, Clay Cook for all of the ideas that he has so graciously given through Black Heart Revenge and Black Heart Retaliation. Again, I am blown away with God's ability to line us up with those who can both nurture and keep us on our path. Thank you for all the research, for allowing me to pick your brain and for just being a great guy who loves God and his beautiful family.

I would like to thank my friend and co-worker, Ashley Torbert for all the times that she has spent being in my corner. I thank you for listening to me and for reminding me to get back to the drawing board. I thank you for the times that you do not let up; the times that you have asked me, "Did you work on your book this weekend?" It is those times, believe it or not, that have helped to keep me accountable. I love you, girl. I thank God for your presence in my life. You are awesome!

I would like to thank my co-worker, and friend, Angela Simon. I thank you for all of the prayers. I thank you for being my spiritual mother and mentor in a dark place where it was so hard to be the light. I thank you for the times that you reminded me that we were set a part to be picked on; for it is those times that you reminded me that I am no better than my Lord and Savior, Jesus Christ. I love you and I am eternally grateful that you are a part of my world.

I would like to thank my co-worker, Mr. Ed for his wonderful insights on the book. He gave me a lot of great ideas.

C H A P T E R

1

Bam....! Bam....! Bam....! Her pulse roared in her ears, like the incessant beating of a drum. Jordan struggled to push her tiny, four year old body, as far back into her closet as possible. One by one she placed her shoes on the other side of her. She scrambled to grab and restack them as they fell. She was trying to build a fort; anything that she could hide behind.

The taunting screams of her mother, begging and pleading for her father to stop hitting her, warred within Jordan's ears. Her tiny hands sprang to her ears, pressing hard against the sides of her head in an attempt to muffle the sounds. Rocking back and forth, while holding her ears, she started to scoot her bottom across the closet floor. She pressed her head back into the paneled wall, as her terror-stricken eyes, searched the darkness for any sign of her father's approach. Her mother's screams dulled into shuttering whimpers.

Jordan strained against the darkness, harder now, trying to see or hear anything. Terrified to move, she waited for her father to enter the room.

"Please. Please. Please", she silently begged. Hoping with all her might that he would not come and at the same time, she was filled with shame: the shame of hoping her father would be too tired from beating her mommy to come after her. Why couldn't she be brave? Her tiny mind grasped the errant thought and then it was gone, as she was brought back to reality by the sound of a thundering crash.

Jordan recognized the sound immediately; it was the front door slamming shut. Fear held her prisoner, a few moments longer. She sat stone-still, waiting. She crushed her body further against the closet wall; straining against the dark, to hear or see anything; afraid even to breathe. Her body calmed its convulsing, as she heard the pardoning sound of her father's truck roar to life. Waiting, but still afraid to hope, or to move, she listened… finally, as if her prayer had been answered, she heard the crush of loose gravel under heavy tires, as the truck mercifully drove away.

She crept, mere inches at a time to the closet door. She dared to lean her head out, but saw nothing amiss in her room. She moved into the light of her bedroom and eased to the door, careful to tiptoe. She couldn't make any noise. Her father could still be in the house. His truck could have left, but he could be in the house lurking around a corner and waiting for her to brave the endless-stretching-hallway, so that he could ambush her. It had happened before.

The scene changed, again. She could see a panoramic view of her old-family-home. Pornographic images plagued the living room and bathroom in the form of magazines. Beer and cigarette stains, inundated the floors and walls.

She had been told by her father not to come out of the bathroom without clothes. Her father's beliefs were so confusing; too hard to follow. Jordan tried to understand; to comply with all that he wanted. Never had she wanted to anger him, but trying to understand was just too hard. The way that he acted in no way held with his words.

He had warned her on multiple occasions, but Jordan had forgotten. She couldn't stay in the bathroom with no clothes. Staying in the bathroom for too long held a stiff penalty as well; she had had no choice, reaching up to the cabinet, she grabbed the biggest towel she could find. It was one of the beach towels that drug the floor and resembled a dress on her small stature.

Jordan had always liked the scene depicted on the front of the towel. There were lanky palm trees, resting around a silent cove. The water lapped, endlessly, against the shore. She wanted to be there. She wanted a different life for her and her mommy. Unfortunately, that was not a life for her; everyday was a test of survival. Whether she would ever enjoy the safe haven of the lazy shore, of the beautiful hidden cove was a mystery to her, but she had no time to dream of such a future. Any lapse of concentration could cause her agony beyond her imaginings. Her father was as cruel, as he was imaginative in his punishments.

Jordan peered out of the bathroom door. Seeing no one, she ran as fast as she could to her bedroom and shut the door behind her.

She blew out the air that was burning her lungs with the need for release… she dare not even breathe, as she raced across the hall. So afraid was she that he might hear the slightest sound and come for her. Relieved to have made it into the safety of her bedroom, she tossed the towel to the bed and reached for her gown. She had made it. She would never do it again. She just had to get to her room, just this once and she would never forget again. About that she had been right.

The door thundered open behind her, as Jordan swung around just in time to see her father's angry-beer-soaked face contort into a mask of rage. She shrieked and started for her closet, just as her father caught her hair and snatched her back. He held a flyswatter in his right hand. The moment that her body boomeranged back, he started the angry thrashing. He swung the flyswatter with all of his might; leaving Jordan in a whimpering heap on the floor.

Her mother waited until he left the room and the house for that matter before coming to check on her. Kneeling down beside Jordan, her mother took the towel and dabbed at the smears of blood that covered Jordan's arms and legs. V-shaped marks were dug into her skin where the flap had fallen off of the flyswatter, but her father had continued, undaunted by its absence. Jordan had never left her room to take a shower without her clothes after that and she had always been aware that her father may not appear to be present, but the possibility that he was, was very real.

The scene changed, once more as she was, again back in her room, waiting to check on her mother.

She opened the door to her room and listened first before looking into the hall. She could still hear her mother's moans of pain, but she did not see or hear her father. She walked slowly to her parent's bedroom, praying with every step that her father was truly gone. The door to her parent's room was pulled up, but not closed completely. A hole was in the middle of the door, a reminder of her father's last rampage. Jordan shivered, as the memory fled her mind. She pushed timidly at the door.

An eerie, creaking, noise boasted of the doors movement. She eased around the door's bulk and pushed farther into the room.

No sign of her father, she crossed the room to where her mother lay, crumpled on the floor. Blood was smeared across her face and matted in her hair. Jordan knelt down next to her, patting her arm, lightly.

"Mommy...?" Jordan's urgent tone begged for her mother to show some sign that she was going to be okay. Her mother did not respond. She lay still now... no whimpering- no crying. Barely breathing. . . her arm was bent in an odd angle. Jordan looked at the other arm, noting the difference.

She remembered what her grandmother had said on one of her visits. She had pulled Jordan into her lap and told her something very important. She knew, because her grandmother had told her that it was very important. She had made Jordan promise to remember.

"Jordan if you ever see anyone hurt for any reason, and they can't help themselves... you can call this number." Her grandmother had taught her the number. What was it? Jordan strained against the fog that enveloped the memory. She had to remember the number. It was something with a '9' in it. And then she did remember!

Running to the phone, Jordan picked the receiver up off of the cradle and listened for a dial tone. She slowly dialed the numbers one by one, remembering what her grandmother had told her.

"If you don't dial with care the robot woman who sounds like she is speaking through her nose will come on the phone and tell you that you have the wrong number."

Finally, Jordan sighed with relief, as she heard a tiny voice on the other end say, "911, what's your emergency?"

Jordan sat very still, afraid to move or speak for a long while. The woman again, prompted her with the same greeting.

"I'm... I don't know." Jordan struggled with an answer to the woman's question. What was her emergency? Her Mommy's arm! Jordan assessed the arm again and decided that was definitely, an emergency.

"My mommy's arm is crooked." Jordan confided.

"Okay honey..." The woman on the other end soothed. "Is your daddy there?"

Jordan jerked around. Scanning the room at the woman's question, she relaxed after seeing that he wasn't there. Minutes had gone by without her giving any thought to where her father was and when he would be coming back.

"No I don't think so. He left. My mommy's hurt bad..." Jordan said, as she started to cry.

"Okay honey... You're okay. Don't cry. We're going to help mommy, okay." The woman offered her comfort, as she tried to calm Jordan down.

"Do you know your address?" The operator asked with resounding hope filling her tone.

Jordan spouted off her address, another thing that her grandmother had insisted on Jordan remembering. The woman had assured Jordan that help was indeed on the way. She had also insisted that Jordan remain on the line. Soon the sound of sirens filled the air as Jordan waited by her mother's side. Still, through all of it one fear crippled her... what would her father do to her for calling the number? What would the horrible punishment be? It angered her. How could she be so selfish?

Then, without warning, the scene changed, once more. One minute Jordan was sitting on the floor next to her mother crying; crippled with the fear of her father's return and the fear for her mother's safety. What if her mommy didn't wake up? Where would she be?

The next minute she was running. Black fog encroached, with its otherworldly-eerie-blankness. The feeling that something though she did not know what, scrambled for her as she tossed terrified glances over her, now older, more mature shoulder filled her every thought. Her legs felt so heavy with the fear. She was running down an alley; sounds filled the air and bounced off the walls. But the sounds made no sense. It was all whining and whimpering and yet it was laughing and taunting calls, promises of bad things to come. She ran and ran; her limbs becoming like rubber. She had nothing else to give and yet the fog lurked forward, ever closer with its promises of terror in tow.

Perspiration broke out on her forehead. Her breaths came in bursting pants. She could now feel the icy fingers of the fog, as it grazed the ends of her hair and caressed the backs of her calves. Reaching deeper inside, she tried to find some store of energy that she had yet to put forth, but there was nothing. She had given the escape all that she had. She had nothing left to give.

The fingers closed in on her and began to shake her with a determined force, demanding that she do something, but what? She couldn't make out the words. What did the fog want? She could let go. She could just release herself, wholly to the fog's desires. Couldn't she? She could, for once, not run. She could just fall back into the waiting arms of the evil beneath… Who would it hurt?

With shuttering reality, she knew the answer and she did fight. She could see their faces one by one and she knew in that instant that she could not allow the fog to win. Her family needed her: Lane, Amelia, Tristan, and even the Cadotion tribe. Reality strained through the darkness of the dream; trying desperately, to pull her from the dreary arms of the past. She could feel the fingers of that long-ago dreadfulness, staking its claim. She felt as though she were pushing against tons of darkness toward a faint glimmer of a light that she had no shred of evidence, to prove its existence, represented hope. Still, the familiarity of the tugging that she could feel against her arms and the far away voice that beckoned in a low tone, straining against the darkness, claiming her consciousness; beseeching her to join it in the real world... was so effortlessly pulling her along on its calming tenor that she could almost give herself permission, to give way to that reality.

"Jordan..." the wonderful, familiar, voice pleaded for her to join it. "Honey, can you hear me?" The wariness in the tone was becoming more evident, with every syllable spoken.

She knew exactly in that moment where the wonderful voice was coming from. It was her husband, her other half, her gift from God. .. it was Lane.

Jordan strained harder against the darkness holding her prisoner. She clawed at the outer edges of the darkness for the small shreds of light. Each time the dream came it was becoming harder to wake. Changing each time, the dream flowed from scenes of her abused childhood to the depraved moments spent under the power of the demon's demands for bloodshed. Though, the ending of the dream had remained unchanged, a constant in the world that plagued her nights, it was the most unsettling part. She could not think about the angry monster that she was certain, lay just beneath the murky deep of the foreboding mist.

At that moment, there was but one thing that called to her with fervent desperation... She would make it back to him. And just as she had never fallen from the precipice of reality and into the darkness of the past—she was awake and peering into his liquid blue eyes.

✷ ✷ ✷

"Jordan?" Lane coaxed. "Honey, are you okay? You were having another nightmare." Pulling her into his arms, he pushed the errant strands of her dark auburn hair away from her face, while allowing appreciation for the way the sun's rays had lightened some of the strands with a more golden hue. The lightened strands seemed to compliment Jordan's beauty—lending an angelic quality that suited her unique countenance.

"We need to talk to Aniahi about these bad dreams you are having. Maybe she can prescribe some kind of herb that could help." Lane continued, as he tilted Jordan's head back and only then realized how quiet she was being. The feeling of concern that was mounting inside of him must have been a desperate enough cry for Jordan because mercifully she allowed a weak smile. Her hand lifted to his face. Then pulling him closer to her, she placed a tender kiss on his lips.

"I'm okay, Lane. I think the dreams are coming because of the trip." Jordan offered.

The trip had been planned for weeks and Jordan had been anxious. She hated to fly that was certainly true, but it was more than that. She had planned to try to make contact with her sister-in-law and niece. Jordan had explained it all to Lane. The idea left Jordan feeling drained and hopeless. The fear that neither would accept her apology nor want to be a part of her new life was staggering. Lane knew how important it was to make amends with her family. She was different now and she wanted to share her new found faith with all those that she loved but the uncertainty was killing her.

He could understand how she must feel. How she must blame herself, though the demon and the lifestyle she had been forced to endure had certainly played a crucial part in her actions that day; Lane knew that Jordan couldn't blame Erica or Penny if they never wanted to see her again. He hoped and prayed that they would be willing to listen to an explanation and give Jordan the chance he felt, she so richly deserved.

Jordan had been a very different person back then. She had thoughts and ideals that she was adamant were the only way. Those beliefs had all but killed Erica, her sister-in-law and Penny, her niece. Jordan tried to force her beliefs on her family. The doctrine of her new world order was the only thing that mattered to Jordan. She believed with absolute finality that if she trained women in combat and taught them to have confidence that the scales would tip in their favor and would in essence lead to a better life for all women. Women would no longer be at the mercy of men who treated them as slaves in their own homes.

Jordan would never forget the look on Penny's face, as she turned with the six-inch blade in hand and thrust it to Penny's throat. Penny had approached Jordan mere seconds after Jordan had killed Garret, her brother and Penny's father. Garret, along with Jordan's father, had managed to make every waking moment of Jordan and her mother's life a tragedy. For so long, Jordan had hated the two of them with a fervor that had defined her whole existence. It was that hate that had decided the course of Jordan's future back then and had eventually led to Jordan being possessed by an upper level demon. The demon had taken over every part of Jordan and in the end had not only alienated her from all those that she loved but had almost caused her to kill the love of her life, Lane.

Now, as Jordan lay next to Lane, in the middle of the Cadotion village where Lane had grown up with his adopted missionary parents, she thought of her life. Amelia, the beautiful, Cadotion child who they had adopted—after her mother had died during birth and her father had been killed in an attack on the village led by the Manerky, a then enemy village—and their biological son, Tristan lay only a few feet away from them in the same tent. Jordan could hear their even breathing as they still succumbed to sleep. This life that she loved so much was a far cry from the life that she had once known.

Pelts of fur made up their makeshift beds while a long-leather-hide split the tent in half, giving the children a room separate from that of Lane and Jordan's. It wasn't much, but at least they were together.

Though Lane and Jordan had a more lavish lifestyle that they could return to at any time in the United States continuing Lane's adopted parent's mission of bringing the truth of Christ's love to the world was more important than their comfort level.

Their son, Tristan, was a miracle. Amelia was gladly adopted a decision that had been made earlier before they had even taken vows. Jordan had been left barren due to the vicious beatings of her father during his drunken tirades. It wasn't until Jordan and Lane had gone to pick up Amelia from the medicine woman, Aniahi; where Amelia was an apprentice that Aniahi had been the one to tell Jordan that she was pregnant. Lane was staggered by the news. He knew that Jordan could and almost certainly would die during the birth of any child sired by him, an offspring to the fallen angels.

The histories were grim for women who had the misfortune of being intimate with Nephilim; being impregnated was nothing less than a death sentence, one that Lane had no intention of inflicting on his beautiful, Jordan. Lane's mother had, like all the other human women, died during childbirth.

Jordan, on the other hand, was elated to hear that not only did they have their beautiful daughter but now she would know what it meant to carry a child beneath her heart; to bring that child into the world. She had never faltered; her path was set and she could not have been happier to be on it. Jordan had instinctively known the instant that Aniahi had told them that she was pregnant that it was God's power, through Lane, as he cast out the demon; the power had healed her physically, as well. Every wound ever inflicted at the hands of her father and brother had been healed entirely even the psychological scars no longer existed. As long as she pushed into God's grace, Satan had no power over her. She had to be reminded of who she was to God. Satan's lies no longer had a claim to her.

The enemy was ever ready and would attack with every weapon at his disposal. Lane and Jordan both knew all too well the importance of staying in the word. A Christian must always keep his or her eyes on the Lord. They must always listen to the Master's voice; sometimes it could be hard; sometimes the enemy could win battles in a moment of weakness. The dreams that Jordan was having were proof that her resolve to hold onto the Father and His promises for her life had faltered to some degree. But Jordan had been strong enough, so filled with faith that she could do the impossible. It was with that knowledge that Jordan had gladly embraced their son and had never wavered in her resolve that God would protect her during the birth of their son. She would find that faith again.

Lane knew all too well the snares of the enemy. Satan was crafty. He would stop at nothing to make God's people question what God had done in their life. Jordan was strong; one of the strongest women he had ever met, but she was human. Satan would sift her, as he had done Jesus before the cross. He would try her, as he had done Job and it would be up to Jordan to remember the truth of her situation. She would have to lean on God and away from Satan.

Jordan lay in Lane's arms now as she silently cried out for God to be with her. It was not just the fear of flying that was worrying her. She was certain to move past that. More than anything, it was the fear of what existed behind the fog in her dream that was really the source of her terror.

She could still feel the icy grip on her flesh as goose bumps prickled her skin and in that instant, her fears were met with the resounding truth. No matter how much she tried to deny it; she knew. The entity behind the fog was none other than Hate and it was beckoning to her to once again allow it to be in the driver's seat; to forget all of the truth that God had given to her and all of the healing. Satan was trying to bring it all into question. He would cast his net of lies and hope to catch her in its terrible snare.

2

Animal calls died on the wind, as Lane pulled the leather strap into place around the animal-hide door. The Cadotion tribe, a meager people wasted nothing. Survival was of the utmost concern in the village. Not given to the same desires to hunt and kill animals to have the heads or hides for bragging rights, as some of the poachers that Lane had seen on a documentary; the Cadotion people did everything for one all-consuming purpose: survival.

The tribe used every part of any animal or plant life that was sacrificed to ensure its survival. The tribe had a wonderful life philosophy, in some ways they were everything that Lane would have wanted to infuse the life of his children. However, Lane could not deny the reason that he was there in the village. He had to realize his parent's dream to bring the truth to the people. To allow them the opportunity that was afforded all mankind through the sacrifice of Jesus Christ, to spend an eternity in Heaven with the Creator of all. It was that legacy he intended to leave behind; his parting gift to the people that had been so pivotal in the molding of his thoughts and beliefs.

It had been an honor to raise his family in the same place that his own life had been so greatly influenced. In so many ways the people of the Cadotion tribe had lent much beauty to his world. Lane was sure that he would have not been the same had his parents chose to raise him in a more privileged environment. It was the sacrifices and unity of the tribe that had strengthened his resolve to be all that God had desired of him. The things that he had learned from the tribe could never have been replaced. The simple way of the people: the love that they shared for one another was so great that it was even used as a means to keep civility among the tribe's people. The threat of being cast out of the tribe was more than any member could stand and it was that innate desire to remain among their loved ones that burned in the hearts of every man, woman and child in the Cadotion village that ensured order. There was no need for any of the usual penalties that would be in place to reprimand crimes for the love that lived in the hearts of the Cadotion people was so alive it was like a tangible being, living and breathing the same air.

Aniahi, the tribe's medicine woman, had explained many of the tribe's beliefs to Lane when he was a young boy waiting for his parents to return from their trip to the states; a trip that would prove to be their last.

Lane's parents had adopted him at birth. He would find out about this later in a near death experience during a battle for his life.

He had been forced to defend himself against the upper level demon that had claimed Jordan's very freedom. She was imprisoned in her own mind by the demon that she had for so long believed her only ally. Finally, in a battle for her soul, Jordan had been forced to crouch in the recesses of her own mind and watch hopelessly as the entity thought to be a trusted friend attempted to dismember the love of her life. Lane recalled the tortured anguish that was made apparent on Jordan's face, as she described every moment she had spent prisoner to the demon during the altercation in the woods. The demon had made many demands on Jordan; most of which she had gladly followed in a blind belief that she was fighting for the good of all woman kind. The last day, however, the demon had seen that she was starting to second guess its desires. For once, the demon had shown its true nature. There had never been any truth to all of the whispers. .. the demon was never concerned with helping her make the world better. The men that Jordan was killing were merely feeding the demon's desire to meet with its master's approval. Satan's agenda had never changed. He was still roaming to and fro; seeking whom he may devour. He was still sending out his evil-scouts, demanding the souls of humans. He was still trying to fill the bottomless pit with as many of God's beloved creation as he could.

Lane turned to the sound of movement just behind him in time to pull Jordan into a gentle embrace. She came to him easily, as she tangled her arms around his waist and rested her head on his chest. An impressive five foot ten inches tall, Jordan's lean body was sculpted with graceful muscle and sleek curves; gained by time spent as a CIA operative, a unit headed up by the government: Black Heart. Unfortunately, it was here that she had learned to satisfy the cruel demands of the demon lurking in the shadows of her subconscious.

Jordan lent her mind completely to the intoxicating allure of control. Allowing herself to believe that she held the reigns. She basked in the strength she felt. Soon the demon that had only been watching and waiting for the perfect opportunity to pull the proverbial rug out from under her, took center stage and claimed the full wealth of her anger.

Lane stood a majestic six foot five inches tall. A descendant of the fallen angels, his height and width dwarfed Jordan. Errant strands of her dark auburn hair played on the breeze, as Lane collected the stray strands and tucked them into his fisted hand at the nape of her neck. using his free hand he gently, lifted her face to his kiss. His breath caught as he gazed into her deep emerald green eyes; for it was there that he could see more than the stunning beauty that he held so adoringly, in his arms—he could see the true wealth of her fear. The fear in her eyes was so real that it felt more a part of the moment than the wind, the animal cries, or the gentle voices coming in hushed tones from the other tents. Lane felt her fear more than he felt her warm body, as it crushed against him.

"Hey..." was all that he could manage; he was crushing his lips down on hers, determined to change the anguished torture that stole over her visage. The kiss deepened and he pulled her up from the ground into his massive arms, her feet dangled in the air like a child. His determination to take away any of the thoughts that had claimed any part of her forcing this tortured look, filled the kiss. It mounted and grew and even Lane could feel how dangerously close he was to losing himself in the moment. Their little ones would be stirring soon. They had always been careful to keep their passion shrouded under the veil of night or to allow one of the other villagers to take care of the children while they enjoyed a few stolen moments. This moment was more than anything the two of them had experienced. He wanted desperately to erase all that he could of the fear that was so evident in her eyes. He knew that their time was growing short in this village, their home. He could feel the finality of that truth. It all culminated into this desperate moment; both of them starving to impress upon the other how much that truth paralyzed their every thought...

Entangled in the need to vent, to heal, or to just cling to however many precious few moments they had left to enjoy life among the people they so desperately loved and longed to remain with but could not. It had to end. The Cadotion tribe had embraced the truth and soon it would be time for them to venture forth. Lane, gathering all of his strength, reluctantly broke free of their embrace and placed Jordan gently back on her feet.

"Wow..." Jordan stammered with simple appreciation.

Lane allowed an awkward apologetic laugh, as he nodded in the direction of the children. Her cheeks filled with embarrassed-shame, as he could see that the moment had done more than he had hoped. Not only had he erased the fear but apparently, he had at least for the moment, wiped out all memory of anything but the two of them and the obvious hunger that burned between them.

"Yeah... that's putting it mildly." Lane said, as he touched his lips, which at the moment, he noted was a mirror response to that of Jordan.

"Tonight?" Jordan announced sheepishly.

"Tonight" Lane agreed with a sly grin.

Jordan moved quickly from Lane's side. He knew her well enough that she was maintaining her focus in the moment. If she did not fill the space between them with ample distance, one of them would be going to collect Aniahi to sit with the children while they borrowed her medicine hut for a few hours. The idea was intriguing, Lane had to admit but he knew that with the trip to the states in only two days, there was so many loose ends to tie up that there was no time to be getting their days and nights confused. Unfortunately, they would just have to stick to some semblance of a schedule, as applied to stolen moments of passion. Having children was a rigorous responsibility that neither of them would trade for all of the stolen moments in the world.

Lane and Jordan walked through the day with expectant hope for the coming night. Every attempt was made at keeping their distance; yet at the same time it seemed a lost cause. Stolen glances of the promised passion to come and touches that ignited the coals never quite quenched from that moment were starting to make getting prepared for the coming trip impossible.

Finally, coming to the conclusion that this night would definitely be more than the two had ever imagined. Lane cornered Aniahi. Confiding in Lane, her desire to spend time with the little ones before their departure for the states, she agreed without so much as a thought. The trip would have them away for week's maybe even months and Aniahi would miss them very much. She too had grown attached to Amelia and Tristan. Lane had believed and even accused jokingly Aniahi of being willing to go with them so she wouldn't lose a moment with the children. Had it not been for her obvious responsibilities, as medicine woman to the tribe, he knew in his heart that she would.

It would not be until Amelia's sixteenth birthday that she would move from apprentice to the medicine woman's partner. Then Aniahi would be able to take her long hoped for time off in the form of a journey walk.

A journey walk was a long walk in which the older members of the village would take to see the other parts of the world. Some may choose not to go, but it was not often that this happened. One would have to fulfill their duties to the village and once they had trained another to take over those responsibilities, then the elder was able to leave and explore; a time to live without responsibility to be true to their spirit man as the villagers referred to it before their soul returned to the Creator. Some of the special members of the tribes hierarchy were given the right to go to other parts of the world before taking on their responsibilities as tribal leaders: this was to improve the intellect of the leader. It was believed that learning from abroad could profoundly increase the leaders ability to lead.

Before Lane and his parent's time with the people they had believed that each part of creation had many spirits responsible for taking care of it. For instance, the ocean was cared for by the water spirit that kept all of the aquatic life in check and the air was taken care of by the wind spirit and so on and so forth. Lane's parents had brought a new understanding to the people and through the Holy Spirit were able to speak to the people's hearts. The Cadotion people were able to see the truth of his parent's words. The people had been very satisfied with the explanation and had felt the love and companionship of the Christian beliefs. The tribe's affinity for family and togetherness made their acceptance of the truth almost too easy.

Soon Lane knew that he would have to move on to other areas that needed the truth. He would have to leave his beautiful daughter to her duties as medicine woman in order to fulfill his duty as a missionary of The Truth. His job, as was Jordan's now that she too had accepted the responsibility was to bring the truth of Jesus Christ's love and devotion to humanity. Unfortunately, not all areas of the world had the easy knowledge of something as powerful as the love of Christ, a love that would change the very existence of all that were allowed to share in its saving grace. So it was with a heavy heart for the first time since Lane could remember that he would move forward in his mission for God but he knew that God would protect their daughter.

He and Jordan had agreed to only work in the surrounding areas for the time being. There were many villages that surrounded the area that would need the benefit of the truth. So for now, all would be well. They could spend all the time they needed allowing their daughter to grow in her confidence and embrace her path. All too soon, life would separate them and Lane did not want to think about how much that bitter sweet day would tear at the very fabric of his existence. For now, he would revel in the fact that his daughter was a mere four years old, and still had many years before she would assume responsibility of the village's care.

Lane felt strongly that Aniahi would be the first elder to refuse her journey walk. He felt the weight of that selfish thought. It was not her place to give up her own happiness to stay and keep watch over Amelia but Aniahi and Amelia were so interconnected spiritually that it was as if she were Amelia's own grandmother and in many ways she had been. If Lane were being honest it was more like Aniahi had been his grandmother first. She had always been willing to give of herself so that the good of all in the village would be realized. However, with Lane and his children, he knew that the bond went deeper. It was more than a sense of duty that kept Aniahi by their sides. She had taken over after the death of his parents. Changing roles from a grandmother figure to that of mother was an easy step for Aniahi; one that she filled with grace.

The plans were made and most of the packing had been completed for the upcoming trip. Lane walked past the other tents in the village enjoying the cool breeze that swept the valley floor. The great mountains on either side of the village made for beautiful scenery but the area had not been chosen by the people for its beauty. The elders of the tribe had reasoned that the breezeway made by the mountain pass would keep the tribe cool in the baking hot summers and offer refuge against the cruel winters. The people had erected a large fence of sorts that closed in the mountain pass on either side during the winter months; keeping the harsh winter winds at bay.

The structure, some ten feet high had been erected much the same way that walls are raised while building a large house. All of the necessary amenities needed to keep out the wind were added such as tree sap. Vines were interlaced around the small saplings, found around the water's edge just outside the mountain pass. Easy access to a water source had been another reason that the area had been chosen. After wrapping the vines around the small saplings and tying them off as tight as possible, the sticky sap was glazed in copious amounts to glue the vines and saplings together. Finally, with some effort, the strongest of the villagers were enlisted in the struggle to raise the structures on either side of the mountain passes. The mouth that the mountains made was small, a scant fifteen feet on one side while the other end was only a few feet wider. While the stronger villagers were charged with holding the fence in place, the more agile of the villagers such as the young men and women were sent up the mountain to tie off the fence. Boulders and trees were used up the mountain as makeshift stakes to anchor the structure in place. On the bottom of each enormous gate, a small opening had been left in order to exit or enter the village. The openings were easily closed off by sliding a large boulder into place to keep any wild animals seeking refuge from the winter storms at bay.

Snow was not an issue most of the time, as it did not snow in the Cadotion village often. In the unlikely event that it did snow, the villagers would gather as much of the snow as possible outside their campsites and store the substance in clay pots kept against the mountain walls. As the snow melted, it was used for water rather than having to venture out to the river.

Lane continued his scrutiny of the village as he moved on to the tent that he and Jordan shared. Standing by the tent, was a small woman with long braids and flowing tan robes. A big smile lit her eyes as she pointed in the direction of the water.

As moonlight cast a luminous light on the woman's face, Lane noticed a hint of red coloring her cheeks and realized that she was blushing. Casting a simple glance in her direction, Lane tried to keep the confusion from coloring his own face. He nodded his thanks before continuing passed his tent to the small river that he knew to drift lazily on the other side of the grand mountain.

He felt a hint of irritation. He wanted to spend time with his wife. Wasn't that the reason for the babysitter? He tried not to allow his irritation to be apparent as he passed yet another blushing-young-woman. This one was sitting on a small boulder weaving a basket. She, too, pointed in the direction of the river. Lane nodded his thanks to the young woman again, struck by the fact that she was blushing. What was going on with the villagers tonight; had they all lost their minds?

He side-stepped another villager; this time it was an elder. The elder clasped her arm around Lane's as her long robes gracefully fell forward in a quaint curtsey. She, too, pointed in the direction of the river.

Lane was about to allow his irritation to show. He didn't want to be pushed toward the water for some ritual that the tribe had orchestrated in order to say goodbye. He loved the villagers; bringing them the Word had been his entire existence, before Jordan, and he was still in for the long haul when it came to that dream. He had to be. It was his mission but he and Jordan had been hinting at things to come all day and now his body ached with need for his wife. He wanted to feel her in his arms. He wanted to claim her mouth, again and not have to hold back from the promised passion of earlier that day. He had a babysitter now. He wanted to tap into the passion that flowed between them to unbridle and explore it. The feeling had been new, something that neither of them had ever before experienced and now the villagers seemed to have other plans. Try as he might to keep control of his irritation, Lane was losing his grip.

He stepped passed another unwanted, helpful village elder; as he saw the trees open into a clearing that he had not seen before.

It was a lost cove that he could not remember having explored, even as a young boy. The trees seemed to open up as though they were great hands, opening in a grand attempt at showing something so beautiful that words would never be enough. Moonlight danced on the small ripples that ravaged the water's glossy surface. A trail of light, in the shape of an arrow, growing from the shore out into the water made its end at a graceful tip that pointed to someone in the water. Lane strained against the dark night. He allowed the angel half of him to take over; clearing up the murky vision of human sight. There at the end of the beautiful, subtle luminous light was the most beautiful creature he had ever known: his wife.

Lane took in the sight of her. The shear naked sight of her milky skin against the light as the water lapped luxuriously against all the places that would forever be his, alone. He too stepped from his robes without another thought and headed straight for the only place on earth he wanted to be at that moment: by her side. Hours passed, as they played, loved and laughed under the cover of the water. Lane felt the sting of guilt as he realized the women had not been detaining him from what he wanted as he had thought. Instead, they were making it possible. The village was full of children and other adults; tent walls made for a very flimsy, source of privacy.

"How did you do all of this? I was only gone for a short time." Lane laughed, as he pushed back the wet tendrils of hair sticking to Jordan's face. He searched her eyes, waiting to be amazed.

"I talked to Mozeria about what had happened between us earlier." Jordan began, as her face filled with the same redness of the young women who Lane now realized was not only acting as guides to show him where Jordan was, but they were also lookouts. "Mozeria said that she and her husband were married for many moons and they too had been very much in love." Jordan explained, as she looked away very briefly and then found his eyes again.

"They had much passion. Finding places to hide in a village with this many people was not easy. It was Mozeria's love, Edenar, who found this place. It was their special place." Jordan's eyes misted over, as Lane could see that she wanted desperately for him to comprehend the gift that Mozeria had given to them. "Mozeria said that never had she seen another couple in the village that deserved this gift." Jordan touched his cheek then and claimed his lips with hers in a tender kiss. She pulled away only briefly as the next words came in a strangled cry. "Thank you for loving me like that."

Lane took her then pouring all of the passion that he felt into every kiss, every touch. He prayed that God would allow her to know the simplistic and yet extremely, complicated way that she had of filling him with wonder. He loved her, that was true, but the pleasure was all his. He would have told her that but at the moment words did not seem enough.

3

Lane had made all of the necessary accommodations for their flight to the states. There weren't a lot of issues involved; it seemed too easy. He had talked to the HOD (Head of Department) for The Truth, Anderson and made him aware that he and Jordan would be arriving on the first of March. They would be staying long enough to deliver data and to make certain that their new assignment was still a go. He had talked to Anderson a week earlier. At that time, Anderson had liked the idea of talking with the Manerky tribe first. It made sense to go after the most problematic, historically speaking of all the tribes.

The Manerky, for years, had been a thorn in the side of most, if not all of the tribes that surrounded the Cadotion people. So the plan was made and they were set to move forward with the trip. He had talked to Anderson about staying in the renovated portion of The Truth's headquarters. Lane had explained that the habitat would be a good experience for their daughter, Amelia, who was studying to be the tribe's medicine woman.

With all of the details complete, he was proud of his efforts. He had almost become boastful in his own mind about being the best husband. He had thought of everything, made every effort to keep as much stress off of Jordan as possible. He had wanted to keep as much of the issues that usually occurred during travel at a minimum as pertained to his wife.

Lane was still concerned about the dreams that she was having. It seemed that every morning she was waking up in a deeper fog than the morning before. As if her ascent to consciousness was somehow being inhibited. That was of course, an absurd notion that normal people, given normal circumstances, would dismiss. But it was hard to imagine anything in their little world as being, beyond irrational. After all, the very notion that they would end up together was absurd. Jordan had been possessed by an upper level demon that she had unwittingly lent control to during a search for retribution while Lane was an offspring of the fallen angels.

Lane had been sent by an organization known as the Truth to bring Jordan back. It was thought that with his particular set of skills that he would be able to disarm any aggression that Jordan may harbor against the opposite sex. He would most certainly be able to bring her back to Black Heart so that she could be recycled by the organization and set back out into society with another mission.

Lane, however, was readied by the Almighty with another mission entirely. He was sent by God to bring Jordan to the Truth that Jesus Christ had given all to save her and that He loved her. Lane had thought that he was in breach of the mission when he started to feel things for Jordan that he had deemed not of God. To the contrary, Jordan had been meant to be his path, from the beginning. Lane had forgotten a very profound truth: God knows the plans that He has for us, and they are not to hurt us, but to prosper us. (Jeremiah 29:11).

Now, as they sat in the airport waiting for not the first flight that Lane had made with the airline, but the second; Lane could not help but scrutinize his wife as she catered to their children. He hated the stress that had been placed on her. All of his careful planning and plotting to make things go off without a hitch had seemingly been for naught. Now they sat in section D16 (the letter and numbers over the doorway that marked the narrow entrance to where passengers boarded the plane) waiting to enter the new flight at D3 because it was closer to the restrooms and the Quiznos Sub. At least, they would be able to feed and relieve themselves while they waited.

He noted the illuminated restroom sign adjacent to the Quiznos. "Ten hours to the next flight." He thought. The present circumstance was the best that he could do. Lane couldn't help but think about the older woman at Customs as she screamed out her disapproval of the airlines care of her luggage. Lane had been bereft to see anything that the airline may have done to cause such irritation from the aging woman.

"The last time I flew with this airline, you all caused me to be detained." The old woman snarled while casting a withering glance at the customs employee before continuing. "I missed my flight all together." The woman accused as her brow furrowed with irritation. "Just be careful with my bags, young man." The frumpy-woman with an embellished hairstyle that rose high on her head and a red scarf around her ample neck, scowled at the young man who was obviously no older than twenty five.

Lane was impressed with the tactful way, in which the young man was handling the woman's slanderous claims. A few of the other passengers stood in line behind the elderly woman, taking in the whole fiasco with humorous comments. One woman had actually made a comment that seemed logical, if not downright ironic to Lane.

"She'll probably look back on the grand scheme of things one day and discover that it had, in fact been her own useless-tantrums that had caused all of the delays in the first place." The woman surmised as she smirked at the older woman and then turned her attention to Amelia.

The woman had been consumed up until that point with how cute Amelia had been in her light pink dress, with its lacey borders that stood out in stark comparison to that of the dark-hazel-hue of her skin. The golden-honey-brown of her eyes made it difficult to tear away from her lovely gaze.

Lane knew that the woman was lost; after all, he too, had been beyond hope when scrutinized by his gorgeous daughter as she tried to get her way. He and Jordan had been determined not to spoil the children but at times they had fallen short... during those moments, they would try the tag-team approach to parenting.

"Get the fresh man in." Jordan had jokingly, dubbed their attempts at not turning their children into spoiled, self-indulging adults concerned with no one else's wellbeing but their own.

Lane stood, soothing Tristan's sleeping form while assessing the woman's philosophical, point. He liked it. He wondered how many times in life had he done things that had caused him to wait on God's blessings rather than just move forward... How many times had he forfeited something so wonderful just to sit on the sidelines pouting or questioning God about his present circumstance?

"Hey, earth to Lane." Jordan teased as she captured a rogue piece of wavy hair that had managed to claim its freedom from the leather tie at the nape of his neck where the rest of his multi-hued hair of light brown and blond tendrils had been tightly kempt.

"Sorry, just distracted I guess. Hey, I'm really sorry about all of this." Lane admitted as he captured her hand and caressed her warm fingers. "I wanted all of this to be smoother for you." He tried to keep the moment light. He did not want to tip Jordan off to the true wealth of his worry for her. Jordan didn't like to be the source of his concern; a part of her that she had carried over into their new life together. Some things would never change, he mused.

Jordan would always be independent. She would always feel that it was her place to be more responsible for those around her than they would be for her. He loved her tenacity. He just longed for her to sometimes allow him to hold things together for her; to be her soft place to fall.

This trip was supposed to be his chance to do that. Unfortunately, it had all unraveled beginning with the woman at Customs and then with the airline giving bad information about how to find their initial flight which had been 66 on terminal N at D2.

Now, their son was starting to become cranky. He was two and a half and while his dark auburn locks and cloudy blue eyes testified of the angel descendants of his past, his behavior seemed to identify at times more closely with that of the demon that Jordan had been possessed by.

Lane laughed at the thought, as he caressed his son's head. Jordan would not be amused if she knew what he had been thinking. Only once had he confided his 'little joke' but he had learned that it was not funny to Jordan at all. Something about that time, still had Jordan captive. She had accepted Jesus as her Savior; that was true, however, the fact was he could not deny that she still seemed a prisoner to the past in some ways. And now, that they were returning to the states, he was starting to see just how real that prison was, in the form of her dreams.

Jordan stood, as she pulled Tristan into her arms. She leaned down and touched Amelia on her arm.

"Stay with daddy. Ok?" Jordan moved her hand to Amelia's satiny-black-hair and caressed the tender new growth back in place. "Thank you for being good. You are such a big girl. I'm very proud of you." Jordan scrunched her nose as she adjusted the ample weight of their son and then winking at Lane she started for the restroom.

"Someone needs a potty-break." Jordan announced as she playfully bounced Tristan while glorying in the musical sound of his laughter.

No matter what the situation of her mind, Lane loved this. He loved the way that she had of making things feel okay. She had the uncanny ability to make everyone around her feel calm, whole and though, Lane knew with all of his being that it was an illusion that he could not afford to get caught up in; he just could not help himself. That, more than anything, was a good reason to be back at the compound surrounded by those that knew and loved them. He needed to have someone that wasn't so close to the situation, help him figure out what to do about the dreams. He feared what might happen to her; the dreams more than anything else in her life scared Lane. How could he fight the unknown?

Lane watched, as she walked away. He felt so helpless. He wanted to protect her but in the end, he did not have a clue where to start. He reached over and lightly brushed Amelia's hair.

She was spending time reading a book about herbs that she would be tested on when they returned to the Cadotion tribe. Her devotion was amazing. She seemed to meditate on everything that confounded her and in the end, she would triumph rather than fall prey to the problems of her life. She never complained just persevered with hard work and determination. Lane admired that in his daughter. He longed for that kind of determination. He needed to see the solution rather than always focusing on the root cause of the problems of their lives. As he mulled it over in his mind, he started to realize that the answer was there all along. He needed to meditate to focus on Christ because He was the solution to their problems.

The evil that filled his soul registered completely in his dark eyes as they followed Jordan's every move. He watched as she sat talking with her family. She had it all. He hated that more than anything. He had nothing and that more than anything else… that had happened in his world, was her fault. More than the abuse, suffered at the hands of his stepfather; more than the countless hours his mother had worked; and, yes, more than the years of poverty… Jordan had ended any chance he had of his father entering his ominous world. He had waited for her to be alone but luck did not seem to be in his corner.

Tommy Hayden paced the floor like a large cat, stalking his prey. He had been so patient. He was sure that his patience would soon pay off. He thought that his luck was taking a turn for the better, the moment that the old woman had caused a scene in Customs inadvertently causing Jordan Buckley-Gates to miss her flight. But now, as he watched her carrying the floundering toddler to the bathroom, he was starting to understand just exactly what he was up against. Getting to Jordan, may be impossible. Was she ever going to be alone? For crying out loud, he had been waiting forever for her to return to the states.

Tommy was informed that Jordan would be landing at the Atlanta airport at nine o'clock E.S.T. From there, she would be boarding her next flight by eleven o'clock E.ST. As luck would have it, Jordan missed her flight causing the window of opportunity that Tommy had hoped for. He had booked a flight to New York on the same flight that Jordan and her family would be taking. The hope was that he could get to her before having to board the flight. He had been able to access the entire inside information on Jordan's whereabouts from an old friend at the agency.

James Ruston had made an impromptu visit to The Garden a few weeks before Tommy was scheduled to be released. The usual six months stay in The Garden had been foregone… the staff deemed Tommy unfit for society. Tommy's stay in The Garden had far exceeded any in the history of The Garden's visitors. He hated the place. The darkness inside of him begged to be released from its serenity but no such reprieve was granted, on his behalf. It wasn't until his visit with James Ruston that Tommy knew exactly what he would have to do.

James had explained to Tommy everything concerning Jordan's involvement in his biological father's death. He had also told Tommy that Jordan had been one of the agents responsible for bringing him into The Truth… Tommy was thankful to Agent Ruston.

Tommy had come to the agency after making his first kill. He could remember every detail. It wasn't until he had become a part of Black Heart that he had truly understood what his place in the world had been. But then, just like every other aspect of his useless existence, it had fallen apart and Tommy knew exactly who was to blame.

James had gone on to tell Tommy that Jordan had been jealous of his father. That she had killed the man in cold-blooded-murder. She knew all about Tommy and had personally orchestrated his stay at The Garden. It was her idea to keep Tommy out of the way so that she could kill his father. Ruston explained that Jordan knew that if Tommy was not detained that she would never be able to accomplish her greatest desire... to kill the man that she had felt took everything from her; the man that she felt had taken her parents' love from her because she believed her parents had loved him more. In the end, Tommy's father was just in the way and if she could remove him then she could have what she had always wanted, her father's love.

Tommy's mother had struggled to make ends meet. She worked two jobs simply to pay the rent, water and lights. With such meager paychecks, his mother could not afford cable. They did not own a television, for that matter. They lived in a two bedroom trailer, pale-blue with white trim. The siding was falling away and the underpinning had holes where the weed-eater had been put too close.

He barely laid eyes on his mother most days and when he did, she was, too exhausted to do much more than take a shower and go straight to bed. Tommy had spent most of his days at the school not going to class but hanging out in the basement.

His mother had tried for food stamps once but was told that she made too much money. She would simply have to choose between a place to live and food and if she didn't have a place to live, then she would lose custody of Tommy.

Tommy had been responsible for cutting the grass and weed eating, until his mother had met and soon married his stepfather. His stepfather never fixed anything. Molding strips on the inside of the trailer were falling away from the paneled walls. The once beige carpet was now dark brown from mud being tracked in. The couch and loveseat were a faded tan from years of being baked in the sun; the windows had no curtains to protect the contents of the room. A slender hall rolled from the living room ending abruptly at his bedroom.

He barely had his own room; the actual size of the room would have classified it more as a closet than a bedroom. His mother's and stepfather's bedroom was at the end of the trailer beside the living room which made him an easy target for his stepfather.

His stepfather was very abusive; crushing Tommy under the weight of his iron fist. He had played a double role in the life of Tommy and his mother; tormenting Tommy at night while his mother slept for her morning shift. Every night just as the one before Tommy would escape into his bedroom and wait for his stepfather to enter. He heard the grating scrub of the metal striker as the door pushed open. The footfalls of his stepfather filled the room. Tommy tried to disappear under his thread-bear covers. He listened as the door slowly closed and his stepfather drew near to him. Tommy would cower under his cover until his stepfather yanked the covers free. His body would be covered in the evidence of the abuse. Unfortunately, his cries for help always fell on deaf ears.

His mother had always told him that his biological father would someday come and take care of them. He was a truckdriver with one of the local services in Darlington, South Carolina. Tommy's mother had made the time that she spent with his father seem like a wonderful-love-affair. He often found himself daydreaming about the man that was his father. He could only imagine that anything he might dream up would pale in comparison to the man that his father truly was; a fact that he could surmise from his mother's stories. He knew that his mother would always have feelings for his father. He hated his stepfather for more than the abuse. He hated that he stood in the way of any happiness that he would have in a family made up of himself and his biological parents.

Every day the abuse grew and every day Tommy became darker inside. His every thought was based in the elimination of his stepfather. The days that he spent in the basement of the school, thinking of how he would do it, became one big blur. There was more than enough proof that his stepfather was abusing him, both mentally and physically but old bruises weren't enough to justify the death of his stepfather. Somehow, Tommy had to provoke his stepfather. If only he could be strong enough to withstand the assault and still have enough wherewithal to kill the man; he could, then prove it was self-defense.

Tommy could remember the moment that the idea had become a full-fledged plan. He was at school, ditching math again. His favorite place was among the pipework that ran across the basement ceiling. There was something about looking down on the custodian that made Tommy feel in charge; like a demigod looking down on mere man. The man going on about his usual task of readying his cleaning cart; whistling some showtune, of course, while Tommy viewed from his perch above. It made Tommy feel good to know that he held this kind of control over another human being. It was times like that that Tommy could almost identify with his stepfather. He could almost understand why the man would come into his room and gag him with a pair of socks. He could almost understand why the man would tie him to the bed on his stomach and deliver lashes for every year that Tommy had been alive; every year that Tommy had disturbed his life with his wife, Tommy's mother.

If it hadn't been for Tommy, his mother would have loved his stepfather but it was the union that made Tommy possible; his very existence was a reminder of the man that Tommy's stepfather would never be.

As Tommy looked down on the janitor, he was reminded how good it felt to be in control of someone or something. In that moment, Tommy's mind was made up. He would allow his stepfather his one last beating. He would allow the man to shell out his last piece of justice and the moment that the last tie was removed from his arms and legs would be his stepfather's last.

Tommy went home that night, armed with a piece of old pipe that he had found lying among the debris just below the pipework. He collected the pipe and thought of the duct tape that he had in his drawer. He had found it in the very same place a week earlier. He hadn't decided what he would do with it, until this moment. He waited for the man to leave and then he began to hone the pipe into the weapon that he knew it could be.

He saw it so distinctly in his mind's eye. He would wrap the duct tape around the bottom for grip. He would scrape the end of the pipe on the old-metal pipes around him until the edges were made razor sharp. He knew the moment that the weapon reached the desired sharpness. His eyes glowed with intensity as he relished the heat that radiated up the handle from the red-hot edge. Tommy wasn't sure how long he had been rubbing the metal pipe against the pipe work. He was brought back to the moment, the minute the door to the basement grated on the floor announcing the return of the custodian. He was putting away the cart for the day which meant it was only fifteen minutes until school let out. That gave Tommy only an hour to get home, put the tape on the handle and hide the weapon in just the right place. His stepfather would be home from the job he was working today. He worked for a local construction company that was working a job out of town. He had been gone a week. He would be home for the weekend. He had been a week without venting his anger on Tommy. Tommy knew that he would not miss the opportunity. The moment that his mother was asleep, he would be stalking the floor in search of his prey.

Tommy rubbed the end of the still, warm pipe. A wicked smile filled his face. He was proud of the plan he had developed. He looked down at the custodian once more and then back at the glowing red of the pipe. How easy would it be? He caressed the pipe. He had no time. He would have to run home and prepare for his stepfather's certain death but how he longed to test the weapon. Another smile arched his lips, as he realized then, for the first time the predator would become the prey.

4

Jordan examined her face in the mirror. For the first time since fully understanding what it meant to have a relationship with Lane's God, her God; Jordan realized she was afraid and as she allowed that fear to resonate completely in her mind, she was able to examine it. It was then that she knew the source of her fear. It wasn't for her own safety that she was clutching her auburn-haired, blue-eyed son that was the image of her husband. No. She could feel the fear as deeply and real as if it was an entity sharing the same space with her. It was her children that were sounding the alarm. Their very lives were wrapped up in the Cadotion tribe: their ways, their will, all that was intrinsically the Cadotion people had been engrained in her children. But now, as she stood in the airport restroom clutching her precious little boy, she knew with all of her being that their reality was about to be spoiled.

Why was Tommy here? Why would he be standing in the very same airport at the very same time as she and her family? Atlanta airport was a far cry from the Cadotion village. And wouldn't Tommy have to have inside information in order to be following them? She didn't want to become paranoid but she could remember a time when revenge had been all that she lived for. She thought back to her own days of being lied to and held captive by the demon: Hate. She was determined not to spend time in The Garden, Black Heart's answer to wayward souls.

The Garden was a place of serenity and beauty but it was a place that Jordan could remember all, too clearly that she did not want to be. The demon possessing her, claimed her will, and would do anything in its power to keep her from any establishment, bathed in that kind of peace. At the time, Jordan had believed it to be her own desire to stay away from The Garden. It wasn't until later, as she and Lane stood in front of God and their friends reciting their vows—promising forever that she realized it had been the desire of the demon and not her own that had kept her from The Garden. Now, she was on a trip to The Garden, and to her disbelief, she could not wait to bathe in the Holy-tranquility that filled the place.

Still, Jordan was not so far removed from the time spent possessed by the demon that she could not remember the utter distain for the place that permeated her senses. Though, the feelings encompassing her were flowing from the black heart of the demon, she later learned to be Hate; the feelings were as real and as a part of her as if they were her very own. She could only imagine that Tommy felt the same connection to whatever was in control of his will.

Jordan stood in the large restroom of crimson red doors and black and white checker-board-design-floors that reminded her of a normalcy that she had grown keenly, aware and attached to. Her eyes darted back to the mirror as she examined the image peering back at her. The woman stood clutching the auburn-haired boy. Her green-eyes registered a fear that seemed to remind her of someone in the past and in that moment Jordan knew. Though she was viewing her own reflection, the self-assured, in-control eyes that she had for so long grown accustomed to seeing in the mirror had been replaced. Now, as she looked back at the image in the mirror, it was all too clear who the image reminded her of. It was her mother, her niece, her sister-in-law and it was that three year old little girl that she had dreamed about before the trip-the child that had sat for what seemed like an eternity over her mother's mangled body waiting for the paramedics to show and praying her father would not return. For the first time, Jordan saw her former self. . . a part of her that had been long since buried. Then, she recalled the dead eyes of Tommy. What revenge must he be seeking after, she had helped hand-deliver him to the very place that she absolutely would not have wanted to be? She recalled his dead gaze, the liquid-black-evil that emanated from his eye-sockets and she knew without a shadow of a doubt that Tommy was here for her.

Jordan stroked Tristan's head as he looked back at her with trusting-smiling eyes. Tristan had never known of the evil that had been a part of her past. She and Lane had done everything in their power to keep that ugly past from touching their children.

Now, as she stood looking back at their son, clutching him tightly to her trying to erase any evidence of the fear that she was so desperately drowning in from her face, Jordan knew that the past was here. It was in her babies' world and if she could not think of something fast, it would explode all over their perfect-serene little lives. It would expose itself to their precious children and it would leave a black-ugly scar that would forever blotch out any attempt that the two of them had made to infuse normalcy; to shield them from that horrible time.

Now as Jordan held their son to her heart, praying for the ability to protect their family from whatever evil awaited them, Jordan knew how wrong she had been. It was not all men that were evil. It was the hate and jealousy that had touched their lives and created within them the same demonic spirit that had almost taken everything from her. It was the acts portrayed against them that were evil. It was lending their will to the lie, 'that hate could stop hate'. It was all of that culminated together to create the monster that sat crouching inside of Tommy. And even as Jordan prayed for protection she knew that it would come.

As Jordan stood looking at the image that she and her son made, she thought about all of the bad things that God had used for good in their lives: Amelia had a bad start through the death of her biological-parents but that start had led to them being her parents; Jordan's father had beaten her ruthlessly which had led to her hating all men and being barren but God had allowed Lane to heal her: mind, body and soul which had led to her knew understanding—that she was not the end all-do all; she was not the change that the world needed. Jesus Christ was. God had allowed her to have her precious son, Tristan. So many good things had risen from the ashes of their tortured pasts. (Romans 8:28)

She knew that though God may seem a thousand miles away during the storm—He would be there! He would be right on time! The same way He had healed her and allowed her to conceive their beautiful Tristan, God would show up. He would shield them from that ugliness once again. Jordan just had to have faith. How? It was that one thought that was the biggest source of Jordan's fear. Could she have the faith that she needed? Did she have the faith that it took to move mountains, faith in this very real, very scary time? Could Jordan have faith the size of a mustard seed? As she looked back into the mirror, she did the only thing she knew how to do. The thing that she had learned on the forest floor outside of Beulah County while sitting next to Lane's still body. . . she prayed. (Matthew 17:20)

The restroom door swept closed once again as Tommy watched Jordan return to her family. Something familiar seemed to resonate from her eyes. Something he remembered. Tommy tried to think where he had seen that look before and then it came to him. He licked his lips as a devious smile played on his features. Of course, he knew. It was his stepfather. How could he forget? The same fear that registered across his panicked expression now stole over Jordan's visage.

Tommy had laid there on the bed, the dirty socks tied around his ankles and wrists. He kept completely quiet, refusing his stepfather even the slightest whimper as the whip came down one lash after another onto his back; careful not to hit too hard. He did not want to get caught, after all. This was just between the two of them. Tommy could imagine the demented things that his stepfather would tell himself: he couldn't allow the stripes to become infected; Tommy would have to go to the school nurse or his mother and then what? He would be caught.

"That would be a big laugh." Tommy thought. He had tried to tell once before. It had ended horribly. His mother had been angry at him. She claimed that he was jealous and he couldn't stand that she would be with anyone other than his father. Tommy guessed his mother had been right. He did want his parents together. After all, look at the way that she had represented his father's memory. Tommy would be a fool not to want his father and mother together. . . especially, with a stepfather like Harold.

Tommy lay there gritting his teeth and biding his time. He gripped the bedpost as he thought of the weapon he had made that afternoon. Soon, the post would be replaced with the weapon. Harold would bleed his last.

The weapon was perfect. Tommy had wrapped almost half of the roll of duct-tape around the end of the pipe. He had spent a good twenty minutes, practicing some moves that would be sure to kill.

His stepfather moved in to untie Tommy's hands, the whole while delivering the 'it's your fault' speech. The one where Tommy was reminded that if it hadn't been for his existence then his wife would love him.

Tommy's mother had been a beautiful woman but she was given to the night life which had resulted in her meeting Tommy's father.

Tommy's father hung out at the local bar down the road from his house. Shelby, Tommy's mother, had gone into the bar after a fight with her ex-boyfriend. Tommy's father had talked with her every day for a week. He had been so kind to her. Buying her drinks and taking her home without so much as trying anything. Then the last night he had dropped her off, Garret Buckley had dropped in for a night cap. They had too much to drink and soon their dancing had turned into a more passionate embrace. She had seen him every day after that until she had revealed to him Tommy's existence. He told her that he was already married and that he already had a child. He told her things were not that simple. He told her that he had to break things off with his wife. He told her to wait for him. He said that he would return for her. But he never showed up. Tommy's mother had told many stories of her time with Tommy's father and soon his father became like some character in a fairytale, a character that would never become a reality because Jordan Buckley-Gates, his very own aunt, had destroyed all hope of his father ever returning.

Tommy focused more intently on the fear emanating from Jordan's eyes as at last he allowed the memory of his stepfather's last day to take control of his thoughts. He recalled it so perfectly, it was his favorite memory. As his stepfather was leaning over him, taking off the last of the ties, his hand was sliding from the post to the side of the bed where he had tucked the perfect weapon. He raised the pipe and the final blow was delivered as he thrust the razor-sharp edge of the pipe deep into his stepfather's throat. Tommy stood there as Harold gurgled on his own blood. That deer caught in headlights-'why me' look that filled his stepfather's visage would forever be etched in Tommy's memories. It would forever be a part of him and Tommy loved that most of all.

Now, he was vibrating with the impulse to make another memory. One that was sure to be with him even longer than that of his stepfather's end. The death of the one person that had stolen the most empowering dream of his childhood and had claimed any hope of a future that included both his parents. The one person that had caused the death of not only one of his parents but both because his mother had ended her life, not long after finding out her one true love was gone forever. Jordan Buckley, Tommy's very own aunt, the sister to his biological father. He would kill her and claim the richness of yet another blissful, memory. But as Tommy sat there thinking about the end that would surely come for Jordan, an idea started to grow. Why make it so easy on her? Ending her life would be too easy. It would be over. Why not take out all that she loved right before her very eyes? And then, after she was filled with the vision of that loss kill her slowly; allow her last moments to be filled with terror and grief.

Jordan tried desperately not to look back. She walked stiffly toward her husband and daughter. She was sure that Lane would not be fooled by her attempt at hiding the fear she felt flushing through her veins. Back in the restroom, Tristan had smiled sweetly at her. In that instant, she knew with great relief that Tristan had fell for the calm facade. He was just as happy as he had always been. He was sheltered and with every part of her being, she prayed it would remain that way.

She was already concerned about the Manerky tribe. Though she knew that the tribe had sworn to keep their distance after the raid that had claimed the life of Amelia's biological father, she could not know what their reaction would be to missionaries coming into their midst.

Jordan had been told by many of the elders of the Cadotion tribe that the Manerky people were anything but gracious hosts. They did not allow strangers in their midst. But Jordan had to believe if God brought them to it. He would bring them through it. She had witnessed that fact on many occasion since her relationship with the Almighty had manifest itself in the woods, the day the demon had nearly claimed their lives.

Jordan had begged for Lane's Creator to show up and save Lane that day. But God had done more than that. He had showed up, all right. He had healed Lane and Jordan. He had created within her a love for mankind that transcended her own understanding. He had healed her black heart. He had knitted her womb back together. He had allowed His perfect will to engulf her life. He had touched the hearts of those in charge of her case and opened doors that would never have been opened. After all, to the public, Jordan was a coldblooded killer that should be destroyed. But God had different plans for her. He had put her in front of a judge that was ready to put her away and had softened his heart. He allowed the judge to see the truth that Jordan was not in control of her decisions. God had allowed her to become under the control of a physician at the institution that as a Christian had not only heard Jordan's story but had believed. He helped her in so many ways and He returned her not to her former life but to a more fulfilled life. A life she could never have believed possible. And, just as she knew that God had been there for her then; she knew with certainty that He would be here for her now. (Isaiah 61:7)

5

Lane stood up immediately. Something in Jordan's face was off. She was always there taking care of those that she loved. Lane had put the whole trip together as a way of allowing Jordan to relax; for once to feel as though he could take care of her. Things had started to unravel and all of his plans had seemed for naught... Jordan had come to his rescue as she had always done. Now, as Lane witnessed the obvious distress that he knew in his heart she was trying to hide—it was the same fear that had been ever present the day before he could see that something was off. Something very real had occurred in the time that she had been gone to the restroom with their son. But what?

Lane studied their surroundings as he tried to attune himself to the things that may have set her off. The woman that had been in customs was now sitting across from them waiting at the adjacent terminal for another flight; he knew to be heading for Las Vegas. It only took Lane a moment to dismiss the thought. Jordan was anything but petty. She had probably not given the woman a second thought. Ever since they had moved to the Cadotion village and carved out their lives among the people, Jordan had seemed to take most things in stride. Very little seemed to unhinge her. But in this moment, something had definitely changed Jordan from the self-assured missionary, wife and mother that she had become to the timid-fearful mess that stood before him.

Lane again, allowed his eyes to leave that of Jordan's to try for another scan of the room. He knew whatever the issue... there had to be a clue among the people in the crowd. And yet, he was still coming up short.

A woman stood near the gaunt-sandwich-shop scolding a small child that was throwing a temper tantrum. The boy, not but a year or two older than their own son, fell into a heap at his mother's feet screaming for a candy bar that his mother had denied him. His brown curls bounced playfully around his head. His mother stood over him with her arms crossed tapping her foot waiting patiently for the tantrum to subside. She had asked the child if he was finished which had brought about another fit of screaming and angry words. To the woman's credit, she did not give into the boy's demands but told him that she did not reward bad behavior. Soon the child stood to his feet and plastered his sweetest smile onto his face. Extending one hand, Lane could read on his lips the word please. To which, the woman promptly handed the boy the fruit she had wanted him to eat in the first place. Lane could not help but allow a small chuckle. He felt very proud of the young mother who seemed to have it together in more ways than he. His own children seemed to have the upper hand more times than not.

Lane pulled his attention away from the young woman and child. He was just about to return his scrutiny to his wife when a movement caught his attention. A man with dark auburn hair and dark eyes that seemed filled with contempt stood on the other end of the Quiznos' sign. He adopted a self-assured stance and reminded Lane of someone he had once seen in the past. The man wore a white t-shirt and designer jeans. There was a kind of confident air about the man that seemed familiar to Lane. Something about the way the man carried himself; as though he was all that mattered. The hair, the emerald green eyes, darkened with hate; everything about the man screamed familiarity. But no matter what it was about the man that reminded Lane of the past, it was more than his arrogant demeanor that set Lane on edge. Lane watched the man's evil eyes. He followed the man's intent glare and in that moment he realized to his horror what had the man's attention. It was his family but more specifically, it was Jordan. In that moment, as Lane watched the man glaring at his wife with open contempt, Lane felt his blood run cold because he knew with acuity, exactly who the man reminded him of. It was Jordan's brother, Garret Buckley. The man or more to the point the boy, obviously not much older than Jordan's niece,

Penny, was staring at Jordan with such focus and intent in his evil glare that he did not even notice that Lane was watching him or did he?

Tommy felt the roving eyes as they scrutinized his face and torso. He could tell with his keen intellect that the man was not happy with what he saw. No matter. Tommy was here to do one thing and the man's approval or lack thereof had no bearing on the situation; though he did find that he was strangely intrigued by the man's open disapproval of his presence. Tommy thought he would definitely have to pack the revelation away in his psyche for later analyses.

The disapproving scrutiny of the enemy's husband could make for a sporting time of her death... Tommy mused. After all, he had nowhere to be and all of his time would be dedicated to her, and of course, her family's early demise. He felt a wealth of pride blooming in his dark heart as he mentally patted himself on the back for adding her family to the fun. How else would she ever know the depth of his sorrow; unless she felt it firsthand? It was too bad that he was not willing to leave her alive to swim forever in the mire of that sorrow.

No. He somehow could not stand to exist in a world that would lend its properties to her survival; no matter the benefit of seeing her pain. Tommy would just have to be satisfied that her last memories before leaving this world would be of her family dying. Not just dying but dying slowly. He would just have to make the deaths of her family be a lasting memory that would follow her straight to hell and be so deeply stained in his own memory that he could call upon its richness to satisfy his need for retaliation for all of eternity.

CHAPTER

6

Garrison had walked the floor for three days, wondering whether to tell Jordan and Lane about Tommy Hayden being released from The Garden. He had argued with the powers that be for three days that the boy was nowhere near ready to be released but Judge Harrison had issued the papers to release him on Friday. It was now Monday evening and Garrison had already spoken with Lane. He knew that they were at the Atlanta airport. He also knew that the flight had been missed and that Lane was freaking out that all of the mishaps would just send Jordan into some kind of relapse. Garrison knew better. Jordan wasn't the type of person to pretend. The fact was she was changed, and Garrison could see that it was in a forever kind of way. Lane was her husband and while they had a connection that defied logic; Garrison and Jordan had been a part of each other's world for a very long time.

Garrison had seen Jordan at her best and her worst; he had never seen her fake emotions that she was not truly feeling. She meant what she said and said what she meant. That was the last worry on Garrison's mind at the moment.

He was about to lose control of his sanity. Jordan and Lane, both were bound to be very angry with him about the oversight. Who was he kidding? It was no oversight. It was a downright omission of the truth. He had willfully kept the truth from both of them and now, he could not think of one good reason for doing it.

Now, as he stalked the floor of his office and studied the old clock on the wall that was in the shape of a fifty seven Chevy Bel Air, he could feel the minutes taunting him as they fell away in what seemed like warp speed. Garrison fussed with his hair. It was getting too long. He liked to keep it short; one less thing to worry about. Time seemed to be laughing at him. In only twelve more hours, he would be picking them up at the New York airport.

As Garrison stood in his scantly decorated office, brushing his fingers across his hair again, trying to vent some of the morning's frustration that had been building over the last few days. His eyes roamed the wall adjacent to his high-leather-back chair. The leather felt nice. He guessed he had come a long way since his time in the bureau spent as partner to Jordan Buckley. His office may not have the furnishings of the other corporate-tycoons that filled the offices on the third floor but his were lavish in their own right. His desk was made of oak; a man's wood; honest and strong. Garrison liked that about the desk. It felt good to have something that he knew he could count on. Unlike the counterfeit Fikias that stood in the corner of his office; he hated that thing. He would have gotten rid of the plastic imposter long ago if it hadn't been provided by the company; that and all of the ladies that darkened his door fussed over the thing as if it were the Elvis of plants. Garrison thought of another imposter; himself. He knew that he was a fake and a phony, just like the plant.

Garrison knew he owed Jordan so much more than the lies that seemed to be filling the space between them. He allowed his mind to flow back into the past to a different time, a time when he had first encountered Jordan. She was no more than twenty then. Her head down and her eyes full of doubt—she lived in a one bedroom apartment in the middle of town. Her days were spent hidden away under a pile of books at the local library. Garrison shook his head. So much had changed since that time. Jordan had moved through her own life with fear; like some fly on the wall of her own existence, Jordan cringed back into the shadows away from any promise of a hope-filled future. Garrison believed at the time that he was doing Jordan a favor. But watching her life unfold, one catastrophe at a time, he knew that could not have been further from the truth.

It was James Ruston that had initially come to Garrison with the news that he would be going out on a recruiting mission. Ruston had appointed Simon, an agent that had been with Black Heart for several years to oversee Jordan's recruitment. Ruston, at the time had made the whole process seem simple. It was what needed to happen to make Jordan's life better.

"After all, look at us, Garrison." Ruston had made it all seem logical. Not only logical but the only alternative; as if Jordan's life would be doomed without the help of Black Heart. The organization had changed his life after all. Hadn't he been another person all together before being recruited that faithful day in July? The day that he had killed a gunman that was holding up a convenient store.

The man had been making good his escape when Garrison stepped unknowingly from the cab and started across the street. The guy, stealing a backward glance ran headlong into Garrison. The man dressed in an old pair of blue jeans, with too many holes and a black t-shirt; his face was covered with a stocking, causing his features to take on a sunken-alien appearance. The man began swinging the pistol in Garrison's direction. Garrison, as if being guided by an unseen force, sidestepped the man's intentions and then shoved him face first into the open cab. Grabbing the cab door, Garrison thrust the door closed with overt force. He wasn't sure at that moment if the man was dead but as he watched the man's body fall awkwardly to the ground the reality crept in. He was a murderer. Garrison watched as the man's eyes stilled forever as if testifying to that fact. Not long after that incident, though Garrison did not suffer from an abusive past, the bureau stepped in and claimed his future; in an instant, his life was changed. Garrison was no longer a young idealistic teen that had his whole life ahead of him; he was a murderer for hire.

He supposed that Jordan's experience was very different from that of his. After all, she had practically demanded a pen to sign on the dotted line and had all but flailed her body in excited anticipation onto Garrison and his recruiting partner. Did that make the fabrications okay? Did the fact that Jordan's life was so unsatisfactory, make it okay that the bureau had manipulated the whole situation in order to have Jordan and the inmate meet up outside the apartment at that very moment?

Garrison was drowning in guilt. He had so much to confess to his friend. Would she ever forgive him? And now, he had lied to her again.

He had not told her that he knew all along that Tommy Hayden was her nephew. But it was more than that; he knew the day that he and Jordan had taken Tommy to The Garden. That day, as he looked into Tommy's eyes, had he seen a glimpse of this? He had definitely thought that he was protecting Jordan from the truth. Her state of mind was deteriorating, before his very eyes, even then but Garrison was neck deep in lies; so he could not or would not bring himself to tell Jordan about Tommy. Had those omissions that lie cost his best friend more than she should ever have to pay? Hadn't she been through enough? And, if he could bring himself to unveil the awful truth, would he lose her friendship, forever?

What about Lane and the children? He had grown so attached to the children; Amelia and Tristan, actually referred to him as Uncle Garrison; a fact that Garrison adored. He had no siblings; so his only hope at being an uncle had entered the world through his best friend, a woman that he would have never thought capable of being a mother. But as Garrison thought of the person that Jordan had become, through 'her Savior'--Isn't that what Jordan had called Him? This Jesus person that Jordan spent hours going on and on about not—He was her Savior and though Garrison may not understand or know what that meant, he could not deny the change that her 'relationship', as she called it, had brought about in her. Forgiveness was a word that people tossed around, like it meant nothing special. Jordan, on the other hand, seemed to know what that meant. Garrison could see the light in her eyes. He could sense that something in her being was crystal clear on what the word meant but would that be enough for her when she found out the truth? Would this Savior of Jordan's and His teaching of love and forgiveness be enough to help Jordan to forgive a betrayal of this magnitude?

Jordan had calmed down the minute that they stepped onto the plane. She had seen no sign of Tommy. She had only encountered the boy once a few years ago as she and her partner, Garrison was bringing him into The Garden. Maybe it wasn't long enough to be able to positively identify him in a crowd. After all, that was more than four years ago. People change a lot in four years; especially young people.

Tommy was recruited into Black Heart at fourteen, the youngest agent to ever be brought into the organization. Not to mention, the fact that Jordan had another agenda all together; she was practically salivating with the idea of killing her brother and ridding the Buckley bloodline of all the evil that seemed to inherently follow all of the male children into the world.

Jordan tried every possible explanation in an attempt to calm her suspicions but one by one, they were all dismissed. She knew that she had been trained by the best operatives in the field and like it or not, no matter how she tried to explain it away, she would have taken in the entire situation. She would know every detail about the boy and with the training received by the aging specialist, she could even add a few years onto a person of interest within reason to be able to pick them out of a crowd; just the way she knew in her heart, she had with Tommy only a few minutes earlier in the airport terminal. Thankfully, she did not see him on their plane, but what did that mean?

Jordan looked over at Lane. He was busy satisfying Amelia with one of the coloring books that had been packed in her carryon luggage. The decision for Lane to ride next to Amelia while Jordan rode with Tristan was easy enough. Tristan was still very young and though he loved his daddy very much, he preferred his mommy. Jordan allowed a smile as she took in Lane's easy way of being a dad. She was so thankful that he had been able to experience this; that she had been able to experience this. God had given them this miracle and they would both be forever grateful.

Jordan looked down at her cell phone. She knew talking to anyone at this altitude would not be impossible but she could put her phone on airplane mode and hopefully with any luck, Garrison would be near his own phone. She would send him a quick e-mail.

"Hey guy, I know it's late but you hardly sleep and I can't wait to see you in the morning." She wrote and then hit send. She waited for what seemed like an agonizingly long time for a reply. Thankfully, Tristan was sleeping soundly. It appeared that the tag-team-effort she and Lane had made to keep him awake would pay off. Jordan ran her fingers through their son's dark auburn hair; pushing the dainty curls away from his angelic face. She felt so much happiness welling inside of her at times like these: times when her family surrounded her and the past was a distant memory that had been forgiven and all but forgotten.

"Hey. How's the plane ride?" Her phone buzzed, as the screen lit up, evidence of a new e-mail.

"Oh, great!" Jordan wrote as she allowed a sigh of relief. She wasn't sure if Garrison knew anything about Tommy Hayden but she had to ask before her heart popped out of her chest and bounced on the floor in spasms.

"I know this is an odd question, but do you remember Tommy Hayden?" Jordan waited again. She felt as though she sensed some hesitation though, she wasn't quite sure why. Finally, after a long silence, the phone lit up and buzzed, again.

"Uh, yeah? What about him?" Garrison's question came back. Jordan thought even the question seemed to be dripping with hesitation.

"It's probably nothing. It's a small world after all. But I think I saw him in the airport earlier." Jordan hit send again. Then she looked over at Lane and their daughter to ensure they were keeping busy. She didn't want to alarm Lane. She knew that he had probably picked up on her mood but with any luck, he had passed it off as jetlag. She was bound to tired. The problem was she had been on a lot of stakeouts, gathering Intel on a mark longer than the ten hour stay she had spent with her family in the airport waiting on the next flight. She was also sure that Lane knew that as well, but if he did, he wasn't saying so.

"I think I may have heard from one of the guys in passing that he was released a few days ago. Why, did he approach you?" Garrison's question came as a surprise to Jordan; the fact that he, too would be thinking along the same lines as she, was nothing new but it did not help her nerves to have her suspicions confirmed. There was no denying the truth. Now that she had Garrison's collaboration with her thoughts, she knew Tommy was in that airport for no other reason than to stalk his prey. As the last thought flowed through her mind, Jordan again, touched her son's face and allowed a longing glance at her daughter and husband. What would they be up against? Jordan wasn't sure but what she was sure about was she would have to make certain the children were safe while she and Garrison did what they do best... it was time to turn the predator into prey.

7

Shadows danced around the room as they seemed to chase the light back into the corners. The sunlight scarcely cast shards of light like spindly fingers stretching eerily across the room's expanse.

"There was a certain amount of pride that one had to feel," Tommy thought—finding a place that lent itself to that perfect aura of fear wasn't easy. But Tommy had pulled it off.

The old Maddox farm was both secluded and forgotten. Thirty five miles on the out-skirts of down town New York's Irish district, home of Black Heart, stood the small town of Morristown, New Jersey; population a little over eighteen thousand. The idea was a stroke of genius if Tommy had to say so, himself.

Tommy had spent a good part of a Saturday morning at the library scanning through the local archives for abandoned structures. He had just about given up when the tantalizing shot of an old farm flashed across the screen.

Triple murder/suicide leaves small town in shock. The news clipping boasted every detail. Harvey Maddox, long time resident of Morristown, population some eighteen thousand people, came home late Saturday night after spending time at a local bar. A witness was quoted as saying, "Harvey frequented the establishment every Friday and Saturday night." Another witness claimed that Susan Maddox, Harvey's wife was seen with a local man, no more than twenty five years old. Apparently, the two had been carrying on an illicit affair for some time. The article went on to tell how the police had discovered the bodies of Susan and

Harvey Maddox and their two young children: Aaron Four, and Rose Six years of age. The police report had concluded that Harvey Maddox bludgeoned his wife and children then after several hours of listening to some old records had shot himself in the head.

Tommy stood in the old farmhouse taking in the darkened splotches that lined the floor, wall and ceiling. It seemed there had not been a place in the house unaffected by that dreary night. Tommy felt that familiar surge of pride again. A chill ran down his spine as even he felt a twinge of fear dance across his soul. What horrors had unfolded in this house? He thought of the article again and could almost see the vented-rage as it played out in real time.

Tommy imagined the farmer would have come home after drinking all night at the local bar that the article had spoken of. He would be both drunk and angry. First, turning his rage on his wife and then at some point deciding that the children would be better off in heaven than in a world without their parents, he had taken their lives as well.

Tommy followed the splotches down the hall, running his hand on its surface, as he went. Here and there, as the walkway continued, he noticed that some of the blood-splotch patterns seemed to resemble a handprint in places. Maybe the farmer's wife had been pushing against the wall for support near the end of her life. Soon the dreary-walkway opened into a small bedroom with twin beds. The woman must have fought with all of her strength to stop what she felt was inevitable. She had to know; at some point that her outraged husband would end her life and go after their children.

Tommy wasn't sure how the thought made him feel. He wasn't even sure how he felt about killing Jordan's children. He did not know that he cared at all. The idea of the small children dying at the hands of their father almost made sense to him. What did that make him? He supposed some would call him a monster but he didn't feel like a monster. He felt nothing. He would not want his own children, not that he wanted any to be left in this world defenseless. So taking them out of the equation made as much sense to him, as any other option.

Tommy could remember with perfect clarity, how the nights, when he had been left to his stepfather's cruel intentions had been. He would never want that for his children, would he? Would he stand by as his mother had and make excuses? How did he feel about her? Maybe she did the best that she could with what she had and maybe the farmer had too.

Something inside of Tommy felt absent. The excitement even the fear of his amazing find had been short lived. He could feel the familiar emptiness creeping in around his heart. Every victory in his life was always overshadowed by the vast emptiness that dwelt within him. The emptiness that he was sure had been born of his father's absence; an absence that would forever shroud his life and steal any joy he may have had... The fact was his father would never be a part of his life. He had to make Jordan Buckley-Gates pay. No matter how disconnected or empty he may feel; it did not matter. He would never be able to move forward whatever that meant until she shared his pain.

Tommy scanned the house again. No matter what he felt or more importantly did not feel, he had to admit; this house was the perfect place to be a part of Jordan Buckley-Gates' last memory. He, again caressed the blood-stained walls as he allowed the evil rumbling that had been rolling up his throat to have full reign—the laugh, finally, turning into a maniacal chortle.

He soon left the old house after making some last minute decor decisions just a few odds and ends that would definitely beef up the scare factor; not that the place needed much help.

He made his way back to the one bedroom shack, he had erected deep in the woods. He had wanted to keep his equipment close, but not too close. He had to keep his living quarters small so that he could burn any evidence after he had completed his objective.

Tommy was soon in his workout clothes. He would first run five miles around the perimeter of the properly; three times around, exactly five miles. He had a watch given to him by Black Heart. The watch was equipped with many amenities; one of the nicer functions was the mile gauge. He could set the gauge and the mile detector would simply keep up with his footfalls; it was accurate within a few yards which was enough for what he needed. After running, Tommy would find the old punching bag hanging from the huge maple tree in the backyard and pound out his frustration. After five hundred sit-ups, three hundred crunches and one hundred pull ups, Tommy was ready to end his day.

He had kept up his workout regimen and had even added a few cardio exercises of his own which he would tack on every other day.

Staying fit was not an option; it was the only way to accomplish his goals. Tommy was determined to keep his body honed to perfection. He was proud of his godlike features…his green eyes, dark auburn hair, and winning Buckley smile had already given him a leg up with the ladies. As Tommy stood toweling off, he turned first to the left and then to the right; he almost felt a twinge of sorrow for other men… his golden body glistened with the droplets of water from the shower and Tommy smiled. No one was as beautiful as he.

Tommy thought of Jordan in that moment. How could she not know who he was? Wasn't he the spitting image of his father before the nightlife had taken its toll? More importantly, he was the image of Jordan, herself. She had taken the attributes awarded her through the Schooner and Buckley bloodlines and had honed them to perfection as well. In a different time, under different circumstances, they might have been friends: Tommy pondered that idea momentarily, he could never see them as being anything but what they were: enemies. He hated her and soon she would hate him.

Tommy watched his reflection in the mirror, once again as the emerald green hue in his eyes devolved into dead-empty blackness. He couldn't wait to see what Jordan Buckley-Gates was capable of. He had heard all the details about her time with the organization. She had been one of the best until she had lost control and allowed some demon… isn't that what James Ruston had said? He had told Tommy the day that he had come to The Garden that Jordan had claimed that she was possessed by a demon. Well if that's the way she wanted to play it; the devil made her do it; did he? Okay… Tommy laughed, the dark laugh again, as his head fell back and then he looked into the dead eyes of his reflection.

"Time for Jordan to come face to face with the devil!" He snarled.

8

Garrison flipped his laptop closed. He had been mowing over some files that Jenkins had expected to be on his desk by Friday.

Two of the department new hopefuls were being released from The Garden and placed in the field. James Ruston's name appeared at the top of Jeremy Lewis' file. Garrison thought Ruston's days of not only recruiting but training had come to an end; especially after the incident in the park over four years ago.

Garrison tossed a wary glance at Ruston's name again and then allowed the events of that night to unfold in his mind.

Garrison had responded to the scene a few minutes before the local sheriff's department. The crime scene had his partner's M.O. (Modus Operandi) all over it; not that any of the other detectives or law enforcement agencies would notice.

Garrison ducked under the police tape and followed the hushed tones into the living room. The house was not at all what he would have thought. Thinking back to Jordan's apartment complex, Garrison thought better of his initial assumption. Jordan had obviously come from very meager beginnings beyond that of his imaginings. The walls were shellacked in a viscous-tar yellow that clung to the tattered furnishings as well. Garrison followed a thin hallway to the back of the house. Stepping through the doorway, he saw the body there.

Junior Buckley lay in an awkward heap, with blood splotches, fanning the area surrounding him. Glass particles were splayed on the floor from the shattered window behind him. Garrison could instantly tell that the window had been broken from the inside. The murderer had exited there. He could also tell by the careless mess of glass lining the floor and the large crater through the middle of the pane that he or she had been in a hurry to leave. If Jordan had committed this crime, she would not care to leave in such a manner, something had to of caused her to abandon protocol. Jordan would never do anything so sloppy while exiting a crime scene, doing so would increase the possibility of finding particles of hair or clothing... maybe even blood from the perk.

Garrison turned and headed back to the living room. He would make small talk with the wife; get her attention on serving drinks or whatever; he didn't care... he just wanted to get her out of the way.

The local law enforcement had already started to arrive and were canvassing the place with a fine-toothed comb. It wouldn't be long before they would have all of the obvious spots covered and Jordan could do what she did best: be invisible. Garrison hoped with the destroyed window that Jordan had not already eliminated all possibility of being unseen.

Garrison had pounded the art of invisibility into Jordan's head during training. It could literally be the most important weapon in an agent's arsenal. It could mean the difference between freedom and captivity; more importantly life and death.

Garrison watched as Erica Buckley left the room to make a glass of tea. He bent slightly and tossed the letter into the chimney; making sure not to be seen by anyone in the room. He turned to one of the other detectives that were enthralled with a stain on the wall near a rotting blue chair with a floral design.

"Yummy." Garrison quipped. Then turning away, he quickly headed for the front door.

"Well nothing to see here. Make sure all the evidence is bagged and tagged." Garrison said, as he continued to the door. "I'm beat. I'm headed home for some shut-eye." Garrison walked right out the door, paying no attention to the confused glances. None of the other detectives or law enforcement agencies had a clue who he was. No one knew that Jordan was a secret operative working for the CIA. They definitely had no clue that she was a potential suspect or that Garrison was there to warn her about Black Heart's intentions to recycle her...

more importantly, no one knew that Jordan Buckley was his partner. Garrison had scanned the window, he hadn't seen any signs of DNA, left behind or any clothing… he hoped his initial scan had been enough. He had no other choice but to hope for the best and try to warn her about Black Heart's intentions.

Garrison knew that Jordan would be in the chimney and that she would get his letter; what he didn't know was though, the night was long, it was about to get longer. The letter had requested that Jordan meet him in the park later that night so Garrison could give Jordan vital Intel concerning her status with the organization.

Things had gone from bad to worse that night; causing their meeting, to be even later. By the time they did meet up in the park, so much was going on that Garrison had no time to inform Jordan about anything.

Garrison had ended up at Jordan's family home that night after following his partner for days. Driven by revenge, Jordan had believed ending her brother's life would end the evil taint that poisoned her family bloodline. The rage that Jordan had believed would be forever satisfied by her brother's death only grew. Consumed by that rage, Jordan turned on her niece nearly ending her life, as well. Jordan had jumped through the bedroom window in an attempt to put distance between her and her loved ones. Jordan collapsed not far from the house where she had her first encounter with Lane Gates; the man that she was now married to.

Try as he might, Lane could not curve the demon's insatiable appetite for bloodshed. Undeterred, Lane pressed forward and it was that determination that had almost ended his life. Garrison claimed Jordan's body after injecting her with a bulletlike dart that made her appear to be dead: by lowering her heart rate, lowering her temperature a few degrees and changing her skin tone to a pallor which was normally associated with the dead or very ill. Garrison moved Jordan's body to The Garden where John and Cynthia Benton; a couple of agents from The Truth could keep watch over her from the observation room.

John Benton owed Garrison and Jordan a favor for having Cynthia transferred to The Truth. Cynthia, like Jordan had been a rogue member of Black Heart. Unlike Jordan, Cynthia had not killed in hate or revenge... Cynthia had merely been protecting herself on the way home from the store one afternoon. Unfortunately, Black Heart had witnessed her artful means of self-preservation and like Garrison, they recruited her under false pretenses... stealing yet another, hopeful existence; replacing it with uncertainty and vengeance.

Garrison had kept Jordan's presence in The Garden a secret from all but the Benton's.

Not long after waking, Jordan made good her escape; where she again met up with Lane. Lane soon called Garrison realizing that he was the only one that the two of them could trust. Garrison, again, requested that they meet him in the park.

In the park that night, Garrison, Jordan and Lane stumbled on more than each other; they uncovered a gun and drug cartel; headed up by none other than James Ruston which brought Garrison back to his original query; why was James Ruston's name at the top of a new recruit file. For that matter... why was it at the top of Garrison's former partner, Simon's recruit's file? The very one that had assisted him the night that Jordan had been inducted into Black Heart. The same night that Garrison had first betrayed Jordan by not telling her the whole truth.

Garrison, not only knew about the inmate; he had been responsible for making the scene appear to be authentic. In fact, Jordan was his first recruit. It was her successful recruiting and training that was to take him to the top of the proverbial food chain of Black Heart.

Garrison pushed the file away and started to step away from his desk. Just as he was about to collect his coffee mug and pour him another cup of the steaming brew, he noticed his I-Phone lighting up. The indicator at the bottom of the phone showed that he had a new E-mail. Garrison sat back down. He pulled up the E-mail. His breath caught. It was from Jordan. He answered all of her questions, as usual with as little truth as he could possibly attach to the responses. He shook his head and then pushed his I-Phone away from him. He didn't want to think about all of the half-truths and lies that were piling up between him and his best friend. What was scarier still was he didn't know what bothered him more: the fact that he had withheld the truth or the fact that the truth was bound to come out.

9

Jordan moved to the middle of the isle. She had collected as many of the bags as she could carry. Lane would have to carry Tristan, his car seat and bag; along with some of the other luggage at baggage claim. Jordan held her hand out to Amelia as she allowed a smile. It would not be easy separating from the children; not under the circumstances. The whole reason for bringing the children was to spend time with them. Now, in just a few short hours, John and Cynthia Benton would be moving into their temporary quarters at The Garden in order to assume care for Amelia and Tristan during Lane's and Jordan's absence.

Cynthia had jumped at the opportunity. She had told Jordan and Lane nothing would make them happier. Jordan felt guilty about asking the couple. She knew that their devotion was probably a result of their belief that they owed her in some way. Jordan knew that was the farthest thing from the truth. Her own life had been spared and given back to her as if it were a magnificent gift. She had deserved death; nothing more and nothing less. Instead, someone had gave her life and more abundant. She was happy for the times that God allowed her the opportunity to pay some of her good fortune forward; even in the times that she was not capable of knowing what goodwill was, God was there allowing her a taste of all that was to come. She would have done anything to have served God sooner; to have freely given her life in His service. She had wasted so much time.

Like Jonah and his whale, Jordan had run from her Nineveh. She had denied her purpose on the earth for so long. She had killed God's people in a misguided belief that she was some justice, born to rid the world of all the evil. Satan had lied to her; just as he lies to all that will listen. But God is the bringer of life, the giver of second chances; her second chance had come in the form of her husband, her children... most of all it had come in the form of her salvation. Now, she was returning to the place where she and Lane had promised forever, the place that she had run from for so long; the place that she had not realized was wrapped in an essence so strongly saturated in the peace of God that it was like walking into a small piece of heaven on earth. She was returning to The Garden. She had intended to share its gifts with their children.

The Garden was a beautiful place: as its name suggested, it was a lush garden: full of exotic flowers, cascading waterfalls, decorative fountains, and impossibly, enormous indigenous bird, and butterfly populations. The cacophony of sounds that the birds demonstrated was like an orchestra of the most heavenly music.

Jordan had so looked forward to sharing that world with her children. Now, a twinge of sorrow and if she were being honest jealousy was needling the back of her mind because she knew she would soon be dropping off her children in the world that she had wanted to share with them. She and Lane would be walking away into whatever darkness awaited them. It was there that she knew she would find him... the owner of the eyes, darkened with an evil, so strong that it seemed to blotch out his very being. She would find Tommy. In that place, she would have to return to, at least in part that person she had long since left behind. She would have to remember what it had been to be Jordan Buckley, the Black Heart operative.

Could she do it? Could she lend her senses to that part of her and keep her will? More than ever the dreams made sense. She had learned to listen to God speaking to her in all things. He was in the world around her... yes, but, He was in her dreams as well. He was trying to warn her of the evil that lurked in the shadows of her not so distant past. He was trying to reach her, where she was at; through her own experiences. He was showing her those long forgotten fears. He was allowing her to remember, to experience so that she would not forget not even for the tiniest of moments. She had to keep Him first. She had to allow Him, full reign of her conscious and subconscious mind! If she was slack even for a moment, Satan would again have his way. Whatever this being was that was controlling Tommy Hayden, there was only one way to destroy it forever: God's power. The same way that hate had been eradicated from her own life, God could do the same for Tommy.

If only, she would not allow the wounds of her past to have the upper-hand. She could not allow the old anger associated with distrust: the lies that had piled up around her, back then, the disgust of being abused by those meant to care for her and the false sense of shelter that she had believed existed in her mother's arms to pull her back into the darkness.

It was not until she had her own children that she had realized how wrong she had been about her mother. Jordan had believed that her mother was so innocent, just as much a victim, as she had been. Quite frankly, it had been the deepest, and yes, hardest of all her wounds to heal. Her mother that should have protected her; her mother that should have been her shelter from the storm; her mother that should have left the awful existence in search of a better way for her children; her mother had sat like a squatter in the midst of all that hate and destruction, too weak minded to make a better way. It had been that weakness that had made it all possible and it was under the care of Doctor Schoonhoven, a Christian counselor at the psychiatric ward that she had come to terms with that hidden truth. It was in that realization that Jordan had found the most peaceful place in God's truth, His forgiveness; His all-consuming love had only one way; let it go and so she had.

It seemed too easy to remember God's love; it was in everything... her children's laughter, her husband's touch and the simplicity of her friendship with Garrison. It was all there, all she had to do was focus on the depth of love she felt for them, and yes, received back in spades.

Jordan moved down the aisle with the flow of traffic as she claimed her little girl's hand. In that moment, she quietly prayed to hold on to the innocents she knew existed behind her daughter's eyes. She prayed that when all was said and done; for better or worse that she would still be Jordan Gates: wife to Lane, mother to Amelia and Tristan, beyond all that she would be an obedient daughter to her Savior. As the prayer swelled within her heart, Jordan could feel that tangible peace that always calmed her. She could feel that all would be well. God was filling her with His reassuring Spirit. She had only to have faith.

10

Lane's mind was racing. He had been on the phone with John Benton for only a few minutes. He was confirming all of the details about the couple caring for the children but in that time he could sense something wasn't right.

John Benton was one of the most open individuals that Lane had ever known. He had been with The Truth for fourteen years. John came to The Truth as a missionary when he was twenty. It had been his desire to go overseas and work with foreign missions. During his time with The Truth, God had tweaked his plans. John had met and fallen in love with Cynthia Jacobs. It was through their union that God had manifested his true calling.

Cynthia Jacobs had been wrongly inducted into the government's answer for unpunished crimes, Black Heart. Cynthia, the oldest of four girls had been on her way home from the store when she was attacked. In a bout of desperation, Cynthia had flung rocks and gravel into her attacker's eyes incapacitating them. She had inadvertently killed one of the men by hitting him in the temple with a rock. At the time, she had believed it to be a lucky shot but later she would come to know that God was purposeful. Her path had been set from the beginning.

It was through her induction into Black Heart that Cynthia had been brought like all new recruits to The Garden to be counseled. There Cynthia would be introduced to many forms of spirituality. She had also met John Benton her future husband.

She had turned out to be a bumbling disappointment of an assassin. Black Heart had placed Cynthia back into The Garden where they were making plans to recycle her. Cynthia would be put through intense training sessions, mind altering processes that John liked to refer to as brain-washing and finally plastic surgery.

John had been overseas at the time in a country called Honduras helping to build habitats and reconstruct water supplies. He and Cynthia had not met until later. She had returned to The Garden after another fumbled attempt at taking out a mark. John had stayed by Cynthia's side. Watching over her and even holding her as she cried herself to sleep. She was so broken about the prospect of returning to the field. Another plastic surgery would do nothing to change what was in her heart: Cynthia just did not have what it took to end someone's life. She would continue to be caught and she would continue to put Black Heart at risk. .. she felt so hopeless.

John and Cynthia both had confided that time to Lane one night, when he had returned from the Cadotion village. At that same time, Lane had learned of his new assignment. He would have to convince Black Heart's most dangerous agent to listen to the teachings of Christianity and somehow show her a better way. The Truth had suggested Lane for the assignment; assuring the HOD of Black Heart of his success. Lane wasn't so sure. John and Cynthia had told Lane her story in order to remind him of God's purposefulness. God had a plan and no matter how bleak the circumstance, He would be right there guiding Lane's path.

It was John that had first approached Garrison. He had begged Garrison to talk to his HOD (Head of Department) about the official transfer of Cynthia into The Truth. John had explained that Cynthia was not cutout for the life of a trained killer. It had been mere happenstance that had allowed her to best her would be rapist and possibly murderers that day in the alley.

Garrison had told John that he could make no promises but he would plead her case. Edward Stanton, the Head of Operations was a very busy man and at times very unreasonable. It was he that had ordered Garrison's induction after Ruston had brought Garrison to Stanton's attention. No matter that Garrison was no killer, Stanton had seen something in the way that the murder or rather self-defense killing had been orchestrated and he had felt that Garrison would be an asset to the company. His instincts were rarely wrong.

Cynthia, on the other hand, had been inducted by James Ruston. It was his urging that had led to Cynthia being placed in the department. Cynthia had been a thorn in Black Heart's side from the start and Garrison feared though he had not told John Benton that she would have to be erased if something was not done soon. Garrison hoped that it would be that angle that would help to convince Mr. Stanton that changing Cynthia Jacob's objective could be a better option.

Mr. Stanton had allowed the move admitting that he owed Garrison for not being a bumbling idiot like Cynthia had been. He knew that Garrison had come from a similar background. Though there had been something, both brutal and final, in the way that he had killed the bank robber, Garrison could have been an embarrassment to Mr. Stanton in the same way that Cynthia had been for James Ruston.

Garrison had taken to the company with an excellence that permeated his every decision whether it was a kill or merely recruiting another operative: Garrison was quite frankly, Mr. Stanton's golden boy. So Edward Stanton had happily agreed to the request. He had felt that it like many of Garrison's ideas was a stroke of genius. John and Cynthia had been married not long after her induction into The Truth. They would soon realize God's purpose for their lives was to equip others in similar situations as Cynthia with the means to cross over; they would head up the OAW (Operation, Another Way) a ministry that was aimed directly at the heart of Black Heart. Quite simply, John and Cynthia was working from the inside to recruit and convert as many of Black Heart's agents as possible. Lane knew that doing so would paint a big target on both of their backs and it may even cause problems for Garrison, golden boy or not, for having Cynthia transferred in the first place.

Lane put his phone into his pants pocket and tried to put the thought that something was definitely amiss out of his mind. He could only imagine the stress that would accompany such a dangerous mission as that of OAW. The fact was, like it or not, the two lived behind enemy lines and at any time, they could be caught. John was probably filling the full-weight of that truth and now Lane was asking him to take their children. Unfortunately, they had no other options. John and Cynthia were the only family or friends in the states that led the least dangerous lifestyle. Everyone else on the list was either field agents with a big bull's-eye painted on their backs or they were single like Garrison and had no clue what keeping a child might involve.

John Benton hung up the phone as he began the slow decent into the terror that he had become accustom to lately. What was he going to do? The phone calls had been coming more often lately. He had kept as much of the threatening messages from Cynthia as possible. He watched her becoming more and more involved with the details of getting the wing donated to their stay while keeping Lane and Jordan's children ready for their arrival. How could he blame her? What he wouldn't do for a distraction right now. He was thankful that she had other things to think about than what he was occupying his time with at the moment. Any other time, avoiding Cynthia's full knowledge of something of this magnitude would have been more than impossible.

John kept tapping the phone. He wasn't sure whether he was making certain the eerie voice had really been on the other end of the phone line or just in the other room. The phone call had come almost immediately after he had hung up the phone with Lane.

John was standing in the middle of The Garden, taking in the new additions made to the fountain. Crape Myrtle hung from the outstretched hands of the cherubs in heavy clumps like fatted grapes ripe for the picking. The tiniest of additions, and yet, it had added so much wonder and luster to an already magnificent piece. The fountain made in the image of the Arc of the Covenant had two cherubs standing with hands outstretched facing the same direction. The middle of the fountain, a flat surface made for sacrificing was embedded with rare stones found in mission fields such as that of the Cadotion village: each stone had been brought in by the agent responsible for bringing the truth to that field. The agent would in a ceremony conducted by The Truth's HOD, Kevin Anderson, cement the stone into place; a reminder that another place in the world was now filled with God's holy word. John caressed the stones, regret filled the touch. He had so wanted to be responsible for the placement of one of those stones. He prayed even now that though God's mission for his life was bringing the truth to unfortunate Black Heart recruits that one day He would allow him this one honor. He knew enough of being in God's will to know that regret would not last; still he knew enough of God's love to know that He was a gift giver. God is the best in the business when it comes to knowing what His children want; so John would make his wish known and he would pray for what he knew would come. One day, though John did not know when he would be placing a stone.

John thought of some of his own times in the field. He longed for the dangers that had accompanied the more simple moments in the field. He was a missionary for crying out loud. He had always half expected to receive some sort of slap on the wrist for their involvement in bringing awareness of The Truth to Black Heart recruits but this was so far from his imaginings. The voice had been very clear. He and Cynthia would die. Die? John thought about the word again, as he imagined what his death might have looked like. Maybe an old man next to his girl that's what he called Cynthia, his girl; maybe he would have a massive heart attack and that would be the end of it. But this voice was not suggesting an easy way out; something quaint in the middle of the night. No, he and Cynthia would not just be fading away... they would be dying in a very imaginatively-dark place where the person on the other end of the phone would be able to toy with them. John had no desire to find out how many ways the person on the other end of the phone could bring about one's death.

John stared into the fountain as he thought of his wife; Cynthia had been through so much, unlike him. He had been with The Truth since the beginning. It hadn't been easy; mission work was anything, but easy. But mission work was nothing like Black Heart where the recruits were being trained to kill in ninety nine of the most excruciating ways that he had ever heard of.

Cynthia, a sweet southern bell that did nothing for so long, but help her mother with dinner and care for her younger siblings; Cynthia, who until Black Heart the worst thing she had seen of death was her grandmother killing supper in the backyard was forced to kill in the most vile ways and dangerous settings. Still, somehow, John could imagine that the sinister voice on the other end of the phone could do things that would make Jordan Buckley-Gates, one of the best Black Heart had ever trained, cringe.

John brushed his hand through his light brown hair for the umpteenth time, this morning. He allowed his mind to drift back to the first phone call he had received from the voice. John had stepped out that morning and was running a few errands for Cynthia. She had informed him that if the children were going to be staying that there would need to be some things brought in that would capture their imaginations. John had been sure that Jordan and Lane would not only be aware of this but would be capable of bringing such things. Cynthia had assured John that she was aware that the couple knew their children but they would not be able to bring the things that the children would want on an airplane. They would only be able to bring the bare necessities.

The phone call came, as John was on his way back to the compound. John's initial thought was that it had to be a prank but the more that the person spoke the more aware John became that this was no prank. Chills ran down his spine as the voice informed him that he would be receiving some guests. The voice told John that unless he wanted his precious wife to end up dead along with himself that he would be compliant. John hated the way he had felt every day since; actually, considering the words of the voice. He was now standing out by the fountain trying to think of ways to carry out the orders of someone that was most likely going to kill his best friends. He was too big of a coward to do the right thing. Jordan would know exactly what to do but instead of confiding in her John was trembling like a scared rabbit in the bush.

John thought about the conversation that he had just had with the voice. The voice wanted him to leave the back entrance to the compound open. How could he do that? The person on the other end of the line would surely not leave him and Cynthia, untouched for their troubles. No. John would have to somehow talk to Lane and Jordan. He was certain that the person issuing the threats on the other end of the phone line would not stop until he or she had tied up all the loose ends; including him and his wife.

11

Jordan stood in the small apartment-sized kitchenette. She was feeling claustrophobic in the small space. She thought that she should be used to such confined spaces; living in the handmade tents of the Cadotion tribe certainly did not leave an ample amount of room but there was something about being that close to nature that seemed to open things up; ease her stress. Hear her pulse raced, she had forgotten that the compound was buried so deep beneath the surface. The walls at times seemed to take on a life of their own.

The entrance to the compound was gained through a small pub in New York's Irish district. No matter the distance, beneath the soil it may, as well be thousands of feet because the result was the same—she was away from the people that she loved, the people that had taught her so many things about love, life and devotion.

Her eyes moved around the standard earthy-brown of the cabinets and suddenly, she missed home. Everything here was so button-down-the-collar. What she wouldn't do for some much needed alone time with Lane. It had been a week since their time in the village. Her body tingled with the phantom caresses of their embrace. She shuddered as her mind wondered lazily back to the water as it rippled luxuriously against her naked flesh while Lane's fingers sought the tender places of her body that came alive for him alone.

"Is everything okay?" Lane's voice broke through the memory as his arms snaked around her abdomen, pulling her body against that of his own, melting their shadows into one on the small dining room walls. Jordan turned to him as his hands moved up her spine, setting small fires in their wake. His fingers laced into her hair as he began a slow massage; his way of erasing some of the stress that had been back building over the last week. Jordan sighed as she allowed her body closer access to his. Her mind filled with awe. It never ceased to amaze her; this giant of a man that filled the already miniscule surroundings should add to her stress but it was in his arms that she felt the most freedom.

Amelia and Tristan were safely tucked away in their own beds just down the hall. Jordan couldn't believe how easily both children had gone to sleep after she and Lane had completed their nightly ritual of giving them baths, dressing them in their pajamas, reading from the small children's story book bible and saying their prayers. The children were exhausted from the two day flight from the Cadotion village and the ten hour delay at the airport, only to board yet another plane for New York. It culminated into one big barrage of events that perpetuated an already exhausting and trying trip. Having to fly across country with two small children would have been no easy task under the most favorable of circumstances but to be complicated even further by a delay in an airport for ten hours; how could she expect anything else?

Jordan had already committed to allowing the children to sleep in the following morning. Their bodies needed to stretch out. Having spent two days in an upright position, surrounded by so many strangers would be trying for an adult... Jordan sighed as she thought about her babies and how good they had both been under the circumstances. She was proud of her family. Her children could be spoiled at times, she supposed. But for the most part having spent their lives in a village where each member would have to maintain a job in order to ensure the survival of its people, as a whole, Amelia and Tristan were better than some of the children Jordan had witnessed. . . the thought brought memories back of the little boy in the Atlanta airport; kicking and screaming as his mother tried to lovingly encourage him to make better nutritional decisions. Like Lane, Jordan had been proud of the young woman for sticking to her decision for the child's care, no matter how stressful, Jordan could imagine it became, she had insisted that her child have a piece of fruit rather than the sugar filled candy bar he had wanted. Though the child lay sprawled out on the floor of the airport terminal, screaming to the top of his lungs; the young mother never wavered. In the end the child took the fruit. Jordan imagined that the trip could not have been easy on the young woman with such a small child in tow.

Jordan allowed her head to fall lazily against the wall of Lane's chest as again she emitted a throaty sigh. Just being near him like this felt so right. How had she fought him for so long? It was Lane that had known, however subconsciously that their paths becoming one had been in God's plan from the beginning. Lane too had fought the idea at first, feeling as though it was his own flesh that was lusting for Jordan and not his soul being compelled to be with her... in time the push was so strong that neither Lane nor Jordan could fight the inevitable.

Lane removed his right hand from the slow massage he had been administering as he circled his arm around Jordan and moved his other hand to her chin. With a gentle tug, he could see that his intentions were made clear. Jordan lifted her face to him as their eyes danced in the pale light casting an eerie glow that bathed its soft luminous aura on their bodies causing their shadows to mimic their motions.

Lane lowered his lips to Jordan's, moving, slowly at first then more eagerly. Threading his fingers into her beautiful dark-auburn hair with a gentle tug he tilted her head back exposing the flesh of her long neck. Her usually milky skin had been kissed by the sun's rays during their time in the Cadotion village; adding a tropical-exotic allure to her already stunning features. He moved with the authority of a man that knew every dip, every subtle detail of his wife's body as he trailed light kisses down her neck. It had been too long since their last touch and Lane could not be sure when they would be allowed the time to be this way again; to explore the terrain of the other's body enjoying the gift of pleasure that could be found there; a gift that God had meant for man and wife alone. It was that thought that lit the already smoldering flames inside of him. Lane dipped low as he claimed Jordan's legs and pulled her into his arms. Like a stealthy car his body moved with ease as he maneuvered the dim lit corners of the small apartment to the bedroom that they shared. Gently pushing the door closed with his foot and locking it with his free hand, he moved across the room as he placed his wife onto their bed.

Jordan's mind abandoned all thoughts of anything but this moment. Her heart beat with wild abandon against her chest... she savored the new reason for her galloping heart. She loved the effect that her husband had on her. She loved that despite everything that they had been through, and all that was happening in their lives at this moment that he still could take her to this place. She loved that everything about him said he wanted her, loved her, and needed her: it was all evident in the touch of his hand, the way his eyes lingered over her body; the smolder of desire in their depths, the way that he spoke to her in a tone that seemed almost reverent at times. She loved him with all of her being. Lane was God showing mercy on her. She loved that God loved her enough to allow her this. .. the oneness of their spirits, the way that they seemed to think and move as one, everything about them culminated into a uniqueness that was theirs alone. All of it had been perfectly, and yes purposefully orchestrated by God's own hand.

They spent the night loving each other. Each touch, embrace, kiss, and lingering glance moving them forward as one to that place where their love could sweep them away from all of the problems of the here and now to the place that existed for them alone... in a torrent of bliss they were whisked away to their very own paradise.

✳ ✳ ✳

The room was filled with small toys of every shape and size. The Head of Department had even said that the colors could be changed as long as Cynthia and John agreed to return the room to its former state. Cynthia wasn't sure if she wanted to return the room to its former state. This time of preparation had taught her well what her own desire for the future was. At first she had been afraid of the possibility that her life could change so dramatically. Would she make a good mother? Would John even want a child? Did she want a child? Now as she took in the soft blues, cool yellows, and pale pinks her heart filled with the possibility that their future held.

Cynthia's eves filled with unshed rears as she rubbed the small bump at the base of her abdomen; a possibility that she only now knew would be sooner rather than later... but how would she tell John? Hadn't he been dragging his feet the whole way?

In the last two weeks since finding out that Amelia and Tristan would be staying with them for a while, John had grown distant. More than once she had found him withdrawn by the fountain speaking in hushed tones but to whom? Cynthia did not know. 'Was he having an affair? She couldn't imagine her John doing that. He loved her, of that she was sure. But who then? Who was he speaking to? She had been so preoccupied with the details of preparing for the children's arrival. Had she missed something along the way? Could John be facing something?

Something she had been too busy to notice? Her brow furrowed as she turned from the room and headed for where she knew she would find her husband... the fountain. It was rime to ger to the bottom of all of this.

Cynthia moved with determination. She had something to tell him and whether he was ready to hear it or not; she had not gotten pregnant on her own. John Benton had some listening, and explaining to do...

12

Two days had passed since Garrison had talked to Jordan. By now, he was sure that they were settled in at their new quarters. The Truth had gone all out. The idea that a family could need to be housed at the facility had opened up new possibilities for ministry. Garrison could not understand the big deal. Why not just rent an apartment for the family? But that was not his concern. Right now he was up to his eyeballs in figuring out what to do about the Tommy Hayden situation.

Garrison had devoted countless man hours to finding Tommy; so far his best efforts had been met with utter failure. He had tried to return to the basics. What was he missing? He wanted to treat Tommy, as he would a mark that he was profiling in order to get close enough to take him/her out. Even that idea had fallen short. There simply was nothing, no one that Tommy was that attached to. No roots, no ties that bind, as would be true with other marks. Tommy Hayden was like a feather floating on a breeze; like a ghost. Every person that had ever touched his life was simply gone; dead.

Garrison exhaled forcefully, as he pinched the bridge of his nose while throwing the file he had found on Tommy back onto his desk. He had been through every detail of the file with a fine-tooth-comb.

Tommy had attended Bellflower academy, a private school that allowed two charity borders a year. Tommy was selected by his case worker, Ginger Ryan. Ginger was notified by the school counselor, Tim Bridges, after he had noticed a drop in Tommy's grades. Ginger started to make visits to the house and had not seen anything other than a very impoverished environment that may have caused such a change in Tommy's overall behavior. The young-idealistic counselor was determined to reach Tommy. She thought that the small setting of a private school may be just what Tommy needed to bring him out of the darkness.

It was the private school that had prompted the meeting between Tommy's mother and stepfather. He had been a truck driver that frequented the truck stop where Tommy's mother had gotten a job to be closer to Tommy's school in case of an emergency. Tommy's mother had been on a downward spiral at the time as well. She was starting to give into the nagging possibility that had always been at the back of her mind like a cancer eating at her hope that Tommy's biological father would never come back to her. Tommy's mother had started to blame Tommy and was spending more and more time at work. The nights soon became longer and Tommy spent a great deal of his nights alone.

Tommy had confided in Ginger about his concerns for his mother. He had told Ginger many things after she had gained his trust. Every detail that Tommy had entrusted Ginger with was all in the file that now lay on Garrison's desk, and not a word seemed to help him. He still had no idea after reading the file who Tommy Hayden was. He had no idea where he was. He could not imagine what his next move was and time was running out.

Garrison slumped in his chair, as he looked first from the large bank of windows that lined the outer wall of his lavish office and then to the fake plant in the corner he so hated for its reminder of how counterfeit he felt... not only as a friend to both Jordan and Lane, but as an agent. Never before had Garrison met with such a wall of opposition as this. He had the file. Why couldn't he make the profile? Why couldn't he just figure out Tommy Hayden's next move?

Everything about Jordan as crazy as it seemed made sense. Her father and brother had tortured her. They had treated her and her mother with utter disrespect. Jordan had done what any serial killer would do; she had killed those that met with the profile. She had deemed herself the salvation of all those that she believed to be cast down by the sins of those that shared the likeness of her father and brother. Jordan truly believed that she was protecting the world by her actions.

But Tommy, he was another story. He wasn't killing people that fit the profile of his mother who had cast him aside to lick her own self-inflicted wounds. He was not killing people that fit the profile of his sadistic step father that had tortured him for countless years because he blamed Tommy for stealing his wife's affection. Who was it in Tommy's past that had wronged him? Who had set all of these events into place? What was the one transgression that could not be forgiven? He had read the file and he knew that Jordan was his aunt, but so what. He didn't know Jordan. He probably had no clue that she was the one that had taken him to The Garden. So why would he care about Jordan? What was it about Jordan that would cause Tommy to go to where she was? Why follow her?

Garrison eyed the file on his desk with a frustration that was becoming more and more familiar to him. It was there. Whatever it was that was driving Tommy, it was in the pages of that file. Garrison thought for a moment, as he looked at the Fikias in the corner of the room, yet again, frustrated with its imitation of life. He inhaled another deep cleansing breath trying to clear his head. His eyes moved from the counterfeit plant in the corner of the room to his coffee cup. It was empty. He needed something to help him through the long hours ahead of him. Standing, Garrison purposely, ignored the file on his desk as he started for the door of his office. He needed to get out of this room. He had to get some air. The office walls were getting smaller by the minute and his patience was wearing thin. He needed to call his best friend. He needed to talk to her personally about some of the things that had happened in the past during the darker season of her life.

Garrison pulled his phone from his coat pocket. Sliding the illuminated bar across the screen, the icons came into view. He started to ignore the pictures depicting each file, represented on the face of his phone. His finger lingered, only a moment over the contacts icon and suddenly his attention was drawn to an icon at the lower left corner of his phone. It was Jordan's file. He immediately pulled the file up, as he dropped back down into his high backed chair. Of course, the answer had been there all along. He had to compare the files. If he could somehow cross reference the two files maybe he could develop a profile that could bring into focus the piece of this puzzle that he could not see. With that in mind, Garrison grabbed his coffee cup and headed to the coffee maker in the hall. He was certain this would not be anything less than a long grueling process that may not prove to be anything but a huge waste of time... but it was a chance that he would have to take. His best friend's life may be counting on it.

The smell of eucalyptus played on a light breeze filtering through the air duct. Jordan was so happy to not be allergic to the plant as her mother had been. The loved nourishment of the koala bear had many uses as Jordan had learned during her time among the Cadotion tribe. She stretched her body languidly as she thought of the day ahead. She still felt very unprepared to deal with all that she knew would be before her that coupled with the dreams that had been coming more often, seemed to be sapping her of all her energy. What she wouldn't give for one night sleep uninterrupted by any outside force; be it dream or otherwise.

She looked at the phone as she again thought of how badly she needed to get in touch with Garrison. She had been in town for two days and had still not touched base with her best friend and former partner. There had been the e-mail concerning Tommy Hayden but nothing that could say she had really made an attempt to communicate with the one person that had stood by her when no one else seemed to understand her or care to. The plans made for Garrison to pick them up at the airport had fallen through; Garrison was swamped. He was involved in a case at the office and could not get away. The thought saddened Jordan. She had been looking forward to the time she could spend with Garrison on the ride back to the compound.

Instead, John Benton had picked them up. Jordan and Lane had decided to spend a day or two with the children. The children needed time to acclimate to John and Cynthia before just taking off after the enemy. The time may not be practical, especially given the dangerous circumstances of which they faced but leaving their children with strangers, at least, as far as the children were concerned, felt wrong to

Jordan. It in of itself would bring about its own level of psychological damage.

With a sigh, Jordan stepped from the bed as she made her way to the small bathroom attached to their modestly decorated bedroom that was a mere eight by twelve cubic feet. She relieved her bladder, brushed her teeth and checked her reflection in the mirror.

"Yikes!" She complained as she stepped quietly from their bedroom into the hall. Today she would have to make the necessary preparations for the children to be placed in their friends care. It would not be easy. Other than the short time that she and Lane had flown back to the states for the birth of Tristan, they had never been separated from their children. This would be different, somehow. Now, they would have to find within them the ability to stay focused on the task at hand and not allow thoughts of their children to cloud their minds.

Easing the door open, Jordan peered inside the small bedroom where her children still slept. Refusing to sleep alone, their small bodies nestled together on the toddler bed. Tristan laid cuddled his dark-auburn hair curled around his angelic face in ringlets. Amelia, the picture of a hazelnut princess with dark hair, shrouding her now older features lay with one hand over her head while the other stated her claim as guardian over her brother. Jordan stifled a giggle, as she closed the door and headed for the kitchen. She would need to hurry if she was going to get breakfast on the table before the pitter patter of little feet claimed the silence.

She continued down the scarcely lit hall, as she noted the embellished wood wall on the opposite side of the hall separating the bedrooms from the living room area. Chorded spiral wood rose from the halfway point of the wall stretching to about three inches from the ceiling. The garnishment was meant to give the small apartment a more open appeal, incite thoughts of beauty but a shutter claimed Jordan's body as she could think of nothing more than prison walls. Stepping away from the small divider wall, Jordan had full view of the phone that hung on the kitchen wall. She sighed again as she then realized it was time to make that call. It had been put off long enough.

13

One more phone call would have to be made in order to convince that sniveling idiot, John Benton that he would do exactly as he was told. Tommy's patience was wearing thin. He had tried to gain access to the compound in other ways, all of which had been a waste of time. Now, he sat in the middle of the abandoned farmhouse, taking in the accessories he had added to beef-up the scare factor.

Strobe lighting was placed in the four corners of the room, and worked on a timer that was remote controlled through a mini motion detector. Tommy eyed the darkened windows, as a chill ran wickedly down his spine. Burnished streaks blazed their way down the full length of the floor to ceiling windows. The eerie fingerlike etchings that the varnish made on the windows filled the room with the perfect amount of gore. His eyes moved to the walls, as he spotted the blood stains. There was nothing that he could do that had not already been done to them. The farmer's moment of crazed jealousy had lent its own gruesome influence, so Tommy had just let the walls be.

A novelties shop on the outskirts of town had given Tommy the find of a lifetime. The small shop with a large picture window had oddities on display. A shrunken head doll with a creepy iridescent glow radiating from a lone hole in the center of its head stared ominously back at Tommy from vacant eyes. The doll called to Tommy in a way that nothing ever had; like an invitation boasting of another time and place that Tommy had never been; the doll beckoned to him to enter the store.

Old English lettering hung from swayback hooks above the door on a tattered wooden board that looked centuries old. A scorch mark hindered the view of the first letter slightly but was not enough to change the name totally as 'Remember When' waved back and forth reminding Tommy of an old saloon.

An antique hair curler device that was used in the early thirties stood alone in the dungeon of days gone by. The hideous addition stood on a single pole with clawed feet at its base. The top had an umbrella shaped dome made of metal. Long wires dangled from slight metal rods protruding from the umbrella like hood, ending in bronze covered metal clips. The hair was meant to be placed on curlers that would then be clamped with the bronze colored hair clips and then plugged into a wall outlet. Heat would pass through the clips, resulting in the hair being curled. The machine was found to have a horrible flaw when a few women were discovered electrocuted. As with all such discoveries, the curling device soon fell into the hands of the more depraved members of society, earning its place among the relics in the antique novelty shop. The older gentleman in charge of the shop had been none too subtle about his love and knowledge as pertained to every item in the shop.

Tommy had nearly walked out of the shop when the short balding man clad in a pinstripe suit with a little too much middle section, made his way to the strange looking torture device. Tommy's eyes glazed over with the need he felt to possess the item. His eyes traveled lazily from the curler torture device to the shrunken head doll. The man had been adamant that he would not sell the doll; no price named would part him with the piece. Tommy was determined to have the doll. Something about it called to him. The doll seemed to mesmerize Tommy with its uncanny ability to reflect in perfect clarity the darkness that filled his heart. Never before had he felt so tied to an object as he did this shrunken head doll. He needed the doll to complete the room's horrific decor in a way that was something akin to putting a bow on a present. It was like putting his own touch on a song; making it his own. The doll would do that to the house in a way that Tommy knew with certain clarity nothing else ever could.

Tommy stepped over to the shrunken head doll, as he glared into the blacken pool of evil in the center of the doll's head. Pulling the doll into his hands, Tommy began caressing the doll, as the memory of the day he claimed it from the window to be a part of his house of horrors washed over him. Every offer that Tommy made, no matter how obscene the amount, the store clerk continuously rejected... Tommy had looked back at the old man as he was just closing the lid to the box storing the ancient torture device. Tommy had one all-consuming agenda and no matter the obstacle standing in his way, he would have to remove it.

Crossing the room, Tommy moved slowly behind the old man as he reached into his pocket. His fingers caressed the small pocket knife. He had tossed the weapon into his pocket that morning not knowing that he would need the instrument until this very moment. He would make it quick. Yes the man had stood in Tommy's way but could he blame him? Tommy could never part with the wonderful object. Unfortunately, he had left Tommy no choice.

A bald spot shining from the top of the man's head was covered with scant sprigs of light-brown hair. The bulky build of his short stature spoke of a sedentary lifestyle. Tommy hated that. There was no excuse for a person being obese. Exercise and eating properly were a must, a choice that should be made correctly. If the man was intent on wasting his life in the shop, then Tommy felt he was doing the man a favor. He would end the man's miserable existence.

Easing up behind the man, Tommy claimed his mouth with one hand as he glided the blade effortlessly across the man's trachea. He could feel the violent shudders as the man's mind rejected the loss of air and then the gurgled attempts at breathing. Soon the store grew silent. Tommy pulled his limp body through a wall of beads hanging from ceiling to floor into a hidden cove of the store. He, then returned and claimed his prize. Blood still marked the gory scene that had just taken place but Tommy ignored the evidence. He had an agenda.

The list was almost complete. Tommy had ticked off every piece of the puzzle in his mind. He had procured the perfect place for Jordan to die. He had collected every amenity needed to set the tone for the perfect stage. Now he had, but one important piece of the puzzle hanging in the balance and all that stood between him and claiming the revenge he desperately wanted, maybe even needed, was gaining entrance to the compound. He had to get in.

Tommy had talked to James Ruston multiple times this week, trying to gain access through his clearance at the compound. Unfortunately, that would not be possible. James Ruston had been alleviated of his duties and no longer held the level of clearance required to enter The Garden, at will. Now he had, but one hope... John Benton would cave. He had to. It was the only way that Tommy would ever be able to kidnap Jordan's children. It was the only way that Jordan would come to him. He had to get her on his turf, He wanted Jordan at her best. He wanted to see what she was made of. If she, was in fact, the best that the bureau had to offer then it was time that he remove two very real obstacles from his life. He would have his revenge on his Aunt Jordan for cheating him out of the life that he should have had and in doing so, he would finally prove once and for all to himself and the bureau the one thing he already knew: he was ready. He was capable of doing the job; making him sit in The Garden for three years had been a mistake. It was a waste of his talents. After dealing with Jordan there would be no mistake about how talented a killer he truly was. In order to be the best, you must beat the best. If Jordan Buckley was indeed the best, then it was up to Tommy to prove that she was a washed up has been and he was the new improvement on the best that the bureau had to offer.

Tommy had access to Jordan's file and from what he could tell, there was never a time that she was more at her best than when she truly believed in what she was fighting for; what better way to make her rise to the occasion than giving her a mission? She would have to save her children. If she proved to indeed be the best then she could walk away with her children's lives intact, if not then...

Tommy stood, as he, again relished the room. A slow smile claimed his lips. There had never been a more perfect stage set. The only thing missing was the guest of honor.

14

Hanging up the phone after the fourth consecutive call that morning, John thrust his hand into his hair. The stress was overwhelming. He moved to one of the benches that surrounded the fountain. He felt as though the weight of the moment would cripple him. He couldn't keep going like this. Cynthia was bound to find out and what about his friends? Jordan and Lane were already in the newly, refurbished west wing with the children. Today they would be entrusting their precious children to him! What kind of guardian would he be?

"John?" Cynthia's voice came as a mere whisper. She moved closer as she took in the site of him. John was definitely dealing with some pretty heavy trouble. But what? Was he this distraught over having to accept responsibility of someone else's children? If so, what would he do with the news that she was now carrying their own child?

Cynthia wanted to run back to the room and throw as much as she could into the small yellow tote bag that she had tucked away in the bottom of the bedroom closet. Did she know him at all? She had hoped to leave secrets, deception and the unknown behind her when she left Black Heart to be inducted by The Truth. Now, as she watched this strange man before her, battling with some inner demon that he was not confiding in her about; the man that was supposed to share her life, the man that was to trust her with things no matter how big... her husband; she felt that she did not know him at all.

"Cynthia..." John gasped, as his eyes met hers. His obvious shock at seeing her, see him in this moment of utter distress was bewildering. How could he let her see him; the man that she had trusted to care for her, so out of answers? What was he doing? Was he actually considering the possibility of giving this mad man access to his wife? He loved her! He could never let anything or anyone hurt her! So what was the problem?

Sure the voice had said that he would be exposed for some things that he had done in the past, but wasn't that what the blood of Jesus was for? Wasn't it His sacrifice on the cross that had washed it all clean? He had told Cynthia everything or so he had thought. Now, as he sat looking into her deep-brown-eyes, he knew that there was one horrible truth from his past that had been forgotten... one omission that he had even kept from his own consciousness, something so horrible that he could not imagine that even this trusting beauty before him could forgive; not after what she had experienced in the alley. She would never understand. But could he sacrifice so many lives to keep his darkest secret buried in the rubble of his forgotten past?

John scrutinized his wife for a moment. Could she forgive him? Had he forgiven himself for that matter? Cynthia stood, her dark-blond hair caressing her face; soft ringlets were glued to her neck and face in some places with sweat. Her beautiful-soulful-brown eyes searched his for answers he was not sure he could or would give. Her creamy skin was exposed modestly under the gray t-shirt that had a cross made up of silver jewels. The outer edges were set in gold and silver flames. Her body was slender all except a few inches she had been packing on in the midsection.

John smiled to himself, as he thought of all the caramel coffee drinks she had been unable to stop drinking. He loved that most about her; the insatiable appetite she had for life. The wonderful way that she had of falling in love with all that life had to offer and never looking back... even the simple things like caramel coffee. She was always exercising, though, so the weight she had put on from the extra she had been drinking lately, he had to admit did not add up. So he could understand why she would be frustrated that she had been gaining a little around the midsection, but it did not take away from her beauty.

John loved her. She was all he had ever wanted, besides serving God to the fullest. Now, as he looked at her and took in all that she meant to him, he was forced to think of that long ago day.

The day had been too long. John Benton was in a college fraternity. How could he ever forget? This was the day that was the defining moment, the pivotal moment that had changed his life, and set his course, forever.

Jeanie Clearheart was one of the most desirable juniors at Middleton State University. She was in line to be the valedictorian of her graduating class. She had a spotless record and was one of the people that would most assuredly fight for a cause; John had never known Jeanie to be without someone or something to fix. . . from the planet all the way down to bumble bees in the south possibly becoming extinct; Jeanie was the go to girl. She knew exactly what the score was and the best possible plan to put into place in order to bring about a change.

John had had a fight with his father that morning, as he left for work. He was still living at home to save all of the money that he could for his future plan of moving to Santiago, California. It was in the cards, back then for John to be a computer programmer for an up and coming Software company.

John would have a cushiony job, as one of the many members of a geek squad. He had studied hard and his grades more than reflected that fact. However, he had met up with one of the less than future hopefuls, Clint Rider—as far as grades would testify, Clint was going nowhere. In truth, Clint sailed through college on his father's liberal contributions. He made nothing over a 'C', but that did not matter. He was going to be working as head C.E.O., one day for the biggest company in Middleton, Tennessee. Clint Rider Sr. was named head C.E.O. after graduating college just as Clint Rider Jr. would be.

John had fell in with Clint after lunch one evening. Clint sat three tables behind John and the other hardworking book worms. The class clowns and muscle heads sat in a neat cluster of mayhem waiting to unleash their next bout of treachery on the students of Middleton High.

On this particular day, it was a food fight that had filled the need to make drama. The dean of admissions was not impressed. John was collecting his plate to leave in the middle of the war zone when a stray baked potato landed square in the middle of his plate causing a landslide of Jell-O and sweet tea. The mixture oozed onto Jeffrey Davis, splattering bits of the liquid onto the dean. John was subsequently brought up on charges, along with his now partner in crime: Clint; though the two had never before been formally introduced they now shared in a detention sentence. After that Clint and John were inseparable. Though, something inside of John testified to the fact that he should put a wide gap between himself and Clint, the allure of being popular that accompanied being in Clint's presence outweighed the urgency of his common sense. Soon John's grades reflected the lack of study time he had put into the subject matter.

John joined the fraternity that Clint and his rat pack headed up. John began attending the frat parties. He was drinking too much and using some of the drugs that passed from person to person. He gave no thought as to what tomorrow may bring. He quite simply no longer cared.

The frat party, the night that had changed his life was in full swing. John had been drinking since noon and was now standing in the fraternity house doing a line of cocaine with Clint. John could no longer recognize his own reflection. His once combed to the side three piece suit persona had been replaced by blue jeans, t-shirt and a hairstyle that the jagged edges reflected the tears in his soul. His eyes were sunk back in his head. Black circles carved a path around his once bright eyes. He was losing weight and rarely cared to shower though he had for the frat party. His head lifted from the white powder, as he heard the front door open again.

Jeanie stepped into the vast expanse of the fraternity house taking in the grand staircase. The rolling stairs was not unlike that of the stuffy two story-three winged mansions that she had ventured into while heading up one cause or another. It was the upper class's blatant disregard for what really mattered that claimed her attention: the homeless, the hungry and the planet's constant slip into oblivion while social lights like those she visited, stood by oblivious or just plain unconcerned sipping on cocktails.

Jeanie had led a simple life with her parents. She loved that simple life. Her mother and father had infused her with the zeal of life that pushed her to make a difference. Though, they could not afford more for their own children, they had always filled each of Jeanie's siblings as well as herself with the drive to be that difference that would bring more for others. Jeanie's parents had in no way ever tried to cripple their children by the impoverished nature of their lives. Instead, they had pushed each of their children to go further in life, to love life and had explained to them that the events leading up to their own lives, ending in poverty would in no way predict the future of their children.

In the days that Jeanie had stood in the kitchen learning to cook with her mother, she had always talked to Jeanie about tools. She had told Jeanie that knowledge was a very important tool that could be used to change the course of one's future. Knowledge, her mother had explained, was gained through education. If you so choose you could throw the very important tool away or grab hold of the tool and refuse to let go—drain every useful aspect out of the tool until it gave you all that you needed to move forward to that future. Those words had translated in other ways, as pertained to Jeanie. She had heard a mountain of wisdom in her mother's words and she had used her ability to gain knowledge to unlock a brighter future for others as well and to make a difference in the world.

Jeanie ignored the cherry-wood varnish of the staircase, as she slouched angrily across the marble floor. Not missing the opportunity, she stomped across the emblem in the center of the room; a lightning bolt engulfed by flames, represented the team.

It's not that she did not like football but more that she felt that football represented more of the cancer that ate away at the world's priorities: millions of dollars spent to pay an athlete's salary, obscene amounts of cash given to an artist that was perceived to be the next Van Gogh or Michael Angelo; the whole while every penny, if any given to world affairs was begrudged.

Her head was reeling as she moved further into the room. What had she allowed Cara Moon to drag her into? She had no business here. What did fraternity parties have to do with saving the world? Did no one care, but her? She wanted to be a part of the solution; not living it up behind enemy lines.

Cara belonged with this class of socialites. She was a part of the mansion people as Jeanie referred to them. Jeanie, on the other hand never rubbed elbows with the likes of the fraternity goers unless she was trying to solicit for some cause or another.

A flustered sigh made it passed Jeanie's lips as she flopped into one of the stuffy high back chairs lining the walls. Oh what she wouldn't give for a good day of picketing out by the new zoning site.

She had spent the week before up to her eyeballs in questions about what to do next. She was part of a committee of activist determined to save the three hundred year old trees that stood on the edge of town. Progress, always progress... that's all the entire world cared about, anymore. She thought. Ironic... it was that progress that was killing what was left of the foundation built by all of their forefathers to make it all possible.

The night had moved on hurdling, John toward the change that would stop the floundering palpitations of the dying heart that represented his future. He could not see how unraveled his life had become. His father had been right about him throwing his future away that morning. Though John had not had the where with all to listen to his father's warnings. All John could do was stand in the middle of the kitchen rolling his eyes at his father and shouting back at the man that had sacrificed everything so that John and his siblings could have more.

By the time John had found Jeanie Clearheart standing in the basement, confused and looking more beautiful than ever, the evening had become a blur of drinking and illicit drug use. He had started to just return up the stairs in search of another beer or fix anything that would take his mind off of how horribly he was wrecking his life but something about the way that Jeanie's eyes searched the room compelled John to go to her.

Jeanie had taken just about all that she could stand by the time Cara had returned from her fourth consecutive dance with Charlie Walters. Why had she even tagged along? Was this Cara's plan all along to bring Jeanie to the party and then abandon her while she chased after Charlie Walters, the quarter back for the Middleton Lightning Bolts?

Jeanie huffed as she pushed her body up from the high-back chair she had been seated in for the better part of the evening. She was pulling on the mint-green-knit sweater that matched the mini sundress she wore when Cara returned to gush about her time with Charlie. Jeanie cast an irritated glare in Cara's direction as she continued pulling on the sweater.

"Don't be like that, Jeanie. You're just not trying to have a good time." Cara accused as she allowed an exaggerated sigh. "Come on. Let's go get you something to drink." Cara eyed Jeanie quizzically.

Jeanie knew that her friend was waiting for the usual goody-two-shoes speech about how she did not drink. She could see the wheels turning in her friend's head. She had always pushed this on Jeanie but tonight, Jeanie just didn't feel like fighting. She didn't even know why Cara bothered to hang around her; they were as different as night and day.

"Cara... I..." Jeanie stopped for a moment as she thought about what she was saying. Wasn't she tired of it all? She was the only one that seemed to care about the planet, the homeless or the hungry. She was hungry! But for what? What was she so hungry for? She wanted more! But, what more did she want? Jeanie fell back into the chair as her expression changed from aggravation to defeat and then acceptance. Maybe this is just what she needed. Yes! Jeanie smiled affectionately at her friend,

As she nodded, "Go... get me that drink. I probably need it worse than anyone here." Jeanie scoffed.

"Amen!" Cara teased. "Just kidding. .." Cara offered with a sheepish grin and then walked away heading for her friend's much needed drink.

Jeanie had sat in the same spot nursing the drink until she realized she needed to go to the restroom. She had not been gone long but when she returned she could have sworn that her drink seemed a shade darker and that maybe it was closer to the middle of the table than when she had left for the ladies room. Passing the concern off as paranoia, Jeanie shrugged.

That was the last cognitive thought Jeanie could remember having before waking up the next morning, lying in a pool of her own vomit. Her clothes were torn and her body felt put together wrong. She was lying on the floor of a basement. She pushed her body up from the floor, as every muscle testified to the exaggerated movements. She wiped disgustedly at her mouth. Her eyes swept wildly taking in her surroundings. She did not recognize the place that she was in; instantly, fear had the upper hand.

The walls were lined with cubical shaped holes. In each, was what appeared to be a bottle of wine. In the middle of the room, a brown-plush-leather loveseat sat next to a matching chair. A small odd-shaped table, filling the space in front of the chair and loveseat was lined with magazines of all genres.

Jeanie pushed at the floor, as she moved to her full height. Her head was swimming and she could feel another wave of nausea. She turned away from the scant furnishings as rays of sunlight filtering in from a modest-wooden-door with stained-glass-windows captured her attention. Ignoring the stairs, leading to what Jeanie could only assume had to be the house she had come to for the frat party, Jeanie moved painstakingly to the door. Thankfully, the door was only locked from the inside by a deadbolt. She exited the door and never looked back.

John sat huddled in the corner, as he watched Jeanie leave the room. He had woken that morning to find that he was lying next to her. The state that she was in could only suggest that the time she had spent with him had not been pleasant for her, though he could not remember anything about the night. He moved quickly into the shadows of the room when he saw her stir. He could not face her. He wasn't sure what had happened that night but whatever it was, he could not stand to see it register in the eyes of this beautiful, idealistic woman that had always seemed so fearless. Now, nothing was left of that person, as she lay in a pool of her own vomit, her clothes disheveled and her hair mangled. The once fearless activist would be forever changed by a useless drug addict that had tainted her once noble existence.

John left that night in the fog that he had awaken to and never looked back, until now. Standing in this serene place, looking into the eyes of the only woman that he had ever loved... eyes that were demanding truth. John shivered as he crossed the distance and took Cynthia into his arms. He had to figure this out and fast. He didn't know what had happened that night but by the looks of things it wasn't good.

Cynthia would never understand and no amount of drugs would excuse the fact that he had possibly raped Jeanie that night. Cynthia would not understand, she could never understand. How could he expect anything less? Hadn't it been the intent of the men in the alley to rape and possibly kill her? How would he confess to being no better than her would be attackers?

John eyed the phone in his hand as he thought about the possibilities. He should call Jordan or at the very least, Garrison. But what would he say? He would definitely, say that a madman was calling him every day and demanding to be let into the compound. He would say that he was threatening to kill his wife and to kill him, but that made no sense. He could hear anyone that he told now... 'So don't let him in', that would be the common sense thing, right? Ignore the calls and put it all behind him. After all, if the person behind the voice could not get into the compound, then how could they carry out their threats? The answer was evident. They couldn't. But, what of the phone calls? If the crazy person behind the calls had found a way to contact him... couldn't the same be done with Cynthia?

Each time that he rationalized it all, in his mind, he ended up back at square one. He was trapped between a rock and a hard place. Soon, he would have to make a decision... give into the threats of the madman or tell all to Cynthia. One way or the other, life as he knew it, would come to an end.

CHAPTER

15

Something seemed wrong with John but Lane could not place it. He didn't want to leave his children with so much tension in the air but he had no choice. He was sure whatever the issue John and Cynthia would find a way through it. Love was a decision; one that he and Jordan had made on a daily basis. He made a mental note to confide his concerns to Jordan the minute they left the compound in search of Tommy Hayden.

Jordan had made a quick phone call that morning before leaving the apartment to take the children to their friends. Something was up with her best friend and old partner. Jordan was sure of it and wanted to get to the bottom of what the problem really was. She had asked Garrison to put aside whatever he was working on for a short time in order to meet her and Lane at the pub.

Garrison hung up with Jordan that morning and knew that his time was growing short. He had known Jordan for a long time. He could not keep her in the dark much longer. She had an amazing intuition. She could see trouble from a mile away and this was just about the biggest trouble that he had ever seen, much less been involved in. He had reluctantly agreed to meet with his friends. He wanted to talk to her alone but if he was being honest with himself, he knew that having Lane present would be better for his wellbeing. Lane had a way of calming her down and that is exactly what Garrison would need once he had confided in Jordan all that he had done and all that he had known... yet, he had never told her any of it. His heart was heavy and it was time that he unloaded some of the baggage he was desperately trying to keep intact. He was close to a nervous breakdown. Enough was enough!

The heat index outside was growing. Sweat poured off of Jordan's back. The grass surrounding the park had turned a dead-yellow as even it had ceased to thrive in the wilting heat. There had been no rain for days, although, in other states rain would not stop falling. Jordan was told that Florida had received a foot of rain in the last week. She wasn't sure she would want that either but this heat could possibly be her undoing. The park was completely empty; not a jogger or dog walker in sight. The weather man had urged everyone to stay indoors. The temperatures were at a record breaking 105 and climbing.

Jordan had told Garrison to meet them at the Irish pub, just outside the entrance to Black Heart. She didn't want to waste time finding the perfect hiding place for the three of them to talk. After all, sometimes the best hiding place was the one that you didn't try to make; in plain sight. She knew all too well that everyone that was anyone at the bureau knew that she and Lane were married and for that matter, that she and Garrison were partners. So there was nothing to hide. Just order drinks, sit and have a little small talk; blend and then after everyone was satisfied that this was three friends getting together after a long absence; they could finally get down to brass facts. But, Garrison had insisted that they meet somewhere more secluded. That somewhere was in the middle of the park, outside.

Jordan pushed at the stray hairs that had defiantly refused to stay tucked in the hair tie at the base of her neck.

"Good grief, but it is hot! This is New York, for crying out loud!" Jordan griped but this was everywhere. The weather was going crazy. She gave a frustrated sigh as she spotted Garrison coming toward them.

"What did I do to you, chief?" She growled, as again, she tried with no luck to get the rogue hairs out of her face. . . the strands stuck to her neck in a sticky mess. Her clothes gathered in sweaty clumps refusing to be straightened. She cast an irritated glance over her shoulder at Lane who was standing tall and perfect, not a hair out of place. Though, he too was sweating, he just seemed to be doing a better job of dealing with it than she.

"Okay..." Garrison's face was plastered with conceit. "It's hot as crap out here!" He smiled innocently at his friend. "I guess, we should have stuck to the pub." A shadow of doubt was cast over his features, but only for an instant.

Still, Jordan knew him well enough to have caught the change in her friend's demeanor; for whatever reason, Garrison seemed different. Jordan took in the heat for only a moment longer, and then just as quickly decided to ignore the agonizing waves. She understood. She could see from just that fraction of a second that whatever this was that her friend was dealing with, they needed seclusion to discuss it. The pub would not do and as crippling as the heat seemed at the moment, it was nothing compared to what she was waiting to hear. A chill ran up her spine and suddenly, the heat did not seem so foreboding.

"I'm listening." Jordan coaxed, as she cleared her throat; not sure if she was really ready to hear all that he had come to say.

"Jordan there's a lot that I need to tell you, but I'm not sure that this is the place." Garrison waved his hands around, and then wiped at his brow.

"This heat is intolerable!" He griped. "What I have to say is already bad enough. I don't want to add to your reaction." Garrison was choking on his words. It wasn't like him to do that.

Jordan eyed her friend for a moment, and then took a step forward.

"Garrison?" His name was but a timid whisper a child could have spoken. "You know that you can tell me anything." Jordan offered, as she caressed her friend's hand in an attempt to reassure him. Again, the same chill traveled her spine, as she looked into his dark brown eyes. There she could see that what he had to say wasn't just Intel on the case he was working, it wasn't more information on Tommy, though that may be wrapped up in it somewhere... this was more, it was deeper. Whatever, her former partner and best friend was about to tell her, she knew it was life altering. It would somehow change things about their relationship; it would move them into a new place that she was not sure she was ready to go.

Garrison pulled his hand from hers, as he turned his back for a moment. When he, again faced her, his eyes seemed older. He looked as though he had aged just in the last few seconds that he had gained years on his life and whatever, he was about to reveal to her could possibly be the end of life as he knew it.

"You're scaring me." Jordan admitted. She again, stepped forward in an attempt to take her friend's hand but this time Garrison moved away from the attempt. His eyes cast down for an instant and then he was facing her again. This time there seemed to be a mask in place as though the agent was in charge now; he was no longer her friend but a Black Heart agent delivering the fatal blow. She was the mark and he was set to make the kill.

16

Garrison was so numb inside that he no longer cared about the heat or anything else for that matter. Now, more than ever, he felt just like that fake plant in his office: dead. There was no life in him, as he stood before his best friend that would soon be a part of his past. He knew her too well. She would never be able to trust him again. Maybe she would be able to forgive him of that he was sure. But his time at her side, being a part of her life, playing uncle to her children... it was all finished. He had to tell her the truth, he had no choice; no matter the consequence, he could not live this way anymore.

"I have a story to tell you, Jordan." Garrison moved to one of the park benches. He didn't wait for the two of them to sit as well. He couldn't. He had to get it out while he still had the nerve. He had already allowed the agent to take over. No longer was he her friend, her old partner now, he was the agent. He had a mission and if he wanted to maintain what was left of his waning sanity, he had to unload all of it; every last lie; every half-truth.

Jordan was still looking at him with that fear in her eyes. It was the same fear that he had seen the day that he had recruited her in the apartment. Good... He thought. She needed a healthy dose of fear. This was serious. All that he had done was in the name of protecting her and even that was a lie; for he now knew that he was protecting himself all along. He did not want to lose her. His friend, his partner; she was the one person on earth that knew him and did not judge. That place would be gone now; that safe haven would be forever destroyed and after today he would have nothing. Not even the ability to find the place that Jordan had found, a place of peace and a place of renewed hope because he was beyond redemption. He had allowed Black Heart to take his soul; he had given them everything, and now, he had nothing left. All he had was the truth to give to his best friend and after he had laid it all out, he would end it.

Garrison allowed another uncertain glance at the ground before beginning.

"I was twenty years old, attending college. I was on top of the world. I came from a rich family and I was next in line to take over the company." Garrison stopped for a moment, as he looked into her green eyes. He wanted to make sure she was listening to him. He didn't think that he had the strength to repeat any of it.

"My father was the head C.E.O. of the company that he worked. I was nothing like him." Garrison allowed an exasperated laugh. "That would be putting it mildly." Garrison scoffed, as he rolled his eyes. "But my father was a go getter! He never took no for an answer. And, though it was not my dream… Like my father, I would take on the company that he had built from the ground up. Even my grades didn't matter." Garrison thrust his fingers over the shorts waves of his hair, as he watched a squirrel run up a nearby tree and disappear into a hole near the top.

"How ironic." He thought. He felt as though he was disappearing into a hole that was filled with lies and cover ups; mountains of them.

"I'm not who you think, Jordan." Garrison admitted and then he looked straight into her eyes. "My name isn't even Chad Garrison. Who has that name?" Garrison threw out the rhetorical question, as he again, started with the story. "The day that I became Garrison, the man that you see before you, a Black Heart agent; I was running from life, as I knew it, the spoiled rich kid that did not want to be tight cast in his father's stuffy shadow. Little did I know that I had the world at my feet." Garrison stopped, then, as he again looked in Jordan's direction.

"I was scared Jordan. I felt like my whole life was mapped out and there wasn't a dang thing I could do about it. I wanted to do something with my life; I'm sure, but for the life of me I can't even remember what was so important that I couldn't just do what my father wanted and run the company.

"The man was running from the convenient store that he had just robbed." Garrison looked at his hands as the hardest part of his past crept into his mind's eye. "I was leaving the cab that I had hailed in order to get away from my father for the umpteenth time that week. I'm not sure where I was going that day, just away, I guess. The man ran into me and maybe he thought that I was trying to stop his getaway. Who knows? All I know is he started to swing the pistol at me." Garrison turned to Jordan, as he studied her features for a moment. His eyebrows arched, as if to accent the magnitude of what he would say next.

"That maybe the last innocent decision I have ever made. I was simply protecting myself. I killed that man that day, Jordan, same as you and Cynthia, in self-defense. And same as you and Cynthia, I was inducted into the bureau for my efforts." Garrison looked at Jordan, then, as he waited for some recognition that she could remember the day that it had all happened to her.

"Garrison I don't understand what all of this has to do with anything. You look like life is over, as you know it. But we all killed. That's why we're here. That's how they got us. We made our first kill in such a way that it raised an eyebrow in the agency. So what? What does it all matter now? Why can't you let it go? As you said it was innocent..." Jordan was still ranting when Garrison started to shake his head.

"You're not listening, Jordan. I said it was the last innocent act I have probably ever had." Garrison stood, then, as he started to pace. He couldn't sit any longer. It was coming out wrong. He had to be more direct. Story telling was not the way to go. Maybe, if he just spit it out.

"I recruited you, Jordan. The same way I was recruited."

"I know that Garrison. I was there, remember? What is the point Garrison? It's hot as hell out here!" Jordan was looking irritated now. She was ready to walk away.

Garrison knew he had to do it. It was now or never.

"It was a setup, Jordan! The whole thing was a set up. It was set up by the company. Don't you see? How else could the bureau have known that the kill was made to specification?"

Garrison stopped, as he, again looked for recognition in her eyes. This had to be it. She had to get it. The words were too hard to say. He couldn't make himself tell his best friend that he had stood by all those years ago and waited to see if she would be the victor to the spoils.

"You were there? In the alley... I mean... while the man was dragging me into the..." Jordan stopped, as she leaned into Lane. Her hand was on her throat and Garrison could see that she was swaying in the heat.

"What's going on?" Lane questioned Garrison as he claimed Jordan with his arms. "Garrison what are you saying to her? That you stood by and did nothing..." Lane was unable to finish. Jordan's hand went to his lips as she shook her head.

Garrison could see that she was starting to walk away but he had to stop her. He had so much to tell her and this was just the beginning of the lies and half-truths. She had to listen, as he purged himself of if all. She had to know it all. He could no longer carry the weight of it around with him. It was killing his spirit. It was claiming all of his happiness. He felt dead inside. As he thought of all the reasons, he should tell his best friend of his many betrayals he knew that this too was an act of selfishness. He was doing this to save his soul to stop the anguish inside of him, even if it meant destroying his best friend in the process; he couldn't stop himself. He needed it to end.

"Jordan there's more... Whether you like it or not, you have to hear this. It's killing me! I have to tell you everything." His eyes were desperate, as he pleaded with her. "It all matters. It will not only clear the air between us, but it can help you with Tommy Hayden."

Garrison watched as Jordan's head instinctively sprang to attention. "You need to know who you are dealing with." Garrison moved back to the bench, as his eyes begged for her to do the same.

"Please Jordan..." Was all that he could manage. "After I am finished and you have heard everything you can go. You can decide what you would like to do about our friendship after you have all of the facts but I owe you this Jordan." Garrison again begged with his eyes.

Jordan moved to the bench reluctantly. She didn't want to hear anymore. Her mind was already shutting down. Even now, she could feel how dangerously close she was to vomiting and Garrison was saying this was only the beginning.

"I'm not sure I can hear all of this, but I'm listening." Jordan whispered, as she too sat on the bench.

"I'm not proud of the fact that I stood by and watched as you struggled with the convict in the alley. But I can tell you that it was my first time. Whatever solace that brings… However, you need to know that recruiting happens interactively. It's not as you think. The bureau doesn't just get calls from stationed-operatives in the police force or the hospital. That would leave too much to interpretation." Garrison again looked at Jordan.

Jordan nodded that she was listening. She could see in his eyes that he knew she was no longer listening as his friend, but as an operative collecting Intel. It was the only way that she could make it through the next few minutes.

"Continue." Jordan prompted flatly.

Garrison nodded and did as he was told. "George Daniel was the guy's name that you killed in the alley. He was taken from his cell early that morning Mr. Stanton spent the better part of the day in a room with the man telling him how he would gain his freedom. He was told that he would be put through a test and if he survived it that he could have his freedom."

"Wait! You are telling me that if this guy had raped and killed me that he would have gained his freedom?!" Jordan was livid. Her body vibrated with anger.

"Oh God, no! Of course not! It was a lie to make the man rise to the occasion. Jordan you know full well that Black Heart would never be able to sanction the release of someone, as vile as that onto society. My God it's what we are supposed to be ridding the streets of. Not turning loose onto…" Garrison dropped his head, as Jordan could see the point was just now becoming clear.

"But it was sanctioned and he was released! He was set loose on me, Garrison!" Jordan vented, as she stood and paced the heat stroked grass. She felt lifeless and barren like the dead grass beneath her feet. She felt that same old anger and disgust rising up in her as she settled back onto the bench next to the man she had believed to be her best friend, a man that she now knew she did not know at all.

Garrison felt there was nothing left to do now, but continue on with the rest of it. He had to get it all out and let the chips fall where they may.

"That is just the beginning of it Jordan. There is so much more that you don't know. I need for you to prepare yourself for all that you are about to hear." Garrison looked into her eyes then and there he could see what he had hoped would not come; the wall that she had erected once before, against men. It was there now brick by proverbial brick being put into place behind her emerald green eyes. He was now her enemy; just a piece of the puzzle to help her on her way. He was of no consequence to her and though, he knew it would change nothing he had to continue. He had to keep going because it may be too late for him but he owed her. He had to set her free. She deserved to know the extent of the lies, the cover ups, all of it, everything that had been set into place to create the world that had held her prisoner for far too long. It was then that he knew she could truly move on. No more dreams.

"Wait. You said that your name isn't Chad Garrison. So what is it?" Jordan asked, as she glared at this man that she was meeting, it seemed for the first time.

"Clint Rider." Garrison said flatly. "My real name is Clint Rider."

"Why was your name changed? It makes no sense. I am still Jordan and Cynthia still has her birth name. It's not like other operative programs where we have to die to who we were. I mean that's a part of the cover up. So what was so special about your situation that you had to have your name…" Jordan stopped mid-sentence as the facts came into view "Your family was rich. Your father would have stopped at nothing to get his heir back. Is that it?" Jordan asked as she rolled her eyes at the idea.

"Exactly!" Garrison admitted, as he allowed the ray of hope playing over his soul to have the upper hand for only a moment.

"Okay, so you were a rich kid that had it made. What about that would raise a red flag for the bureau? I'm not completely stupid Garrison. I know enough about Black Heart to know that before I was fed to the lions, something about my life had to capture their attention. I mean. I was abused, the trips to the hospital, the 911 calls, but you?" Jordan gave Garrison a once over as if to say 'look at you'.

"There's nothing. You were a rich kid with the world at your feet. No one would be watching you." Jordan surmised. She was looking at Garrison now, as she tried to fight through the fog for the truth.

"I had the misfortune of sharing a college dorm with a member of Black Heart. One that you know all too well: James Ruston. He had his eyes on me from the beginning. He could see the restlessness and hear the incessant complaining. He knew that I was unhappy with my plight. Unfortunately, I was too stupid at the time to know what I had and James Ruston was too corrupt and in love with the bureau to care. He started to follow me. He painted a picture to the HOD that didn't exist." Garrison looked up for only a second, as frustration lined his features.

"I guess you could say that he set me up. He was the one that talked me through your induction. He explained that you would be better off. He pointed out how awful your life was."

"Don't! Don't you do that! Don't sit there and try to pass the blame onto James Ruston!" Jordan was practically screeching by now.

"I'm not Jordan. I promise. I just want you to hear it the way that it is. The way it all played out. How I viewed it; what my thoughts and experiences were." Garrison again begged with his eyes for Jordan to sit and allow the entire story to come out.

"Garrison, Chad or whatever your name is. What does all of this have to do with Tommy Hayden?" Jordan asked as irritation replaced anger on her face.

"I'm getting to that." Garrison said, as he forced air out of his lungs. "Tommy Hayden is closer to you than you think Jordan." Garrison ebbed.

"Enough with this cloak and dagger nonsense, Garrison! For the love of God, spit it out!" Jordan spat as she moved again from the bench.

"He's your nephew, Jordan. Your brother, Garret Jr., is his father." Garrison confessed, as he waited for her to respond.

Jordan swayed again as she flinched away from the news. Some residual part of her past igniting, she felt the low burn as the realization made its way through her consciousness.

"How can that be?" Jordan asked. Her mind was in a stupor. Of course, she knew how one conceived a child, but how did she have a nephew that she didn't know about but more than that she had been in contact with him? She had been the one to deliver him to The Garden. Jordan's blood ran cold, as her throat seemed to shut off and the air whooshed mercilessly from her lungs.

"I need you to answer the next question as carefully and honestly as you possibly can and then I need for you to get the hell away from me... At least, until I've had time to sort through all of this." Jordan said with a calm that was so matter-a-fact that it made a chill run up her spine. "Does he know about me?"

Garrison dropped his head, as the word slipped through his lips unbidden. "Yes..." Jordan jumped to her feet then. She was a frenzy of action.

Lane was there holding her arms; forcing her to look at him. "Tell me what you're thinking?"

"Lane, the children." Was all that she could manage as she looked into the direction of the bureau.

17

The sky had seemed to open up and water burst forth drowning everything in its path. Thunder sounded its deafening boom, as lightening streaked the sky, filling its vast expanse with a luminous silver glow. The rain wasn't just falling from above; it seemed to be coming in from every direction; as if it was somehow trying to make up for the days of drought. There was no escaping its incessant plunder, as Tommy stood in the alley just outside of the pub. The weather man had said there would be a break in the heat. A thunderstorm would be coming through, making way for a cold front. The cold front was expected to be ushering in a blizzard. Tommy was happy to see the heat go but a snow storm he had to admit was not high on his agenda. He had plans and a blizzard was bound to limit those plans in some way.

Still, Tommy had been hounded relentlessly by the heat all day as he stood by waiting for John Benton to make the decision that he knew he would and maybe the cooler weather would be a welcome change. His eyes sought the pub's entrance. Soon he would receive the phone call telling him the code that would allow him the access he so desperately desired. It was just a matter of time.

Tommy licked his lips, batted his eyelashes and dabbed uselessly at his brow as he tried without success to clear the rain from his face. He would go into the pub but it would be taking too big of a risk that someone would see him. He didn't know how long it would take for John to make the call. Standing in the middle of the pub where other agents of both The Truth and Black Heart frequented was quite frankly, a bad decision. He needed to get in and get out without being noticed.

The back entrance to The Truth had been finished right before the New Year. That was just a month after he had been released from The Garden. He knew his way around the place, but getting in was like trying to break out of Alcatraz; it was a nightmare. The only alternative was to have someone on the inside that would allow you access. His someone had to work out.

$$* \; * \; *$$

John crossed the room to his wife. He knew the truth would come out. He had no other alternative. What was he going to do, allow Tommy Hayden access to the place? Allow him to just waltz into The Garden and have access to the people that he loved. No. He would never do that. He would do the only thing that he could do.

John took Cynthia's hands into his own and led her to a bench that was engraved with old English lettering. The inscription read simply 'In God We Trust'.

"Cynthia." He began, as he took both her hands and looked into her trusting eyes. "I have so much to tell you. I don't even know where to begin." John sniffed, as he looked down at their hands. He allowed a silent prayer that this would not be the end. He begged God that He would give him the words.

"I love you. You know that, right?" John beseeched, as he moved closer to Cynthia and caressed some of the stray strands of hair away from her face.

"John, of course I know. I mean I think I know. You've been acting... I mean. You know erratic, lately. But, as a rule of thumb, yes… I know that you love me." Cynthia babbled, as she nervously rubbed her thumb across John's hand.

"I know the way I've been acting lately has been crazy, but you must never think that I don't love you." John pulled Cynthia into his arms. He put all of the desperation to never lose her into the hug. He hated this. He wished he could tuck this awful part of his past away and never look at it again, but Tommy's entrance into his life, their lives, had made that impossible. He pulled back away from her. Placing a hand on either side of her head; he leaned in and kissed her head.

"I was a different person when I was younger, Cynthia. Once a long time ago, I made really good grades and was up for an easy job as a member of the geek squad at a predominant company. But, I fell in with a bad person. Well it's not that he was bad. It's just that he wasn't focused. He was very popular. We met by accident." John stopped for a moment, as he stood and crossed the cobblestone floor to the other identical bench just across the way. He turned to Cynthia, then and started to head back for her, but he stopped.

"It was intoxicating being around Clint. I was nobody and he was larger than life. I was less than a fly on the wall. I wasn't even picked on. I was a ghost in the room. I didn't even exist as far as others were concerned." John smiled awkwardly at her and then started again.

"It's hard for you to imagine what that is like, unless you are in it. Are, it, I mean. I worshipped him for so long. I would do whatever he wanted. I started to drink and do drugs because it was what Clint Rider was doing. I ruined my life because it was what Clint Rider was doing.

"He was in line to be the next head CEO of the company, his father built from the ground up, and he threw it all away. And I allowed him to throw my future away as well."

Cynthia stood then and went to him. "Baby what's wrong? What does all of this…" Cynthia waved her hands in the air, as though she were desperate to find the right words; as though she would somehow find them floating out in the air between them, and then at last she continued. "The past… What does it have to do with us now, and how you are acting?" She laid a gentle hand on the side of his face and looked deep into his eyes, searching for the truth. The truth, John knew he could no longer hide from. John took her hand from the side of his face and gently kissed it.

"It's the path I took then that is causing the trouble I'm in now." John confided, as he moved again to the bench that they had been sitting on. "I've been receiving phone calls lately."

"Yes. I know. I've wondered about those. Why do you come out here to talk on the phone? It's as if you don't want me to hear. It scares me. I feel as though you don't want the baby." Cynthia froze. Her hand flew to her mouth as if she were trying to capture the words to stop them from leaving the place she had held them captive. Her other hand reflexively claimed the tiny bump in her: stomach. Her eyes filled with tears.

John made no decision to be at her side. It was like he was pulled across the expanse in an instant. He had her in his arms, and he too, was crying. For a moment, he forgot what he was telling her. In that moment it was like time had frozen and all else ceased to exist. The pieces that had for so long left him bereft for an answer, all of the sudden fell into the puzzle and were crystal clear. She wasn't gaining weight because of some dumb coffee drink that wouldn't adhere to her exercise program... of course... she was pregnant.

Cynthia's laugh was muffled with tears. "I thought you didn't want the baby." She admitted, again, as she pulled back and looked at John through watery eyes. She placed her hands possessively on either side of his head. She searched his eyes for any sign that he did not understand the gravity of the situation. She had just however, accidentally revealed a definite change in the course of his future.

John wished that this moment could last forever. That he could just be sharing the news that he and his wife would be having a new addition to their world; expanding their love. Oh that it were that simple, but the truth was far more morbid. He was trying to tell the woman that he loved that the one thing that she could never tolerate, from the man she loved was the most horrible part of his past.

"Cynthia, I can't believe it!" John tried to drench the words with all of the pride that he felt. He was proud. He was happy for them both, but it did not erase the fact that they were standing on the precipice of the most life altering truth. He had to tell her and now more than ever he did not want to. He would not only be taking the chance of losing the woman he loved but a child that he had just learned about and already felt tied to in some concrete way that escaped his understanding.

John held her to him, willing the moment to never end and even as he held her, he knew that it was inevitable. He would tell her everything and he would stand by while she held his heart in her hand. He would wait to see what she would do. Would she shelter it—keep it safe in her loving and capable hands or would she shred it; leaving nothing of him.

John peered into her eyes, as he tried to gauge her reaction. She was an ocean of emotions. He could see that but exactly what emotion was predominately in charge at the moment, he had no clue. After what seemed an eternity of searching for clues, as to how she was doing so far; how well she was taking the news, he could see that nothing would be surmised. He had no other alternative but to continue.

"I wish that hearing about the baby was all that needed to be done here in this beautiful place." John admitted, as he gave Cynthia a warm smile. "But the truth is... well the truth is that I've recently remembered a very dark part of my past. A part of my past that I'm not sure you will be able to forgive." John took her hand and pulled her along toward the bench. He wanted her to be seated, at least. In her delicate state it would be bad enough telling her what kind of monster she was married to but for her to have to hear it while carrying their child?

John's whole body felt as though it were having a physical reaction to what he was about to say to Cynthia. As though even the primitive parts of what made him man, knew that she was all that kept him tied to this world.

"There was a frat party that night. The night that my life changed, forever I mean. I had been doing drugs, and drinking since early that morning. I had a fight with my father; it didn't take much those days to set him off where I was concerned. I was floundering wildly. I had gone from being this hopeful child to a drug-induced-zombie overnight, it seemed. My father was terrified." John placed a hand on the tiny bulge at Cynthia's waist. So much was made clear now: the mood swings, the weight gain, the sleeping, and yes, the nesting. He smiled at the tiny person that he knew to be growing under the warmest heart he had ever known. "I can only imagine how he must have felt." John confided.

"Jeanie Clearheart was an activist with so many ideas about how to save the planet that it was scary. She would probably have done it, too." John looked away, then, as the guilt of a lifetime seemed to pour down on him, crippling him. "I had never met her. I had heard about her yes, but I had never been formally introduced to her." John shifted his weight.

"The night that she showed up at the fraternity house; I was honestly shocked. Clint had come into the kitchen announcing her arrival... well, let's just say that he wasn't nice in his choice of adjectives." John cast a weary glance at her, before returning his thoughts back to that long-ago-dreaded night.

"I don't remember much about that night, but what I do remember is waking up in the basement next to her." John stopped, then, as his voice broke. The agony of that morning was filling every part of him. It was swimming through his veins like poison. It was cutting off his air, and shutting down his hope. He had taken her future. He could see it in her eyes the morning that she had left. While he stood hovering shamefully in the corner like a frightened child, Jeanie Clearheart, the determined activist pulled her battered body from that dusty floor, as she left in its place, her pride. He could see it. He could see even from the shadow of his shameful hiding place that she was changed that whatever was left of Jeanie Clearheart, the larger than life world changer, had died. It was lying in a fetal position, having been choked to death by the shame and disgrace she felt; the shame and disgrace of waking up in a place that she did not know and concluding that she had been raped.

"It's okay John. I'm here go ahead. Get it out." Cynthia crooned, as she reached out to him.

Something in the way that she was looking at him made him feel, as though she somehow had an inside view of that time, as though she too had been in a corner of that dark and dusty room watching John chided himself. Hoping that she would truly understand would not make it so. It was time to tell her everything and good or bad he had to accept what was.

"Please don't Cynthia. Don't comfort me. I don't deserve anything less than your anger." John moved a few inches from her. He couldn't stand to be touching her now. He had to get it out. He did not want this wonderful woman to have to be in contact with the likes of him. He was vial. She was beautiful. He was corrupt. She was pure. He was hateful and putrid; she was light and hope. No matter her response to his news, he now knew that he would have to make the decision, even if she could not. He would have to take his taint away from his family. He did not want to corrupt them. He would not allow his brand of ugly to seep in and destroy what beauty that lived within them. With that, he was ready. He would tell it to her, all of it. He would lay every last sorted detail out for her to see and he would hope that she would see him for the monster that he was; so that she would leave and take their baby as far away from him as possible.

"I woke that morning after the party. I wasn't alone. I rolled over. I saw her, then; Jeanie Clearheart. She was lying on the floor next to me. But what I saw was not a picture of two people having spent a wild night in the froes of passion." John stopped, again, as he felt his nerve waver. Just say it... he thought.

"What I saw was Jeanie laying there on that cold floor with her clothes torn and disheveled. Her hair messed up and she had bruises on her face. Her lip was cut and eyeliner collected in a dark shadow beneath her beautiful eyes. Streaks of it ravaged her innocent face. I was terrified. I immediately thought of my own safety. I scrambled for everything that was mine; anything that would incriminate me; I took and I moved as quickly as my aching head would allow to the nearest corner to squat like a criminal." John stopped then. He was overcome with the sadness he had never allowed to have control. He had never purged himself of the self-loath of that time. He had never asked forgiveness. He quite frankly had never remembered it. He still had no memory of what had truly happened.

"That's it! That's your proof that you raped that girl? That is what you are trying to say, right? That you got so drunk and wasted on drugs that you actually blacked out and raped that girl in the basement of that house? That's the big secret!" Cynthia was laughing uncontrollably.

John looked at her. At first he thought she had snapped and so she should. But after a while, he felt angry, as though she were making fun of him; making light of a very dark time in his life.

"What's so funny?!" John barked.

"I'm sorry babe. Of course, this is not funny. My God you must have been devastated. To sit in that corner, hiding behind that furniture..."

"What? I never described the room to you. How did you know that there was furniture?" John felt the blood drain from his face. What was going on? Was the whole world in on the joke? Did everyone know what happened that night, but him?

"John... I can't believe we've never had this talk. I had no idea you felt this way. John I rolled down the stairs. We were so drunk that night. We were barely able to move. I remember hitting my head and…" Cynthia was waving her hands in the air. She was trying to say something about that night but John couldn't understand. His mind was spinning. He felt as though he would lose consciousness.

"Cynthia? Have you lost your mind?" John asked stepping from the bench, afraid to be near her. What was she saying? That she was there? Is that what she was trying to tell him? How? How could she have been there? He had waited in the corner until after Jeanie had left. He did not see anyone else in that room.

* * *

"John I thought you knew. I mean, being as close to Garrison or should I say Clint Rider as you are. I thought you knew what my real name was. I'm so sorry baby. I swear I didn't know that you felt this way. I left that room that day; yes, that's true, but the look that you saw on my face was not disgust about anything that had happened that night between us. It was about my own failings. It was because I was so busy trying to save the world that I didn't know a thing about myself. I found out that night that someone else lived inside of me; someone that I didn't know until that night with you. The night that we spent talking and laughing." Cynthia tilted her head to the side and tapped her right index finger to her chin.

"I remember, now. I couldn't for so long. I had gone to the restroom and when I came back my drink was moved. I thought nothing of it. I drank it anyway." Cynthia moved closer to John. She felt so terrible for him. She could have saved him all of this anguish, if only she had not gotten so drunk that she could not remember that night. It wasn't until John had started talking about the room that she remembered the in between. For so long, she had thought that they had gotten drunk and had sex. That she had woke up in the room with him gone; she was left there in a basement just another statistic, a dirty secret. But now, as she saw the rest of it through his tortured eyes, she knew she had to tell him. She had to tell him everything that she remembered.

"Who are you?" John asked as he moved away from this woman that he had loved for so long. This woman that he now realized he knew nothing about.

"John I swear I thought you knew my former identity."

"You are not... You don't look anything like her." John stammered.

"John I was a horrible agent. When you came to my rescue, I had already had plastic surgery once. I bumbled up my first mark. I was caught and processed. I'm not sure what would have happened to me if not for you and Garris... eh... Clint." Cynthia moved across the room to his side again.

"Please sit down John, you don't look so good." Cynthia encouraged, as she pointed toward the bench.

"Are you saying that you were... that you are Jeanie Clearheart?" John asked, as his hands automatically pulled free of hers.

"How can that be?" John felt cold. A lifetime of guilt came crashing down on him and dissolved in an instant. He had such an overload of thoughts, memories and expectations; every part of who he had been, the pivotal moment in his past that he had believed so long to have defined the John that he had become... suddenly, the past, the present and then the future that had been his, was gone; his thoughts careened out of control, his mind could not contain them all. The outer edges of his vision were darkening. And then there was nothing.

CHAPTER

18

S hards of light pierced through the cloud-cover. Tommy was still standing outside the pub. He was angrier than he had ever been. He had not gained entrance to the compound. That sniveling idiot John had probably gone and done something stupid like telling his wife the truth. What bargaining chip did that leave him now? He had no way to get into the compound. James Ruston was a pile of information, but he was of no real help. If he couldn't get into the bureau, then he had to figure out a way to get them out; but how?

Tommy pulled off the pale-blue parker he had been wearing to keep his clothes dry. It had been no help keeping the rain out of his eyes but he had still managed to see Jordan running through the pub entrance. Something was going on. He could tell by the way that she was moving. Something or someone had obviously lit a fire under the infamous, Jordan Buckley-Gates, but who? And just like that it carne to him. Of course! It was him. John Benton may not be useless after all. Maybe all that was needed to bring Jordan back to her old self, was a little truth telling. Maybe she just needed to think that he could get to her children. Yes. Now, all Tommy needed was a way to get Jordan to come after him.

Jordan's heart raced as she rounded the bar and made her way to the drab-wood door that led to the high-stakes-poker room. Lane moved through the crowd, not more than a few feet behind. While Jordan's once best friend and partner Garrison brought up the rear. All three stepped beyond the door and waited for the retina scan to begin. The feminine voice noted that the heat sensors had picked up three bodies inside of the tiny access room. Due to the discovery, three retina scans would be required.

Jordan felt the frustration mounting, and dispersing across her nerve endings. It was just about to drive her insane. She felt that all-consuming desire to just rip the door open. She knew it was impossible, just as thinking that she could get out and run faster than the bus could commute across town but it did not matter. She wanted so desperately to get to her children that everything that stood in the way had become an obstacle worth removing by any means possible.

The silver door to the elevator finally slid open as the smell of lilac and honey suckle arrested Jordan's senses. She raced down the cobblestone walk that mapped out the pathway to the middle of The Garden. Her eyes scanned the area near the fountain as she at once caught sight of Cynthia hovering over someone that was obviously sprawled out in the middle of the floor. Jordan's lungs seized on a shocked inhale. Something was wrong. Jordan looked away from the couple, fearing the worst. Where were her children?

Jordan's eyes trailed the inner workings of The Garden's sanctuary. The sound of birds crying rang out with intensity. Jordan knew all too well that what seemed a cacophony of beautiful songs illustrated by some of the most colorful tropical birds she had ever seen was really a warning. Not that the birds would do anything to an intruder, the calls were meant more as a scare tactic. Unfortunately, for the indigenous bird population, the calls invited those in that were meant to be discouraged.

A water fall cascaded from the ceiling, ending in a small lagoon that dispersed in fingerlike trails filtering out to the many fountains throughout The Garden. Tropical flowers of every kind filled the outer edge of the trailing water source and butted up next to the cobblestone walk that snaked the entire length of The Garden.

Jordan again turned her attention to her friends in the middle of The Garden. John seemed pale.

"Cynthia what happened? Where are the children?" Jordan asked as she rushed up next to Cynthia, taking a knee on the other side of John.

"The kids are fine. They are laying down for a nap. John passed out." Cynthia eyed Jordan for a moment and then passed Garrison a wary glance.

Garrison gave a defeated nod. Cynthia dropped her head for only a moment. Jordan detected the smallest bit of anxiety pass across Cynthia's troubled glance as she, again faced Jordan.

"I was telling John who I truly am." Cynthia confided.

The wind felt as though it had been knocked out of Jordan.

"Cynthia, not you too?" Jordan turned to Lane as the color drained from her face. The reality of what she and Lane had done was finally making its impact on her already over loaded psyche. "Are we the only two people that we know that are truly who we say we are?" Jordan asked Lane as she then turned her attention to Cynthia.

"I think you had better tell me who you are." Jordan tossed a glance over her shoulder in the direction she knew the apartment John and Cynthia were housed in was located. "You better hope that your time spent as an agent is the worst thing I'll find lurking in your past." The ominous threat filled with an air of menace hung between Jordan and Cynthia for a moment.

Cynthia stiffened for only a moment as the underlying threat in Jordan's statement made its intended impact. She then, returned her attention to John as he still lay unconscious. Her hand started to gingerly caress his blonde hair away from his face and then a tear slid down her cheek.

"Jordan you know everything you need to know about me. Everything you know is all true. The only difference is my name and my face. I look different than I once did but I am the same person that you have always thought me to be. I was inducted into the bureau after killing a man in self-defense." Cynthia stopped, as she started to sniff. Her eyes were brimming with tears.

"I thought he would be able to handle what I was saying." Cynthia said, as she touched first one of his light-brown eye brows, and then the other. "I thought it was funny. I really thought that John would be relieved to hear the truth; especially, after discovering that he believed he had raped me."

Cynthia lifted her eyes then and faced Jordan. "Can you believe that?" She turned back to John.

All at once, Cynthia was on her feet. She was moving in Garrison's direction.

"You!" She screamed as she pounded her fist against his chest. "Why didn't you tell me that he didn't know?" Cynthia wailed as her head fell helplessly onto Garrison's chest.

"He's coming to." Jordan informed as she moved quickly to John's arm and placed a hand under his shoulder.

"Easy does it John." Jordan soothed as she tentatively pulled her friend to his feet and helped him to the bench. Lane had done most of the lifting on the other side of John but Jordan would not move. In that moment, she felt as though the two men at her side were the only two people that she knew; the only thing real in her world. John's ashen face seemed to embody the emotions that were a torrent wave rushing through Jordan's senses. She understood.

Jordan turned her attention to the man that she knew as Garrison, but he wasn't Garrison at all. She could only imagine what Cynthia had shared with John that would make him pass out. After all, hadn't she discovered that her entire existence save a few minor details was a complete fabrication?

Jordan moved from the bench to Lane's side. She cast a lethal glance in Garrison's direction. Though he may not be the man that she had always believed him to be; she was the same. Jordan had not changed so much that Garrison would not understand the threat emanating in the glance that she had given him.

Lane pulled Jordan closer to his side. Jordan supposed that the threat had made it to more than Garrison's attention. Moving closer to Lane, Jordan allowed a small smile for John. She felt bad for the guy. He seemed a strong enough sort. So she knew without a doubt what Cynthia had told John something that was so beyond anything that he could fathom. It had literally caused his mind to reject the information.

Jordan had seen this before. She had underestimated someone in the past; it had almost cost an innocent woman her life. Jordan had vowed to never be fooled by a facade, a mirage, a hoax; it was all a visual lie that she could not buy into. Lives had counted on her, and she had become too invested in her own idea of evil to see that evil standing in front of her.

Jordan was a very different person before her marriage to Lane. She had been inducted into Black Heart the same as other recruits but unlike Cynthia, Jordan loved being an agent. She relished the kill. The demon in charge ensured that she pursue more and more individuals that would satiate its bloodlust.

Jordan had encountered a man during the hunt that had seemed more than what he had equated to. He had not stopped, instead, he kept telling a young woman at the bar what he would do to her. Jordan was in a window seat staking out the establishment for her next kill. The man had not caught her attention; he did not fit the profile of her usual kill. It wasn't, until she saw the cringe registering on the young woman's face that Jordan moved to the bar to be able to listen to the conversation between the man and woman. It turned out that the man was not whispering sweet nothings to the woman, but on the contrary was making threats. It seemed that the man had his own agenda. He too, had a profile to fill; apparently, the young woman fit the image registering in the man's head that inspired the most hate. Jordan moved away from the couple and waited for the man to leave the bar. She followed close behind, watching the man as he weaved in and out of the shadows. He had efficiently filled his intended victim's mind with fear. Now, he would stalk her until he was able to find a satisfactory place to fulfill his every threat, his every desire.

Jordan moved along the outer edges of the foliage, just beyond the man's notice. The electric spark that was pulsating through her veins, fueled by what she knew was to come was invigorating. The man stopped just outside the young woman's house. He faded into the shadows, waiting for the young woman to make her way into her home. The sanctuary that she believed would keep her safe. Her long red hair a wavy-silken texture bounced whimsically down her back; errant strands cascading over her shoulders. Her creamy skin puckered a rosy red in the icy cool wind. She pulled the long duster up around her neck and face, trying to ward off the cold. She shivered so violently that Jordan could see it from her hiding place.

The man stood, waiting; ever waiting. He wanted her to hurry. He wanted to be in that apartment alone with her. No prying eyes. Just him alone with her screams that could not be heard. Jordan knew, all too well what the man was thinking; it was the same as what she was thinking about him.

The woman disappeared into the apartment and the man started to make his move. He lunged for the open window, just as Jordan closed the distance. He turned to face her and in that moment as he stood eye to eye with Jordan as she held the six inch blade to his throat; she could see in his smug eyes that he believed her unworthy of his abilities. He reached for her hand, the one holding the knife but Jordan was faster. In an instant, she was gone. Like smoke after a brush fire, she climbed the wall disappearing into the nothingness beyond. She saw then the frantic need to find her, register in her would be victim's eyes. In an instant, she landed on his shoulders as she, again brought the knife to his throat. A strangled whimper made its way through his clinched teeth. The hunter he had been only moments before lost to the moment; the moment that would be his last.

Jordan was brought back to the present, as Lane, again pulled her to him. She shivered as she thanked God that she was no longer that person. Her eyes, again moving to John, Jordan scrutinized his blanched appearance. Again, she was baffled. What could be so big that John would take it so poorly? And hadn't Cynthia said that John had believed he had raped her? John? Lovable, happy-go-lucky, John Benton, raping someone? It made no sense.

Jordan crossed the distance to John. She slowly sat down as she took his hand into hers.

"John?" Jordan started as she waited for John to acknowledge her.

John turned to face Jordan. She could tell that he was still quite shaken.

"Yeah?" John's answered reply was but a whispered cry.

"I know that you've had a very trying day." Jordan said, as she peered up at the others. She noticed the tear-stricken face of Cynthia. As she cast a small smile in her direction;

"I don't mean to put any more on you." Jordan soothed and then continued. "What was it that you reacted so poorly to? What was it that Cynthia told you that caused you to pass out?" Jordan again turned to the others. By the looks on their faces she could tell that the line of questioning had them baffled. Jordan turned back to John, as she realized it was time to ask what she had wanted to ask.

"John this doesn't seem to add up. Please tell me what you are not telling us." Jordan turned her pleading gaze in John's direction.

"I know there has to be more to this John. So you found out that you didn't rape your wife; that she's not the person you thought she was, but who is? This is normal, Black Heart M.O., you should be used to nothing being as it seems." Jordan turned to Garrison, then.

"I recently come to realize that someone wasn't who I thought. I remember, all too well how that reality made me feel, but John we've been through too much for something this..." Jordan looked around, as though she were searching the air for the words. "It's not trivial, that's not what I'm saying. It's just nowhere near the crap we're used to dealing with."

Jordan again faced the others. This time she could see that they too were starting to get the bigger picture. Jordan turned back to John who was now looking a little less lucid. She moved quickly to hold him in place, before he lost consciousness again.

"Please..." Cynthia groaned, as she pulled John closer to her. She soothed his head with one of her hands, holding him to her chest. She rocked him slowly; methodically. Her eyes seeped and her lower lip quivered.

"No." John was pushing away from Cynthia and holding onto Jordan's hand. Tears poured from his eyes, and he, too had a quivering lower lip.

"This can't wait." John admitted. "I have to tell you something." John cleared his throat.

"What you said is right. There is more to this than just what Cynthia told me. Though I have to admit, it was very disturbing to find that the person that you are married to isn't quite who you thought them to be. But let's face it that's not something unheard of in the ranks of Black Heart."

John faced his wife and allowed a comical smirk. His eyes shone with the humor he wanted desperately to feel inside. Then he turned his attention, once again on Jordan.

"Yes. There is more to it; much more." John stood then, as he crossed to the fountain. He thrust his hands into his hair. The look in his eyes, as he faced Jordan was enough to make her lose consciousness.

19

The shroud of darkness hunkered close as Tommy stood in his shadowy cove, hidden from the prying eyes of those around, meandering the busy New York street. The streets were teaming with the sounds of life. Traffic zoomed this way and that in its usual New York style of hurry up and wait; it was the heart beat that thudded with every pulse of the organism that was New York City and tonight, as Tommy Hayden stood in the shadows it was no different.

Some of the finest cuisines nestled together as the smells wafted into the street, causing an angry growl to reach through the silence. Tommy jumped as the sound took him by surprise. Then as he allowed the reality of what had happened to settle in on him he calmed a little. He had been preparing his house of horrors for Jordan and her family for the better part of the day. The other part he had been avoiding the phone calls that never seemed to stop coming; Ruston was a determined if not desperate man. Now Tommy was standing on the corner of Bowdon and Groves, waiting for an opportunity that may never present itself and along the way he had managed to ignore the basic functions of life. He had not eaten a thing.

Tommy, again, turned to the night life around him as he again tried to ignore the low determined murmurings of his abdomen.

On the corner of the adjacent street, he could hear the false laughter of a young woman. He strained his eyes, as he peered intently in the woman's direction.

A small leather skirt hung snugly to her hips ending at mid-thigh. Long boots that Tommy wasn't sure of the color, flowed up her milky legs to just below the knee. The woman's hair, a long wavy bright-red danced like fire around her head. She smacked mercilessly on a piece of gum while leaning in the driver side window of a black sports car. In the shadows behind her, a dark figure stood watch. A long duster flowed from neck to boot camouflaging the man's appearance even further. He puffed on a pipe while clearing his throat as the woman negotiated the price of her services with the older man behind the steering wheel.

Tommy strained to listen to what portion of the conversation he could catch. The man in the shadows, Tommy assumed was the woman's pimp and she a prostitute. Her pimp was obviously directing the woman to jack up prices. Tommy looked again at the woman as he took inventory of the long-sleeve-sweater she had on. The midriff bodice showed off her very thin abdomen. Her ribs bulged like an emaciated animal. Her face seemed more than a casual thin. Tommy rolled his eyes as he thought about how desperate the man in the car would have to be in order to actually purchase a date with such an uncouth woman. He could only imagine where all of the money was going. He could tell by the looks of the young woman that precious little went toward her upkeep to say little of her diet.

To Tommy's shock, after a few minutes the woman disappeared into the man's car. She had not been in the car long when the man produced something black in his hand. The light from the street lamps bounced off the of the object, and for an instant Tommy was able ascertain what the thing the man was holding actually was. Tommy grunted a laugh, as the woman let out a string of cuss words. At which time, Tommy was absolutely certain that the man was holding up a badge.

A series of vibrations pulsed in Tommy's pocket as he yawned. He was bored out of his mind. He knew exactly who was on the other end of his phone and he wasn't in the mood to deal with James Ruston for the umpteenth time today. He pulled the small-burner-red-flip-phone out of his front pocket and rolled his eyes again, as he could see that he had been right all along. It was Ruston. He would have to deal with the coward once and for all.

Tommy had called James earlier that morning. He had mistakenly believed that after Ruston's history with Garrison and Jordan that he would be thrilled to hear about the plans that Tommy had for Jordan and her family. To the contrary, Ruston had begun shouting in desperation on the other end of the phone. The man was out of his mind. He insisted that Jordan's children had nothing to do with the vendetta between Tommy and Jordan...Was the man insane? Of course, the children had something to do with it. It was about retribution, retaliation; it was about getting even. How better to get even with someone than to meet them on their own playing field. After all, hadn't Jordan decided the name of the game? She had made the rules, right? Tommy was just trying to be a good sport and play along. It had been Jordan's idea from the start to end the taint of the Buckley bloodline... Tommy was just giving her the chance to do just that.

✳ ✳ ✳

The phone rang incessantly on the other end yet no one answered. James Ruston paced back and forth in his small shoebox apartment like an angry panther ready to pounce. His mind begged for Tommy to pick up the phone. He prayed that the man had not done anything rash. He guessed this was what he deserved. After all, hadn't he created this monster and wasn't it the good doctor Frankenstein that in the end was forced to face his monster and pay with his very life for his evil creation? James thought he was no better. He deserved his fate but Jordan and Lane's children didn't.

It had been his freshman year of college that he had met Garrison or Clint Rider as he was known back then. The two of them had been inseparable; nothing could ever come between them or so James had thought. The year ended as always with James and Clint making plans to spend a beer soaked summer together while in the arms of whatever 'hotties' were available to fill their nights. The following year started much the same. Clint and James sat in the same classes, paying little attention to anything that the professor had to say.

Lunch was greasy, as usual and no one in their right minds was interested in taking the plunge except Joe Daniel. Joe, was an even more hopeless case than Clint and James. He was a wide receiver for the football team and would eat anything. He had even once held his niece and wiped the spittle off her mouth and then thrust the dribble into his own mouth. James had nearly lost consciousness in a half laugh-gagging fit. Clint asked Joe why he would do such a thing. To which he replied, "I wanted to know what all the fuss was about." After that James would put nothing passed Joe's appetite.

The day that the food fight had ensued, had seemed no different than any other day. But in the end, it had been the precipice, the jumping off place that had changed James' whole existence. The moment that Clint had flung the grease-soaked liver and onions at James, was the beginning of the end of Clint's and James' time together. Never again would they spend days hashing out plans to crash the local bars in search of women. It felt so normal being with Clint. The parties; all of it... James wasn't apart of Black Heart. He wasn't an agent waiting for his next mark; in the times that he spent with Clint Rider, he felt like he was truly a college student discovering himself for the first time.

After the incident in the lunchroom, John Benton did not prove to be the tattletale that Clint and James had thought him to be. Clint had pulled John under his proverbial wing and unfortunately, for James there just was no room for anyone else. James had vowed to get even with John Benton for taking away his life. It wasn't enough that John had replaced James at Clint's side but James had turned into a 'nobody', at the school once the class clown, everyone looked to for a good time—he had become a shadow on the wall—no one wanted to hang out with Clint Rider's leftovers.

James was left to evaluate his existence; again the agent for Black Heart with no shadow of make believe, he sat like a squatter in his life, frustrated and alone.

Ruston had seized his opportunity to make good on a lifelong promise to get back at John Benton and Clint Rider. Finding Clint Rider outside of his father's company one day, while staking out a mark was a stroke of luck. He had known that the day would come that he would at last bring an end to Clint Rider's all-American persona. He would at last know the dead-end world of Black Heart.

James Ruston, like many of the other agents housed at Black Heart, did not resemble his former self. His name back then was not James Ruston, but Bobby Thornton.

A mark had been given to James but during the elimination faze James had gotten the execution code confused; he had never been one to study. The code given was thirteen. James had executed the mark using code thirty three. Thirteen was the standard issue hanging that was orchestrated many a time in prison in order to make an operative appear to have committed suicide while thirty three was not standard at all.

Thirty three was inventive. James had found it most satisfying of all the codes used to kill a mark. The mark would be placed in a prone position while being tied in a spread-eagle pose to four stakes drove securely into the ground. Because of the mark's position, they would be rendered unable to see anything that may happen to them. The idea was to up the fear factor, thus confusing the cause of death. The coroner would obviously be able to detect that some sort of restraints had been used at the time of death but to what outcome was another matter altogether. A drug that was undetectable in the blood stream because it had a short shelf life would be administered behind the mark's ear. This would usually keep the coroner from detecting the tiny prick. The drug was an adrenaline based drug that would speed up the heart rate.

A sharp metal rod was scraped languidly down the mark's back, as the agent spoke in harsh tones through a voice distortion device. The distortion of the agent's voice would normally cause the mark to search unseeingly as they strained against the blindfold over their eyes. A drawer was filled with metal components of no real use such as: broken pipe pieces or corals of wire. All of the metal pieces raked against one another causing the mark to strain to hear anything that may give them a clue what they could be up against. Everything orchestrated was in an effort to quite simply cause fear, thus accelerating the heart rate; no real harm had ever been inflicted on the mark. It had all been in the mark's imagination. And in the end, it had been the fear of what might be but had never been that had killed the mark.

The cleanup crew had been dispatched that day. Unfortunately, the crew had come, expecting to check for any discrepancies that would disqualify that the mark had been hung but had been caught off guard. The man lay prone still held in place by the restraints, his eyes were covered with the blindfold; thinking that the cleanup would be minimal the crew had called the incident in. The crew had no other recourse, but to change the description of the murder scene. Pretending to be a CSI team, as the police arrived that was called in by the local medical examiner's office after discovering the horrific nature of the crime, the crew went on about the menial tasks of collecting hair samples and such.

At the end of the investigation, James Ruston was found to be an up and coming serial killer and true to Black Heart procedure, he was thrown in prison. There he faked his death and underwent plastic surgery. He was then reassigned after three months of The Garden and some brain washing by the upper management. James spent his time healing from the surgery. Realizing that he had a world of opportunities to uncover; it was all up to him to see his cup as half full and not half empty and it was with that decision that he set out to induct Clint Rider.

One decision led to another as James moved forward in his plans to bring down the infamous Clint Rider and his friend John Benton. It was a shear stroke of good luck that he had been thrown into The Garden. It was there that he had discovered John Benton was one of the missionaries.

James bit his tongue, as he acted like the good patient. He allowed John to pray over him and perform whatever religious ceremony made him feel the coziest. He had nothing but time and the best laid plans took time. He moved every pawn into place, careful not to push too hard. He started by introducing Garrison, Clint Rider to John Benton so that the old reframes of friendship could be rekindled; or so they thought. He then started to sift through some of Garrison's past accomplishments in his profile sheet and thought it best that Mr. Garrison become as high as he could be in the company in order to ensure the fall be that much more devastating.

James took Garrison on his first recruiting detail which by another shear stroke of dumb luck ended up being Jordan Buckley who was by the way aunt to a future member of society's un-hopefuls, Tommy Hayden. James wasted no time after discovering Tommy was Jordan's nephew; he set Garrison and Jordan up on the recovery detail. The two of them were charged immediately with the safe recovery of Tommy Hayden. He was to be brought to The Garden. Soon all of the pawns would be in place and James could sit back as he pulled the strings of all his carefully placed puppets. Unfortunately, for James he hadn't counted on one of the puppets having a mind of his own.

Tommy Hayden had turned out to be the most evil being that-James Ruston had ever had the misfortune of crossing paths with and that was saying a lot. James, after all worked for one of the government's most tightly kept secrets, Black Heart. He had recruited some of the most underhanded vengeful sociopaths imaginable yet, Tommy Hayden caused chills to run down James' spine .

Because of James that monster was off his leash, planning the deaths of an entire family and there seemed to be little to nothing James could do to stop him.

20

James stood in his understated New York apartment, pacing from the door to the small kitchenette. The open floor plan of the small apartment left little to the imagination. His bed, a modest full size that had taken the place of a lavish-king-size-four-pollster, monument to comfort, sat nestled close to one of the cream colored walls. A two drawer night stand close beside the bed was littered with a black ashtray full of cigarette butts and a large-clear-blue cup filled halfway with watered down sweet tea. A ring of water circled out from the bottom of the cup, boasting of a time when the drink had been freezing cold. James ignored the urge to throw all of it into the floor, as he thrust his hand hopelessly into his pocket to check for any return messages or phone calls on his small forty-dollar-flip-top phone.

He felt like a stealthy cat caged. What was he going to do about Tommy Hayden? He felt he was running out of options. How many phone calls and text messages had been sent just this morning? It was to no avail. Tommy had made his intentions clear and nothing or no one would stand in his way. He was a virtual robot set into motion and until the mission was at last complete, he would remain in motion. James would have no other alternative; he would be forced to shut him down. The issue would come in the how. Tommy was no easy kill; he was not just some mark that James had been charged with; some individual that had caused untold amounts of aggravation for the government but in the grand scheme of things for all of the trouble they had caused it would be a menial task to disarm them. No, Tommy Hayden like his Aunt

Jordan, would be a formidable enemy. In fact, he could possibly be the worst thing that James had ever had to face.

Something would soon have to give. James had to put an end to all that Tommy was about to do. He could not stand by and allow the man to eliminate an entire family. James checked the phone again for a dial tone and again it was there. A time or two he had wondered if he was getting any service; maybe he had forgotten to pay the bill. Things like that did happen especially after having a phone supplied to him for more than ten years; sometimes trivial things like paying the bill escaped his remembrance.

The organization had let him go after he had been found to be involved with the gun and drug cartel and it had been a blow to his ego. But, it had been a far cry better than having to go to prison. His higher up had insisted that the charge be pushed under the carpet and the names of anyone involved that was associated with Black Heart be removed from blame. The fact of the matter was that Mr. Cochran was in it up to his neck and he could not afford for some of the other members in the bureau to find out his involvement. It had been that act of self-preservation that had saved James from a fifteen year prison sentence.

Fortunately, James had been put out of Black Heart but not without some perks. He was still allowed a recruiter's fee. This was a contingent plan thought up by Mr. Cochran to keep James from telling all to Garrison or anyone else in the organization that might listen. Mr. Cochran had sited that the organization could not take the chance that the members would be put back out into society and just have to survive. After all, the members of Black Heart only knew one means of survival so could the bureau fault the members for doing what the government had trained them to do. Oh, how the man fought for the new plan. James was astonished that no one had sense enough to see through his false bravado. How could highly educated members of an elite government organization not see the truth behind his unexplained need to champion fallen comrades after years of caring for no one more than himself unless someone higher was involved?

Trying to figure out who was at the top of the Black Heart food chain would not be hard to do. James had been around long enough that he could recite the pecking order by heart. The trouble was which one of the 'powers that be' was the guilty party. That was the million dollar question.

James flipped his phone open again as he thought about the once lavish office that he had possessed on the third floor. The wall to wall plush carpet and high back chair that had served as a medal for those that had served the bureau without complaint taunted him now as he peered at his meager surroundings. He was once one of the elite. Now, he was in a small apartment taking scrap jobs for Mr. Cochran. The very thought burned a whole through his ego that would never mend.

His mind raced, as he again started to make yet another attempt at reaching out to Tommy. James jerked his hand back from the send button as the tiny phone buzzed to life. His eyes seemed to be playing a cruel trick on him as he witnessed the name in the indicator window. It just could not be. Had he wished it into being? James flipped the phone open, as Tommy's voice filled the airways and lit a small flame of hope deep in his heart.

"Hello." James addressed the menacing voice on the other end of the line, as he tried without success to erase any evidence of fear from his tone.

"Why, James Ruston! How have you been?" Tommy Hayden crooned with an over exaggerated southern drawl. "I'm certainly sorry that I haven't been able to return any of your texts or phone calls but I've been very busy. You do understand?" Tommy added for good measure as again the line became deafeningly silent.

James pulled the phone away from his ear, as he considered hanging up for a moment. What would he do about Tommy anyway? He wasn't really trained in the retrieval of one as deranged as Tommy Hayden. James guessed he did have some responsibility for what Tommy had become but he was certainly not the one that had initially created this irrational threat to society.

James had read Tommy's file. He was well aware of the struggles this young madman had faced. James knew that the day that he had entered Tommy Hayden's life had been a drop in the bucket when compared to the more challenging history the boy had suffered through. No, he would not claim all of the credit.

James cleared his throat, as he considered his response for a moment. He had harassed the man all day; certainly he had given some thought as to what would be said once he had reached Tommy. He would have to say something very profound in order to stop this fleshly-machine from carrying on with his predetermined mission. But what could he say? He had begged and pleaded with the man all morning through texts. He had left multiple voice mails of various content ranging from nice even energetic messages, trying to convince him of the need to meet with him and then the more threatening voice mails where James had promised to do his worst. But in the end, James truly had no other recourse but to end it. He would have to quite simply kill Tommy Hayden. Nothing else would do. He would not listen to reason begging promises or threats… James had only to figure out the best way in which to end it all. Would he make it look like a suicide or maybe a good-ole-fashion serial killing gone wrong? Whatever the tactic, James was certain of one all-consuming truth; he would have to do it and fast. Jordan and her family were running out of time.

"Tommy", James began, "Thanks for returning my phone calls." James figured stating the obvious; that he had indeed made many attempts at reaching Tommy, couldn't make the matter any worse than it already was.

"I would like to meet somewhere." James cleared his throat again as a chill ran down his spine. How could he even think of meeting-someone like Tommy anywhere? Truth be known, he didn't want to meet the man in public among thousands of witnesses, let alone somewhere secluded enough to kill the man. But what choice did he really have?

James brushed his hand across his forehead. It was then that he truly noted the profound affect the man was having over him. James' head was drenched in sweat. He felt nauseous and weak. He wanted to sit, but couldn't. He had to be doing something. Even if that something was simply pacing the floor, it was better than nothing at all.

"I'm listening." Tommy's sinister voice broke through the silence. "I am a busy man, Ruston." The line was quiet for another moment. "Well?"

"Oh yes." James babbled. He felt like a child standing before an open closet in a dark room. He shivered as he again tried to clear his throat. The fear inside was becoming more than just a feeling. It was an all-consuming entity, raging through his body, choking off his air supply and realigning the chemicals needed to maintain his equilibrium.

"Um… yes… could you meet me somewhere, like later this evening?" James sputtered.

"Where did you have in mind?" Tommy's voice filled the phone line again causing an involuntary shiver to make its way up James' neck where the tiny hairs stood on end.

"I thought maybe the back side of the park on Jenkins Street." James was proud of the way, for the first time since the conversation had started that he actually sounded sure of himself.

"Are you familiar?" James asked. He waited as again he mopped the sweat off of his brow.

"Yes. I've been there a time or two to let off some steam or clear my head." Tommy informed James in a decidedly nonchalant manner or so James thought.

"Okay that would be great." James tried to keep the fear racing through his veins—boosting his epinephrine and causing his head to spin from registering in his voice. He had to keep Tommy guessing. The last thing he needed was for Tommy Hayden to have the upper-hand. If he could somehow keep the proverbial ball in his own court and Tommy guessing it could prove to be a grand ally.

"What about six sharp? I can finish up what I'm doing here and meet you there. Is that good for you?" James smiled at the way his words sounded calm. He no longer sounded like a child standing face to face with the boogieman. He sounded sure. He sounded ready for anything. If only he could truly be ready. If only he could meet with Tommy Hayden, and end it all. If he could turn it all around and no longer have to be concerned with Jordan and her family's welfare; it would be a victory of monumental proportions.

"Six O'clock sharp." Tommy agreed and then there was nothing but defining silence. James pulled the cell phone from his ear. The screen seemed so dark and lonely with no name or number flashing across its darkened-glassy-surface. He had no one to call. It was done. He had made plans to meet Tommy in the park and there was no turning back. In less than three hours one of them would breathe their last. James hoped it would not be him.

CHAPTER

21

Lane stood as he faced the four other people in the room and all at once he knew that he had never known them. His life was a chaotic mess; a hand-me-down existence not quite his own: his parents, he had found out were not his parents at all but two people working for The Truth, as missionaries that had adopted him after his biological mother had died during his birth and his father had taken his own life. Those two people had been good to Lane but they had been taken from him too soon in a terrible plane crash on the way to the states. The woman he was sent to supposedly bring back to The Truth was in truth meant to be his wife even his history was a murky picture fraught with the grays of uncertainty.

A descendant of the fallen angels, Lane's path had been set from the beginning. Nothing in life had been left to chance. All of his choices made for him from the start. Lane felt the finality of that truth as it weighed down on his subconscious. His breath caught and his mind raced. His chest started to tighten and all at once he couldn't breathe. He had never felt anything like this before.

Lane's eyes started to glaze over, as the weight of it all pressed down onto his shoulders. He moved with the vigor of an old man, crippled by time to a nearby bench. He felt his life was spinning helplessly out of control. Who or what could he trust in a world where everything and everyone around him slowly turned to vapor? Nothing was real? Lane allowed the desperation brought by that question to have free reign over his frayed senses. Head in his hands, he peaked through the openings made by his fingers, being spread wide across his forehead. Staring absently across the room, his eyes finally settled on the bench adjacent to where he sat. Old English letters stood out in stark comparison to the soft eggshell tint of the cement bench they were carved.

Lane sat straighter, as he moved his arms allowing them to lay loosely on his legs so that his hands dangled across his knees. Again, he read the words. 'In God We Trust'. The truth of that profound statement took root in his mind. Of course, he could trust in God and hadn't it been God that had ordained his future? Lane could look back on his hand-me-down existence and see the hand of God as He purposely orchestrated people, places and even things to be perfectly in line; all of which had brought him to the exact purpose he had been created for.

He pushed himself away from the stone bench. Walking over to the fountain in the middle of The Garden, he cast a reassuring smile in Jordan's direction. She looked so frail under the weight of the last few days; that coupled with the dreams was really taking its toll on her. Even with the dark circles forming under her emerald green eyes and her hair pulled back in a loose ponytail, she was the most beautiful woman he had ever seen and she was his. God was good to him. What did he really have to be unhappy about?

Lane moved to the fountain, as he reached out to touch an onyx stone. The small cylindrical stone shimmered like black glass under the florescent lighting; what should have been an ominous black was made beautiful by the soft iridescent-glow. Lane's fingers glided across the tiny gemstone, as he remembered the day that Aniahi, the medicine woman for the Cadotion tribe had given it to him.

Aniahi had pulled the stone from a clay pot on a weaved carpet, sitting in front of a fire pit at the center of her tent. Smoke rose to the top of the tent, billowing through a hole in the tent's center. The smell of burning pine bark filled the small enclosure causing the tent to smell clean, though dust settled on all of the unused clay flasks. Mud and mint leaves were splashed on a large tree stump set to the side of one of the tent walls. Obviously, Aniahi had been brewing a mint poultice. The concoction was usually used for boils caused by mosquito bites becoming infected. However, the mint leaves had a calming effect and was sometimes rubbed on an ailing individual to help with sleep. Lane had had many occasion to need one of Aniahi's mint poultices.

He caressed the smooth surface of the black-stone, as a dull ache filled his heart. Aniahi had provided the stone to Lane because his parents had found the stone during their stay with the tribe. Aniahi had told Lane that his mother cherished the tiny stone and had asked her to keep it safe until their return from the states. Lane's mother and father had been playing in the water when she had found the stone.

It was then that Aniahi had shared with Lane the legend of the great mountain that had once lived where the Cadotion River had been. A powerful storm had risen from the center of the mountain. When the storm had subsided, the mountain was no more. Huge pathways had been formed by a lake of moving fire; each pathway surrounded the place where the great mountain had once been. Rains came and filled the void left by the powerful storm and moving fire. All that remained of the great mountain was beautiful stones that could be found on the bottom: some black as glass, others as green as the meadow grasses and still others were as blue as the skies.

Lane thought of the crystal blue waters of the Cadotion River; water like he had never seen before or since, untouched by man's abuse. The water shimmered in the sunlight and was so clear that he could see his feet on the sandy floor beneath the surface. He missed his home more now than ever. What he would not give to be standing amongst the Cadotion people; his people. He longed for their ideals, the love that they shared that seemed to poor out over all that shared the sanctuary of their holy home. Lane looked around at the manmade version of a tropical paradise in which he stood. No place on earth could match the essence that filled the homes of the Cadotion tribe; not even The Garden came close.

Jordan watched as Lane caressed the small black stone. He had been adamant concerning the placement of the stones. Many discoveries had been made during the missionaries' time in the field but the onyx stone was one of the more compelling finds. It was not until the day that he and Jordan had married that the stone had been placed at the bottom of the fountain.

"Let the greatest among you be your servant." Lane had recited the words from the Basic English Bible. He stood tall in the simple robes with his beautiful hair pulled tight at the nap of his neck. His blue eyes shone with the determination Jordan knew he felt to make every word clearly understood.

He had waited for the right time to place the stone. It was the day of their marriage that he had said he felt the most capable to allow his parent's memory to rest. Jordan could understand the sentiment completely. She too, had symbolically let go of the past on the day of their marriage.

A small tube of perfume had been given to her as a child. Jordan had only to smell the scent and instantly it would transport her in her mind into her mother's presence. The tiny sample of her mother's favorite perfume, White Diamonds by Elizabeth Taylor had been like an aura of hope placed over a life that was darkened by the treachery of her father's alcohol-induced-belligerence and her brother's determination to follow in his unfit footsteps.

Jordan had stepped to the center of the fountain. The fountain was made in the image of the arc of the covenant. A flat surface took up the space between two cherubs where the Israelites would make burnt offerings to God for their sins before the death of Christ. Jordan poured the contents of the small tube on the surface as she prayed that God would forgive her of her transgressions against not only Him, but Lane as well. She prayed that just as they had paid homage to the people of the past that had paved the long and arduous road to a better place that one day she and Lane would be able to blaze a trail of servitude to a mighty God that had loved His people so much that He had sent His only son to die on a cross in pain and anguish so that they would not have to. It was her hope that their path to serve the Lord would be so bright so well defined that there would be no question for their children as to what their choices would be.

Jordan took in the quiet strength of her angel husband as he stood touching the stone left to him by his parents. What legacy would she and Lane be leaving to their own children? What would their lives say to Amelia and Tristan? Jordan stood, as she walked over to the man that God had chosen from the foundation of the earth for her. Wrapping her arms around his vast chest, she allowed him to enfold her in his arms. In that moment she was completely aware of what that legacy would be. It would be their great love. It would be the knowledge that no matter what the circumstance or how insurmountable the trial may seem, their parents would stand together. Fight together. They would now and forever trust in God. The same God that Abraham, Isaac, and all of the others that had paved the road to Christianity had served. That would be the legacy that they would leave.

22

The room spun into view as reality slowly crept to the forefront of his mind. His eyes searched the walls for any sign of a door, a window, any type of an exit leading away from this place. James tried desperately to stay in the moment. This was not the first time he had gained consciousness.

He searched his mind for his last memory before darkness staked its claim. He had been in his apartment. Yes that's right. He had made a phone call to Tommy Hayden. He had made several phone calls and sent many text messages in an attempt to stop the inevitable. He felt the same old desperation creeping in, as he, again tried to strain against the restraints holding his arms and legs. Where was he? He glared into the corner of the room.

There was some kind of an old shrunken head doll, a dark eye filled with a glaring ominous glow bursting out the center of its forehead blackened out the entire countenance of the horrific doll. The walls were shellacked in darkened pools of what James could only perceive to be blood. A faint smell teased his nostrils. He tested it against his memories, but could not bring up anything in the archives of his mind that would match the smell. It was neither pleasing, nor unpleasant. It seemed to originate from a farther point in the structure he was being held.

"Ah it seems you are awake again." The voice came from behind his head.

James struggled against his restraints again. A small light drilled through the darkness casting an eerie glow across the wall just to the side of where he was laying. Fear trapped him to the cold slab of metal.

He knew that voice. It was Tommy Hayden and James knew he was not in this place to view the structures erected to enhance fear. Though this room and the rooms beyond may incite fear, James Ruston knew without a shadow of doubt that he would have to focus on a way out of the house of horrors. He would have to ignore the resounding truth crippling his mind; he would probably never see the outside of this horrible place again. This would most likely be the site of his death. The thought pierced his mind with fear and seized his spine with chills.

James wanted to ask what Tommy wanted with him, but there was a gag in his mouth. It tasted of a strong sweet smelling vapor. The substance was having an anesthetic effect on James.

"Let's remove this for the time being, shall we?" Tommy said in a soothing voice that made James feel anything but calm. "A little chloroform never hurt anybody." Tommy stated with an uninterested sigh. "Besides I have lots of little surprises to show you and if you keep going to sleep you'll miss the fun." James heard a loud snap, as the table he was attached to swayed upright. He was immediately facing the room. He stood encased by cloth ties, his head straight up. He was unable to move his head or torso. The table he was tied to started a slow turn.

"No worries, Ruston. I spared no expense. I wouldn't think of having you lay down on this table and not see all of the wonderful trinkets I've provided for your horror." Tommy laughed, as he strolled slowly over to the corner of the room. "My personal favorite in my house of horrors is this little number. Sort of reminds me of myself. I feel it captures the essence of who I am." Tommy said, as he replaced the horrific distorted doll back on its stand. He walked to the wall next to the shrunken-head, as he began trailing his fingers across the darkened stain on its eggshell surface.

"Quick history lesson." Tommy offered, as he turned to James. His face was lined with false concern. "You don't mind do you? I mean I wouldn't want to keep you from something." Tommy stopped for a moment, as he walked over to James and pulled his face into a tight grip. His fingers bit into James' flesh. He twisted his head but stopped, as he felt a sharp edge stab into the temple on the right side of his head. His neck and head muscles were throbbing their protest.

"I'm speaking to you, Ruston." Tommy ground his teeth together emphasizing every word. "When I speak, you listen!" Tommy moved his hand from James' face, as he straightened James' shirt. He pushed his hand over the glossy surface of his dark auburn hair and turned back to the wall. "Now where was I?"

James' heart was pounding. He could think of a thousand things he wished he had done. Anything would have been better than getting in touch with Tommy. It wasn't his fault that Tommy was demented. He did not kill his father, he did not treat him as if he was a mistake, clouding up his life, and he did not throw him into The Garden. None of those things had been James' fault. He had only recruited Tommy; just as he had recruited Jordan and Garrison. Tommy even seemed thankful for the gift of being an agent of such an elite force such as Black Heart. Garrison, too had admitted that his life was all the better for Black Heart's interruption. Jordan was the only one of his recruits that did not embrace the company's values. Though she had in the beginning, after she had met up with her husband all of the things that made Jordan Buckley-Gates happy and satisfied had shifted. Jordan was practically a tree-hugger these days. She had moved to some country on the other side of the earth and had joined up with a tribe.

James studied his captor. Tommy stood, pacing the room, boasting of all the trinkets he had collected to beef up the scare factor of his haunted house. He wore a black t-shirt with black jeans. His shoes were black, as well with black laces. The black he wore stood out in stark contrast to his emerald eyes. His face chiseled to perfection was that of a flawless-angelic-creature, standing before his captive. His hair was slicked back to his face. His eyes a deep shade of emerald green, changed colors, ranging anywhere from a dark green that bordered on black to the emerald green that James witnessed before him now. Tommy's eyes danced with the possibilities he seemed to be contemplating. James had a feeling that he did not want to see one of those possibilities come to fruition.

Tommy pulled a dark curtain back from the large picture window. He stared out into the night beyond. "I wasn't always like this, you know, I was young and idealistic. I had hopes for the future."

Tommy allowed the curtain to fall, as the burgundy material careened across the window's width and settled on the floor—looking like nothing more than pooling blood. The thought sent waves of revulsion through James. He wanted with all his might to be able to look away, but his head was glued to the spot. A turn in either direction embedded the razor sharp edge of the metal object into his skull. The same metal objects were mounted on either side of him following the entire length of his body.

"Why do you have me here?" Though James was sure he did not want the answer, he had finally assembled enough courage to ask the question.

"Now, now, let's not put the cart before the horse, Ruston." Tommy soothed with false compassion. "I'm sure you would like to know what will become of you. That is a very good question." Tommy said, as he raked a finger across his chin. "You see I hadn't prepared for you. I was ready for Jordan and her family. But I must admit you were quite the surprise." Tommy smiled, as he walked closer to the metal table where James was being held.

"I didn't realize that I would have the opportunity to practice before the big show." Tommy nodded his head once in James' direction, as he turned again to the adjacent wall. "I guess thanks would be in order." Tommy said, as he crossed the room and pushed open the top of a rolltop desk.

James felt the blood drain from his face. He wanted to fall asleep and never wake up. His mind raced, as he took in the arsenal that Tommy had unearthed inside of the roll-top desk. Rows upon rows of metal objects, some with sharpened smooth or serrated edges and others were equipped with hinge points to pivot the device open with one hand. Those objects James was sure to hold in place skin or organs that had been cut away so that a surgeon could more easily explore the bowels of a patient.

Tommy opened a drawer just beneath the rolled up portion of the desk. He searched for a moment and then James saw him pull out a bag with tubing. Next Tommy pulled what appeared to be an IV needle, still in a plastic wrapper out of the drawer. He then, satisfied to have all of the instruments to start his impromptu surgery, crossed the distance to the other side of the room where a metal tray on wheels sat unencumbered.

The wheels of the table squeaking, Tommy pulled it slowly to the side of the metal bed that James was strapped to. Laying the looted objects on the table, Tommy left the room briefly. When he returned he was holding several bags of liquid. The first two bags James had no trouble identifying: blood and normal saline. James' throat started to dry out as the realization of what Tommy was about to do to him poured through his psyche. Tommy moved to the side of the metal table that James was strapped to and again pushed a button that allowed the bed to recline. Pushing a second button, the bed proceeded even lower allowing Tommy more access to his patient.

Tommy stepped to the head of the metal bed and started to unscrew a locking mechanism on a long metal pole with four hooks at the top. It was then that James realized that the pole was actually an IV pole. Tommy busied himself hanging all three of the bags from the pole. Then, as if he were a nurse in an operating room, he explained to James in a soothing tone that he would have to start an IV. Returning to the metal table at James' bedside, Tommy opened the bag with the plastic tubing. Once the bag was open, James was able to see that the bag was not just limited to the plastic tubing but was a surgical kit. There were about four plastic tubes, three blue tourniquets, and several other objects that at the time meant nothing to James.

Tommy strapped one of the blue tourniquets around James' left arm and thumped the bend of his elbow. Soon a large vein popped up rewarding Tommy's efforts. James tried to turn his head again, disgusted at what was about to befall him but the pointy objects surrounding his head again jabbed him in the temple. Pain shot through James' head and then through his arm as Tommy gained access with the IV. James tried desperately to hold back the tears, the cries of pain; he wouldn't allow Tommy the satisfaction of enjoying his anguish but even as the thought entered his mind, James was whimpering like a small child.

James could tell by the blood and IV fluid that Tommy intended to keep him alive for a long time, while he played with his arsenal of medical instruments. The thing that had his attention more than all of the other bags was the scalpel that Tommy held in his hand, as he spiked the last bag and attached it to the IV port. James had a total of two IV sites. One side had the blood hanging, while the other side had the saline and the fluid that James couldn't identify.

James watched in horror as Tommy used a pair of shears to cut his shirt open, and then he was cutting away the material of his pants. James lay on the metal table his entire body exposed; the only thing left covered was his genitals. A flush of relief filled James as he physically relaxed if only a little.

"I'm not a monster, Ruston." Tommy laughed as he carried on with preparing his patient. He pulled a can of shaving cream out of one of the other drawers on the role top desk. A pack of razors lay just beside the shaving cream. Tommy pulled one of the razors out and pushed the drawer closed again. He stepped away from the desk and across the room and then back to James' side. He placed all of the objects but the can of shaving cream on the metal table. Tommy gingerly smoothed the shaving cream in a vertical line down James' chest. James stared on in horror. A surgeon completely engrossed in his duties, Tommy paid no attention to James. Tommy washed down the shaved area of James' chest with a white cloth doused in alcohol. He then collected a dark colored pen of some sort and traced a straight line down the middle of James' chest ending in a downward V formation. Replacing the pen on the metal table, Tommy collected the scalpel. A sardonic glare colored Tommy's expression, as he leaned in and looked straight into James' eyes.

"Hold still now. This may hurt a little." Tommy moved his hand closer to James' chest. James stopped caring about the metal objects lining his body as he prepared himself for the pain that he knew would accompany the impact. He struggled to move his body from the path of the oncoming blade. He hoped that if he impaled the metal objects lining his body hard enough he could possibly end his suffering before Tommy had planned. It was then that the contents of the third bag became apparent to James; it was a paralyzing agent. James struggled but his body remained still as a stone. He searched his mind for the controls to his arms and legs. He was desperate for a way to stop the effects of the drug. His eyes froze in place, as Tommy sneered down at him.

"I told you I spared no expense." Tommy, then placed the scalpel against the top of James' chest. He pressed the blade down and a sharp tearing sensation forged its way through James' senses. "Sorry I didn't get anything to numb the pain." Tommy said as he continued to pull the scalpel in a straight line down the center of James' chest.

Screams ripped through the air, as James' mind lifted to a conscious state. It was then that he realized it was his own screams that had awakened him. Tommy was hard at work. James tried to blink his eyes but felt a tug as he strained to close them. Vile surged into James' mouth as he realized that Tommy had sewn his eyelids to his eyebrows in an effort to keep them open. Every time James blinked a ripping pain pulsed through his head. Blinking was an involuntary motion and James could do little to stop the action. He dared to peer down at his chest. His eyes went wide as he witnessed an avulsed layer of skin. A metal instrument hung, loosely to either side and was attached to a flap of skin holding it clear of the incision. Tommy's hands were moving to clear out pulsing blood, as he clamped off an artery.

"Ahh... He awakens, again." Tommy scoffed, as he removed his gloves and turned a dial down on one of the bags.

"Not trying to kill you yet." Tommy said with a smirk. "Just a little epinephrine or adrenaline to keep the patient alert; wouldn't want you to miss a thing." Tommy stepped away from the table and again left the room. He returned with a small instrument with a serrated edge on the end. There was a long electric chord hanging from the end which Tommy plugged into a wall.

"This will have to do. Sorry. I couldn't get my hands on a real bone-saw. Not to worry though I'm fairly certain that this will cut through bone." Tommy seemed to be testing James for just the right reaction to every comment or action he had taken. Judging by the sheer jubilation on Tommy's face, he was no longer disappointed.

James could only imagine that his face was matching the terror rolling through his psyche. Tommy had every intention of sawing his ribcage open, while he laid paralyzed on a metal slab and with the blood, IV fluids and adrenaline being pumped into his veins, James wasn't sure how long he would last but one thing he was certain of... it was longer than he would want to.

23

Jordan entered the small bedroom. She hadn't realized that she was holding her breath. Her head swam as she eased down next to Amelia's sleeping form. Jordan caressed the tiny shape of her leg. Her eyes filled with tears, as she took in the protective pose of Amelia, as her little girl arms claimed Tristan's chubby body. Oh that it was that simple. Jordan at that moment would have given anything for Amelia's actions to be a prediction of their future. She wanted to believe that her children would be safe. She touched the creamy face of her son and noted the difference in the hue of her children's skin. Amelia with her hazelnut skin stood out in stark comparison to the more pale color of Tristan's creamy face. Both of her children were an immeasurable part of what made her life wonderful. Though Amelia had been adopted from the Cadotion tribe, she held just as much of Jordan's heart as Tristan.

Amelia had been a tiny gift that had lit up their world with the tenacity of a comet, flashing across a midnight sky. Jordan had been diagnosed unable to bear children due to her father's cruel beatings. Her womb had been so traumatized with scar tissue from wounds in different stages of healing that the doctor had delivered the final blow to Jordan during a head to toe workup. Every agent had to submit to a series of tests that would allow the agency some incite as to their capabilities concerning the job. At the time, Jordan hadn't realized how much she would someday want children of her own. The day that Amelia had been placed in her arms her heart was healed of wounds she did not even know she had suffered.

Tears streamed down Jordan's face, as she touched Amelia's satiny, dark hair. Like a raven's wing in flight, her beautiful locks, enfolded her tiny face and body. Jordan tried to subdue the urge to bring her daughter's body into her arms but everything that culminated into making her a mother screamed from within her psyche. Jordan scooped her daughter up and rocked with fierce abandon, as tears cascaded down her face.

"Mommy?" Amelia's little girl voice breaking through the darkness of the room brought Jordan back to the reality of what she was doing. Jordan pulled back, as she peered into Amelia's beautiful eyes. Her little girl; her season of hope had begun with this miracle that she now held in her heart and arms. Jordan smiled at Amelia. The action broke something within her. Nowhere in her mind, heart, body, or soul did she find the smile that she now produced for her innocent daughter. Jordan cleared her throat, as she silently thanked God for the strength He was giving her that she did not even know to ask for.

"Hey baby girl." Jordan managed, as she again pulled her daughter into her arms.

"Hey, what are you still doing up?" Lane's voice came from behind Jordan. She brushed back Amelia's hair, as she laid their daughter's head on her arm and allowed her hair to fan out so that every tendril was laid over the bend of her arm. Jordan turned to face Lane then, and in his eyes she could see that she had not been successful in disguising her anguish.

"Why don't daddy read you a bedtime story so that you can fall back to sleep." Lane said, as he moved to Jordan's side and scooped their daughter up into his massive arms. "That way mommy can go out and check on Uncle John and Aunt Cynthia." Lane prompted.

Jordan gladly took the disguised opportunity as she freely offered their daughter to Lane and brushed passed the end of the bed to the door.

"I'll be there soon." Lane offered while laying their daughter back in the bed next to her brother.

Jordan hid just beyond the door frame out of sight of her family. She could not yet leave them. Everything in her wanted to be near them all. She leaned her head forward and listened, as Lane told the story that his parents had told to him many times; the story of the great mountain that had blown up and filled the sky and valley, surrounding it with liquid fire. The liquid fire had formed huge trenches that had filled with rain water and was now the Cadotion River. Jordan smiled to herself, as the moment filled her spirit. Her children lay on the other side of the wall listening to her husband, their father tell the story that had once been shared with him by the people that had raised him as their own. Her heart felt so full and yet her soul cried out within her to grab them up and run from the threat that awaited them.

Even as she listened to the story unfold and thought of the love that filled their every moment together, Jordan knew what she had to do. She had no choice. The children needed Lane. They could not lose both of their parents and besides out of the two of them Lane was the one who had more to offer as a parent. He had a wealth of history to be shared. He had been raised soaking up the love of the Cadotion tribe. He encompassed that love; exuded it. She had to go. She was the only logical choice. She would have to face Tommy alone. It was her bloodline that had produced that evil; it had been so when she was possessed with the demon and it was so now. She had seen the truth that day in the airport; yet, she had denied it. Now, she had to end it. This time she would be fighting for her family. She would not be fighting for some misguided belief that she alone possessed a knowledge that could change the lives of every woman and child for the better. This time, she was fighting to protect her husband, her children and her friends from an evil that was so dark that it had sent chills through her entire being.

She had decided that she would wait until everyone was asleep. The plan was set; no one would leave until the morning. John had been through too much and he would need time to recover. Garrison had offered to stay the night to help keep an eye on the children. Jordan was upset with him, but she knew that he would never harm her children. The love that he felt for Amelia and Tristan was evident in all the time he had spent with them. But, it was the love that her children felt for him, their Uncle Garrison that kept Jordan from throwing him out of their lives. No, she and Garrison would, never again be the same but her children had nothing to do with it. Their happiness was the most important thing to her. Jordan was crying inside to think that she may not be there to see her children's future unfold but she was thankful that

Lane, Garrison, John, Cynthia, and the whole Cadotion tribe would be there to watch her children grow.

She reluctantly pulled away from the wall as she moved blurry eyed from the small apartment. She headed to the apartment provided for her family. She crossed the room and started to lie down on the queen size bed when she felt arms come around her body. She hadn't even been aware that anyone was there. She froze to the spot. Her senses were so stricken with all of the new discoveries about the people she knew but didn't know and then there was the situation with Tommy. Nothing was real; everything about her life was out of focus.

"Hey..." Lane managed to say, as he pulled Jordan's trembling body into his arms. The sadness that had been welling up within her seemed to pour from her like an avalanche.

She crushed into his arms, not feeling she could be close enough. She knew that their very souls had been fused as one by God, Himself and yet in this moment, she felt as though even the Power of that union would not sustain her.

She found his lips then, as she doused the kiss in all of her worries, anger, confusion, brokenness but mostly her love. She wrapped her arms around his neck and climbed his body as if he were a large tree and she a small child seeking refuge in its branches high above the ground. She wrapped her legs around his midsection; using the strength of her leg muscles, she arched her body further into the air so that she could claim even more of the sweet nectar promised to her from his lips. She felt like a caged animal that the only way out would be through the exploration of their love.

Lane allowed her the access that she so desperately desired. He never questioned where the passion emanated from. Instead, he too sought refuge in her love as he pulled her body closer to him. He, then tenderly lay her down on the hard mattress of the queen sized bed that seemed barely enough to support his body. With every touch and every tender kiss, she could feel the determination that he felt to illustrate his love and knew it could only be matched by that of her own determination.

Time seemed to stand still in those moments, as they claimed their prize in the arms of the other. Soon Jordan heard Lane's slow even breaths, as he fell deeper into sleep. She kissed his massive hand and confessed her love. Then, she slipped from his arms a little at a time, holding her breath as she felt him stir a few times. She knew that he would never allow her to go alone.

She stood for scant seconds that seemed infinitely longer as she watched him sleep. She took in the sight of him, praying that it would give her strength later as she stood face to face with her nightmare in the flesh.

Jordan made her way passed the fountain and down the long corridor to the back entrance. There was an eerie quiet that settled over the compound. Save the insistent, trickling of the waterfall the place was deathly quiet. All of the indigenous bird population had bedded down for the night and even the crickets had sung their last mournful song. There was nothing but the slight patter of her feet on the cobblestone walk as she pushed passed all of the beauty encompassing The Garden and with every step drew closer to the ugly beyond.

Her heart stuttered, as she climbed the stairwell leading up. At the top of each section of stairs was a flat plateau designed to cut some of the climbing down. The new exit had been put in after the tragedies of the twin towers. The building fund for Black Heart was an ever growing fund; it had to be. No expense would be spared in providing security for the agents of Black Heart. For their safety ensured the safety of the higher ups in the bureau as well. Anonymity was everything and every stop would be pulled in order to keep the agents' identities hidden. Any breech in the tapestry of that anonymity could not, would not, be tolerated.

Somewhere out there beyond this little heaven on earth, The Garden... was her nephew. He would be waiting on her. For all she knew, he could be waiting just beyond the door for someone to exit so that he could gain access.

24

A gust of icy wind slammed into Jordan's body as she exited the compound. She wanted to listen to her surroundings but the blasts of snow flurries made it impossible. She hadn't paid any attention to the weather. She had barely had time to unpack when the bomb had been dropped about Cynthia.

Jordan pulled her coat more tightly around her neck and tugged on the black hat she wore to camouflage her features. She had slipped into the bathroom and put on the black suit after leaving the bed. She hoped that the suit would help her cause. If she didn't die of frostbite before finding Tommy Hayden then maybe she could live long enough to mount an attack on him. She hoped that he would sustain wounds that would be bad enough that he would languish even if he had killed her. He could not walk away. If he survived the attack, then her death would be in vain.

Jordan had done her homework well. She had spoken with Garrison about the last known whereabouts of James Ruston. She knew without a shadow of a doubt that it was Ruston's handy-work that had led to all of the horrifying events that her family and friends were being faced with. It all made sense. James Ruston was the link that had tied all of them together. From the beginning, he had been pulling every string to ensure that all of the people of his past, like pawns on a chess board came together at just the right moment in order to fulfill his lust for revenge. Ruston had manipulated everyone involved. She was sure that if she found Ruston that Tommy Hayden would be close at hand.

Jordan could not understand what she had to do with it all. What about her had set Ruston off? Why had Ruston wanted to hurt her by telling Hayden that she was in fact his aunt and that she had killed his biological father? She was the one piece of the puzzle that did not seem to fit. She had not attended college with Garrison and John. She had nothing to do with them before that day in the alley when Ruston had sent for her to be recruited. As a matter of a fact, that had been the first time that she and any of the other people had come in contact. To her knowledge that was the beginning of her time with all of the others: Garrison, John, Cynthia, or Ruston. So how did she fit into it all? Jordan knew enough about field operations to know that if she was going to find someone she first needed to understand them. She would have to gather as much Intel as possible on Ruston in order to better understand him. It was then and only then that she had any hope at finding him or Tommy. She would have to start at Ruston's apartment.

Jordan quickly disappeared into the cab that she had hailed. She had scanned the area for any onlookers. A few homeless people were scattered in the shadowy corners of the street huddled under newspapers or pieces of cardboard in an attempt to ward off the cold. Jordan made a mental note that she would have to talk to Lane about what could be done to help the people. The number of the homeless population was growing with each new day. There had to be a way to put an end to the senseless reality. She wanted to be a part of something bigger.

She wanted to leave behind the past and know that no matter what it would not come careening out of some darkened corner and drag her and her family into the murky shadows erasing in an instant any semblance of happiness they may have forged.

She eyed the cabdriver's reflection in the rearview mirror, as she recited the address of her destination. The cabdriver, a heavyset man with graying hair greeted her with a nod, as he quickly pulled away from the curve. After a U-turn, they headed south. Soon Jordan would have the answers needed to find Ruston and hopefully that would lead to Tommy Hayden.

Darkness, uncommon to New York shrouded the city. The blizzard had knocked out the lights. A blanket of snow covered the power lines while the wind whipped with heated, frenzy disarming the cables.

Several deafening booms had sounded in the distance. Jordan knew that sound, all too well; it was the sound of transformers blowing. A deep-urgent voice echoed from the speakers of the cab's factory-installed radio. The man advised everyone to stay in for the night. This storm would be unlike any that the city had witnessed in the past. Jordan shook her head, as she thought of all the people in the city. Most would listen to the man's common sense pleadings while others would claim to know all about the snow. There would be talk of how they had chains on their vehicles and after all, some of them had been dealing with snow for years. No one could tell them anything that they did not already know. Jordan hated to see so many lives senselessly lost due to pride. Why couldn't people just realize their limitations?

The cab driver grunted with the effort of holding the cab steady in the road; even a seasoned driver was having trouble negotiating the extreme conditions of the brutal storm. Jordan thought, as she collected the man's information from his credentials hanging from the dash to the side of the steering column.

His graying hair, laugh lines, and crow's feet around his eyes told of a jovial man in about his late fifties. Jordan noticed the gold band on his left ring finger. She didn't know why maybe, it was the nerves of not having been in the field in so long or maybe, it was just the storm but she just couldn't stop herself from making conversation.

"How long have you been driving a cab?" She stuttered the last of the sentence, adding driving a cab at the last minute. As much as she needed to hear another human being in a normal conversation, she didn't want to waste time having to edit her words after the fact. She hated it when someone felt the need to correct all of the mistakes another person made in a sentence, before answering a question or simply continuing the conversation. Ruston was bad about that. Jordan had a different way of speaking; it was as if she came from another planet. She had grown up in a very uneducated family. However, she felt that she had done well for herself, despite her earlier shortcomings. She had once told Ruston that a folder he had asked for was on the side. To which he had stopped and screwed his face up into puzzled-confusion.

"The side of what?" Ruston had asked. Jordan had turned a heated glare on him, as she walked over to the folder sitting on the cabinet top right next to Ruston.

"The side" Jordan's heated gaze warned, as she walked away in frustration.

"Thirty three years, be thirty four in January." The cab driver confessed with a proud glint in his gray-blue eyes. Jordan had been so deep in thought that she had all but forgotten that she had asked the cab driver how long he had driven cabs.

"Oh... Well, that's a long time." Jordan offered, as her cheeks heated to red from embarrassment.

"You okay, ma'am?" The driver asked, as he pulled in front of an old apartment building.

"I'm okay, thanks." Jordan lied, as she tossed the man a fifty and stepped from the cab.

"Hey, don't you want your change?" The man asked, as he leaned across the seat.

Jordan waved him off. She heard the breaks groan, as they released and the cab pulled away. All at once, she felt utterly alone. Her mind was reeling, as she stood back and took in the meandering building. It seemed to be out of balance with itself in some way. No set pattern existed, as the right side of the building jutted bluntly from the ground and ended only a few hundred feet in the air; no more than three, Jordan surmised. The left of the building burst into the night sky, as it seemed to be scraping the clouds above while the center with its curved roof connected the two ends in a lazy-snake formation. The engineering, Jordan could tell was meant to be whimsical but had taken on more of a tacky gaudiness that took away from the surrounding establishments.

Jordan stepped up on the curb, as she pulled the small paper from her pocket. Normally, she would have burned the slip of paper housing the information of a mark but this was not the same. She was not in search of someone for the bureau; this time it was personal. This time she was fighting for family and for her own life. She knew all too well that Tommy would not stop. She had been driven by evil before. She had felt the claws of that retched demon, as it sank them into her very soul a little further each day taking away every piece of what made her human. She knew that place that Tommy Hayden now existed. She too had once lived to appease a desire that burned within her very soul; a desire that had erased every other ambition, she had ever known. It too had become all that mattered. It had stolen her very life and in turn had nearly taken all that she loved.

She remembered the days well leading up to her time in the woods outside of Beulah County. She could still see the faces of her victims in her dreams. She could hear the cries of their loved ones demanding to know why their time had been cut short. She could hear their own souls, crying out for answers. Jordan had repented and she had come to know the peace that only God could offer. But, at times she had abandoned the safety of His love to wallow in the same disgusting mire of the past. She had, too many times forsaken her Redeemer in the name of doubt; but not this time. She had spent the better part of her time begging God for his protection. She had pleaded for the sanctuary of His loving arms. She would not forget. She would not walk away. She would hold tight to His unchanging hand, she had no choice. She could not do it any other way.

She brushed off the chill that tried to make its way down her spine. There was no time to allow poorly constructed buildings to have the upper hand; she could not succumb to the fear that inanimate objects could sometimes embody. She had to stay focused on the task at hand.

Jordan moved into the shadows, as she followed the building around to the back entrance. Garrison had been clear, during his time debriefing her and Lane by the fountain on the best possible route for gaining access to Ruston's apartment. The back entrance had a service elevator that led up to the fifth floor of the south tower where Ruston lived. When exiting the elevator, she would cut back to the right and step into a small maid closet. There she would be able to find a smock used by the maids to cover their clothes while cleaning the rooms. After that, she would be just another worker on the floor and could easily gain access to the room through the usual means of breaking in and entering. Jordan had a fingernail file that she had used on more than one occasion to jimmy a lock. She had, also been forced to use it as a weapon in a pinch.

She had finally made her way into Ruston's poorly decorated apartment. She felt sadness creep into her core, as she thought of how far the man had fallen. Ruston had a lavish office with all the trappings. Once the lead recruiter for field agents, his lush apartment supplied by the company was equipped with leather upholstered furnishings and a state of the art entertainment center that descended from the ceiling with one touch on a remote control. The blinds too, were opened and closed by a timer that was set for the same hour every day.

Jordan and Garrison had been invited to a party held by Ruston during one of his attempts to show off all of the finer things that his time in the bureau had allotted him. He never missed the opportunity to pay for an overpriced meal. Any attempt would always be made to remind others of all he held in his grasp. Jordan had never been impressed by the man's fortune. Even at her worst moment in life, she knew that all of the inanimate objects in the world could never replace love. She felt a kind of sadness for him, then that she had not been able to truly understand until now.

She lived in a tent on the shores of a beautiful river among a serene people desirous of nothing more than on being in each other's presence. Her home was lavished not in things to up its value but in the love of her family. She bathed every day in the warmness of that love. She would trade that existence for nothing. Even now, as she walked through the remnants of what remained of Ruston's once lavish world, she longed to be back among the Cadotion people; her people.

Something was wrong. Every part of the place, however, poorly decorated it may have been was tidy except a space near a small table that huddled in the corner. Some books lay in a clumsy heap on the floor. A scrunched up portion of sheet at the foot of the bed in a starburst pattern that almost seemed to fit the shape of a fisted hand hinted of a struggle. Jordan was sure that there had been a struggle in the apartment. Someone had taken Ruston by force; but who?

Jordan moved around the room with keen awareness, careful not to tamper with anything that could help officials to prove who had taken Ruston. She mentally cataloged the crime scene so that she could place everything back in the exact position it had been. Then, she moved to the table. There was a pad of paper near the desk. She looked through the top drawer for a pencil but didn't find one. There had to be one somewhere. She moved from the desk to the nightstand near the bed. A small pad lay next to a large wooden lamp with a simple white shade. Right next to the pad was a small green pencil that seemed to have been harshly used. On the sides of the pencil was what seemed to be teeth marks. As though whoever had used the pencil did so under duress. Jordan collected the pencil and then pulled the piece of paper just under the top of the first sheet out. She then walked over to the small table. She moved to a chair set next to a large picture window near the door. She sat down in one of the poorly upholstered chairs and started to slowly and lightly rub the side of the pencil on the first sheet collected from the pad. After a few seconds she realized that there would be no reason to continue. Nothing was on the paper. Evidently, Ruston had either not yet used that particular pad of paper or he had simply not been as upset as the abused pencil might suggest.

Jordan rubbed her hand through her hair as frustration threatened to take center stage. She only had one more piece of paper and if it had as much to tell her as the first then the trip to Ruston's home could have been for nothing. She began the slow-methodic-rubbing of the pencil on the second sheet of paper and like magic, a luminated white background started to appear through the darkened pencil strokes. Jordan stopped and stared at the paper. Her heart was racing. If the paper revealed a number or an address, then she could be halfway to solving a very big problem. But if the shiny white area in the dusty gray backdrop only revealed a petty list of some sort that Ruston had been working on then... Jordan could not finish the thought. She picked up the small chewed up green pencil and started to lightly rub across the paper again. After finishing, Jordan realized that the lighting in the room, left something to be desired.

Jordan carefully pulled the small multifunction knife from her belt and switched on the light at the end of the knife handle. A piercing light filled the small area. Jordan leaned over the table where she sat and scrutinized the highlighted words. She scrutinized the address for a moment longer. What was Ruston up to and who had taken him from the apartment against his will? She didn't like the questions that were starting to pile up; not enough answers seemed to be available. Her mind was reeling. She tossed a quick, glance back at the room. It was time to find out what Ruston had been up to before his plans were interrupted.

C H A P T E R

25

The room felt so empty like too much space existed in it. He moved to the other side of the bed to claim his prize, Jordan. Just as he had done every morning since they had married. Lane loved to wake up next to her. His massive arms crossed the expanse of a too small queen size bed. Rubbing first up and then down, he searched for her small frame. He found nothing. His knitted his brow as he opened his eyes and took in the tiny eight by ten foot room. The apartment space provided to them by The Truth was immensely larger than the small tent that they lived in while among the Cadotion people. Yet, it somehow seemed smaller. Lane could not be sure if it was the fact that the compound was so many feet under the earth's surface and he and Jordan had become used to living outdoors among nature. Or maybe, it was simply that they missed home all together. Maybe, the depth of the apartment made no difference. That was probably the truth of it, Lane decided as he moved to a seated position. He scanned the room for any sign of Jordan, nothing. There was no light coming from the bathroom. Maybe, she had gotten an early start in the kitchen to make breakfast. It would be a long day, after all.

Lane walked past the spare bedroom where Tristan and Amelia would normally be sleeping. The children were fast asleep in the bosom of their friend's love. He and Jordan had said their goodbyes the night before. Lane had to usher Jordan from the room before she broke down in sobs terrifying them both. It was not like her to lose it this way. Something wasn't right. He would get to the bottom of it as soon as he found his wife.

Lane frowned as he noticed the kitchen too was empty. The overhead light above the stove was burning bright as usual but there was no sign of breakfast or Jordan for that matter. He was beginning to become a little antsy. Maybe, she went next door to say goodbye to the children again. He moved to the front door as a small-yellow-paper taped to the front door caught his attention. Lane felt the blood drain from his face as he grasped the paper and read the message inside. His mind felt numb. The air seemed to be thicker than before. His eyes scanned the note again as he took in each word.

Lane,

I know that you don't approve. I'm sorry. I just had to do this "My Way". I can't allow the children to lose both of their parents. Besides, you're better at the parental stuff anyway. I love you with all that I am. Please tell the children every day that their mommy loves them. If I don't come back, Lane make sure they know that I will always be looking over them. I will always be looking over you, too my love, until we meet again in our Father's house. . .

Always in Christ;

With all my love;

Jordan Gates

Lane read the letter again, as the words 'if I don't come back' seemed to mock him... he stared at the offending yellow piece of paper. It was so small and yet, it held within its tiny space words that could change his future. As if he had woken up for the first time that morning, he was a frenzy of motion. He ran to the bedroom and grabbed the first thing out of the closet that he could fit into. He threw his hair back into a clumsy heap at the nape of his neck. He grabbed his phone and dialed the first number that came to mind.

"Hello." Garrison sounded groggy. Clearing his throat he started again.

"Hey, sorry. Who is this? Lane?" Garrison prompted while sounding confused.

"Garrison!" Lane said interrupting Garrison's sleepy greeting. "Have you heard from Jordan?" Lane asked as he tried to calm his nerves.

"Jordan?" Garrison sounded confused. "Why would I hear from Jordan? She's with you, right?" Garrison asked. The sound of mattress springs filled the line.

"Lane, are you there? What's going on?" Garrison sounded more coherent now.

"Listen, I woke up this morning... She's gone, Garrison. She left a note." Lane stammered through the answers. All of the possibilities slammed into his mind. He felt swimmy headed.

"She left a note? Lane, you're not making any sense. Where are you?" Garrison asked. Lane heard lots of movement and what sounded like clothes rustling in the background. Lane guessed that Garrison was putting his pants and shirt on.

"I'm coming there. Are you still at the compound?" Garrison asked.

Lane could hear all of the questions that were being asked by Garrison. He just couldn't seem to react to anything. He felt frozen in place. He had missed all of the signs. Why did he not know that Jordan would go off by herself? Of course, she would. It was her way. She didn't know how to share the load with anyone. She had always taken the brunt of any issue that they faced as a couple and just handled it. It had been the main reason that he had wanted the trip to go so smoothly; the reason he had made the flight plans. He had wanted to be the one for once that took care of everything.

"Lane?" Garrison's voice filled the line with resounding urgency.

"Yeah. Sorry. Look Garrison, I think I know where she went or at least where she would have gone first." Lane offered as he looked at the small note again.

"You think she went to Ruston's place, don't you?" Garrison's question dripped with surety.

At that moment, Lane could sense that Garrison was recalling the briefing on Ruston and Tommy the night before.

Lane studied the note a few seconds longer and then stuffed it into the front pocket of his old jeans.

"Yeah. I do." Was all he said, and then he hung up. Lane knew that Garrison would meet him there. He also knew that Garrison would understand two irrevocable truths: first, Lane would not want to waste time on the phone when he could be talking to his Father about what to do, and second, Lane would not want to be wasting time that could be spent looking for Jordan.

Lane moved through The Garden, as he began the prayer that he knew would not end until he saw his beautiful Jordan again. His spirit groaned with the pain of her loss. He felt as if he had been transported back in time to the day that she lay on the forest floor outside of Beulah County; the day that he believed her to be dead. Lane's every nerve ending vibrated with the need to find her; to know that she was safe. He made the path that he had been certain she would have taken.

Lane had spent quite a bit of time monitoring Jordan's every move, after he had been charged with her safe return to Black Heart. The Truth had been enlisted on numerous occasions to bring one of the rogue agents back. It was thought that the tactics of the missionaries of The Truth were preferred to that of the agents of Black Heart. But, Lane in particular had been chosen to bring Jordan back for one all-consuming reason; He was a man of God with a very unique ability to follow after the statutes set before him by God. Lane had never exhibited any kind of a desire for the opposite sex. He had shown nothing, but unending kindness toward any member of the bureau that he had been charged with in the past. What better person to bring her back than a man that could rekindle her faith in men with Jordan's belief system about men? Or, at least give her faith of any kind.

Jordan had lived a life of an abuse so horrible that it still had a lasting impact on her today. After three years of holding her and reassuring her that it was going to be alright, Jordan was still waking in a sweaty frenzy of tears and agonizing screams.

Lane exited the cab in front of the oddly shaped apartment building. He threw a twenty dollar bill to the cab driver and thanked him. "Keep the change." Lane directed, as he stepped further onto the curve and cast the man a wary smile.

"Thanks." The cab driver offered, as he cast an appreciative grin in Lane's direction.

"Place sure is getting a lot of visitors." The cab driver surmised, as he raced the engine and started to pull off.

"Wait!" Lane was nearly shouting, as he grabbed frantically at the still open passenger window. "You had another passenger come here? Last night?" Lane felt the hope that he had compiled earlier double. There was a chance that Jordan had come here; that she could still be here.

"Yeah, it was about two this morning. It was snowing like wild." The man explained. He shook his head, as he recounted the events of the night before. "Picked up a lady same place as you, pretty lady." The cab driver shook his head, again. "Brought her right here, and she was a good tipper, too." He confessed. "Couldn't understand why a lady would be out so late in such an awful storm especially, a lady that pretty." The cab driver tilted his head toward the backseat as if the lady he spoke of were still in the cab.

"But what do I know? I'm just a driver. I'm not her guardian that's for sure." The driver nodded in Lane's direction, as he pulled away from the curve.

Lane stood, staring after the cab for a moment. He didn't know whether to laugh at the assumption that the cab driver was obviously making about Jordan's ability to take care of herself or to allow the shudder that was threatening to course through his body to have its way. He knew in the core of his being that Jordan could take care of herself. It just felt somehow wrong to him that she was out there facing whatever, alone.

He had seen her at her worse. He had to face her in the past. He knew what she was capable of but that did not negate the fact that she was going through a lot. She could in no way be getting enough sleep; the nightmares plagued he sleep. She was worn out with the efforts she made to keep up with their young children as well. Jordan, quite simply had an insurmountable mountain of stress on her that in Lane's opinion would not help the amount of focus that she would need in order to face a foe as formidable as Tommy Hayden.

Lane had read Tommy's file. It wasn't that he was anymore trained or capable than Jordan; it was more the ruthless, no holds-barred way that Tommy had about doing things. Tommy had been placed in The Garden early. He had been one of the bureau's youngest recruits. His first kill had been so gruesome yet, it was ruled self-defense due to the nature of abuse that he had endured at the hands of his stepfather. Lane had never seen anything like the things that he had read in Tommy's file.

Black Heart had stepped in due to the prompting of James Ruston but not before Tommy had made another kill; more gruesome than the first.

Garrison had filled all of them in on Tommy's history; history that would fill in the blanks in Tommy's file... blanks that had been purposefully left empty by the bureau in order to obtain what they believed would be their greatest weapon. But Tommy was different from any other agent. He killed for a greater need that exited within the confines of his deranged psyche. Tommy thought himself to be a god. He believed that the lives of the people or animals that he had taken fulfilled a greater purpose. He believed his mind was like the sacred grounds of a heaven of sorts. Each person or animal killed became a legendary part of that world and in that way, they would be able to live on forever in his thoughts.

Tommy had in some way felt sorry for the custodian. He liked the guy. He just felt he was ignored, forgotten. So in the end, in Tommy's mind he had done the man a favor by taking his life in such an unforgettable way. It was the least that Tommy could do for a man that had shared his world, so willingly with the young god. The man deserved better; he deserved to live among the legends of those memories created by Tommy. The police had found pieces of Carl Shelton hanging from every corner of the janitor closet. In the middle of a large white wall to the left of the door was a message written in Carl's blood:

Carl Shelton will live forever in the land of my memories. Gone but not forgotten. He shall live as an immortal, walking through the vast lands of my eternal-heaven.

The note had been written in dripping blood with Tommy's finger but had been erased... the bureau had cleaned up the place and had closed the case saying that a serial killer had escaped from the local prison and had sought refuge in the school's basement. Unfortunately, Carl had had the bad luck of happening across the fugitive and had lost his life. But all was well because local law enforcement had neutralized the killer. Due to the delicate nature of the case, it was advised that the situation be kept quiet. A large donation was made to the school and the dean of admissions had agreed that the school's reputation would be better served if the elderly janitor's cause of death were to stay a secret.

Fortunately, for the school and the bureau, Carl Shelton was alone with no children. He was an eccentric-hermit that had horded his money and talked to no one. He rarely had anything to say to the children in the halls as he passed from one cleaning site to the next. Ironically, Tommy had given 'immortality' as he delved it to a miserable old man that hated the world. Carl was not forgotten as Tommy had believed him to be; rather he was self-exiled into a lonely world of his own making.

Garrison had explained every detail that had been purposely kept from Tommy's file. The bureau had intended to set a killer, not someone that had had the misfortune of having to take someone's life in order to survive a very bad situation... a killer... a killing machine on the public. They believed with intense training that they would be able to control the monster. Ruston had manipulated the HOD into letting him personally, head of the Tommy project. Who was playing god now?

No one knew in the bureau at the time that Tommy Hayden had been Jordan's nephew aside from a handful of people including Garrison. Lane shook his head at the very idea that Garrison had been privy to such a crucial part of Jordan's history and had chosen to keep it to himself. And then there was the night before with John Benton.

The things that John had thrust upon them in the form of truth had changed so many things about what Lane thought he knew. The people around him were just dried up and discarded husks of humanity. None of the people before him that night had been whom he had thought them to be, except Jordan. How ironic that in the end, it would be Jordan; his mysterious wife, with all of her uncertainties that would be the only one left standing in his midst that was remotely who he thought her to be.

John had confessed that he had been on the phone with Tommy Hayden for about a week, maybe more. It had all started to run together. He had confided that he couldn't be sure even what day it was. All he seemed to live for was the next phone call and what could be done to negate all that Tommy threatened to do to those that he loved. Tommy knew about his past. He knew that he had gotten drunk and raped a girl in college or so he had thought. He was using that dark secret of John's past as torque. He would tell Cynthia that it had been John in the basement of that house the night that she had woke to discover that her innocence had been stolen away. The man that she had spent years by his side loving and trusting; her very own husband, the man that she had shared all of her dreams and all of her fears; John Benton was not the man that she had believed him to be. Instead, she would be finding out that he was a former drug addict and a drunk. She would be finding out that the man that she had believed was John Benton was no more than a conjured phantom, a figment of her imagination. John would have done almost anything to keep the look of betrayal—of pain that he was certain would fill Cynthia's eyes the moment that she knew the truth about who he really was from emerging... He could not peer into those beautiful, trusting brown eyes and see the anguish that he had caused.

Lane had never known all of the things that John had confessed about himself that night. He felt a sense of loss and sadness for John. Lane felt as though he had somehow failed his friend. That John should have known that no matter what, no matter who he believed Lane to be, he could talk to him about anything; somehow that had gotten lost in translation. He had failed his friends. So, among all of the people in the midst of The Garden that were not who Lane had believed them to be, was Lane himself. He too had been some fabricated ideal of himself. He had failed them all. He had deceived himself into believing that he was the kind of friend that someone would talk to because they knew that they could. He believed that he incited trust in others. How could he have missed something so simple? How could he have believed so blindly that his friends would come to him, because they felt safe in doing so? John had taught Lane that he had some changes to make. He would spend time with the Almighty. He would allow God to improve the things within him, things that lived in his spirit that he was not even aware of. Things that stood in the way of Lane being the kind of man that he desperately wanted to be. But for now, he would have to focus on the things that he could work on at the moment.

Lane looked around. Dawn was just beginning to break. Deep purples and blues clustered on the horizon looking like brush-strokes just before the painter created the ultimate master piece. Somewhere in the distance, a dog barked its loan protest probably some jogger trying to keep in shape had passed by.

Lane squinted against the sunlight, as it strained through the trees casting streaks of white across the purple and blue hues putting the final touches on the master piece. He longed to have Jordan here with him, enjoying this moment; lying under a clear sky with scarce clouds in various shapes. Her head on his arm, as they play a guessing game with the children—guessing what each cloud reminded each of them of the most; a game that Amelia had been best at. Untouched by life's taint, Amelia's imagination was extraordinary.

Bright lights pierced the still, too dark morning. Lane didn't have to play a guessing game to figure out who might be in the cab that was now pulling over to the curve in front of where he stood. Garrison stepped from the cab, shutting the door. He moved to Lane's side. His eyes told a story that Lane was already aware of and afraid to admit; Jordan was in over her head.

26

Jordan had read the message over, again to make sure of the address. Though she had tucked it into her pants pocket, she did not want to have to fumble for it later. Thanks to a nervous or frustrated state, Ruston had pressed down with every stroke. He was obviously determined to relieve some of the stress he had been feeling in one way or the other. She knew the address. She had spent many days at the library on West Tenth Street looking for information to help her in cases she may be working. As well orchestrated, as the Intel had often been, some holes were left in the information. Jordan had gone to the library to fill in those holes. For instance, in times when the mark she was trying to find had been placed in witness protection because they had turned state's evidence on a bigger fish that the FBI wanted to catch; like in drug cartels.

Jordan would go to the library and look up obituaries. Not many people were aware of the system that the government used in relocating someone and giving them a new identity, but Jordan had privy to such information due to the connections Garrison had with members of the FBI.

Charles McCabe was one of the top agents working in field operations for the FBI. He and Garrison had been friends since preschool. Any and all of the connections that McCabe may have, was made available to Garrison and vice versa. Jordan had benefited from that long term friendship in many ways, but none so much as the wealth of knowledge the man had possessed and lavished upon Garrison.

Moving through the woods, Jordan reflected on her time at the library. Something had lurched inside of her the moment she had read the article about the Maddox family in Morristown, New Jersey. She had read through dozens of articles, but none had incited the kind of fear that she knew her nephew would be looking for. She had witnessed it in his eyes that day in the Atlanta airport. She knew that he would be craving a certain kind of energy to be housed in a place that he intended to bring his victims to.

She had been very straight forward in the way that she killed. Jordan didn't like the game playing that seemed to litter the book at the bureau. She had no desire to be creative; just get in, get it done, and get out. She had no desire to make the death scene match some criterion that could best suit the proper clean up scenario.

Tommy, though, that was another story. He thrived on the kill. The exact way to kill a mark would be important to him. She had read in his file that his favorite scenario in the kill criterion manual was number thirty three: the scene that was set up to appear to be orchestrated at the hands of an up and coming serial killer.

Jordan pushed the thought from her mind, as she pulled her coat up closer to ward off the chill. Something about the way Tommy Hayden's file read didn't feel right. Jordan had been a born killer; an efficient killing machine. She had been the best that the bureau had to offer, a fact that she was not proud of, but once had been.

The cab had dropped her off two miles from the entrance to the old farmhouse. Jordan had run the remainder of the way. She kept off the main trail leading to the house. She didn't want to be spotted by Tommy or anyone that he may have as an accomplice though she doubted anyone that crossed his path would remain alive long enough to help Tommy do anything.

The brisk wind tore through the trees, dropping the chill factor about ten degrees. Her legs felt numb. Her face was raw and her eyes burned with the tears that felt frozen to her irises. She pushed onward as she longed for a summer day back on the banks of the Cadotion River. She had no time for wishful thinking. All that she had was the here and now. She would do whatever it took to keep her family safe.

Running across snow covered ground, sinking to her knees was just the preliminary to what she was yet to face and even that was not too much.

A pale light pierced the darkness, as the thick wood opened into a clearing. An old two story dilapidated farmhouse stood in the forefront of an old red and white barn covered in shrubs and tall grass that had not been tended in years. A tractor was pulled to the side of the barn under a slanted metal lean-to shack that was held up by little more than several two by fours nailed together. Snow covered grass, and weeds snaked up the length of the tractor holding it captive in their unrelenting grip. Gloom closed in on the old farm, wrapping it in its foreboding darkness around what once had been a home to the old farmer and his family.

Jordan pulled her attention from the white powder wrapping everything in its light glow. It did nothing for the mood that seemed to haunt the old farmhouse; a mood left behind by those that had once filled the structure with song and love. Now, just a memory in some article about the death of those that once had occupied it, the old house was resolved in its commitment to be a symbol of destruction. Inside, Jordan was not certain what she would find. She had read the article and she was afraid it may be more of the same. If James Ruston was beyond the walls of the old house, his fate would probably be a reflection of the house's history.

Inching her way as close as she dared to the house, Jordan thanked the Lord for the light of day. Her nerves were tight as a rubber band, and she could not imagine having to attempt what she had in mind under the shroud of night. Though, the brightness of the sun glaring off the snow would no doubt foil most of her attempts to stay hidden, Jordan had been careful to read up on another article, before leaving the library that she was certain would ensure her success. The blueprints for most of the homes in the surrounding area had been another one of the archives that the library attendants had been gracious enough to keep on file. Also, a map of the town, and underground tunnels for the sewage and water to circulate had been public knowledge as well; in case an evacuation of the town's people was ever needed.

Jordan had scanned the plans of the old farmhouse. She was very pleased to note that underground sewage was not the only tunneling that the house had access to. According to the document, the old house was one of a few of the homes in the area that had been designated during a town meeting to have a bomb shelter that would be built with revenue provided by the town's building fund. The money had been set aside during a harsh storm that had left destruction of over half of the town's business and private district. The town had suffered such a great loss in the rebuilding but it was the loss of life that had led to the raising of money to erect storm shelters and other precautionary structures or devices throughout the town. Jordan had to commend the town's people for not being willing to be victims over and over before coming to a conclusion that would save lives if not structures.

Leaning to the right, Jordan tugged on a metal handle that was protruding from a wooden plank in the ground. She had to wipe the snow away, but with some effort she was able to gain access to the shelter beneath. Jordan ducked into the structure after scanning the area surrounding the opening for any sign of Tommy. After being satisfied that she was indeed alone, she moved quietly down the wooden stairs that were in severe disrepair. The farmer had obviously, allowed the place to depreciate long before he had lost his senses and killed his family and then himself in a fit of rage.

Descending the stairs, Jordan felt a shiver inch its way up her spine. The squeaking-wobbly staircase boasted of the years they had stood guard over the entrance to the small darkened room beyond. Jordan pulled the small knife from her pocket as she illuminated the darkness beneath with its flashlight attachment. She tested the room for movement. There was none. She moved further into the enclosure with dreaded misery. One hand holding to the small light as though it were her only saving grace, the other tracing the wall, as she continued her eerie descent into the nothingness below.

Once at the foot of the stairs, Jordan shined the light to be certain the door leading to the tunnel that led to the house was closed. It was. She moved to the center of the room, and pulled on a slender chain that was protruding from the ceiling. Nothing happened. Her heart sank as she shined her tiny light up to the light fixture. The bulb was broken. A crunching sound broke through the darkness, startling Jordan. She shrunk into the corner of the room, and turned off the small light that she had counted on with her every breath. Jordan stood in the corner with expectant terror. After nothing happened, her cheeks filled with heat. She realized then that the crunching noise she had heard would be the shards of broken glass from the destroyed bulb. She had stepped on the pieces, unable to see them in the darkness.

Jordan took a deep cleansing breath, and then turned back on the light. Her eyes focused on the space directly in front of her first. She had to calm herself, Everything in the room was lending itself to the terror that was building within her. She searched the cabinet on the wall next to her for a bulb or a candle; something that would help her to be able to see the room more clearly. She needed to establish a base; somewhere that she could run in case the worst happened. She needed to familiarize herself with the inner workings of the place. But at that moment, she was a ball of nerves. She felt nothing of the old Jordan. She was hideously afraid.

Jordan scanned the small cabinet quickly. There was no sign of bulbs or candles. She felt anger well up in her for the first time. What kind of a storm shelter had no candles? She moved to a small wooden box under the staircase. Opening the lid, she discovered extra blankets. She moved a drab-brown blanket from the top of the pile, and just underneath was a large box of matches and two wooden candle holders. She felt a smile spread across he lips, as she moved the supplies onto the floor next to the box. Then with some care she lifted the next blanket, a more ornate blanket with yellow and pink flowers to the other side of the box. Just under the blanket were about a dozen candles. Some were short and stubby, others were long and slender but all were plain white in color. Jordan claimed her prize. Returning the blankets, she picked up her small knife and shined it around the room. In the far corner she spotted a small table with four chairs. Jordan crossed the room and mounted two candles in the wooden holders. She quickly struck a match and lit the candles, filling the room with ample light.

Jordan turned, again to view the newly lighted room. Her breath caught, as she took in the arsenal before her. Weapons of every caliber lined the cement walls of the cluttered room: swords, knives, muskets, pistols, grenades... the list went on. Jordan crossed the room, and began claiming some of her favorites of the loot. A short sword with silver and gold plating on its handle rested on a wooden shelf. The handle had a silver swooping-wing-like mechanism that exited the base of the blade and flared out to about two inches from the knife. The handle was indented with finger grips that traveled the length of both sides. Jordan collected the sword. She took a piece of leather from a deep-green bowl and tied the sword around her thigh. She moved to the other wall where she claimed a small black pistol. She stored it in the waist band of her black jeans after checking for ammunition. She then, turned to a small drawer set below the gun. The top drawer was loaded in bullets. She took the proper ones needed for the long black gun. She then, opened the bottom drawer. Moving some papers out of the way, her eyes lit up. Her hand claimed the tiny handle of the silver derringer. The chamber was loaded. Jordan collected a cartridge of bullets for the small gun, and then pushed the drawer closed again. She placed the gun in her boot and then checked for her own weapons.

The six inch blade that she had kept for so long was strapped to the inner thigh of her right leg. She caressed the knife, and asked God to guide her in what she must now do. She tugged on the long sleeve, black-button-up shirt she wore. Just under the edge she noted her own pistol. It was loose in the waistband of her pants. Jordan took mental inventory of all the weapons she had on her person. She was ready to wage war and yet, she still did not feel safe.

Jordan moved to the wall next to the small drawer set. She leaned back and allowed her head to fall back, until it touched the smooth-cool texture of the cement wall. She would give anything to not have to do this. She was no longer this person. She had been a killer. She had been in a dark place; a place so deep; so without light that she would have walked into this house and killed James Ruston and Tommy Hayden just for being men. Now, as she stood trying to gather courage, she was afraid, she lacked the resolve needed to do what had to be done, she had to end it.

Tommy Hayden was a killer, a cold-blooded-predator that would stop at nothing less than the destruction of her family; but more than the destruction of her family while she watched. Jordan felt like a hypocrite.

She was about to destroy this man for the very thing she had once been. She thought about that. She needed to take mental inventory of who she was, and who she had been. Sure, she was a killer; no denying that. She had enjoyed it. That was true, as well, but had she ever been willing to kill someone just to make another person pay? The answer was no. Jordan would never hurt someone she had deemed innocent; like the old man that had given her a ride into Beulah County the night she had killed the two women and the man at Holsters.

Jordan's mind swam with the horror of that time. The wide eyes of the woman in the backseat as she straddled her and pulled the blade across her milky-throat, filling the woman's ample cleavage with the oozing-dark-red of her flowing blood. Jordan shuddered, as the memory claimed her thoughts. She did not want that life anymore. She did not want to have to do this. Killing Tommy would most assuredly be a reminder of the life that she had left behind.

Jordan turned to the staircase. Moving to the steep wooden escape route, her eyes filled with tears. She felt her throat close, as she grabbed the railing. Her foot sought the first step. A distant scream filled the room. She turned to see the door to the hall burst open.

27

Time seemed to stand still, as the split second decision was made. She had already doused the candles, thank God she thought on her way to the staircase leading out. So there would be no one to know that the room had been tampered with. She had no time to think; just react and she had. She grabbed the banister leading to the exit. Pulling with her arms, Jordan swooped up into the air. A long board careening from the top of the slanted ceiling to the end of the staircase was nailed in place for stabilization of the roof. Jordan pulled her body silently into place and waited breathlessly as the door creaked open further into the room. Her heart pounded relentlessly against her chest. She almost couldn't catch her breath. It felt as though her breathing was being amplified on a loud speaker. Jordan closed her eyes only momentarily as she pulled breaths through her nose. It was as though the breaths were being funneled through the tiny straw that she used to stir her coffee that morning. Finally, she could breathe.

Tommy moved into the room. He walked purposefully over to a small green cabinet in the far corner. Jordan watched from her lone-perch just above the staircase. Her heart stuttered recklessly within her chest. Pulling the cabinet door open, Tommy stepped back just far enough from the cabinet that Jordan was able to see the contents inside. Bottles filled with amber liquid were stacked on the shelves. Each bottle held a body part. One had a finger, the other an eye. Some of the parts seemed foreign to Jordan; something she had never seen on a human body. She strained against the board trying not to make a sound. She wanted to know what the objects were. She had heard of serial killers needing to have a trophy from each of their kills, but this was beyond bazaar. If not human parts, then what were the parts in the lower containers?

An urgent need like she had felt before lit her curiosity on fire. Jordan tugged at the short sword o her left leg. It was making any attempt at getting a closer look impossible. The sword was caught on something. She was frustrated. She kept her eyes on the target and pulled with one final focused, jerk. The banister that she was on pitched to the left and metallic ring filled the room, as the sword raked across a long nail in the outer edge of the board. Jordan froze to the spot.

She held her breath, as she watched Tommy turn toward the noise. He stood there for a moment, as if he were making a decision, and then turned back to the task at hand. She watched, as he sealed the jar, and then replaced it on the second shelf of the green cabinet. Then, turning back in her exact direction, she thought she saw him smile. She cringed back into the darkness and waited for what she thought would come. Had he seen her? Was he about to make the move that she had not been willing to make? But then, as she thought for sure the decision had been taken from her, he exited the room.

She waited a few beats to be certain he would not return. She pulled her legs up under her, and sat on the board in a crouching position. She reached for the top of the banister and pulled with her arms, lifting her lower body into the air and quietly, purposefully, she sat her feet on the top of the long-cube-shaped banister. She walked to the end of the banister and plopped silently to the floor. At that moment, she was thankful that she and Lane had committed to staying in shape even though they were no longer in field operations.

Crossing the cement clad floor, she reached for her knife and turned on the light. She moved with purpose to the green cabinet in the corner of the room. Pulling the door open, she reached in to pull the jar out that had just been deposited on the second shelf. A pink-spongy-tissue with a white-webbing-substance floated in amber liquid. Jordan pulled the jar up for a closer look. Here mind seemed to pitch forward, as darkness claimed the outer edges of her vision. She staggered a few inches, causing the jar of amber liquid to pivot in her hands. With a jerky motion, she tightened her grip on the jar before losing control of it. She breathed deep as she replaced the jar back on the shelf. The realization of what the part was swam unrelentingly through her mind, boasting its horrible truth. It was the bottom apex of a human lung. The prize collected by Tommy must belong to James Ruston. Who else could it be, and if so, then where was he now? Was he still alive? She had heard screaming coming from beyond the tunnel. Ruston must be in the house of horrors waiting for Tommy to return and finish whatever sick-twisted plan he had for him. More importantly whatever plan he had initially concocted for her family; her children.

Jordan clutched her stomach, trying to ward off the rumbling there. She squatted before the cabinet and pulled one of the jars from the lower shelves. The same amber liquid filled the jar but the organ in the jar was something other than the human parts that filled the other containers. She moved to the small four-chair-table and lit one of the candles. The light from her knife just would not be enough. She pulled the candle closer, allowing its soft glow to touch the contents of the jar. Jordan partly closed her eyes as she moved her face closer to the jar. The object floating in the liquid shifted to the side and Jordan could make out a pointy-boney prominence, sticking out from under a pinkish sheath that almost seemed to be a skin-like substance. Just to the top of the skin-like substance was a knotty-black structure that jutted out a few centimeters from the rest of the appendage. Jordan searched her mind for anything that she had ever seen with this formation, on or in its body. She had taken biology in school and had to dissect cats and dogs... Jordan gasped, as she tilted the jar. Repulsed, she walked hastily back to the cabinet and returned the jar back to its original resting place, as the contents of the jar became disgustingly-clear. It was the top half of a dog's snout.

Closing the cabinet, Jordan moved to the table where she blew out the candle. She took a moment to strengthen her resolve. She had to go through the tunnel into the old house; if for no other reason, than to make sure that Ruston was in fact dead. She would never want to be left to the devices of a mind, as dark and morally repugnant as that of Tommy Hayden. She could not be sure that Ruston would ever do the same for her, but if she left him in whatever state, waiting a slow agonizing death; could she live with herself?

The moment the door opened, a cool stagnant breeze gusted through, taking Jordan's breath. The tunnel, all of the sudden seemed to be thousands of feet under the earth. She felt trapped, as she had back at the compound but this was more real. This structure had been erected years ago by the town's people, wielding crude tools and an emaciated budget. Jordan filled her cheeks with air. She was finding that the person she had been before, the killer was all an illusion. She was not the one who had craved the blood; it had been the demon. She was left alone, here in this place feeling abandoned with a killer like none she had ever seen before and she had worked for a government organization that facilitated and trained professional killers.

Jordan examined the emotions accosting her senses: doubt, apprehension, uncertainty but did she feel fear? Was she afraid, really afraid to face Tommy Hayden? Was she afraid that she may end up like Ruston; lying somewhere on a table or bed, waiting for him to grow tired. Waiting for him to end it all? She was to some degree apprehensive about being so far underground. She certainly did not like it, but was she afraid? Jordan thought for a moment longer and decided emphatically that she was not afraid, just cautious. She then examined how she felt about facing Tommy. She needed to get it all out, and leave it here in this bunker with all of the other clutter. She had to sacrifice it and move forward. Doubt or fear would do her no good. She stopped as she silently asked God to be with her. She prayed that He would erase all doubt, and if possible to allow her to do what was necessary to save Ruston. She knew that would be a tall order for a physician, but not God not for the Great Physician. Finally, with her resolve thickened and her doubts at bay, Jordan placed one foot in front of the other as the echoing sounds of her footsteps shouted to the darkness beyond her approach.

CHAPTER

28

Cold air ravaged Lane's face, as he ran through the woods. Garrison was a few yards back. Lane had tried to pull back and allow him to keep up, but after a while he had insisted that Lane move on without him. Lane's long legs and powerful stride had made it impossible to keep pace with Garrison's slower trot, so he had reluctantly agreed to split up. Moving to the side of the old house, Lane shot a concerned glance over his right shoulder. He knew that Garrison was slower, but this was ridiculous. He had been standing in wait next to the old house for about ten minutes now. Shouldn't Garrison be approaching by now?

Lane moved closer to the house, looking for a better entrance that would allow private access. He was about to move to the back of the house when he heard a female's groans of pain coming from a window behind him. Lane froze, as he listened. Surely, he was hearing things. Jordan wouldn't be in the house at the mercy of Tommy. She was a former agent. He had witnessed her stealth and wit in the field. He had almost been killed at the hands of her uncanny ability to not only know where her target was, but how to bring them into her mercies. If anyone knew what a formidable enemy she could be, it was Lane.

Moving to the window, Lane scooted just underneath the glass pane. A burgundy curtain obstructed the view into the room beyond, but Lane could see the silhouette of a man. The pacing gait of the shadowy form seemed to be that of someone nervous; a man out of control. Lane moved closer to the window, careful not to allow his own silhouette to be viewed through the curtain.

"You never do anything the easy way, do you?" Lane heard the angry voice of Tommy admonishing someone in the room.

Lane was desperate to know to whom Tommy was speaking in such harsh tones. He desperately, arched his neck in an attempt to get his ear closer. He pushed his body closer to the house. His hand was gripping the edge of the wooden frame on the outside of the window. He held tightly, trying to keep his balance and not make a sound. The awkward way in which he held his body away from the house, but his head close, caused his weight to pitch forward. Losing his balance, Lane careened into a briar patch to the right of the window. The thick branches with snarls of angry thorns raked at his face. The wind chapped-redness burned, as the briars scratched mercilessly at his cheeks and eyes. Lane scrambled for purchase. One hand pushing the unrelenting blades from his blistered and bloody face while the other worked to find something substantial to push himself back up and onto his feet.

Garrison had moved from the cover of the trees just in time to see the distress that Lane was experiencing, but not in time to stop the inevitable capture that was upon him. Just then the window above Lane's flailing form burst out, as a large metal object that looked to be a hammer came down on top of his head. His blonde hair filled with crimson as a spider webbed starburst formation dented in the front of his skull. Lane's huge body went limp in an instant. A blood curdling scream protruded from the house followed by a sickening crunch.

The sound of a body crumbling to the floor filled the winter wonderland around Garrison. His legs were glued to the spot and his body was rigid, as if he no longer had possession of his gross motor skills. He didn't want to think it, but he knew that the sound inside; the falling body... it had been his best friend. It was Jordan. Tommy had killed her in a fit of rage. Garrison's lungs filled with something not quite air. The air around him seemed void of oxygen. Sweat beaded on his forehead. His vision tunneled into a tiny scope. He took one step that was little more than an awkward stagger; something like he had seen Jordan's children do while they were toddlers.

He pushed against the unseen force that was dulling his senses. He was about to lose consciousness. He knew that if he didn't stop this somehow, he would be no good to his friends. There was no time to give into the darkness that was creeping in; threatening to take him to a place where he would no longer have to think of his best friend lying on the floor of a dusty old farmhouse in the middle of nowhere. If he gave in he could be anywhere in moments, if only in his mind, it would be better than what he knew to be true in this moment. She was gone and there was nothing he would be able to do to bring her back. More than that though, their last moments had been spent in anger. Her anger at him; the anger she had felt in finding out that he had been nothing, but a phony. The Garrison she had believed was no more than a fabricated whim of her imagination. He was created by Black Heart and placed in her life.

Now, as he stood on the edge of the woods, looking at her final resting place, he wished for another chance. He wanted to be the person she had believed him to be. He would give anything to live up to her expectations; her idea of who he was. But there would be no second chances, no do over, this was it; standing at the brink of the rest of his lonely existence, he had but one choice: walk away or avenge his friend.

29

Standing in the cement vault, Tommy knew that Jordan was in the room. He could sense her: he smelled the wax of the recently burning candles, the scent of her shampoo; he knew. Then he had heard the metallic ringing as the blade raked across the nail. He wondered for a moment how she felt. Did she enjoy the view from above, as he had so many times watching over the janitor?

He had knelt in the rafters for too long. It was his stepfather who deserved to die that was true, but something about watching the man go about his duties made Tommy feel right. He felt godlike, as he stood over the tiny man going about his day taking care of menial tasks.

It had not been his intention to hurt anyone, but his stepfather. It was just too enticing, kneeling there in the rafters above the man, watching his every move. He belonged to Tommy. He would forever be a part of his prized possessions. Hadn't the man—living his life unnoticed—no one caring about his pitiful-existence—deserved at least that much?

The dog down the street was just the beginning. The dog was annoying. He had barked incessantly at nothing. The neighbors screamed from their respective homes for the idiot dog to be quiet but the tiny beast had continued. Tommy almost respected the dog's defiant banter when so many wanted the insignificant animal to stop, he had pressed on. He had to admire the dog. It was his, too.

The dog had earned a place in the treasure vaults of Tommy's mind. He had stayed up late the night that he took the little Pomeranian. Its rust-colored-fur filled its tiny body like a giant puff ball. Tommy thought that the dog was cute. It's not that he did not recognize the beauty of the thing it's more that it was his. It had no real existence outside its true purpose of belonging to Tommy. It had deliberately chosen to make itself known to him. He was the god of his existence. He was the all-consuming reality. Anything that had stepped boldly into his path deserved to be taken into his treasure house of memories.

Tommy would make a memory of Jordan just as he was making a memory of James Ruston. Just as he had made a memory of the insignificant animal that no one else had understood—he had understood—the animal was merely calling for its place—no one understood. No one would heed its call—no one, but Tommy. It wanted him to come for it; to claim it. It wanted the same as the janitor had wanted for Tommy to make sense of its insignificant life.

Tommy had gone to the school that night. He had knelt in the jungle of wooden planks, watching the janitor again as he went about his meaningless existence. The bone thin man with worry lines ravaging his face had nothing. Tommy would turn it all around. He would take the man to the memory place in his mind. There the man would live forever among Tommy's treasures. Tommy smiled, as he recalled the wonderful night. The night the man that had not lived became something in his mundane world. The night that all of his years of hard work and living a good life had finally paid off. Tommy had come for him and it would be alright now.

He watched the janitor, as he pushed the mop bucket back into its usual resting spot; an old dirty-high-back-sink that filtered into a drain in the floor. The sink, blackened with grease, groaned with the effort of supporting the metal-bucket as he pushed it over the tiny hump. The bucket slid down a small ramp, coming to rest under the long-neck of a silver faucet. He stepped away from the bucket and over to a cluttered desk in a corner. A silver ring protruded from the wall above the desk where the man hung a ring of keys.

Tommy slipped lower from his perch. He held the weapon that had been formed for his stepfather, tight in his hand. "It wouldn't hurt, though." Tommy thought, as he caressed the handle, still warm from the sharpening on the pipework. Just a little test; after all, the man deserved it. He had earned his place among the archives of Tommy's memories. What an honor for him to be the second human that Tommy would take.

The man turned to collect his coat after hanging up the keys. He was startled at first to see Tommy just standing there but then he offered a welcoming smile. His eyes moved from Tommy's young face to the forged weapon in his hand. Tommy could see that he had made the same mistake that others had made—that his stepfather had made. The man had thought Tommy just a boy. Tommy smiled, as the man's face lit with knowing. His troubled eyes moved from Tommy's face to the metal rod suspended from Tommy's outstretched hand. Tommy could tell that the man sensed his greatness. The man knew that Tommy was here for him. It would be okay now. Tommy had come to claim his treasure. The man would live forever among the wealth of those treasures.

With practiced ease, Tommy set the metal plate to spinning. His fingers played along the pipe's smoot surface. He thought of how the grip would be much better with the tape around the handle. No time for that now. The man deserved his undivided attention. Tommy moved closer circling the man, savoring the fear that existed behind the man's eyes, knowing it would soon be over.

"It will all be okay, now. I am here for you. I have come to claim you. At last your worthless life will have meaning. It will all be okay." Tommy smiled patiently at the man, as the thoughts burned through his psyche. He moved faster now, the time had come, the man had waited long enough.

The man's eyes bulged like the dog's had, as Tommy made a wide arch with the metal pipe. The tip raced across the wrinkled skin of the man's throat, filling rustic-colored flesh with crimson. The end seemed to come too quickly; the memory had to be more in order to live in Tommy's memory forever. Tommy knew that now. With that, he started to lift the old-forgotten-man higher into the archives of his immortal memory, as he used the tools in the janitorial closet to heighten the death scene of the man's mortal-existence. Now, he would live in the vaults of Tommy's memories.

The memory flashed into Tommy's head, solidifying its place among the treasures there.

Tommy turned to the steps where he knew Jordan to be; suspended in the place above the steps, like a goddess, watching over her possessions. She had a lot to learn. It was a shame that he could not teach her. He would have taken her in, his aunt, and honed her skills into a razor's edge of exact homicidal intent. She could have been his greatest achievement. He smiled to the place he knew her to be; allowing her that moment of his affection. He had come to claim her. He would do as he must. She had earned her place among the memories, as had his stepfather. She had taken something from Tommy that she had no right to take; she had taken his right to be happy. His stepfather had abused him for years. Their place would not be the same as the simple-forgotten-custodian… theirs would be a place of higher torment; a place that existed only for those that dared to impose their unlawful authority over such a being as he.

Tommy placed the jar on the second shelf of his token cabinet. He had moved all of his beloved souvenirs here, after finding the place. No one was ever to see them, they were for him, alone. He thought about Jordan hanging above the staircase looking down on his things… He liked it. But, he liked sharing this with her. It seemed fitting; to share his greatest achievements with his would be prodigy. He mused. He could allow her that one favor; just a tiny glimpse into what could have been what should have been.

"Pity." He thought… "things bad to end this way." How much sweeter would it have been with her at his side. The only other being on the planet that was close to his equal.

Moving through the tunnel, he sorted through the many ways the end should come. How many wonderful ways could Jordan Buckley-Gates take her rightful place among the archives of his treasured memories? "It was only a matter of time," he thought, as his mind filled with the possibilities.

Stepping into the room where Ruston was strapped to the metal table, Tommy slowed to a stop. He took in the amazing treasures that he had amassed for Jordan's benefit. What a shame to let all of his hard work go to waste. Sure he could kill her swiftly; get it over with, but why? Didn't he deserve to enjoy the look on her face, as she took in the wonders that he had collected on her behalf.

Tommy made the decision, then, as he peered mockingly at Ruston. Lifting his index finger to his mouth, he cautioned Ruston to be quiet. The man lying on the metal slab with his eyes bulging was on the brink of death. Tommy pulled the remote into his hand and pressed a button. The bed groaned with the effort of lifting into the air. Soon Ruston was suspended vertically, just another pawn melting in with the other treasures. Tommy allowed an approving sigh, as he took his place behind the burgundy drapes and waited for his most coveted treasure to take her place among the museum of artifacts filling his mind's eye. She would be his greatest accomplishment. Jordan Buckley-Gates would live on forever, her last moments suspended forever in his memories.

30

As Jordan moved further into the house, a dripping sound melted in with the beeping noise filling the already eerie farmhouse with a more intense repulsion than before. She heard a moaning protest filter from the room just to the other side of the large wooden door that closed off the drab dining quarters from the rest of the house. Jordan pushed the door open with caution. She was sure this would be the room she would find Ruston; if not Tommy. She would have to be careful. She felt that Tommy knew she was in the house. Something felt wrong to her; she knew to walk into the scene without invisibility would be a mistake, but she had no other recourse. She couldn't leave Ruston, no matter how much she did not approve of him as a person. He was after all, a human being, howbeit a vile one.

The long tunnel had seemed to go on endlessly, but Jordan had at last gained access into the old dilapidated structure beyond. She had half expected Tommy to come out from the darkness after the cold grin she was sure was meant for her benefit back in the bunker. All the way down the tunnel she had filtered out every noise, listening for any movement: the tiny pitter patter of the rat feet, as they scurried away from the threat Jordan posed, the tinkling of a distant water source as it filtered down the cement walls of the darkened tomb and even the creek and moaning of the cement vault, as it settled deeper into the surface of the ground with every step she made... But nothing had happened.

Pushing the door to the house open, Jordan peered inside with caution. She kept waiting for the inevitable whack on the head that would render her unconscious and at the mercy of Tommy's dark desires;

still nothing. Jordan's face screwed up in confusion, as she moved further into the low-ceiling-kitchen. Tongue-and-groove walls varnished cherry red melted together in the four corners of the room. An old refrigerator with a bubbled door and a silver handle about middle ways, stood across from a wood burning stove. The door left open, allowed ashes to filter over onto the wooden floor of the kitchen. A bulky sink dipped low into silver galvanized piping that exited through the floor beneath. Walking into the room was like stepping into the past.

Jordan moved from the large drab room. Her eyes and ears focused on what existed beyond. The sound of a distant beeping pierced the silence, as she moved into a giant empty room with a long wooden table and eight simple, low-back-wooden chairs. No embellishments donned the table and chair set; it was just a simple-drab wood design made for the occupants of the home to sit and eat. The walls were devoid of pictures or any sign of flowers; no fixtures to spruce up or bring festivity to the room. Jordan had seen tents more beautifully adorned in the Cadotion village than this large farmhouse.

As she moved further into the house a glowing form filtered into the darkness of the next room. Jordan focused on the object and then with stark realism the object filtered into her vision. A small doll with an over-sized body and a tiny head peered from its perch. A glowing demonic-hole that almost seemed to be an eye looking out from a dark world filled the doll's forehead.

Jordan stiffened, as the room filled with light. All at once, seeing bits and pieces of the surrounding room, she felt assaulted by everything at once. The walls, an egg-shell-white were faded from time. A darkened blackness that Jordan knew to be blood, long dried and petrified lined the walls in splotches. The marks testifying of the gruesome murder and suicide at the hands of the farmer, fused with the shrunken head in the corner in such a way that gore met with an evil so dark that it seemed to be filtering into everything around it. Chills splashed across Jordan's body, as she dared to turn to the dripping and beeping that had been calling to her from the rooms beyond.

Disgust replaced caution, as the metal table pivoted upright. James Ruston's body was being held in place with metal straps. Tiny shards of metal cocooned his entire body; one move and the shards would pierce his skin. Jordan's stomach convulsed, as she witnessed the avulsed skin on his chest. His rib cage flayed open, was being held apart by an object with long fingerlike protrusions. Each of the protruding rods curved around one half of his severed sternum and pulled apart his rib cage. His heart pumped in a lazy staggering beat not yet dead, not really alive. Jordan allowed her gaze to go even further, as she took in the sheered portion of his left lung. The bottom lobe was missing. Against her will, she ventured further. Dozens of feet of linked glossy brown and red-corded links clumsily relieved themselves in a haphazard puddle on the floor. A heap of intestine lay in a lazy pile on the floor in front of Tommy's patient. The long some large some more slender-sausage like wet material hung by a flimsy tag in the upper part of the stomach.

She pulled her eyes away from Ruston's exposed innards and forced them to his face. His eyes sewed with a black thread to his brow, bulged in protest; seeing but not seeing.

Jordan, not knowing if he was still here, turned away refusing to allow Ruston to see the horror she felt. She couldn't let him know how bad it really was. In his mind there could be some shred of hope and that could be the only thing keeping him alive. She wanted to close her own eyes to refuse all of the evil that was filling the house. She needed to focus. Tommy Hayden was here somewhere. She knew that he was probably watching her, as she witnessed the haunted extravaganza he had erected on her behalf.

"You never do anything the easy way, do you?" Jordan heard the icy tone in which Tommy Hayden had delivered the words. She stiffened as she witnessed the burgundy curtain seem to come to life. It folded back and Tommy stepped forward.

Jordan moved to close the distance while tugging the rope on her leg, releasing the short sword. She pulled the blade into her grip and crouched forward in a ready stance. She had, but one opportunity to sink the blade into his flesh; silencing his reign of terror, forever. If she failed she would become no more than a hapless victim in his twisted museum. Allowing a quick appraisal of Ruston strapped to the table, Jordan cast a sympathetic nod in his direction. She could make no promises, but if something of the former man still existed behind those wide, pain stricken eyes she wanted to send him a message that she would do her best to save him though the gory sight he engendered did not incite much hope; she would try.

Jordan's attention moved back to the window, as the slight sound of a struggle played out beyond. Her eyes darted back to Tommy just in time to see him lift the silver handled hammer high above his head. She had thought the attack would be meant for her. She stepped to the challenge, but then at the last minute Tommy's body twisted to the window as his arm came down in a menacing blow. The sound of shattering glass bled into the deafening silence. A howling wind tore into the room, lifting the burgundy drapes so that they seemed to reach for her; beckoning her to stop some unseen tragedy. Jordan heard the sickening crunch of metal meeting human skull. Her world tilted on its axis and she became a blur of action.

With speed borrowed from adrenalin soaked terror, Jordan arched the sword through the space between her and Tommy. The sword became an exaggerated blur. She heard a distant agonizing scream born of anguish, and realized it was coming from her. Blood split the air casting sprayed droplets on everything in its wake. Tommy howled, as his severed hand dropped to the floor at his feet. He squeezed the bloody stump, as his face contorted into a mask of anger and rage.

Her mind was racing. She was sure she had just witnessed the death of her beloved. On the other side of the mass of burgundy drapes and broken glass lay the body of her sweet husband. Rage mingled with anguish, as she dropped the sword and reached for the pistol in the front of her pants. Her eyes had left the enemy for only a split second, but it may as well have been an eternity.

Tommy seized the opportunity. Grabbing the turkey carver he wrapped the cord around the end of the severed limb. Pulling the gory arm in the opposite direction of the turkey carver he wielded the blood spattered tool in Jordan's direction. Slicing through the air with practiced precision, Tommy slammed the serrated edge of the saw into the pistol, as it cleared Jordan's belt. The tip of the blade sliced easily into Jordan's hand, tearing a gash into the flesh. Blood dripped from the jagged wound, mingling with the red gore, making for a slippery surface.

Her feet slid apart, as she scrambled to a nearby-wall. She grabbed a long piece of cloth hanging from the metal table set up next to Ruston's metal torture chamber. She wrapped the cloth around the wound on her hand, tightly trying to stop the bleeding. She reached for the other gun strapped in the back of her waist band. Pulling the gun free, she cocked the hammer back and pulled the trigger. Nothing happened. Jordan cast a wary glance at the silver gun. Her eyes narrowed, as the stark realization flooded over her. How could she have known? The gun was a prop! All of the weapons in the room had been for looks. The farmer had obviously been in a few wars and was a collector.

Tommy glared at Jordan. His face filled with mocking finality, as he moved toward her. He swung the serrated edge of the carver wildly. His eyes glistened with expectant triumph. Jordan not to be outdone, flipped the gun around. Gripping the barrel of the gun, she flung the weapon in Tommy's direction. With lightning speed the gun closed the distance, striking her assailant with lethal intent in the side of the head. Tommy's body crumbled awkwardly to the floor.

Stepping to the metal table where Ruston was being held, Jordan touched his arm lightly.

"Hang in there." She whispered, and then moved to the shattered window. "He's still alive." Garrison reassured while lifting a cell phone from his pocket.

"Thank God." Jordan said, as she slumped against the window. Her mind felt exhausted, a web of intense anguish and joy rushing together. She yanked the drapes from the window and shoved them through the broken glass. Garrison claimed the warm treasure. Enfolding Lane in the mountain of material, he began giving coordinates to the person on the other end of the phone. He cast a simple smile in Jordan's direction.

"Wrap things up in there, partner. I got this." He said while pulling Lane closer to the warmth of his own body.

"Thanks Garr..." The words hung in the air, unsaid, as Jordan's head pitched forward, bashing her skull into the wooden remnants of the broken window.

CHAPTER

31

Fear slammed into Garrison like a brick wall. He gripped Lane's shoulder as he gingerly laid him on the ground.

"Okay, angel-boy, heal thy self." Garrison offered as he made the only decision he knew that he and Lane both could live with. He would do all that he could to save Jordan's life. In the end, it was all that mattered to either of them.

Jordan's body lay limp for only a moment over the broken windowpane. She was breathing, but her face was ashen.

Garrison pulled himself out from under Lane's heavy unconscious form. He appraised the wound on his face. The starburst pattern of blood spatter protruding out from the dented in hole on the front of his forehead made for a gory sight but Garrison knew that things could look much worse than they really were. Lane would be okay, Garrison assured himself. He had to be. Right now Garrison would have to leave him to the Creator that Lane was always assuring Garrison could take care of everything.

Garrison reached for the gun just inside of his coat. He had no idea what the plan would be. If he were being honest he had believed that Jordan and Lane would defuse the problem. He believed completely that he would only be moral support while his two friends stopped Tommy. Now, it seemed that he would be their only hope.

Moving to the side of the house, Garrison pushed his body as close to the wall as he could. Going in through the window was not an option. He needed the element of surprise. He hoped that Jordan, calling his name or at least trying to call his name, had not tipped off Tommy.

Garrison scanned the outer wall of the house for anything that could help him gain access. Nothing was coming to him. There had to be another way inside. His grandparents had lived in an old farmhouse; he had visited for whole summers as a child. During his time there, he had explored most of the surrounding landscape. As far as Garrison knew each house built by a farmer would be for the most part the same. Farmers were practical people and most of the time governed by survival. His grandfather had been a simple man as were most of the men who visited his grandfather's farm. No nonsense, the man had built his home with the bare essentials: a bathroom, bedrooms for the number of people living in the home, a kitchen, and of course, a dining room. There were silos to contain feed or grain. Places for the animals to be housed but nothing about the house was grand. It was a simple life. Garrison thought about that for only a moment, as he remembered his grandfather hiding a key around the front door for access in case he had ever locked himself out.

Hope flickered through his mind, as Garrison moved away from the broken window and around to the back entrance of the house. He first looked for a mat where the key could have been hidden. Not seeing one, he lifted up on his tip toes and felt with the pads of his fingers for any sign of a key on the lip of the gutter system, protruding from the small awning. The back porch was very small, just about four feet in width; so looking for any sign of a key did not take long. Nothing! Frustration started to set in, as he thrust his hand across his raven-black hair. He couldn't go in through the window; that was out. Tommy would kill him the minute that his head entered the house. If Tommy hadn't seen him, or if he didn't realize the name that Jordan was trying to call out when he thrust her head into the windowsill then maybe the element of surprise was still on his side. But, what was he going to do if there was no other way in the house but through the open window.

Garrison crossed the small cement patio. He held on to the wooden banister holding the ceiling of the porch in place. His eyes scanned the area surrounding the dark oak door. Where would this man put a key? Maybe Tommy had already considered the possibility. Maybe that was how he had gained access to the house in the first place. Garrison started to leave the back entrance of the house when he spotted a large green plant broken and browning from the snow fall. The weather had been cruel but the plant undeterred had pressed on determined to live. Garrison smiled at the plant and again started to leave.

A gust of wind that seemed to come from nowhere blew the haggard plant causing the potting soil to be exposed. A tiny red box lay in the pot. Garrison, not wanting to allow the hope budding in his heart to gain root, moved to the box. Reaching in, he claimed the aging box and immediately opened it. There, inside the box, under a bed of yellowing-cotton-balls was the silver key. Garrison snatched the key up and hurriedly moved to the door while thanking God for the gust of wind that had brought the key to his attention.

The woman's face swirled into view; anguished fear colored her features, as she squirmed hopelessly against her attackers unwanted advances. Her ample bosom heaved with the effort of breathing as her attacker pressed down upon her. The silver blade shimmered against the street lights, as they cast a faint illumination into the rear of the vehicle. Honky-tonk music bled in muffled tones from the building behind them. The florescent glow of the illuminated sign on the top of the building served as a beacon to entice customers to come into the trashy-unkempt-dwelling. Modeled fear colored the landscape of the woman's too made-up face as she stared helplessly into her attacker's unyielding eyes.

From somewhere behind, a man was drawing out an admonishment; something about starting without him. Then the scene changed, as the killer shoved the cold steel of the blade hard into the seat and straight into the man's back. Eyes bulging, the man asked through strained-gurgled attempts at breathing. "Why?"

The scene changed again.as the killer stood outside of the car and tore a piece of the leather interior off of the seat and shoved it into the gas tank of the car. Igniting the makeshift wick, the killer turned for the cover of the trees and stood, watching as the car blew into the air with a whoosh.

Fog rolled in through the trees, as the killer sat peering from the hidden cove, admiring her work. Cold realization slammed into Jordan, as again, she recognized not only the killer in her scattered dream but the approach of the unknown.

It was Jordan the day that she had killed the three people outside of the bar on her way to Beulah County where she and Lane had fought almost to the death. She was there, again, crouching in the wooded debris, admiring her work. Her mind raced, as she searched without success for a way to leave this place. She did not want to be reminded of the horrific time. The past where she had taken countless lives was creeping in. But more than that was the terrible truth... she was here, again with the encroaching fog; underneath was the real threat. Somewhere in the fog was the beast that had nearly claimed all that was important to her. Fear doubled, as she moved away from her hiding place into the open.

All at once, she was no longer the predator. She had become the prey. Her mind screamed for some exit; a way to be released from this horrendous nightmare that had claimed her every sleeping moment.

The darkness that had claimed everything was now starting to recede as the room came into focus. A low moan escaped her lips. Her head was pounding. Her eyes ached, as they fluttered to awareness. Jordan immediately jerked away from the unseen threat that she knew to be there. Suddenly, as if she had never fallen from the precipice of reality, she was sitting upright, her back to a corner. She could feel the fold, as the wall came together behind her back and pressed unyieldingly against her ribs. Relief poured into the moment and then she realized there was a greater threat. Though the fog was gone and the shadows of the past were back where they belong; she was back in the real world. Her chest tightened as panic sliced through her.

Tommy Hayden was nearby and somehow she had allowed herself to become his hapless victim.

"Lane?" The name was but a tortured cry. Jordan tried to turn to the broken window. Tears streamed unbidden down her cheeks, as she recalled the blood spatter on his beautiful face. Her love was forever lost to her. She had to survive for her kids, but somewhere deep inside, she just wanted to die. Let Tommy do his worst. She had no desire to be in a world that did not include Lane.

"Not quite." The menacing voice came from across the room. Jordan squinted against the darkness, trying to locate her captor. A blurry form closed the distance. Again, she tried to clear the web of white blotchiness coloring her vision, but it would not yield its hold. Her head spun and ached with the effort. She pulled against the ropes that held her hands too tight behind her back. The room swirled like a water spout, never quite coming into focus.

"What do you want?" Jordan asked the words; yet they seemed to come from somewhere else in the room. "Kill me if you want, but stop this game!" She spat the words at her would be killer. She hated this wait; it was too much. The not knowing whether Lane was alive or dead was torture enough without the drama that Tommy had in store for her. Her mind spinning out of control, stopped in an instant, leaving her unmercifully to ponder his fate.

"Oh, in good time;" Tommy jeered from his hidden cove. "All in good time, you really don't think that I put this whole thing together just to walk up and end it all in an instant... do you?" Tommy paused on the last word, as he, again dared to come closer. "Oh, the thought had occurred to me in the bomb shelter. I wanted to take you, then, but how could I deny you all of the fun that I have prepared for you?"

He abruptly stood before her. Kneeling down his handsome, menacing face came into view. He pulled her hair back exposing her neck. The carotid artery in the right side of her neck pulsed with adrenalin pounding out the anxious desire that she felt to rip his heart from his chest. Jordan could see in Tommy's eyes that he had mistaken adrenalin for fear. Good! She thought as she eyed him, allowing her face to become a contorted mask of anguish, she cried out for him to let her go. She knew it would spur him on. This is what he wanted... to feel her fear. It would be the one thing that he could not deny himself. Like chocolate to a small child, he lived for the taste of fear's sweet nectar. She too had once thrived off of the fear of her victims.

"Don't test me, Jordan!" Tommy growled, as he yanked her hair even harder. He slammed her head forward. The muscles in her stomach ached against the forced contortion. Her legs were sprawled in front of her, tied together at the ankles. She pushed her head back into an upright position, forcing herself to pay attention to her attacker. If she couldn't get him to kill her, then maybe she could get him mad enough to make a mistake.

"Test you?" Jordan feigned innocence. "I don't understand." She lied.

"You act as though you are afraid of me." Tommy thrust his hand up against her throat, holding her head back to prevent her from slamming it into his own head. "You have been through worse in training." He scolded. "This is nothing." He informed, as he indicated the room with a wave of the bloody, now wrapped in cloth and tape stump. "This little party of sorts that I have concocted for you..." Tommy said with a flourish, indicating all of the objects in the room and then he turned to her and continued. "This is nothing. You have seen worse. But. .." Tommy was face to face with her now. She could smell the peppermint on his breath. "I will change that. You will be afraid when I'm done." Tommy threw his head back in a menacing chuckle. His eyes flashed with a malevolent promise just under the surface.

"You see, Jordan, I know that you would never fear for your own safety. That is not the way to bring Jordan Buckley-Gates to the brink of insanity." Tommy was crushing her throat with his massive hand. He moved his eyes mere inches from hers. "Oh no, that would never do; But Lane? Oh yeah, that is definitely the way to unleash a fear so deep, so irrational that it will take you past the brink of insanity." Tommy moved away from Jordan then. Crossing the room, he flipped a light switch on the wall. The room filled with a bright florescent light: pure white illuminating, and welcoming settled on every corner of the room, leaving nothing to the shadows. Jordan's eyes followed Tommy's outstretched hand. Her heart sputtered, threatening to falter as the blurred vision cleared and Lane's unconscious form lay helplessly on the metal table that had once held James Ruston.

"Wasn't easy, you know?" Tommy sneered. "I had some difficulty moving him into the house—would have been easier with two hands." Tommy growled, as he moved to her side, again. "But I think I can work this." He admitted, as he returned to the table near Lane's massive sleeping form. Pulling a large serrated blade from the metal table; he pretended to fasten the blade to the end of his bloody stump.

"What do you think? Huh? Look good?" Tommy returned the blade to the metal table, as he again approached Jordan. "Yeah, I think I can work that, armed and dangerous." He moved in close to her face.

His breath fanning her nostrils, Jordan felt sick. Her stomach was heaving, as she tried to pull her face away from his unwanted advances. Tommy thrust his hand hard against her throat as he moved in closer than before. He brushed his lips against hers and then with a mocking appraisal plastered on his dark visage, he continued.

"At all times!" Tommy's eyes glistened with delight, as the threat he had heaved at her filled the space between them. What havoc could he reek on society if his bloody stump were equipped with an instrument such as the serrated edge of the bone saw?

Fear slammed into her chest, then taking her breath. Her eyes could scarcely take in what was playing out before her. Her mind refused the sight. Denial caged her thoughts, refusing the truth access to her conscious mind. She was not here. Lane was not lying on a table. She would not be watching her nephew, a depraved murderer butcher the love of her life. She was at home on the banks of the Cadotion River, lying in his beautiful arms, listening to the sound of his even breathing and the thumping of his heart. But, even as she tried to tell herself that none of this was the truth, she knew that was truly the lie. Her nightmare had finally come true. If she could not soon find a way to free herself from the binding ropes around her wrists and feet, she would be forced to witness Tommy Hayden butcher her husband right before her eyes.

CHAPTER

32

Garrison claimed the red box and moved, quickly to the door. He thrust the key into the lock and listened as the tumblers moved into place. Relief and fear filled his senses, as he twisted the knob and moved cautiously into the old farmhouse. Oh that he were back in his office. He would even love to see the Fikias that he hated so much. The plant that he had hated for its imitation of life; he had been too hard on the plant. So it was not real, it was not the plant's fault that it was a synthetic version of the truth. Sometimes that was all that you could hope for. He wasn't Jordan or Lane; it had been years since he had been in the field. He was a recruiter; he spent his time training. Jordan had moved on to The Truth, and he had moved on as well. His last assignment had been to retrieve Jordan, now as he entered the old house the irony of it all seemed bitter sweet.

Here he was again, collecting his partner but he was uncertain of his possible success. Could he be what he needed to be? Could he tap into the long dormant agent that lived inside of the business man that he had now become? He prayed again to Jordan and Lane's God. That too seemed ironic. He was now praying a lot. Fear had a way of doing that to you. He thought. He did not believe in God. He thought the idea of an all seeing, all knowing God, absurd. But as he moved further into the house of horrors orchestrated by one of the most demented minds he had ever seen profiled, he found that he was getting more and more familiar with this all knowing, all seeing God that he had never believed in. If he survived this, he would have to ask Jordan to tell him more because a God who could pull them back from the clutches of such a demonic force as Tommy Hayden, was worth knowing.

Dim shadows played on the kitchen wall, dancing from flickering candle light held in bronze sconces on the wood paneled wall. Crouching as close to the wall as possible Garrison strived for anonymity. Hushed tones, creeping in from the outer room, mingled in the air, becoming little more than a blurred beeping and whirring. Garrison arched his brow to the sounds, trying to familiarize himself with the even cadence of the distant humming. He had heard the sound before and then as if summoned on cue the memory came ushering in... it was at the hospital. Of course.

As an agent, Garrison had spent many a day in the hospital: receiving stitches for a knife wound, sometimes cleaning glass out of places that he could not reach and still other times being observed after a concussion. He had his assumed identity; the person that the world believed him to be was always ever ready. He could not go into the hospital as Garrison, the Black Heart agent. That would never do. Instead, he was Roy Peterson, a bouncer at a bar on the outskirts of town; he was bound to sustain a few scars for his trouble. The cover wasn't iron-clad, but it did the job. Most of the doctors and nurses working at the local ER had far more troubling issues to concern themselves with than checking to see if Garrison was really who he claimed to be. Also, it helped that the hospital was located in a tough neighborhood of gang bangers; therefore, it was not uncommon to see gunshot or knife victims. Garrison probably didn't need to make up the story about being a bouncer. The medical staff would have most likely been satisfied to think he was just another thug, with too much time on his hands, but with every part of his life always being morally in question, it felt good to be the focus of less brutal scrutiny that being a bouncer afforded. At least, as compared with the life of a trained killer.

The darkness of the house seemed to be competing with the noises for first place at disarming Garrison's nerve. Jordan had warned him when he took the office position that he had better keep his skills honed. He had laughed at the notion. Those days were well behind him; he had assured her. He would never again be in the field. He had seen enough death and destruction and after fifteen years of loyalty to the bureau, it was time he collected on some of the perks of being an agent. Time In the field could be long and lonely. He had had to watch his back be aware of his surroundings at all times; one mistake could result in his demise. Death was the game, it's what he did but his own death was last on the agenda.

Now, as Garrison pressed further into the house telling himself to be calm and not pay any attention to the darkness, the muffled whirring and beeps and even the clicking-scurry of rat feet against the wood floor, it all seemed for naught. Every sound just seemed to solidify the dread building in his frayed senses. Every step into the house honed the anguish crushing down upon his soul. He prayed that though, he had been neglectful of his skills, there was somehow some dormant part of that time lying in the recesses of his mind that he would be able to mercifully call upon now.

The dining room was dull; Garrison allowed himself a normal thought in an abnormal situation. He needed the normalcy; it calmed him in some way. In the very next room was the predator he had hoped to never meet in a dark alley; yet here he was in an entire house, wading through the misshapen horrors, pieced together purposefully by that predator.

The tiny hairs on the back of his neck prickled, as he moved from the dining area into the next room. He felt as though he should be standing behind a rope, in a line of people huddled in front of a dark curtain waiting for something though he did not know what, to jump from the darkened recesses beyond the rope, maybe. . . a howl of terror from the tortured soul on a table covered in fake blood and entrails. Whatever it was that he would see in that fake haunted house of fabricated horrors, he was sure would pale in comparison to the things he was about to encounter. His heart pounded out every step. His mind, insisting that he was making a mistake, common sense beckoned for him to leave this place and put it in more capable hands and yet he pressed further still into the museum of death.

His fingers trembled, as he reached for the wall and searched for a light. Relief mingled with terror, as he was rewarded with a florescent glow that fell upon everything in its wake. His eyes settled on the large sleeping form of Lane. Confusion crippled his senses momentarily, as he knit his brow and cast a wary glance to the broken window. Just beyond is where he was certain he had left Lane. Instead, he lay on the metal table, his massive chest exposed. A darkened blue line ran from his throat to his abdomen and his breathing was slow and deep. Metal rods only a centimeter in width lined his mammoth body. To turn his head or any part of his body would result in agonizing pain as the metal rods would pierce the skin.

Garrison turned his head from such a horrendous site. What depravity would be required for a mind to produce such darkness, as was exhibited in this room. His eyes closed, Garrison's subconscious was already filing the sight under things that he did not want to recall. He moved reluctantly into the room as something moved to the side of the room. He turned in horror as his mouth gaped at the picture before him. Jordan was sprawled on the floor, never had she looked more helpless. Not even in the alley the night she had been recruited had she looked so out of control as she did now.

Her eyes brimming with tears, Jordan seemed to beckon him to leave and yet somehow, in the deepest part of her soul he could see through those emerald eyes that she wanted him to stay more. His eyes moved back to Lane, as he cast Jordan a knowing glance and then moved to her side.

Jordan was flinching away from him. Garrison wanted to tell her to stop. He had taken the knife from his boot and was about to remove the ropes from her feet when she reflexively pulled her legs away from him. You would have thought he was the enemy. Garrison was agitated at the way that Jordan was conducting herself. He would have a stern talk with her about cooperation as soon as they were clear of this place. Jordan's eyes searched his as she grunted against the tape on her lips. Desperation filled her eyes, all at once and she flinched even further into the wall behind her.

At that moment, though it was clearly too late, Garrison was crystal clear on what Jordan had been trying to warn him about. Just as the thought entered his mind, everything around him was filled with darkness and then there was nothing.

✶ ✶ ✶

Tommy stood archaically, as he watched with bored disinterest for Garrison to finally make the decision to leave. He had just about given

195

up on Garrison when he scooted out from under the weight of Lane's massive shoulders. Up until then the man had looked to be torn in an unseen enigma. Tommy knew all too well the question that was the driving force behind Garrison's indecisive behavior. For one, the man was a blemish on the face of Black Heart; he had stayed marooned in his lavish, corporate office far too long and was definitely no match for Tommy. Then, there was the decision between saving Lane or Jordan.

The choice would have been obvious had it been Tommy's to make. Lane was no more than a bona-fide tree hugger, as far as Tommy saw it, whereas Jordan was a warrior. In the end, as Tommy watched from behind the heavy curtain, Garrison had at least made the right decision. He had chosen Jordan.

Tommy slipped out the door to the right of the window where he had been hiding and stepped out into the icy wind. He didn't have long. Garrison would be bumbling his way through entering the house and Tommy though it was not needed, did not want to miss the element of surprise. In truth, he could face and defeat Garrison without a problem but to lose the opportunity that would be afforded him at sneaking up on Garrison and dismantling him... It was beyond Tommy's will power to walk away from such a memorable moment. He had to have that fear that would surely accompany that moment; the precise moment that Garrison realized Tommy was upon him.

Tommy smiled to himself, as he knelt to the task of collecting Lane. The stump where his right hand had once been ached, but Tommy welcomed the pain. Grabbing Lane's left hand with all his strength he hauled him to his feet long enough to thrust the bloody stump under Lane's knees; in a fireman's tote style carry, he heaved Lane into the house and laid his unconscious form onto the metal table where he had already removed James Ruston's body. He strapped Lane to the table and then taking a moment to catch his breath; he leaned over and placed his good hand on his knee.

"Good grief," Tommy grumbled. "You are heavy man." Throwing a disapproving glare in Lane's direction, Tommy lifted to his full height and strode to the window.

Tommy listened to the fumbled attempts that Garrison was making at being quiet. He felt almost sorry for the buffoon. It had served him no good to relax in that lavish office of his and soak up the gifts that the bureau bestowed upon its elite. Now, as he listened to the once victorious killer who had moved with the precision of a shadow on the wall, Tommy felt disgusted to see the mockery Garrison had become.

"And they put me in The Garden..." Tommy thought bitterly, as he moved to the hidden cove behind the maroon drapes. He had quieted Jordan with some duct tape around her mouth. He would never render her unconscious at such a pivotal moment as this. How could he? She deserved better. Though, she had cost him everything: hope, happiness, a future with a loving father; Tommy could not bring himself to diminish the experience for her. She, Jordan Buckley-Gates, deserved the finest place among the trophies that littered his mind's eye. She would be his finest moment and he would be hers.

He crouched behind the heavy drapes and watched as Garrison entered the room. He relished the fear that, so clearly registered in his eyes. Fear seemed to radiate off the man in waves. Waiting patiently, Tommy watched as Garrison came to the slow realization that Jordan was indeed tied up in the corner.

"What a pathetic agent he must have made." Tommy thought. This would be too easy. Tommy almost felt it not worth his time; first Ruston, and now this. All of the agents had been seemingly gift wrapped for him tonight. He deserved a challenge. He had visualized a chase, danger. He had waited for this moment forever and now that it was upon him, it seemed to have lost its luster. Every person who he had ever wanted to bring down was sprawled around the room, either dead or awaiting death. Though, he had lost a hand, the memories that he had envisioned in his mind's eye were still more...

Tommy shook his head, as he wrapped his good arm around Garrison and pulled him with little effort away from Jordan. He had spent time as a child learning to use both hands. Someone of his obvious standing could never allow any sort of handicap to deter him from the greater purpose that was his to accomplish. Tommy hated that his right hand was missing to be sure but there was no turning back now. He would just have to find a way to use it to his advantage. For now, he would relish the pain that it caused, as he continued his work and he would visit as much pain as he could on the one who had brought him to such glorious agony. Pain was good. It helped him to think. He loved to feel to know that he was alive that he was not dead in the way that he had felt inside for so many years. Now, as he relished the pulsating-agony of the severed hand, he felt more in the moment than ever. Good! It would help to solidify the memory of her death in his thoughts forever.

Appraising the room, Tommy bent to the task as he pulled a looped rope over Garrison's head. He then, with a sudden and final yank, cinched the rope around Garrison's neck. A gasp of disapproval came from behind. Tommy turned to see tears melting out of Jordan's eyes. A slow smile etched on his sinister visage, as he moved to her side. Crouching before her, Tommy soaked up the haunting beauty that was Jordan.

Emerald green eyes, the twins of his own sparkled with unshed tears. Her tan skin was a caress of golden brown from the time that she had spent on the banks of the Cadotion River. The change in her already arresting beauty was a good addition. Her dark auburn hair was pulled back into a ponytail but stray pieces of unkempt curls twisted defiantly down the side of her face. Her lips were a full satin pink that quivered now with the obvious distress his treatment of her longtime friend had placed her under. A skin tight black suit pronounced every curve of her body as she strained away from his unwanted advances. She was more than beautiful. Just as he, Jordan was perfection personified. She was the female counterpart to him. How he would ever part with one so obviously meant to be at his side he did not know, but he knew that he had no choice. The desire within him to own her, to allow her memory to live in that special place burned with intensity brighter than the urge to hold her close.

For a moment, Tommy abandoned caution, as he placed his good hand on one side of her face while placing the stump on the other, as though the hand were still there. Blood from the stump made a fingerprint type impression on her cheek, as he moved still closer. Finally, with his face mere inches from hers, he tilted his head to the side as he claimed a fallen tear. A smile born of pure evil enveloped his face as he glared unwaveringly into her eyes.

"I've always wanted to taste your tears. Now to hear your screams." Tommy said, as he moved his hand to the back of her head and tightened his fist around her hair.

33

The walkway leading through The Garden seemed a little longer, as John Benton made his way back to the small apartment where Cynthia and the children were sleeping. He hadn't been able to sleep. Something had been weighing on his mind since the conversation with Garrison the night before. There was something underneath the surface that just did not make sense. Why would Tommy Hayden just take it upon himself out of nowhere to go after Jordan? He was an individual. Without the resources afforded an agent by Black Heart, profiling would be impossible. It would be like taking a one in a million shot in the dark. A lot went into analyzing a target. The agent had to know all of the possible venues in which to obtain the target and eradicate the subject without implicating the organization.

Tommy had spent years in The Garden. He had never made it to agent status. He was what the agency referred to as a rogue; a chance too big for the organization to place their confidence in and the future of the agency. So how would Tommy have gotten all of the necessary Intel in order to take out Jordan, one of the top agents that had ever come out of the academy? Ruston? That's what Garrison had said, that it was James Ruston but John couldn't help but think that there was a bigger link to Tommy Hayden. Someone who was above it all, someone who had a lot to lose by Jordan being moved to The Truth. Someone who had wanted her to fail and had been offended that she hadn't, but who?

No matter the answer to that, John knew he had but one alternative. He had to contact the HOD of Black Heart. The man could possibly find out what was going on. He had all of the files on everyone involved.

John would fill the man in on the things that he might not be aware of and hope for the best.

There had been enough secrets and deception between the two of them to last a lifetime. He felt the need to be translucent about everything. John moved to the apartment then. Cynthia was standing in the midst of the small breakfast nook. Pots and pans of every shape and size hung, loosely from an overhead rack. Steam billowed from a frying pan, filtering the aroma of bacon into the small apartment. His stomach gave a hungry growl of protest.

Cynthia was spoiling him. Eating was almost simultaneous to his feet hitting the floor in the morning. He had never been a breakfast person but with her that was not an option. She was a sweet southern girl who had taken on the traits of her mother. Though, her life had taken her a long way from that young girl carrying groceries home to her mother, she had somehow maintained the wonderful-hospitality of her past. She quite simply loved to care for others and he had been fortunate enough to be a part of that experience.

He moved into the room, stepping over to the stove, he turned the burner down and pulled her off to the side. After a slight-admonishing-glare, she conceded and headed into the small washroom to the side of the kitchen. He cast a concerned look at the table where the children were sitting. He had no intention of alarming either of them. Both had already experienced enough some of the things, they were not even aware of and some were yet to pour down like acid rain; burning away the innocents of their young lives, forever.

"John what is this about?" Cynthia fussed.

He noticed that she couldn't help but cast a concerned glace in the direction of her now cooking breakfast.

"Let it be, Cynthia." John gently scolded, as he took her hands into his own. He pulled her further into the scant-privacy that the washroom afforded.

"Look, I'm worried about Lane and Jordan." John tilted his head out passed the doorway craning his neck, he could see that the children were still at the table, interested in the coloring books that Cynthia had given them. Keeping their minds busy every morning had afforded her the time needed to prepare a meal without the begging that accompanied hungry children. Though, he and Cynthia had been astonished at the patience the two could actually show in times that other children, their same age would have melted into a puddle of begging and over-exaggerated sighs of protests. John had thought it was growing up in the Cadotion village that had instilled such patience in children so young.

"I know John, but can't this wait until after I have fed the children, and put them in the playroom?" She cast a worried glance in the children's direction. "Those books will only last so long."

John turned to the table where the children sat. though he knew what he needed to discuss with her was too important to wait; he could certainly see how getting the children interested in their toys after filling their bellies would afford them much more of the needed privacy. After all, he had no desire to upset the children and as he watched the two of them working away, undaunted by any of the shadows of evil that lurked in the corners of their tiny existences, he could do nothing but conceded the point. He would wait.

Breakfast had passed quickly to his surprise. The children were now in the small room not much bigger than a walk-in-closet where their toys were held. He sat on the edge of the couch, barely able to sit still, at all. He felt, at any minute, his heart would come flying out of his mouth, and flounder on the carpeted floor, in protest of all the tension it had been put through, over the last few weeks.

Cynthia sat across from him on a small matching loveseat with plush-hunter-green upholstery. The carpet, a cream color that seemed to be the prefect backdrop to the deep green of the couch and loveseat flowed through the room, lending an aesthetic-balance to the comfortable room. The combination had a calming effect on him that he had normally enjoyed. Now, though it did little to help him relax.

Cynthia sat, legs crossed; trying to exhibit as much patience as possible but he could tell, even she with all of her sweet southern hospitality was coming to end of her patient-good-nature.

"I was thinking that I should contact the HOD." There he had said it. John threw the thought out into the open like a grenade and waited for her reaction.

She normally wanted nothing to do with Black Heart. She was afraid to be noticed by them. Her life had forever been changed due to the meddling of the organization. She had not taken it well that Garrison or Jordan were an active part of their lives at first, but soon she had come to understand that it was not their intent to bring trouble into her life. It wasn't that she was not grateful to them for helping her to make the transition to The Truth; it was more that she was afraid of what their presence in her life meant to the serenity that she had discovered as a missionary of The Truth. Her life had changed immensely and though she would never be allowed to return home to her mother and father she had made a new home with John. It was the fear of losing that home that drove her fear of allowing anything associated with Black Heart to touch their lives.

"I think that is a great idea." Cynthia conceded, as she touched John's hand. She moved to the couch next to him. "John, whatever this is…this situation with Jordan and Garrison… Well, it's bigger than us. We need to do everything to help save the people that we love; the people who those little people in the next room love." She sniffed as she looked deeply into his eyes. She was searching their depths for understanding. John could see that she needed him to listen. No matter how shocking her declaration may be, she just needed him to let her put it into words.

"I know how that feels." Her voice was but a whisper, now as she strained against the tears that were fulling her throat. A flood of unspoken-anguish filled her beautiful-deep-brown-eyes, threatening to topple his resolve not to say anything.

He wanted to comfort her to have the perfect thing to say that one thing that would erase all of it and make her feel whole…but, as he sat there on the plush-couch in the small-stuffy-apartment on the cusp of her emotional-breakthrough he knew that it was his silent-understanding that she needed more and she would have it.

She pulled back a little, as she cleared her throat and began. "I know that…that pain. I know it well and I will do anything to make sure that precious little girl and boy never have to go through it. I did no crime. I was eighteen years old. I loved my family very much. My mother was a stay-at-home-mother who loved to cook and sew." Cynthia allowed a small laugh, as she moved from the couch.

John thought that she just needed to move around not to feel confined to a certain space as she allowed the story of her past that she had guarded so tightly to unravel.

"My daddy worked in the mines. He was a hard-worker but never complained. One time he had come home with his thumb sliced nearly off. He had my mother to sew it up for him. We did not have extra money. All of it was spoken for. So I watched as my mother sewed my daddy's thumb up and my daddy kissed her lightly on the cheek. He walked out of the house and headed back for the mines." Tears filled her eyes, now, as she shook her head, pitifully. Anguish and pride colored her visage as she continued. "My mother begged him to stay home but he just shook his head. He made a joke out of it; told my mama they had made a deal a long time ago. He would bring home the bacon if she would fry it up.

"My mama cried that day after my daddy left. She made me promise never to tell him. I promised but little did I know how easy it would be to keep that promise. I left that day right after my daddy did. My mama needed me to go to the store." Cynthia cast a small smile, through the cascade of tears, now filling her beautiful face. "Well, you know the rest." She offered, as she moved back to his side, on the couch. "I need those children to keep what I was not allowed to have. If their parents are taken..." A gasp escaped her lips, as she crushed herself into his chest. "...it will take with them, their childhood."

She moved from his grasp then, as she placed her hands on either side of his face. "Do it John. Call the HOD. Tell the man everything that you know and after you do that get me the files on everyone involved." A determination like a wall of steel replaced the anguish that had been in her eyes. Gone was the woman that had been seeking comfort, the southern-bell standing over the stove, serving the ones that she loved...in her place was the former Black Heart agent.

John peered at her with confused apprehension. What was she trying to say? Was she going to try to pull from the watered-down knowledge of a not so distant past to try to form a profile or was his innocent, sweet Cynthia determined to go after the monster herself? Chills slammed into him as the thought of his sweet wife being anywhere near the ugly things that Jordan, Lane and Garrison were most likely dealing with at this very moment.

"No!" The word was a command. John had not meant to be so forceful, but the idea of his wife and unborn child in the path of such a deranged-lunatic was more than he could fathom.

Her head snapped to attention. "No?" She moved from the couch, then and paced to a bookshelf lining the adjacent wall. Tracing the spine of a book, she turned to him. Her brow was knit. Her face was a confused, contortion of anger and frustration. "Why do you say no?" Cynthia asked, as she returned to the couch.

"I'm sorry." John admitted, as he rubbed her hand trying to lend her a measure of comfort while he explained his explosive reaction to such a vile thought.

"Cynthia, I can't stand the thought of you being anywhere near this…this monster. What about the baby? Would you endanger the life of our unborn child? I know that you are concerned about Amelia and Tristan as am I, but what about the safety and wellbeing of our child? Have you given any thought to what Tommy Hayden would do to you…to the baby?" John was offering up every argument to support his reasoning. He was a desperate man on the precipice of an unwanted event; an astronomical catastrophe that would erase his life's happiness.

"John, have you lost your mind?" Cynthia was shaking her head now. The anger had taken on a life of its own, as the confusion that had once over-shadowed her visage was now, as clear a summer sky. "Do you think that I would put this baby in harm's way? I would never. I just thought that if I could put a profile together that could possibly make Mr. Stanton's time of finding Tommy's a little easier." She eyed him now, as she moved back to the couch.

John pleased to hear that his worst nightmare had not come to fruition, pulled Cynthia into an aggressive hug. "I'm sorry baby." He crooned. "I didn't mean to assume the worst. It's just with all of the madness…" He waved his hands around, as he searched for the right words."It's hard not to assume the worst in light of all that we have experienced."

Cynthia laughed, as she punched him lightly on the arm. "John, I was the worst agent that Black Heart ever recruited. What on earth would make you think that I would believe for a moment that I could offer anything other than Intel on this case?" She was shaking her head, now, as laughter rippled through her whole body. She shook in hysterics, as she pointed with one hand at John while holding her mouth with the other.

"What's so funny?" A tiny voice from behind asked.

John and Cynthia turned to the sound of pitter pattering feet, as they approached.

"Oh, nothing. Uncle John just told Aunt Cynthia a funny joke." Cynthia said as she moved from the couch. She pulled Tristan into her arms and placed a protective hand around Amelia's shoulders. Pulling the children close, she turned to John as she mouthed, "Get the files."

34

The blizzard had left, just as suddenly as it had begun. Edward Stanton stood staring out the fifth floor window of his lavishly decorated office. His large-dark-cherry-desk was cluttered with files; each held Intel on a member of Black Heart that was of personal interest. He had put all of his calls on hold and cancelled all of his meetings.

Edward had been with the company for a long time; twenty years in fact. He was now the Head of Department. His story was very different from some of the other recruited agents. Most of the agents had been forced into the life. Though, he could not understand the personal vendetta that some of the agents seemed to hold against Black Heart, he supposed he could relate to being in a job that one did not exactly cherish.

Edward did not see his life as a waste of time; some stolen expanse of hope that Black Heat had ripped from his grasp. To the contrary, it was his induction into the agency that had truly set his existence on fire.

He had been in the prime of his life. He was a marketing producer for one of the most prestigious publishing companies in the country. He had brought the company millions, yet somehow, it seemed a hollow victory. He was in so many ways dissatisfied with his life. Something seemed to be missing.

The books that he read spoke of danger and espionage; meanwhile, he wasted away in a four by four cubicle answering phones. The most exciting part of his day was talking authors off the ledge; convincing them to maintain their status with the company. At the root of it all was the need to make money and lots of it. No matter the success of the author, it was the company's success that every decision had hinged upon. And so his life went, until the day that he had been leaving a video store and had inadvertently witnessed a murder.

Edward stood, stuck still as his mind tried to erase the events playing out, before his eyes. This is what came of wishing too hard for a different life and having an overactive imagination. He had finally snapped.

Not ready to rejoin the rat-race, Edward pushed further back into the shadows. He wanted desperately to look away; some dormant part of his brain insisted he go. Yet, as he stood there pressed against the cold cement wall, he shamefully wanted to see more.

Time stood still, as he peered wide eyed across the expanse of people meandering through the street, passed the line of burnished reds, lavish purples and bright-cheerful yellow awnings, covering the top of the store fronts on the other side of the busy street into the dimly lit shadows of the ally where the man was spending his last moments succumbing to the advances of his attacker. To the untrained eye, it seemed no more than a simple mugging but as Edward continued his unwanted scrutiny into the attacker's world, he could see that the killer seemed somehow more: more than the run of the mill mugger, trying to gain unearned riches; more than an attacker that had taken things too far... there was some well thought out masterful element that Edward could not quite connect with and then, as if a book had been laid open before him to precisely the right page it hit him; this was a professional.

Edward licked his lips, as he committed to the plan. No doubt, he would have to be careful. The individual before him would not be easily followed. For all he knew, the killer was already aware of his presence.

Then, just as if his thoughts had been blasted over a loud speaker for all to hear, the killer turned. Edward froze, as the sclera of the killer's eyes shone from the dark mask shrouding his or her face.

Edward glared back with open intrigue. His legs betrayed him, as he took one bold step in the killer's direction. Just as quickly as he had made the decision the killer had disappeared.

Edward turned as disappointment rained down upon him. He had been on the precipice of something great and with the speed of thought it was gone. Contempt for his life started to creep back in, as he despondently made his way back to his tiny cubicle. As the lead marketing consultant at Write Way Publishing, Edward Stanton had pitched more books than most of the consultants in the industry and yet, at the moment, he could not think of one redeeming quality to sell him on his own life.

That night, as he was riding the subway to his high-rise condo, Edward pondered the murder in the alley. It almost seemed a distant memory or a chapter of a book he had read. Though, every detail was alive in his mind, it seemed impossible that it could have happened. He moved to the elevator, as he vaguely considered the empty lobby that was usually teaming with tenants going about their busy lives. The thought banished as the doors closed to the elevator and a poster boasting of a concert in the main auditorium ghosted into view.

The numbers at the top of the silver doors lit up, as the elevator blazed passed each level. With a jolt, the elevator came to a dizzying halt on the fourth floor. The number four lit and held as the doors droned open.

Edward stood motionless, his mouth agape as an exquisitely exotic woman entered the elevator. Her long tan legs were crisscrossed with the red straps of her patent leather sandals. A form fitting black leather dress fell to mid-thigh and dipped low, framing a voluptuous cleavage. Her long neck ventured up and ended at a goddess-like face. Edward dared to allow his eyes to feast upon the electric blue of her arresting gaze. A thin, short nose nested above full lips that were pursed in a tempting pout. She played with a strand of her waste length black hair, as she entered the elevator.

Edward felt oddly out of place sharing an elevator with this apparition. Her hand slipped fluidly to the panel of buttons to the left of the door. She hesitated over the five and then with lightning speed slammed the stop button home. Whirling around, she pushed the length of her perfect body against his. Her mouth claimed his in a simple kiss. Then, she reached up the slight dress she wore to her inner thigh.

Edward closed his eyes. He must be dreaming. That would be the only obvious explanation of the events throughout this day: the murder, and now this. He was an ordinary looking guy: brown hair, brown eyes, with a medium build. He did work out, but so far it had only afforded him a slight muscular definition. Nothing about his mundane existence would ever attract the attention of such a creature as this.

Opening his eyes, Edward peered into the arresting blue of her seductive gaze, as he sank against the wall. He was a lamb to the slaughter. He was hers to do with as she wished. He was bereft to do a thing to save his own life if need be.

Her fisted hand moved languidly up his torso. Expectant desire lit tiny fires throughout his veins, as he arched his body toward her advances. His eyes fluttered closed once more, as he resigned himself to the dream. Alarm replaced desire, as the small barrel of a gun rested under his chin.

"Don't make a sound." She hissed, as she kissed his lips, again.

"I... I don't have any money." Edward stuttered.

"Shh," She crooned. "I'm not here for your money." she pushed into him further obviously trying to hide the derringer from the camera's prying view.

"Do as you're told, and you may leave this elevator alive."

The thought of not living beyond this experience had never occurred to Edward. His body stiffened, as his mind rejected the thought.

"Relax. As long as the people manning the camera," She tossed a lazy smile in the camera's direction, "Believe that we are just lovers in a heated tryst, all will work to that end." She kissed his neck, every bit the lover, lost in a stolen moment on a stalled elevator. "Put your arms around me, and pretend to kiss my neck. No sudden moves, though."

Edward's heart pounded in time with the second hand of her watch. The miniscule silver watch hung loosely from the wrist of the hand holding the small gun. Both delicate and sturdy, the elegant time piece was a perfect match for his captor.

"What do you want?" The words were, but a strained whisper. "Did you enjoy watching me?" Her husky voice breathed across his ear, littering his flesh with goose bumps.

"I..." Edward struggled for a response worthy of the moment, yet, nothing came to mind.

"No need to deny it." She purred.

"I wasn't going to." The response was automatic. Defiance born of lust for more filled his senses, as he squared his shoulders and glared unwaveringly into the electric pools of blue. His arms moved around her body and with a jerk, he pulled her more closely to him.

Her eyes widened, as he moved his lips to hers. He interrupted her simple kiss, as he claimed her lips in a masterful dance of passion. She moved away from him, then, as she returned the derringer to its holster at her thigh.

"We have a lot to talk about." She informed, as she reached to the front of his shirt and claimed his tie. Moving fluidly back to the numbered panel she hit the number ten. The elevator resumed its climb, as Edward watched in open astonishment.

This woman that he had never met already knew so much about him. His mouth felt dry. She hadn't killed him; he supposed that was a good sign. What was she doing in his condo? He started to open his mouth, but she gingerly, placed a finger over his lips, as she whispered, "All in due time."

That had been Edward's first of many encounters with Amorous Dawson. The relationship that had been forged that day in the elevator, born of mutual respect had bloomed throughout his years of service with the bureau. Amorous had been killed in the line of duty four years after their meeting. It had been an expected outcome for any agent, but it had not stopped the aching in his broken heart over her loss.

Edward had thrown himself into the company after her death, not wanting to face her loss. He had blazed the ranks of the company, landing the HOD position just ten years after his induction into Black Heart. Nothing had stood in his way. He had done whatever it took to maintain the coveted status.

He turned from the window, as he eyed the cluster of files on his desk. This time would be no different. When Jay Cochran had approached him about the problems with James Ruston, Edward had thought it a bad idea to keep him affiliated with the company. Edward soon learned that keeping Ruston tied to the company would be better than allowing the company to be investigated by other sections of the government, not aware of Black Heart's existence. A lot of unsavory business deals had crossed his desk, and with that kind of scrutiny,

Ruston and Cochran would not be the only ones who stood the chance at losing their job.

Edward had made all the necessary connections. He had been excellent at profiling during the early years. As the HOD he would need to view the files of agents to better understand the agents under his authority. Spending time with all the agents in such an expansive company would be an impossible task. So, it was the ability to paint an indebt picture of each agent that had proven to be his most helpful skill.

During one of his routine profile searches, Edward had ascertained that Jordan was related to Tommy Hayden. Armed with that information, Edward contacted Mr. Cochran and put into place the most elaborate of all Black Heart plots. He had single handedly orchestrated the meeting and subsequent destruction of several of his most hated agents: Jordan Buckley-Gates, she was a black mark on the face of the company, the very essence of her existence put the company's anonymity at risk. Then there was Chad Garrison, a sad example of how an overactive conscience could destroy a promising future; it was his confession to Jordan about the bureau's methods of recruiting that had caused certain members of The Truth, namely, John and Cynthia Benton to shed unwanted light into some very dark corners of the agency. And how could he forget good old James Ruston, a complete waste of skin; the guy had disregarded every opportunity afforded him. Tommy Hayden was last, but not least on the list of thorns in his side. The rogue agent had been wrong for the company, and should have been put down like a lame horse but he was a necessary evil. He would make for the perfect patsy to lay all of the blame. Retaliation: pure and simple. The guy had been filled with a bloodlust.

Edward pulled the file on the top of the pile closer, as he eyed the name written across the top. John Benton. He moved to the file just underneath, as Cynthia Benton's name came into view. Now, how to make this problem go away.

35

John grabbed his cell and moved into the hall. He followed the cobblestone walk to the fountain where he sat on the smooth surface of a bench. There he dialed the number. He had already been to the file room for The Truth. Everyone involved with the case had at some point been in some way affiliated with The Truth; so The Truth would have access to their complete files.

Cynthia was back at the apartment working away on making the connections. She had been a prelaw student. Her GPA was a perfect 4.0. She had planned to become a civil rights lawyer. Her time at the agency may not have proven that she was any kind of an agent, but she was one of the best profile specialists the agency had encountered in quite a while. Agents still requested her expertise. Though, Cynthia did not want anything to do with the organization, she conceded her help in hopes that it would keep the agency satisfied to let her remain off the payroll. She did receive a compensation for her efforts, though she had been insistent that she would not be taking anything for her time. John smiled, as he thought of how hard at work Cynthia had been, as he left the apartment.

John had started to give up on contacting Mr. Stanton when the tinkling voice of a woman answered. "Mr. Stanton's office. May I take a message?" The woman asked John heard some papers ruffling in the background.

"Uh... Yeah... I mean, Yes ma'am. Could you have him call John Benton?" John rattled off his number, and then promptly started back to the apartment. He guessed that he would probably hear from Mr.

Stanton in a week. He hadn't thought about all the red tape you had to go through just to get a simple phone call from the man. Once he had needed to meet with Mr. Stanton about one of the recruits. He wanted to clear up some of the murky details. It had taken Mr. Stanton a week to return the phone call. Meanwhile, the man wandered around the halls of The Garden. Without knowing the exact direction that Black Heart wanted to take with a recruit, The Truth could not implement their own agenda. Instead, he was forced to wait on a plan of action.

John thrust his hands into his hair. He and the others didn't have a week. What was he going to do?

John had arrived at the entrance to their modest apartment when his cell phone came to life. Puzzled by the ringing, he almost dropped the phone. He rarely received any phone calls that weren't related to The Truth and right now, they were considered to be dormant agents. Taking care of the children of Lane and Jordan had taken them out of rotation. Normally, they would have been next to leave for a mission. Now, they were confined to The Garden on babysitting detail.

John lifted the phone, so he could to see who was calling. Again, he almost dropped his phone. It was Black Heart headquarters. John answered, thinking that maybe the receptionist would be calling back with a definite appointment to see Mr. Stanton. A male voice was on the other end of the line. John pulled the phone back. It seemed off that it was not the receptionist. This never happened. Mr. Stanton was a very busy man. He never got back in touch with anyone in less than a day. This was unprecedented.

"Hello?" John clambered through the receiver. Still uneasy with the record time in which Mr. Stanton had returned his call, his hands shook with anticipation.

"Hello, Mr. Benton." Came the booming voice of Edward Stanton. "You needed to talk with me?" The line went silent. It was a moment before John realized that Mr. Stanton was waiting on his response to the question.

Recovering from the shock, John started slowly at first and then gained momentum, explaining all of the events from the phone calls he had received from Tommy Hayden to Garrison, Lane and Jordan leaving to apprehend Tommy Hayden. Mr. Stanton seemed to listen to the whole story. He never once interrupted. This was another thing that seemed off. Mr. Stanton was a man of few words. He liked his stories short and sweet. With the lack of time, he did not have a moment to waste. Many of the phone calls that Stanton had received, John had witnessed the man tell the agents from either Black Heart or The Truth to make a point; yet, in this moment he showed uncanny patience and considerable listening skills.

A prickle ran up the back of John's neck; something that had often happened when danger was near. John called it his, God-tuition. It was short for the intuition that he had gained over time in the service to the Lord. Once, while out in South America on a mission trip, John was about to enter the tent of a shaman. The prickle on the back of his neck had happened, then as well. He didn't know at the time that he should pay attention to the small sign.

John entered the tent, as he was told by one of the tribal leaders to do so... The man had been in a trance for hours, praying to a false god. John laid a tender hand on the man's shoulder to allow him a kind of awareness of his presence. John had seen this before. The man would have a subconscious awareness, but he would not be able to emerge simultaneous with the moment of contact to acknowledge the other person. Thus, a shaman was well guarded during meditation. John was lifting away from the gentle contact. The shaman whirled around, kicking John's feet out from under him. He, then grabbed a spear, and held it to John's throat.

John was gasping in fear when the tribal leader entered the tent to investigate the commotion. The leaders had believed that the man had been in a spirit battle. In the moment that John had initiated contact with the shaman; the man had believed that John was the evil one. John knew well that the man had been dealing with the lies of the beast. He had been playing with spiritual evil that was probably beyond his understanding. The Truth had sent John and his crew into the tribe to bring the truth of God's Holy Word to the people.

Ignoring the prickling of his God-tuition had, all but cost him his life that day. Now, he was not about to ignore it. John made plans to meet with Mr. Stanton, but instead of that afternoon as Mr. Stanton had requested, John arranged for the next day. He had told Mr. Stanton that something had come up, and he would have to see him the following day.

John flipped the phone closed, as he made his way back to the apartment. Opening the door, he tried to keep the excitement at bay. He didn't want to wake the children. But, as he opened the door, he could see the concern registering in Cynthia's eyes. Whatever it was, she had already made the connection, and John had a sneaking suspicion that it was somehow related to Edward Stanton.

✳ ✳ ✳

Cynthia had laid the kids down for a nap. John was drilling a hole in the carpet with his ceaseless pacing. She had been happy the minute that he had decided to leave the apartment for the phone call to Mr. Stanton.

The files were sprawled out over the small coffee table. She had never had such a hard time of making a profile or filling in the dots. But, this was ridiculous! The files were littered with holes. Something was missing. She eyed Tommy Hayden's file. Though, she knew that he was Jordan's nephew, the file made no mention of it. The weird thing was that she had gone over this same file for the agency the day that Tommy was brought to The Truth. She was sure that the file contained evidence that would support that fact.

She moved to another file. Picking it up, she noticed the name on the file, James Ruston. She had searched the file from front to back, it too made no mention to events that had transpired in Ruston's immediate past; things that she was well aware of. For instance, the time that Ruston had been involved with the drug cartel was nowhere in the file. The history had been covered over; a new picture had been painted. The file now read that Ruston was placed on light duty due to a debilitating injury in the field. It was as if someone was trying to break the connections; but who?

Cynthia was about to put the files back down, citing them a dead end when the door to the apartment opened. She peered up at John. His face was pale. His eyes wide with fear. In that moment, the answer was clear. Someone had indeed tampered with the files, and it was now clear just who that someone was. Chills ran down her spine, as she made her way over to John.

215

"We have twenty four hours to disappear." Was all that he could manage?

Cynthia tossed another glance over her shoulder at the files, and then sprang into action. She would need to bring the files with her. Though Mr. Stanton had made a masterful attempt at erasing the histories of each of the agents listed in those files; no one could be that thorough. He had to miss something, but in order to know what that was, she needed one more file. Cynthia crossed the room and took John's hands into her own.

"I need for you to do something for me." Cynthia admitted, as she moved to the files. "There are huge gaps in the known histories of each of these agent's files... I need the file of the one that I am almost positive made that happen." Cynthia turned, as she gathered the files and placed them back in the small pasteboard box.

"I will have everything ready by the time you return. I need that file." She looked deep into his eyes, as she pleaded with him. "Please be careful, John. I know the risk that you will be taking, now that Mr. Stanton is aware that we are involved. I hate to ask you to do this, but you know, as well as I, the implications here." She licked her lips, as she crossed the room to where John stood. "If we don't figure this out, if we don't connect the dots and somehow hold him accountable..."

Cynthia couldn't finish. John knew, all too well what would be upon them if Edward Stanton was not swiftly dealt with. He had all of the power of one of the government's best kept secrets at his fingertips. Mr. Stanton could erase everyone involved. Just as he had done with the files, their history would be obliterated. He would kill everyone who had any knowledge of each of the agents be it man, woman, or child.

Cynthia turned, as she made her way to the children's room. She had to get them packed. There was no time to waste. Already, they had allowed precious moments to pass them by, as they sat like ducks in the apartment.

John grabbed Cynthia. He spun her around and crushed her to him.

"Grab the children and go. I will catch up to you. You need to be out of here." He kissed her forehead and rubbed the slight bump of her midsection. "I love you both."

Fear slammed into Cynthia. The air whooshed out of her lungs. "I can't leave without you." She held him tight to her, refusing to break contact. He was her lifeline.

"Cynthia…" John started, and then allowing his head to sink a little, he pulled her to him. "Baby, there is no time. Please do as I say. Take the children to our special place. Throw your cell phone away." Do not, for any reason use it. He pushed her back, as he peered into her trusting brown eyes. "I love you. Please honey, do this. I will meet you soon."

Cynthia moved robotically through the packing. She felt numbness inside that seemed to grow with every passing moment that John was away. She gathered their things, and did as John asked. She lay her cell phone down and quickly, searched through Amelia's bag. Grabbing the child's emergency cell phone she laid it on the table. She wanted to devise a way to let Jordan know that the children were safe if she returned. She could not imagine the anguish of returning to an empty apartment and not knowing where the children had gone in the midst of all of this insanity.

Cynthia searched the room frantically for something. To the side of the bed was a teddy bear. It had a hidden pocket no one was aware of. Cynthia scribbled a coded message down and then pushed it into the pocket.

She prayed as they left that Jordan would find the message. It was the only thing that she had to offer.

36

Trapped somewhere between life and death, shards of pain pierced every portion of Lane's body. Agony forced his mind to flee to the comfort of some distant sanctuary, not quite death. It was in those finite moments that he was able to focus on God's love. Then like a vapor in the wind it was gone. He felt more alone, than he had ever felt, in his life in the moments that his mind swam to consciousness.

Evil born of years of hate and murderous rage left a heavy blanket over the house. Maintaining a relationship with Christ, was a choice just as loving someone had been; here in this place, with the bounteous force of evil pressing relentlessly down upon him, Lane struggled for that connection.

As his mind swam once more for the surface of reality, he strained against the fog to stay in the world of the living. He peered at the room through his angel vision. His body flinched away in automatic revulsion, as he witnessed the hordes of demons filling the room; each with a different charge and a different agenda. Four gruesome beings held tightly to each individual in the room while each of them was careful to keep its distance from Lane. The light emanating from every pore of his body flowing straight from the throne of God, however dim, was too excruciating for the demons to look upon.

Jordan stooped in the corner, as the four putrid beings assigned to her crowded in; each whispering lies.

"No one cares." One hissed, as a slimy yellowish-green viscous fluid oozed from a mouth filled with row upon row of sharp serrated teeth.

Long claw-like talons hung from immense hands that were attached to bulky arms that seemed disproportionate to its body. A flat head that bulged out in the middle was adorned with piercing red eyes; each of the red irises was divided in perfect symmetry by a black slit, lending a reptilian appeal to the creature's grotesque features. Its whole body was filled with the same slimy substance oozing from its large mouth. Each of the creatures seemed to be no less than nine feet tall. Lane looked, again at the room, as his mind took in the sheer bulk of all the creatures filling the room in comparison to the scant space of the room. It seemed impossible and yet, he was witnessing it firsthand.

Lane pushed the heightened angel vision back down so that he could see Jordan through the murkier filter of his human eyes. Jordan did seem despondent. Her face was pale despite the golden tan. She seemed so frail. He wanted desperately to go to her, but he could not seem to push past the pain, past the overwhelming evil. He had to touch his Faith. He had to believe. God's power was only limited by the faith of his people. God is a gentleman and he will not tread on the very freewill that he so graciously granted His people. Exhibiting faith is the same, as handing an invitation to God; that invitation, in essence, is saying come and do your best. Lane knew that. It was one of the most powerful things that his parents had ever taught him.

At that very moment Lane felt a thousand miles from ever being able to touch the faith that he knew lived within him. He had called upon that faith so many times in the past. In the woods outside of Beulah County he had to call upon that faith then. He knew that it was there; somewhere buried just beneath the surface, past the fear, past the uncertainty, past the pain; just under it all, his faith burned, waiting for him to call upon it. If only he could push past it all. If there was something so profoundly true in his memories, some seed that had been planted that he could reap the harvest in this moment.

Lane struggled to not leave the cognitive moment. He loved the moments spent with thoughts of the Lord, but right now he needed to be in this moment. He needed to maintain awareness, so that he could somehow figure out how to get out of this mess. Lane was thinking of everything he could do to maintain that awareness when he realized despite his best efforts, he had slipped beneath the deep uncharted waters of oblivion once again.

Letters started to spiral before his vision out of focus at first, and then slowly as if someone had adjusted the lens of a camera the letters moved into perfect focus. Lane held tightly to each of the letters with his mind's eyes. He needed them, as a boat needed an anchor. It was all that seemed to hold him in the world. He felt minutes from slipping off of a deep ravine into the waiting arms of oblivion.

He watched the letters, as they swirled ever closer, each one beginning to fall into blank lines. He squinted with his mind's eye to get a closer look. He found himself trying to guess the ending result of the word puzzle playing out before him. Finally, after his mind had been driven to the edge of madness, in the last moment that seemed he could not take another second of the pain, of the torment; the words landed on each slot forming a perfect line. Spaces existed between words and then Lane saw more clearly it was a message.

'For I am convinced that neither death, nor life, neither angles nor demons, neither past nor the present nor the future, nor any powers, neither height nor depth, nor anything else in all creation, will be able to separate us from the love of God that is in Christ Jesus our Lord.' The message was a Bible verse; Romans 8:38-39. It was one that his mother had shared with him, before leaving to go back to the states. It was the first time that Lane had ever been afraid. He had always felt that his parents would somehow make everything okay, but this time they were leaving and something about it felt final. Lane would learn later that it had been a prophetic thought because his parents had died in a terrible plane crash. The message was the last thing that his mother had ever given to him; it was all that had helped to push him through in the first moments after learning that his mother and father were lost to him this side of heaven. He felt alone, then as well.

He grabbed on to the words, carrying them back to the surface like a life preserver. He quoted them over and over, as he allowed each syllable to take hold and in that moment like a key, the words opened the tightly bound vault and there under the desolation of rotting fear, uncertainty and overwhelming pain, his faith came brimming to the surface and with a triumphant exclamation of determination it swept all of the fear and uncertainty away. Pain that until then had so unequivocally shaken him to his core was instantly pushed to the back of his mind.

As Lane's faith grew, fear and uncertainty withered into nothingness. Strength filled his arms and legs as clarity coursed through his mind. He again gave himself over to his angel half; pure-blinding-light illuminated his body, clouds of fog fail from his vision as the demons, once again ghosted into view. Once towering beacons of pure evil determined to dismantle their charge, the demons seemed to become smaller as they coward in a corner.

Heat filled the light silhouetting Lane's body, and then grew warmer still. The tiny shards of metal penetrating hundreds of painful points around his body melted into liquid steel that puddled on the floor around the bed. The demons fault for refuge in the corner as they pushed their fellow demonic host to the forefront of the swarm. As if waiting to be summoned angelic beings stood battle ready, sword in hand; each one speaking truth as they moved in unison. As the last of the restraints fell away, Lane stepped, determinedly from the metal table.

As if his moving to a standing position were the awaited battle cry the angelic host leapt into action. Not wanting to miss the moment, Lane reached for the legs of the stainless-steel tray. Surgical instruments rained down, clattering to the floor, filling the small room with a metallic ring.

Tommy moved from Jordan's side, as Lane, with a wide flat sweep of the metal table slapped the side of Tommy's head. Dazed, Tommy staggered backwards. Turning the top of the table to the ceiling, Lane swept it in a ferocious arch across Tommy's exposed throat. Tommy's hand flew protectively to his crushed trachea. A gurgling sound emitted from his throat, as frothy sputum exploded from his mouth. Tommy crumbled to one knee, as the bloody stump of his severed limb floated out to Lane in a plea for help. Lane took an unconscious step backward, as he watched Tommy turn a reddish-blue, and then crumble lifelessly to the floor.

Ignoring Tommy's body, Lane moved to Jordan's side. He tenderly placed a hand on either side of her face and smoothed the tendrils of tear-soaked hair away from her face. Jordan flinched away, scooting dejectedly to the safety of the corner. Realizing that Jordan was far from reality, Lane followed her, as he claimed a tighter grip of her face and gently forced her to look into his eyes. He searched her face for recognition, as he lightly spoke her name.

Muffled cries pushed against the duct tape covering Jordan's mouth. Lane reached for her, but she frantically pushed at him; her eyes darted around the room in search of something. Lane moved to the side to allow her full view of Tommy's dead body. Jordan's eyes flashed to Tommy's still form. She studied him with open suspicion, as if she expected him to get up at any moment and again claim control of the scene.

"It's over." Lane soothed as he removed the ropes form her hands and feet. Jordan relaxed a moment and then rubbing her rope-burned wrist made her way slowly to Garrison.

37

A long spiraling drive shrouded by a canvas of sequoia trees finally opened to reveal a small log cabin. Cynthia, at last allowed herself to relax, as she cast a reassuring smile over her shoulder to Amelia. The child had not slept one wink the whole thirty mile drive. Instead, she had sang tribal songs to her brother until he had fallen asleep. The childlike way that she had of mothering Tristan was endearing. Amelia allowed a smile of her own as she lightly patted Tristan's tiny hand.

Cynthia returned her attention to the cabin, her favorite place on earth. The pansies were in full bloom, still nestled in the hollowed out beds that John had made for her in the logs just below the windows. The pale blue of the satin curtains made for a beautiful backdrop for the multihued flowers. French doors were embellished in satin blue curtains that were the twin to the curtains adorning the windows. A winding side walk was outlined on each side with a bed of flowers. Each flower was a mystery to Cynthia, but she had gladly planted the bulbs when John had brought them to her. The reds, yellows and purples gave an enchanted allure to an already dreamy cottage. The rolling brilliant green of the lawn meandered perfectly groomed on the outside of the serene structure. There was no place on earth that could compare.

She and John had worked tirelessly after purchasing the property and putting it in an assumed name. The cabin had been built from the trunks of the sequoia trees. It would forever be an accomplishment all their own and one day when the dust settled from the treachery of Black Heart, they would truly be allowed their own life. She and John had vowed to move here and raise a family. Cynthia rubbed the tiny bump in her lower abdomen, as she thought how soon that time needed to come. She prayed for a miracle. The only hope for a future without the agency injecting its venom into their peaceful lives would be to bring Mr. Stanton to the light of truth. She prayed that would happen soon.

However necessary their separation, leaving John's side was heart wrenching. So much of their lives had been spent at each other's side since the day that they had met.

Cynthia caught a glimpse of her reflection in the rearview mirror. Though she had not allowed the tears to come for fear that such a display of raw emotion would scare the children, she could see that the pain of being away from John with such emanate danger so close to him was just as evident: worry lines ravaged her eyes, fear etched just beneath the surface shone clearly in her brown irises, and her mouth seemed plastered hopelessly in the downward slope of a frown.

Pulling into the small carport, erected from crude pieces of left over lumber and lattice work, Cynthia appraised the wild roses that weaved in and out of the diamond-shaped holes made by crisscrossed cream colored lattice. Again, she was struck by how much the place reminded her of John. So much of his quiet and peaceful nature was represented in the sturdy, yet, serene haven.

Bringing the children here to the cabin had been the right decision, but that did not make it any easier. She needed to be calm, and focused for the children but everywhere she looked was filled with images of their time together; every image brought her helplessly back to the awareness that John was being subjected to a danger that she could do nothing about. Everything felt wrong, off somehow: her arms felt too empty her mind too full and she ached for John to not only be by her side but to be well.

Cynthia sighed, as she made herself go through the motions of getting out of the car. She tenderly pulled Tristan from his car seat, as she savored the scent of baby lotion on his skin. His still, sleeping form draped trustingly over her shoulder.

"I've got you little man." She whispered the words of affirmation, as she placed a gentle kiss on his brow. Moving to the front of the small red Mazda also purchased with cash under an assumed name, she took Amelia's hand and led her to the side door of the cabin.

Once inside, Cynthia turned the main switch on. Instantly, the open floor plan of the small cabin was completely bathed in light, a failsafe John had insisted upon. He had explained that lighting the whole place would leave an intruder nowhere to hide. It was John's ability to think ahead to see and defuse a problem before it could infringe harm upon their lives that filled her with the most peace.

Cynthia watched as Amelia took inventory of their home. She tried to view the small cabin that their future had been wrapped up in through the child's eyes. Though the cherry-wood varnish of the logs made it evident that this was indeed a cabin, it was like stepping into a different world; from rustic beauty to exquisite elegance the difference was as stark as night and day.

A fireplace made of gray, cream and burnt orange cobble stones was framed in mahogany. Crystal candle labrums stood gracefully at each end of the shelf made of mahogany. A large hand-painted picture filling the space between the candles depicted age-riddled-hands outstretched in supplication as majestically beautiful angel wings spread gloriously to the heavens while shrouding the hands as if to say 'I've got you'.

A plush blue sectional-wrapped protectively around the outer edge of the living room. Mahogany tables nestled on either end of the couch were adorned in finely etched crystal lamps. The intricate design was the same as the hand-painted picture over the fireplace. Pale blue shades with lace fringe covered the tops of the lamps reminding Cynthia of the short fringed dresses of the fifties.

An expansive kitchen was equipped with all the necessities that a master chef would need as Cynthia loved to cook. An island made of the same three shades of cobble stone used in the design of the fireplace took fort in the center of the room. Marble, the same shade of mahogany as that used in the living room topped the magnificent piece. The center of the large island was filled with a shiny-blacktop stove. Shelves lined the walls in the same shade of mahogany; brass handles the shape of violins were an elegant representation of their shared love of music. This was Cynthia's favorite room. Cooking calmed her.

Cynthia smiled, as she ushered the children into one of the spare bedrooms. She didn't bother separating them so much had happened and she did not want to take whatever sense of security that they could derive from being in the other's presence.

"Amelia would you mind lying down with your brother while Aunt Cynthia takes a moment and then I will start dinner... Okay?" Cynthia prompted as she carefully placed Tristan on the small full sized bed. She smiled, as his body sank into the thick quilt that her grandmother had made for her. The patches, so painstakingly sewn together were pieces of every girl child's dress upon the day that each had been christened.

"You need a go pray... huh Aunt Cynfia?" Amelia asked, as she endearingly mispronounced Cynthia's name.

Tears slipped from Cynthia's eyes, as she collapsed on the bed next to Tristan. She pulled Amelia tenderly into her arms. Emotions she had been desperate to contain slipped unbidden through her defenses. Her shoulders shook with her sobs.

"I'm... so... sorry." Cynthia choked.

"It's okay, Aunt Cynfia. God loves you." Amelia soothed, as she pushed Cynthia's hair back with her tiny hands and peered more intently into her eyes. "Betides, daddy and mommy will come." Certainty filled the golden amber of Amelia's eyes like a wall of steel. No doubt existed beyond that fortress. Cynthia eased back further, as she studied Amelia's insistent gaze.

"They will, won't they?" It was a statement of fact. In that moment, as she looked upon Amelia, Cynthia understood... It was with the faith of a child that all would be possible. Cynthia sat Amelia down, as she kissed her head and silently left the room.

Somewhere, Jordan, Lane and Garrison were struggling to apprehend a killer thirty miles away under the scrutiny of Black Heart, John was working to gain Intel that would prove Mr. Stanton's guilt and right now more than anything they needed her prayers. Prayers required faith. Amelia had showed her the way. Without delay, Cynthia collapsed to her knees on the living room floor, as she beseeched her Lord for their safety, for their strength, for their ability to be more than overcomers.

38

Rows upon rows of filing cabinets littered the enormous room. Not to bring too much of a penal-code allure to The Garden, the agent histories room was kept in a large storage area that was strategically hidden beneath a canopy of green. The key pad allowing access to the room was well hidden beneath the right arm of a cherub fountain. Pushing a small lever that appeared to be nothing more than an elegant flowing piece of the cherubim's toga brought the tiny box to the forefront of the statue. With a single swipe of his finger, he was able to gain access to the well-hidden files.

John filtered through the rows of filing cabinets, as he made his way surreptitiously to the back wall of files; the cabinets where the HOD and other Black Heart leaders that had a direct connection to The Truth were held. Mr. Stanton's file would be held in those filing cabinets. The files were alphabetized for easy access, so John made his way to the file with the 'STU' indicated in bold lettering.

He took careful inventory of the room, as he opened the cabinet. His heart was pounding against his chest-wall. He wasn't cut out for this espionage nonsense. Getting files for regular members of Black Heart was one thing, but the HOD... He had to be out of his mind. John knew that Mr. Stanton would spare no expense, and waste no time coming after him or his family. As he stood to the back of the hidden room of files, his heart raced as if every beat were a reminder of the danger that he was now in.

The cabinet squeaked open causing another wave of adrenaline to be dumped into his already stressed nerves. Again, John forced a cautious glance toward the entrance. The rows of cabinets, blocking a clear view of the way in, did little to calm his antsy mood. He wished this was over and he could be on his way to the cabin. He was terribly worried about Cynthia and the children. He had no way to get in touch with her. As unnerving as that was, it was the only way to ensure that she not be followed. A phone call would be too risky. A cell could be traced and with the technology afforded to Black Heart, Cynthia could be found in minutes. It was that very reason that had prompted John to take so many over cautious measures.

Cynthia had left in the predawn hours under the cloak of darkness. John hoped it would impair the ability of a tracker to tail her. He had the red Mazda stationed on the outskirts of town in a parking garage. The cab, the car, and even the clothes taken for all of them had been provided by an old friend that had remained anonymous. No one knew that he and John were friends. John had used a pay phone the evening before Cynthia had left. The conversation had been kept brief. John had gone over the details of what to do. Max would collect the sizes of clothes needed and place them in the car. He would then park the car and leave the key in it. He would also contact one of the lesser used cab companies and pay them well to sit out in front of the pub and wait for Cynthia and the children to emerge.

John was so sure that the orders would be followed to the letter that he hadn't even checked behind Max. He and Max had met on a mission trip in Honduras. The time there had been brief but a friendship that would last forever had been forged between the two men. On multiple occasions, Max had to request favors from John; to which John had happily complied. So when John had called Max, he had been only too happy to help.

John was so swept away in the memory of his earlier preparations that he hadn't thought to listen for a breach in the main entrance. Once the key pad was activated, a low whirring tone would begin for approximately thirty seconds. This would give anyone in the vault of files or outside the door a warning that someone was about to enter or leave. His mind raced, as he again, risked a glance. Just then the door opened wide as a man wearing a suit and tie stepped across the threshold.

John's heart slammed into his throat, as he started to jet for the safety of the filing cabinets to the left of him. The cabinets knit in a small cluster, made for a perfect cove in which to hide. John's hand froze on the drawer of the cabinet. He had, but one shot, this was it. If he left without the file, then all would be lost. John reached further back into the cabinet.

The clacking of the man's expensive loafers reverberating throughout the room grew closer still. John fished frantically for the file, as his heart pounded in time with the clack, clack, clacking of shoe to floor. Finally, in the U-section of the file, almost to the very back of the cabinet he saw the desired paperwork. John snatched the folder, though his heart sank at the high probability that the folder had been tampered with. Obviously, someone had misplaced the file. He guessed they had been in a hurry after pulling the file out and taking out or changing whatever materials that suited their purposes. The file had most likely been stashed in the U's by accident. Still, he would have to take the information and pray that Cynthia would be able to ascertain some small clue that may help to prove Mr. Stanton's guilt; only then, would any of them truly be free. John slid the drawer closed as quietly as possible and disappeared behind the small bank of cabinets. His heart stuttered a few beats as just then a large man in a blue Armani-suit stopped right in front of where he hid. Steely gray-blue eyes searched deftly for signs of an intruder. John melted into the gray cabinet, holding his breath. He didn't move. The man finally looped back up the other side of the room making his way to the entrance.

John listened intently, as the clacking moved further away.

"Nothing here." the man said flatly into a small transmitter, John knew to be on the sleeve of the man's overpriced suit jacket.

Careful not to trace the man's exact steps, John moved slowly from behind the cluster of cabinets. He leapt silently into another cube of files and waited for the green indicator beacon to flash over the entrance of the door. His heart slowly returned to some semblance of a normal beat when at last the whirring began, the entrance opened and the man stepped through. John sat between the cabinets for a long while. He remembered, all too well the warnings that Garrison had given him.

"When hiding from an agent, never trail behind closely. Give the agent time to give up on the pursuit. Allow the agent to be satisfied that his search was sufficient. Walking out of a hiding place immediately after an agent leaves is always a mistake. Never make the agent's every step because a lot of agents will leave behind some sort of a device that is sensor activated. The moment that the sensor is tipped off the device becomes active. It could be anything from a camera all the way to something as deadly as an explosive." John's heart stuttered through a few beats, as his mind recalled the last words of warning that Garrison had given as deadly "as an explosive".

John checked his watch. It had been ten minutes since the agent had left the file room. Finally, satisfied that he had waited long enough, John emerged from his hiding place and jumped to the other side of the small-walkway to a wall of cabinets. He weaved in and out of the cabinets as he made his way to the entrance. Stopping to inspect the door for any sign of a sensor, he eyed the door suspiciously. Sure enough, on the inside of the doorframe a tiny almost undetectable green beacon flashed a pale evergreen.

John thought about what Garrison had said and stepped to the outer edge of the door. Careful not to break the circuit, he took the watch from his wrist and pulled a stick of gum from his pocket. He popped the gum in his mouth and then carefully took a small piece of the sticky substance and molded the silver gum-wrapper onto the glass covering of the watch by placing pieces of the gum around the perimeter of the glass; turning the glass into a small makeshift mirror. He then, took the other half of the gum and stuck it to the back of the silver wrapper. Finally, he stuck it to a metal hinge just to the side of the sensor. The mirror would reflect the beam of light back to the sensor, giving the sensor the false allure that the circuit was never broken. John smiled confidently to himself maybe he was good at this espionage stuff after all; if nothing else being a computer geek would pay off.

John quickly keyed in his code and waited for the door to open. He allowed a quick peek around the outside. He did not see anyone. He emerged cautiously from the file room. He quickly ran for the cover of a nearby fountain.

The large fountain trickled water from the basket on top of a beautiful woman's head. The basket was spilling over with fruits; each one had a small hole that water dripped. The water cascaded passed the perfect line of her young face and onto long robes that flowed out to the side. The robes were etched in the marble and painted a royal blue. One hand claimed the basket while the other dipped to the side stretched out in a submissive fashion. Engraved lettering was etched into the bottom of the statue that simply stated, 'Let the Greatest among You Be Your Servant, Matthew 23:11. John loved the verse and the statue. Both demonstrated so perfectly what The Truth's true mission was. The woman, adorned in the majestic shade that a queen would wear was the epitome of servitude as she carried the basket of a servant girl and curtsied in a submissive fashion. Her regal face gazed purposefully at whomever her gift was for. It was the heart of a servant captured in marble, coupled with the elegance of a queen. The beautiful statue was the epitome of what it truly meant to be a Christian.

John crouched behind the fountain. Time seemed to stand still, as he watched the green indicator flash its fluorescent warning, the whirring began and then the door began it's maddeningly slow sweep.

"Hurry! Hurry!" His mind screamed. The door swept closed just as two men rounded a bend in the cobble stone walk leading to the observation room. Suddenly, the steely-eyed agent in the Armani-suit froze. His left hand arced wide, as it landed on the smaller blond headed agent's chest. The younger man in a pinstriped suit that seemed not as lavish as that of the other agent halted instantly. Having stopped the younger agent, the older agent pointed toward the file room door, and then suddenly shook his head. Confusion stole over his visage. After a minute, he said something to the younger agent. Then, giving a dismissive shake of his head, he pointed in the direction of the elevator. John figured that the man wanted to go to the pub to get a drink.

Something felt too easy about all of this. For instance: why was no one manning the observation room? Surely, the agent that planted the sensor did not feel so confident over such an easily foiled device that he would not take more extreme measures to ensure he capture John.

Sitting still for a moment longer, John contemplated his next move. Given the same task that the agents were, what would he do? John thought about that. He knew for sure he would want to be thorough; especially, if faced with a man as demanding and lethal as Mr. Stanton. He would stop at nothing to ensure he did exactly what Mr. Stanton asked. Somehow John couldn't help but believe that the two agents heading for the elevator felt the same. If the high priced suit, the older agent was wearing was any indication of how much the man was being paid for his services... John suspected that Mr. Stanton would expect a handsome return on his investment. With that in mind, John conceded that he would have to be more proactive if he ever expected to escape such a precarious circumstance.

Edging his way through the shrubbery, John disappeared into a small access route; the space had been left during the design of The Garden in order to allow maintenance workers access to the wall in case damage was sustained to the wall and needed to be repaired. Not many people knew about the space, certainly the agents from Black Heart had no way of knowing about its existence. Only a handful of the original missionaries remained with The Truth; John was one of them.

What he lacked in stealth, John more than made up for in good ole fashion knowledge of his surroundings. The agents from Black Heart were out of their element.

John pushed through the cluster of undergrowth. Long since forgotten, the small trail was strangled with vines. He ripped through the mass of greenery, as he searched for the vent that filtered throughout the compound.

Finally, reaching his coveted destination, John pulled a Swiss-Army-knife out of his pocket. His heart sank, as he witnessed the rust covering each of the four screws holding the vent in place. He gently scraped as much of the rust away as possible. He didn't want to be heard though, he doubted with all of the calls coming from the different bird species anything could be heard.

John pulled the Phillips screw driver free of its resting place in the stock of the brown knife. He put the screw driver into the star shaped pattern of the first screw. With a loud snap, the screw loosened. John froze, as a flock of birds nesting in a nearby tree took flight. He hoped that no passerby would equate the disturbance to someone behind the dense growth of exotic flowers and greenery. He waited a moment longer for any indication that someone had been tipped off by the scattering birds. When no one came, John continued on to the second screw. Not able to budge the second screw, John continued on to the final two screws. Both screws twisted off with little effort. John finally returned to the problematic screw. He grunted with the effort, as his muscles in his hands and arms ached with the force he was putting into loosening the screw. The vent was molded in such a way that a quarter inch lip protruded and hinged on the metal frame attached to the wall. Removing the final piece of hardware would be the only way to remove the vent and make good his escape.

"Lord please..." Was all that John could manage. The star-shaped head of the screw was beginning to file away. John slipped the screwdriver into the head of the abused hardware once more. Pushing back any doubt, he focused all of his energy into the violent twist. In that moment his mind and heart synchronized with his spirit, as his whole being had but one focus, one belief: no matter how grim the situation may appear, the screw would come out and he would escape.

39

The screaming sirens of ambulances and police cruisers filled the night. Jordan crouched near the wall, as she held on to Garrison for dear life. He had lied to her, but he was her friend. In that gut wrenching awful moment she was reminded of how much she needed that friendship; how much she depended on its existence.

Tears slipped from her eyes, her lips puckered into a childlike pout, as she slipped the rope from around Garrison's neck. Jordan scooped his head into the bend of her arm, just as she had her children so many times while carrying their sleeping form to a pelt of animal fur to sleep. Tenderly, laying his head on the wood floor, she smoothed a tangle of frayed rope away from his brow. His hair had gotten longer than he was used to keeping it. He needed a haircut. The moment that he woke up, she would tell him. She scrutinized the chapping burn around his neck. Her mind retreated from the image of Tommy snatching the rope home around her friend's throat. She could not think of that now. He needed her.

Garrison seemed so helpless. She had never seen this side of him. In the field, it had always been his direction that had guided her. It was his voice in her head that had talked her through the most precarious of situations. Now, as he lay on the floor, her at his side, her insides convulsed with the sobs that she refused to let loose. She had to think. Her mind seemed frozen, as if nothing made sense. There was something that could be done. She checked his airway again; it was open. He was moving air, yet he made no effort to gain consciousness. His trachea was midline. His pulse was normal she guessed. She had nothing to compare it to. She had never really taken the time to check Garrison's vitals before and she had no real understanding of the medical field; just some crude first aid tips that had been passed along by the bureau.

What was taking those ambulances so long to get here? The question flashed uneasily through her conscious mind. The road wasn't that long. Surely they could have made it down the driveway by now. Jordan turned to see Lane, had already begun looking out the shattered remains of the window for an answer to the same question.

"Are they coming? Have they turned off the lights? The sirens?" Jordan asked, as she took her eyes off of Garrison for an instant. She searched Lane's face for any sign of relief. Nothing registered. He stood in front of the window holding a thick cloud of burgundy drapes out of the way. His eyes intent on something, he leaned his tall, muscular frame toward the window and then just as quickly dropped the drape back in place and moved to her side. Leaning down he scooped up Garrison. Jordan placed a hand on Lane's arm, forbidding him to take her friend. She trusted Lane with her life, with Garrison's life, but in that moment she was not yet ready to part with her best friend. What if these were her last moments with him. So much had been spoken in anger. She had so much to say to him; to forgive and to be forgiven.

"There's no time Jordan. We have to hide him." The words slipped uneasily through Jordan's defense. Her head shot to attention, as her hand fell away from his arm and instantly started trying to help Lane scoop Garrison up.

"I got him baby. Just get a needle and one of those drip sets. Also grab a bag of the saline, the clear liquid on the roll top desk and the needles on the floor over there." Lane called out orders.

Jordan was taken aback. He sounded as though he was a doctor in an ER about to perform surgery but she was not the seasoned nurse at his side. She was a field agent turned missionary. Jordan quickly threw a confused glance Lane's way.

"The drip set is in the cubical in the top of the desk, the one on the left. It is clear tubing." Lane informed, as he moved away from the window with Garrison's unconscious body.

"This?" Jordan asked, as she held up a loop of clear tubing with a blue housing that contained a round white sphere. "Yes. Good. You ready?" Lane asked, as he hurriedly moved toward the door leading to the kitchen.

"Yeah, this way;" Jordan announced, as she reached down to grab the needle that was thankfully still in a protective plastic applicator and then led him out to the hidden tunnel that disappeared into the shelter.

"How did you know about this?" Lane asked. His eyes sparkled with wonder.

"I went to the library. There was a pad of paper..." Jordan waved the prolonged version of how she had come about the information. "Blue prints of the farm are housed at the library." Jordan offered, as she led him further into the tunnel. She pushed the door open, and after Lane passed through, latched a thick dead bolt to ward off intruders.

Lane laid Garrison down on a small cot in the corner. He then, quickly took the supplies from Jordan and started an IV. Jordan watched, as he checked his breathing, his pulse, and then quickly shined a small flashlight that he had taken from his pocket into Garrison's eyes.

"He doesn't appear to have brain damage." Lane said, as he then, peered back at Garrison. "I want lie to you. I'm not very assured by the fact that he is not waking up, but his vitals are good. For now, we will have to leave him here ..." Lane had been trying to explain his intentions when Jordan interrupted.

"I can't... I won't leave him Lane." She defiantly stood, her shoulders squared. In that moment, she seemed the Jordan he had been following so long, trying to bring her to a saving knowledge of Christ before it was too late. He understood her reluctance to leave but there was no choice. With as many agents, as was filling the woods surrounding the farmhouse, if they did not stand and fight together, then they may as well open the door and invite their fate to step through.

Lane pulled her to him. He then, setting her back a few inches claimed her shoulders, as he looked deep into her eyes. He needed her to understand. He needed her help. He needed her not to be Jordan the missionary with a heart for the world, or Jordan the wife and mother that cared deeply for her family. In this moment, he was speaking straight to Jordan the ruthless cold-blooded killer.

"Jordan, I need you to go with me. If you refuse, then we may as well open the door and invite in our fate. .We will be no good to Garrison dead. You have to leave him for a short time, to help me fight. There are dozens of agents littering the woods, Jordan. All are here for one purpose, to kill. We have to take them out before they can take us out; it's the only chance that any of us have. If they get in here, Jordan if those agents find us in here, and you know they will, then all is lost. We will not be able to protect Garrison, while fighting them off. There will be too many." Lane put his hands on either side of her face. "Please, go with me. Please, snap out of this..." Lane waved his hand around, trying to think of the word that best suited the despondent way in which she was acting. "This funk." Lane threw the simple word out. It was not fancy, but in the end it was the truth.

Ever since she had the fight with Garrison in the park, she hadn't been herself. She had been just going through the motions. That was one reason that he was afraid for her to go after Tommy, alone. In her present state of mind, Lane did not trust her to make right decisions.

"You can talk to Garrison when he wakes up. He needs his rest. But, if you don't help me defuse the problem, before us, then that chance will be lost to you. Jordan fight. Fight for me, for Garrison. Fight for our children. Whatever it is that you need to fight for; I don't care, so long as you fight. It is the only way to stop this; to stop Black Heart, to be able to live our lives in any semblance of freedom." Lane was about to carry on with his endless pre-battle pep talk when Jordan pulled his lips to hers. She quieted his bantering with a kiss.

"It seems that you want to fight." Jordan teased, as she walked to a shelf in the corner and started to collect some weapons. Though, this time, she was sure to only gather blunt or sharpened objects... she now knew that the farmer's elaborate collection of war tributes were no more than harmless-relics on display. None of the artifacts with a firing pin were of any use.

Lane stood for a moment longer, stunned. Then smiling his approval at her sudden break into the fierce predator he knew her to be, Lane walked to her side and started to collect some weapons of his own. A bag lay on the floor near the small table. Garrison had brought a few weapons of his own and thankfully, Tommy had been good enough to bring the bag into the hidden room. Lane allowed a moment of thanks for the effort of his would be killer. It seemed that Tommy's greed may indeed save their lives.

Jordan was strapping a knife to her inner thigh when she heard Garrison groan. It was the first sign of life, she had seen him exhibit since he had slumped forward after Tommy had tightened the rope around his neck. She turned on her heel and moved quickly to his side. His eyes were still closed, but his brow was scrunched as if he were dissatisfied with something.

"Garrison?" Jordan spoke softly into his ear. "Can you hear me?" She waited for a response, but nothing happened. She started to believe that she had imagined the sound. She turned to leave with Lane when another groan filled the small room.

"Jordan." Her name was but a whisper. Jordan turned in time to see Garrison's eyes flutter open.

"Garrison. You're awake. How do you feel?" Jordan was so excited to see his eyes open and hear him speak that she had all, but forgot the danger surrounding them. "I'm so sorry. There was nothing I could do. I was tied up." Tears filled her eyes, as they spilled onto her cheeks. Garrison raised his hand awkwardly to her face and tenderly brushed away a tear.

Not being able to say too many words, he lifted her chin and placed a finger to his lips. He then lifted his arm and eyed the IV. His eyes appraised the room that he was in.

"Lane carried you here and started an IV. We called for medics, but they were detained by agents." Jordan stopped on the last word, wishing she had not been so candid with Garrison. In this moment he was not her old partner, he was a friend fighting for his life. The last thing that she wanted to do was cause him undue stress. It could not be of any help.

"Jordan." Lane whispered, as he placed a gentle hand on her shoulder. "We need to go. Time is running out. The more time we allow them to familiarize themselves with this place..."

"The more chance we stand to lose the element of surprise." Jordan finished. She then turned back to Lane and smiled. "You're right." She conceded, as she returned her attention to Garrison.

"You have to stay as quiet as possible; rest if you can. We have a growing problem in the woods. We will try to defuse it as quickly as possible." Jordan informed and then laid a knife in his hand.

"I know you have spent a lot of time out of the field, but if someone comes in here." She stopped finding the words hard to say.

Garrison again laid a gentle hand on the side of her face.

"I will take as many with me as I can." He finished the vow that they had taken as partners long ago.

Jordan had been afraid at first, but Garrison had taken her in and showed her all that he knew. He had told her that it would be okay; that the two of them would never go down without a fight, and then he had appealed to her ever growing need for revenge.

"We will take as many of them with us as we can." He had vowed to her. After that the words spoken in an effort to insight bravery, strength, and fury had become a solemn vow, an oath and from that day forward they had entered every battle no matter how grim with the one thought in mind. "We will not go down without a fight. You may kill us, but rest assured, we will be taking as many of you as possible on our journey to hell Jordan had since changed the last of the oath. She no longer thought of her journey as ending in hell." She now knew she would someday be spending eternal life with her loved ones in the arms of her Creator. She quietly wondered if today would be that day.

40

"Invisible." had been the last word spoken from Garrison before he collapsed into a fitful sleep.

Jordan had turned to Lane, then. "He's right." She had said. She pulled Lane's hands to her chest. She would make him understand. They may get lucky, and open the hatch leading to the outside of the house, and no one would be there to see, but more likely than not, agents would be so congested throughout the grounds that any movement from near the house would be nearly impossible to cloak. The only shot they would have was for her to go back through the tunnel into the house. There she would use the image of the farm's blueprints, burned into her memory to guide her to a secret door in the wall of the kitchen. The door had been added in case of intruders. Inside, the small room broke into a bifurcation, one side of the split led to the roof while the other side led to a hidden door that would exit the house.

Jordan held Lane's hands tightly as she explained the necessity of keeping their whereabouts a secret. She appealed to his better judgment. Reluctantly, Lane agreed, though she could see the hesitation in his blue eyes. He opened the door and watched her as she disappeared into the thick darkness of the tunnel.

Jordan's heart ached for him. She knew all too well the stress of watching a loved one go into battle while sitting on the sidelines waiting, unable to be of help. Unfortunately, Lane's sheer bulk would make invisibility impossible and then there were the confined spaces that would need to be traversed in order to gain the upper hand of surprise on the enemy.

Jordan pressed her ear to the kitchen door. No sound filled the space beyond. Pressing the thin sheet of paneling, the sheer door that melted into its surrounding, seeming no more than another section of wall popped open. Chancing a quick glance into the kitchen, she scanned the large room for any signs of disturbance. Satisfied that there was no one about, she pushed further into the room.

A movement flashed in her peripheral vision. Jordan immediately ducked into a crouch. Extending her right leg out, she swept her foot across her would be attacker's legs, causing him to pivot backwards. The large male figure dressed entirely in black from head to toe, flailed his arms widely trying to gain his balance. Jordan coming to a standing position, plunged her small blade into his chin. With the same heated force, she tilted forward as she kicked her left foot out and up with thunderous impact, she shoved a second attacker's nose into his brain. Instantly, the second attacker crumbled over on top of the first, both were dead.

She quickly made sure no other threats were about and then opened the hidden section of wall. Placing her arms under each man's arms in turn, she drug them into the shadows of the tunnel but not before looting their dead bodies for weapons.

She needed to stay focused, but she couldn't help but allow a moment to acknowledge what had just happened. She held a small victory dance in honor of those dispatched by her capable hands. It felt good to still be able to do what was necessary and still feel very much the woman of God that she had become.

Both men carried black pistols with silencers on the end and both men had two extra clips. With the ability to kill silently from a distance and the extra ammo, their chance for survival had just doubled.

Jordan moved away from the wall and further into the kitchen. Just on the other side of the pantry door was where the hidden room would be located. She searched for a lever that would reveal the hidden door leading into the hidden alcove, but nothing near the area that she knew the entrance should be, caught her attention. Jordan thrust her hand through her thick mane of auburn hair as she turned to the other wall. Something had to be here; somewhere. Just as she was about to try for another exit, time was not on her side, two bronze sconces on the wall caught her attention. She studied the two candle holders; something seemed off with the one closest to the place where she knew the break in the wall to be.

Jordan crossed over to the bronze fixture to get a closer look. Tiny Old English lettering was engraved on the base of the bronze sconce. 'Here in lies the way'. The cryptic message, Jordan noticed, was only on the base of the one candle holder. The other sconce was just a plane bronze color, with no amenities. She smiled as she pressed her index finger into a small fisher just beneath the writing. There was a muffled snapping sound as the wall fell away.

She wasted no time stepping through the secret door. Closing it behind her, she lit her flashlight. Not sure of the integrity of the door, she didn't bother searching for a light switch. She didn't want to take the chance that light may filter through a crack in the wall. If more agents came into the house, they would be tipped off about the room's existence.

Jordan's pulse quickened as she took in the tight space littered with ropelike clusters of dust covered cobwebs. Each of the vine like webs hung loosely like garland. Common sense assured her that no spiders lived in the webs but her skin seemed to grow legs. Her body felt, as though thousands of the eight-legged pests were crawling all over her. She scratched her arms and then mindlessly, her hands sought her head, as she began vigorously rubbing the imaginary spiders out of her hair.

A scripture blazed in her mind, as she started to turn for the refuge of the door and seek out another escape route. The verse had been told to her one night, as she woke from one of the horrible nightmares. Lane had pulled her into his lap, and whispered the verse into her ear. 'For God has not given us a spirit of fear, but of power and of love and of a sound mind. (2 Timothy 1:7) Jordan drew upon that truth, as she pressed further into the slender alcove.

Finally, reaching the bifurcation, she took first the left side of the split. She wanted to go up to the roof and disarm any enemy force that may be staking out the area. By her calculations, there should be two agents on the roof, just as there were two agents patrolling the inside of the house. Also, according to the blueprints, the door leading out to the roof was in a small cube-shaped groove in the roof. A two by two foot section of the roof dipped low to the door leading into the house. The rise of the walls surrounding the door was also two feet. Not a lot of space, but if Jordan was quiet, and careful not to be seen, she could use the silenced pistol to take out any threat.

She silently prayed for God to hide her from her enemies. She then ascended the ladder. Lifting the square board a couple of inches, Jordan listened for movement. She paused, two men were talking. She thought she heard her name. Easing forward, she listened more intently incase the men had valuable Intel.

"Jordan Buckley, huh?" One of the men was saying her name. Jordan knit her brow. What was this about? She pushed the board open a little further. She had never had a problem hearing; she just wanted to make sure with all of the things going on that she did not mistake what was being said.

"Jordan Buckley-Gates, she got married. Remember?" The matter-o-fact response of the second agent made Jordan feel a little uncomfortable. Why were these men speaking about her in such an intimate tone? Neither of them had personal knowledge about her life, yet both were sitting on a roof top, waiting to kill her while discussing her life.

"What a waste." The first agent complained.

"Man. What I wouldn't give..." the second agent drawled while making an inappropriate gesture.

Now Jordan was disgusted!

"Yeah well... You can hang that up. After tonight, that road will be closed." The first agent informed.

Jordan listened to the easy banter of the two men on the roof. It occurred to her that she should probably be angered by the slanderous remarks and sexual innuendos but what was the point.

"That road was never open, boys!" Jordan challenged, as she pushed the door back and aimed at first one agent and then the next. Before either could react, both were lying in a pool of blood and brain matter.

41

Lane paced the floor, causing the small enclosure to seem too crowded. His long strides placed him at the room's edge too soon. What was taking Jordan so long? Something had to be wrong.

"Calm down, Lane." The admonished response to Lane's incessant pacing had been but a whisper. Startled, Lane moved to the cot where Garrison laid, eyes wide. He was obviously distressed by Lane's show of anxiety.

"Hey." Lane chirped, trying to lighten the mood. "I'm okay. Sorry." Lane offered.

"Sure you are." Garrison rasped. His throat was obviously still very sore from the rope that Tommy had cinched violently around his neck. "Look, I may be dead weight right now, but in my day..." Garrison cleared his throat, as the words started to trail off in a series of coughs. He pushed himself up in the bed, as he licked his dry lips.

Lane moved to his side. Laying a hand on Garrison's chest, Lane tried to ward off the attempt that Garrison was making to get up.

Garrison waved off Lane's attempts. "Don't worry. I'm staying put." Garrison assured Lane, as he came to a seated position, and leaned back against the wall. "The point is..." Garrison continued, as he pointed toward the roof. "...She learned from the best."

Lane was struck by how certain Garrison seemed to be of Jordan's whereabouts. Lane knit his brow in an inquisitive fashion. Garrison smiled and licked his lips again.

"I told you she learned from the best." Garrison boasted. The look of admiration in his eyes was hard to miss. This was his best friend, but more than that: Jordan was the person that Garrison had been able to pour all of his knowledge into. All of his time with the bureau; everything that made his time with Black Heart real; all of it had been passed to Jordan. Now, that Garrison was in an office, no longer a field agent Lane could imagine that he felt useless. The foiled attempt at saving them had to be a blow to his ego. Lane could see that even though Garrison was on the sidelines, viewing Jordan from a distance was better than nothing. He took pride in her. She was evidence that he had been an agent. She was living proof that no matter where life takes him, Garrison had left behind a legacy and Jordan had guarded that legacy well.

Lane smiled at the sentiment while crossing to a shelf covered in nonperishable items. There were several cans of various vegetables. Some cans of meat, also were stacked in neat rolls. Lane shook his head, as he ignored the other products and grabbed a bottle of dust-covered water. He quickly wiped as much of the matted dust as he could and promptly opened it. Handing the bottle to Garrison, Lane fluffed a pillow behind his head to help him sit up straighter.

"Thanks." Garrison smiled, and then again nodded toward the roof. "Staying invisible takes time. Jordan will have to take out two agents per so many square feet; that usually equates to two in the house, and two on the roof. After that she will have to ensure that the immediate outside perimeter near the house is clear." Garrison pointed to the hatch at the top of the stairs, while taking a long sip of the lukewarm water.

"While the agents may not be aware of this room, they will be watching from their individual posts for any sign of movement." Garrison pointed to a chair in the corner. "These things can't be rushed. Jordan will hurry as quickly as possible because of radio transmissions. You might as well take a seat." Garrison said, while rubbing his chin as if deep in thought.

"Radio transmissions?" Lane questioned. "What does radio traffic have to do with the time that it would take her to clear the perimeter?" Lane knitted his brow, again. Garrison wasn't making any sense.

"Yeah, radio transmissions. It has everything to do with clearing the perimeter." Garrison said, as he took another long swig of his warm water. He then arched one brow and continued. "Every so many minutes, most likely, on the half hour, each team will have to communicate with the incident commander. So I'd say Jordan has approximately..." Garrison checked his gold watch. "...fifteen minutes to complete the mission, before incident command starts asking for a report."

Lane's eyes went wide, as he moved for the stairs. He ignored Garrison's insistent demand that he not leave. No matter what, he would not leave Jordan out there to defend herself against God only knew how many agents. He knew firsthand what she was capable of but leaving her to face the cloud of agents he had witnessed through the window... Thirty minutes to dismantle two agents per... house, roof... per square footage? How much square footage? The farmhouse, alone was about twenty eight hundred square feet; give or take. Lane's mind calculated the numbers, and then he imagined every scenario that could go wrong. Every extra agent or door that refused to open, every minute wasted on some trivial thing that would cause her to take too much time in a section was another minute that brought her closer to the dreaded scenario that he saw playing out in his mind's eye. The agents would descend like sharks on bloody prey the minute incident command gave the authorization. Meanwhile, he was sewed up in the bunker with Garrison doing nothing.

Lane stepped up to unlatch and push the wooden plank open. His hand froze and then jerked back away from three sharp raps on the door. The sound was deafening as it reverberated through the silence of the bomb shelter. Time stood still, as for a moment Lane contemplated who might be on the other side of the door.

"You should probably answer that." Garrison informed with a tired sigh.

Lane cast an unsure glance over his shoulder. Garrison's flippant attitude concerning a matter that was so important was starting to grate on Lane's nerves.

"It's her. You may want to unlock the door, before she has to face the other agents without you. You don't want to miss all of the fun; do you?" Garrison raised a brow, as he yawned dejectedly.

Lane quickly unlatched the wooden plank and pushed it out. A whooshing sound followed by a muffled thud that Lane could swear sounded like a body dropping filtered through the open space, as Jordan breezed past. Standing on her tip toes, Jordan kissed Lane briefly and then flitted down the stairs to the table. She was treating there circumstance no better than Garrison, as if it were a normal mundane day... nothing unusual.

"Hi honey, I'm home." Jordan called over to Garrison, as she pulled looted ammo out of her pockets, the back of her pants, her boots... Lane stood mouth agape, as he contemplated the amount of agents that would have had to of lost their lives in order for her to have so many weapons. Lane's mind swam with the possibilities. Maybe, he shouldn't have insisted she fight. Maybe, she wasn't ready.

Jordan sifted through the mountain of guns, knives and ammo clips. Claiming a pistol, and a machine gun she tossed both weapons to Garrison. Despite his weakened state, Garrison grabbed both and laid each weapon in turn on the bed next to him.

"By the time they find you, they will know we are here." Jordan informed, as she threw a menacing glance in Garrison's direction. The sheer threat lacing the simple statement sent chills down Lane's spine.

Jordan turned back to the table just in time to catch a glimpse of the mask of concern on Lane's face. The fear and uncertainty registering in his blue eyes broke her heart. She knew all too well the fear in the depths of his eyes had nothing to do with the agents that still covered the woods. This was fear of a threat that had nothing to do with flesh and blood. The threat Lane feared was internal. He feared for her soul.

Jordan gently laid the guns back on the table, as she closed the distance between them. She crushed her body to his, as tears filled her eyes. She found his eyes, then as she searched their depths.

"I'm still here." Jordan whispered. She placed her hands on either side of his face. "I need you to fight with me. If you don't, then we may as well throw open the door, and invite our fate in." Jordan regurgitated the words he had used earlier to break her out of the 'funk' as he called it. She kissed him with a hint of passion. "I fight for you, for Amelia and Tristan. I fight for me. I fight for the freedom to live our lives without looking over our shoulders; wondering when and if Black Heart will send another hoard of agents in to kill us." Jordan answered his call to arms in every word. She then, dropping her head, allowed a rogue sob to be released. When she lifted her face again, she somehow seemed older.

"I fight so this life... those people. .." Jordan choked, as her emerald eyes looked away for only a moment, and then with determination borrowed from an unseen force, she turned her intent gaze upon him; "...can never touch our babies!" Though she was half weeping, Lane knew the words were a battle cry; one that those behind enemy lines would not soon forget.

Lane pulled her into his arms briefly, and then claiming a few of the weapons from the table. Shoving them into his boot, and the back of his pants, he turned toward the door.

Jordan froze to the spot, as she watched Lane stroll heatedly to the door. Turning on his heal, Lane found her eyes, and mischief fought menace for center stage in the depths of the searing blue. "I believe the fight is out there." Lane quipped, as he bolted for the stairs.

"Oh;" Was Jordan's simple response.

As they left the room, Garrison's laughter could still be heard in the distance.

CHAPTER

42

The last screw had finally given way. John was a few hundred feet into the ventilation system, before he realized he would have to pass through the massive fan that pulled air in from the outside of the compound; after the fan, there would be a ladder leading up though an access shaft. The shaft filtered out behind the pub. John felt the weight of those impossible hurdles that stood like sentinels, guarding the path before him; jeering at the danger left behind and the danger, yet to be seen.

He sat on the metal duct work, trying to think just how out of touch one would have to be in order to believe himself capable of getting through the insurmountable task of short circuiting the fan with only a Swiss Army knife and crude electrical knowledge that was gained by watching his father fix problems occurring in the family home. He remembered being eight years old; standing at the ready to hand his father any tool necessary to fix the air-condition unit. It was dead in the middle of summer when the unit had quit. His father never deterred by such a daunting task, grabbed his bag of tools and wrapped his arm around John's shoulder.

"You with me, little buddy?" His father asked. And back then, John was. He was his father's right hand man, his sidekick, and his shadow. John sniffed, as he peered over the edge of the metal duct work. He was a long way from those days, and this was a bigger job. It was a far more dangerous job. If he did something wrong, the fan could start back up. John would be cleaved in half.

He sat, watching the fan a few minutes longer, as he thought about the possible routes for the wiring to run. The shortest distance between two points, including a fan and a fuse box, would always be a straight line. It's not like the fan was a bomb. All he would have to do is find the area of the wall that the wiring was funneled through and then compromise the integrity of that line. The issue would be getting through the stopped blades before the backup generator started. Once that happened, the fan would begin rotating again. The agency had not wired each of the electrical components in the same way that most establishments would have. It was too big of a risk to lay every hope on one source of energy, but more than that the compound was underground. If the wiring from one electrical source stopped working, then the safe odds would be to have the components supplied from completely different wires to the generator. This would ensure that if the electrical issue had been a compromise in the lines, which was exactly John's plan, then the generator would still be able to get energy to the compound.

Searching the wall descending from the fan, John could see a fissure in the middle of the wall. If he could sink his knife into the fissure, he may be able to break enough of the wall away in order to get a clear view of the wiring. Bits and pieces of the sheetrock were sure to fall into the fan. John had no way to protect his eyes. He would just have to be as careful as possible not to allow that to happen. John pulled the collar of the plain black t-shirt he wore over his mouth and nose. Already, his black dress slacks were shellacked in white dust. The button-up shirt he had been wearing over the t-shirt had thankfully not suffered the same fate. He had discarded the shirt in order to better maneuver his arms. The long sleeves would make a long and arduous job even more unbearable.

A large gaping hole now existed where the seam had once connected the two halves of the sheetrock. John was beginning to see the flat surface of the two by four. Ebbed on by the knowledge that the wiring would be housed next to the plank of wood, John dug through the chalky substance with a renewed sense of determination. His eyes were dry and irritated. He had to stop a few of times to clear away the debris from his face and hair. He blinked his eyes rapidly, hoping that the action would cause his tear ducts to over react and wash away the dust caked there. Eucalyptus wafted up from the fan, taking his breath during the moments he stopped his work, and left the safety of his shirt collar to remove the unwanted particles from his face and hair.

At last, the work had paid off. With the board completely exposed down to the plywood that it was nailed to, John could see the rubber sheath in which the wire was housed. John reached for the wire, and then a thought occurred to him. He did have the knife but metal conducted electricity. He did not want the dusty eucalyptus filled ventilation system to become his tomb. John searched the area for anything rubber. The bottom of his shoes was rubber, but he couldn't very well make gloves out of his bulky shoes, it just wouldn't be practical. John thought about cutting away the rubber sheath from around the wire, but that too would be impractical. He had no way to attach the substance to the knife, or scissors to assure it not fall away and despite his best efforts he would be exposed to the electricity either by unintentionally cutting into the naked wire while removing the rubber exterior, or by the rubber particles falling away during the cut.

John took off his shoe. He was frustrated. He was just about ready to throw the shoe at the fan and just face the firing squad waiting for him back in The Garden. He turned the shoe over and there, inside he saw the foot pads Cynthia had placed in his shoes.

John had spent two weeks in Africa on a mission trip to feed the hungry; to teach about Christ. Walking the dusty plains to each of the impoverished dwellings had made for long and hot days. When he had returned to the states, Cynthia had questioned about his feet. John could remember that he was astonished that she would ask such a thing. Though many of the workers had complained about their tired and aching feet, John had little to no trouble.

Cynthia had stayed behind with some of the other women in the group to care for the children of other missionaries. Having gone on the trip a number of times before, she thought it would be good to allow others with families the opportunity to witness firsthand what their spouses had sacrificed to help others. Also, she had confided to John that the beauty of Africa was something that no one should have to miss. It held a magic that healed somehow and seeing so much need, being a part of the solution, had a way of reminding the fortunate just how blessed they really were.

John smiled, as he recalled telling her that his feet felt fine. "Good" had been her simple response. Curious as to why his feet, alone would be unaffected by the vigorous walking, John took off his shoe. He saw there for the first time what had evaded his attention. Just inside his shoe, a declaration had been written on the soles of his shoes... I love you.

John pulled the foot pad out of his right shoe, as the memory faded. Yet, again, the gift given in love would save him pain but this time it may even save his life. The rubber pad clung to the bottom of his shoe by a clear adhesive. The sticky substance made it hard to pull the rubber pad free of the bottom of his shoe, and the adhesive did not lose its ability to stick once free of the shoe.

John laid his shoe to the side. Picking up his knife, he wrapped the pad around the end of it. He captured the wire between his middle and index fingers. He wanted to test the flexibility of the wire. Once John was satisfied that the wire would pull away from the wall a goodly distance in order to be cut, he placed his shoe back on his right foot. He eyed the wire cryptically. Once the wire was cut, and the fan stopped turning, his window of time would be small.

He tried to get a glimpse of the structures below the fan. He could just make out the slight space that would be afforded him. Just below the fan where John would be landing was a metal grate. The grate housed a reservoir that contained eucalyptus and water. A furnace heated the liquid up, turning it into steam that was then blown throughout the ventilation system and subsequently, The Garden. John would need to be careful not to touch the grate with any portion of his body.

He pulled his black t-shirt off and shook the white powder from it. He then put his button-up shirt back on. He would need the protection, however, little of the sleeves. Finally, he put his t-shirt over his head. His face was the only thing showing, as the neck hole rested on top of his head and under his chin; more protection.

John tucked his pant legs into his socks after rolling them tight to his leg. This caused his pants to be tightly rolled to his leg and would not allow any steam to rise up the material and burn his flesh. He scrutinized the fan that was looking more and more like a death trap; this was his last chance to change his mind. He was out of time. It was now or never. The agents were probably already searching the compound and soon enough they would consider the ventilation system. John gripped the wire once more and holding his breath with a violent rake of the knife across the wire, it was severed.

At first, the blade's momentum did not seem to slow. Then finally, the spinning started its slow waning. Putting his hands on two of the blades, John lifted his legs and then lowered them to the grate below. The heat coming from the grate was immediately evident. John had to commit himself to the task. Gravity would prevent him from lifting himself back up onto the blades and then into the vent. He just did not have the strength that it would require. His arms were like rubber after all of the digging into the wall with just a small knife. He had no time left to waste, and yet the heat was so oppressive it made it impossible not to pause. Sweat beaded on his brow, as his clothes began sticking to him. His time was running out. If he stayed in this position he would either be burned to death or sawed in half. Either way he would be dead.

John took his hands from the blades and lowered himself into the direct heat below. The heat covering his body was so intense that he was stunned. Then a buzzing sound filled his ears. At first, he thought he was dying and then he heard a low whirring sound and then felt the first refrains of a light breeze.

John instantly, knew what was happening. The backup generator had become operational, the fan was starting to spin. He crouched beneath the spinning blades of death while hovering over a steamy brew of eucalyptus water. If he did not move, burning human flesh would join the myriad of smells. John heaved his body forward. His hands out stretched, he reached for a thin metal rung of the ladder, leading up and out of the compound. The drop into the room below, seemed no more than six to eight feet, but could surely break an ankle. His fingers touched the rung. John committed to the plunge as he wrapped his fisted hands around the slender rod.

His body catapulted forward and collided with the other metal steps with such force that the air whooshed from his lungs. Taking a minute to right his breathing, he finally scrambled for a higher purchase on the ladder, so that he could place his feet on one of the metal rungs. Pulling his foot up to the next rung of the ladder, he felt as though he was being weighed down. Tilting his head down, John could see the problem. The steam had melted the bottom of his shoes. They were now sticking to each rung as he ascended.

John laughed lightly as he considered the irony. He now had all the sticky substance he could use. The problem was as the rubber cooled it was causing his shoes to mold to the ladder. He reached down and slipped his shoes off. Climbing the ladder without them would be painful but necessary. He held on to the upper rung by draping his arm around it, he then tied his shoe laces together and hung them around his neck.

Painstakingly, John ascended the steep ladder. The arch of his feet ached with the effort of supporting his weight on the miniscule metal rods. His arms screamed for relief to come and yet, it was still hundreds of feet above him. His legs were blistered from the steam and constantly burning. He thought of Jordan and Garrison. Both had lived many years, this being the norm. He could never commit to a life that included days without end of this kind of abuse. He prayed for the abuse to finally end. He longed to be at the cabin with Cynthia. Pushing back the pain, John started to sing. He had always been able to overcome any situation, no matter how grim with praise.

"I can only imagine," his voiced lifted up to the heavens, as he sang his favorite song by Mercy Me. "What it will be like," he continued, not knowing if he had the lyrics right. "I can only imagine what my eyes will see, when your face is before me." John's voice rose far above to the top of the ladder where he longed to be on the last step leaving the miserable place behind. "Surrounded by your glory what will my heart feel? Will I dance for you Jesus, or in awe of you be still?" His voice trembled, as the tears fell washing away the remainder of the dust particles from his eyes. His heart longed to be: with his Lord; to be with his wife; to be anywhere, but in this empty miserable place; fighting for every breath that he took. The remorse he felt started to ebb, as the song grew. "I can only imagine. Yeah. Yeah. I can only imagine." He continued, as the end of the song, came he was truly amazed.

Looking up, John could see that he had finally reached the top of the ladder. His body still hurt, but it was not an all-consuming pain like before. His heart still longed to be with Cynthia, but it was no longer a burning desire that overwhelmed his every thought. He no longer desired to be with his Lord, because as he sang praises to Him, he could feel His presence fill the place. He touched the weathered gray of the metal door. Sliding the latch to the side, he pushed the door open. As the first soothing effects of fresh air caressed his heat chapped face, he realized he was almost home.

43

"Jordan, what are you saying?" Lane questioned, as he searched her eyes.

She held the radio up to her mouth again, and then let it fall back to her side.

"Look Lane, I know this makes no sense to you, but I feel very strongly about this." Jordan beseeched. She needed him to understand.

"What about the element of surprise?" Lane waved his hand in the air, as if trying to make the crucial way in which she and Garrison had treated the precious element clear to her. Now though, to him, it seemed that she was set on destroying what cover they had left. Jordan could imagine how her husband must be feeling.

Jordan couldn't hold back the smile. Sarcasm had never been his strong point; it just did not work well on an angel visage. It was better suited for a scathing human or demonic face.

"This is no laughing matter, Jordan." Lane gently admonished.

Stepping to him, Jordan claimed his hands. She was explaining it the wrong way. Lane was always better at matters of the heart. She, on the other hand, tended to hold tightly to the 'storm the troops campaign, kill them all and let God sort them out'. That sort of thing, until now, had been a fundamental mindset. Lane had changed all of that the day he introduced her to Christ. Now, as she thought about their future, she was forced to recall the second chance that had ensured that future.

"Not even three years ago, I thought like them... worse than them, really. At least they work for a cause. I killed because I thought I was the cause. I may as well have been hold up on an island, wearing white robes while serving up the poison-spiked Kool-Aid." Jordan reminded, as she waited for Lane to make the connection.

"Oh come on Jordan, Really? You were possessed by a demon. It was not..."

"Don't!" Jordan barked. She exhaled. Turning around, she reached for a calmer tone. Frustration would not help her case. It would only breed anger, and Lane would refuse to listen to such childish antics. She had to explain what she felt, what she knew, in a better way. It was never good to be vague, especially in the situation they were presently facing.

"What makes me so special, Lane?" Jordan asked so quietly it was almost a whisper.

"What?" Lane looked really confused now. "Jordan, there's no time. We've already wasted too much; we need to finish this and get back to Amelia and Tristan." Lane's eyes were filled with concern. He was so patient with her, but Jordan knew even his patience could run out. He had committed to the battle. While Lane was no push-over, he was not the trained killer that Garrison and Jordan were. His weapon was love. So he had fully submitted his will in order to, for the moment follow in her capable steps. Now, she was 'flip-flopping' so to speak. Jordan understood how frustrating going against everything you believe in could be. Lane had done just that. Now, she was asking him to turn it all around. She wanted to go missionary in a minefield.

"Lane, please... I'm telling you, this is the right thing to do. Think about it. Am I more than any one of those people out there in those woods? If so, then what is it that makes me so special? Is it that I'm your wife? Is it that I am Amelia and Tristan's mother? What Lane? What about me, makes it possible for me to have that second chance? What about them, refuses them that same the second chance?" Jordan moved to him, then. She reached up and placed one hand on his cheek.

"Help me. If you want this to end, truly end; then it must die with us too, not just them. Because, if we go out there and kill every woman and man in those woods, because of the beliefs they now have never offering them the chance to concede... we become just like them. Just like Black Heart. We are deciding who they are for them. Then, we are callously executing them for being what we accuse them of being. Where does it end? Are they expendable because they are in a sea of faces that we can't perceive? Or, are we going to stop long enough to take a look, to take a chance on them as individuals? To believe that each one of them deserves the same chance that I was given?" Jordan pointed to the woods where the agents waited. "It must die in us, too." She whispered, as her eyes became liquid emeralds. She placed the hand holding the radio over his heart while the other rested over her own heart.

"Grrr! You're going to be the death of me woman." Lane teased as he pulled her to him. Jordan was already doing the second victory dance of the evening.

She whirled around to the sound of leaves rustling in the woods. She was already standing in a defensive pose: legs spread, one arm bent the other straight, and her finger on the trigger. Her protective posture in front of Lane's hulking form seemed comical, but Lane knew, all too well that it was no empty threat.

"Lesley!" A male voice hissed from the cover of the trees, as a female form moved into the open. Her hands were lifted over her head in submission.

"No Nick. I'm done. I want out." The female called from under a black mask. She kept one hand in the air, holding her gun by its barrel. The gun swung loosely from two of her fingers. With her other hand, she reached under her chin, and claimed the bottom of her mask, and started to lift it away.

"No, you know there is only one way out." The male protested.

"Then I accept." The female countered.

A gentle breeze whispered around the silo behind Jordan and Lane. They stood awestruck, as the woman lifted the mask away. Dark auburn hair lifted on the breeze, as emerald eyes peered at them from a very young face.

Jordan gasped, and the gun in her hand clattered to the ground in front of her. She wobbled back into Lane's chest. Lane was already moving her away from the perceived threat. With his right arm, he pointed the silenced pistol at the young woman, while his left hand claimed Jordan's waist and moved her behind him. Jordan felt like dead weight. She made no move to counter the action. It was not like her. She had always been ready in a situation like this, but now she was as limp as a wet dishrag.

"I wouldn't hurt her." The young woman objected with a defiant tilt of her chin.

"Isn't that precisely, what you came here to do?" Lane accused, never taking the pistol from the woman's head.

"Yes. I mean no." The woman countered.

"Well. Which is it, yes or no?" Lane demanded through gritted teeth. The young woman ignored the question. Peering passed Lane; she staggered forward one step and reached her hand out.

"Aunt Jordan," She begged. Lane's head was spinning. What had Lesley, or whatever her name was said? He turned to Jordan. She was leaning over with her hands on her knees.

"Penny." She breathed, as she held her right hand out, pointing in the young woman's direction.

It was Lane that was shocked, now. He moved to Penny then, and pushed her behind him to stand with Jordan. He never lowered the gun, but now it was pointed toward the woods where the male voice had emitted.

The leaves started to crackle, again, as the young man stepped from behind the tree line.

"Where's Lesley?" The man demanded.

Lane moved to the side to allow the man a better view of the woman he now knew was Penny. Jordan was holding both sides of Penny's face. Her eyes were filling with tears. She crushed Penny to her. Sucking in a breath, Jordan stepped around Lane, and leveled Nick with a menacing glare.

"It's Penny!" Jordan spat.

"Aunt Jordan, Please don't. It's not his fault. Nick doesn't know me as Penny." Penny urged, as she caressed Jordan's arms in an effort to disarm her growing anger.

Lane watched, as Nick peeled away his own mask, and for the first time really looked at Jordan. The emerald green of Penny's eyes, Lane was sure Nick thought to be a one of a kind trait afforded only her, was actually passed down through generations of Buckley's.

"Beautiful aren't they?" Lane offered up the rhetorical question, as a life line to the drowning young man. Lane watched, as he seemed to lose ground while falling into the sea of green in both Penny and Jordan's eyes.

"Gorgeous." Nick breathed, as he pushed passed Lane, no longer concerned about the gun to stand at Penny's side.

Tears filled Jordan's eyes, again. "Where's Erica?"

The breath seemed to be forced from Penny's lungs, as her body appeared in some undeterminable way to be smaller.

"They... killed her." Penny panted. Tears poured from her eyes. Her breath came in ragged pulls. "They said we were here hunting the agent that did it." Penny cried, as she fell into Jordan's arms.

"Penny I never touched your mama." Jordan insisted, while rubbing one hand up Penny's back.

"I know." Penny sniffed. "I knew it was you that we were coming here to hunt, but I never believed what the bureau said about you being the agent that killed my mama. I came here to help you." Penny looked out at the woods where she and Nick had been stationed; when she turned back, she was shaking her head.

"Though, I didn't know that you would just walk right out of the house... I was shocked when I heard your voice; when Nick and I saw you standing here talking to this man..." Penny shook her head, as her eyes filled with disbelief.

Lane could see that Nick was still shocked to see the uncanny likeness that Penny bore to her aunt.

Jordan winced at the "this man" part of Penny's explanation. She cast a surreptitious glance in Lane's direction. With a nod, Lane stretched out his right hand to Penny.

"Hi, Lane Gates, Missionary for The Truth." Lane introduced himself with the simple explanation. Penny's face contorted into a confused mask, and then she looked at Jordan.

Lane cast a sheepish grin at Jordan. "How was I supposed to know that hanging around a missionary would be harder to swallow than me being your hu...?"

"Lane!" Jordan growled, while rolling her eyes.

Nick laughed.

"He's your what?" Penny asked in a casual offhanded tone. She turned her quizzical, expression on first Lane, and then Jordan.

Jordan pushed passed Lane with an aggravated glare. "Later!" She hissed her threat to deal with Lane's silly antics when they were alone.

Lane's eyes lit up with desire.

"Good grief! Could you at least show some characteristics befitting an angel" Jordan fussed.

Lane and Nick laughed. Penny's brow knit in confusion.

"Oh no!" Jordan shook her finger in Penny's face. "There isn't enough time in the world to explain that. All you need to know is that's Lane, a missionary for The Truth, and my husband." Jordan enunciated each word. "Anything else you want to know can wait." Jordan said, as she cast another accusatory glance in Lane's direction.

"Husband! You got married?" Penny asked, while sizing up Lane. Nodding her appreciation at what she had seen in Jordan's direction, and then she continued. "I get it. But you Aunt Jordan, defender of women everywhere! Every man must die!" Penny was now enunciating every word.

Nick looked decidedly uncomfortable at the last thing Penny had said.

"You married... their... leader?!" Penny threw out the last word with a comical smirk on her face.

"Hey!" Nick protested, no longer laughing.

Jordan all of the sudden aware of how vulnerable she felt for Penny, started pulling her to the safety of the bunker. With three sharp raps on the door, she ushered everyone through door, and down the stairs.

"Garrison, don't shoot." Jordan called down the stairs.

"Hush honey. That takes out all the fun." Garrison's snide remark floated back up to meet Jordan. Jordan ignored the comment, as she locked the door, and moved down the stairs.

"Since when do we take hostages?" Garrison complained.

Jordan heard the hammer move backwards on the pistol that she had left with Garrison. She reached for the top of the wooden beam above the stairs, and then swinging her legs back and forth with as much force as she could gain in only a short window of time, let go of the beam. Gliding in the air, she landed on the floor in front of Penny.

"You are not going to want to do that." Jordan challenged.

"I think I am." Garrison huffed. "The idea was to kill the agents, not collect them, Jordan." Garrison pointed out through gritted teeth.

Jordan rolled her eyes. "Penny. Garrison. Garrison. Penny." Jordan introduced, as she pointed an outstretched hand to each of them when their respective name was mentioned.

"Penny?" Garrison waved the gun, theatrically. "That means what to me?" Garrison asked sarcastically. Which decidedly, was better suited for his face than Lane's, Jordan thought.

"Oh... Oh!" Jordan gasped, and waved her hands, as she nodded her head in understanding; "My niece." She and Garrison had been so close that it wasn't until that moment that Jordan realized how much of her past remained a mystery to him. She had assumed that Garrison knew about Penny. He probably knew she had a niece, but her name? That would be something too intimate for the Jordan she had formally been to share. She had not begun to give up details that were closer to her heart, until after Lane had cast out the demon, and she had formed a relationship with both Lane and Christ. It was through Lane's love and understanding nature that Jordan had come to reconsider her once ironclad opinion of men as a whole; Then, and only then, could she give up the intimate details of her life. Now, as she considered her friendship with Garrison, she realized that she had trusted him, solely, because he had been the first man in her life not to demand those intimate details and more. Garrison had been content to let Jordan be Jordan, whatever that meant.

Jordan moved into the tunnel. The small glow of the flashlight she held offered little illumination to the darkness beyond; darkness so devoid of light it seemed a living thing. She pulled Penny along with her, as she listened for Nick and Lane pulling up the rear. Having listened from the cover of the woods, Nick and Penny were already familiar with the plan. Jordan did not want to chance being outside the safety of the bomb shelter, or the tunnel with Penny in tow. With Garrison lying in the bomb shelter recovering from the brutal attack, Tommy had launched on him, Jordan did not want to chance upsetting him any further. Garrison would not understand what Jordan wanted to do. Garrison, like Jordan had once been, was an agent to his core.

He would carry out the mission. He could understand Jordan salvaging her niece that he could tolerate, but to ask him to grasp something so completely opposing of what they both had understood to be logical thinking would be too much. She would give the call to every man and woman that desired something beyond what they had found with Black Heart, and at the end of that call whoever was left standing against them would die.

Jordan prayed that a good number of the agents would respond to her call. She had no idea how many men and women were in the woods, waiting for an opportunity to take them out, but she hoped that God would soften their hardened hearts, and allow them to see the truth. In so doing, no matter how many, the numbers would be staggered.

Jordan couldn't help but be concerned for Penny. There were too many questions. How much training had she received? Or, was she merely a diversion tactic, placed by the bureau to throw Jordan off her game, and make her vulnerable enough to take down without too many lives lost? Whatever the reason that the bureau had enlisted Penny, she had planned on acting of her own volition of that Jordan was sure. Jordan had spent a long time in training learning to read people's eyes; there she could ascertain their real intentions. Penny had meant every word. She had indeed come to help Jordan.

Jordan pulled everyone close as she explained the gist of her plan, of God's plan. She then turned to Penny.

"Do either of you know how many agents are on scene?" Jordan asked. She knew the likely answer would be no. HOD rarely tipped his hand when on a recovery. The less an operative knew, the less they would be able to divulge to the enemy.

"We weren't briefed on our numbers. The information that we was given is very simple by nature, nothing too invasive." Penny shrugged. "I wish I knew more, but other than where some of the teams are stationed around the perimeter..." Penny lifted her hands, and then let them fall to her sides. "I guess I'm not of much use." Penny admitted.

Jordan's mouth fell open. "You actually know the exact coordinates of the other units?"

"Well, not longitude and latitude." Penny explained.

"Of course not," Jordan arched a brow, and sent a jubilant smile in Lane's direction, as she grabbed Penny pulling her into an energetic hug.

"Wow, Aunt Jordan! You sure are chipper these days." Penny accused, while casting a confused look in Lane's direction.

"Amen." Lane conceded dully.

Jordan cast another warning glare in Lane's direction.

"Okay so let's have it. Where are the other operatives?" Jordan asked while ignoring Lane's smile.

"Well there are two stationed to the west of the silo about two hundred feet from where we were." Penny pointed in the direction she knew the silo to be in. "Two are stationed on the south wall of the barn, and two on the roof."

"Gone," Jordan interrupted with a nonchalant wave of her hand.

Penny gave a slight nod.

"Two in the house," Penny pointed to the door leading into the house with an uncomfortable glance.

"Gone," Jordan informed.

Penny cast an unbelieving look in Jordan's direction. Lane nodded his concurrence that they were indeed taken out.

"I did a sweep of the perimeter before meeting up with you. There seems to be no immediate threat, just outside the entrance to the bunker, as far as I can tell." Jordan waved her hand in a side to side fashion to indicate the hatch leading into the bunker.

"Thar's true." Nick added. "Penny and I had just been ordered to break post and move closer to the house by central command."

"Break post?" Jordan's brow knit, as her eyes fit Nick with an uneasy glare. "Since when does central command ever advise operatives to break post?" Jordan was moving now. She shifted her weight from foot to foot. Her finger resting on her chin, Jordan's eyes narrowed in concentration. Something felt off She couldn't shake the feeling that she was somehow missing something. Central command lived and died by sticking to the post. You never left the position given. It was important that operatives did not move freely about on a detailed mission. It would leave open the very real possibility that someone get killed on their side. The operatives were never given the position of other key players in order to keep them from being able to give up their own people when captured, but the team was given the exact position of the person of interest.

Each team was told to stay put and watch closely for any movement. The perimeter was to be guarded at all cost. No one moved. There would be only one reason for Nick and Penny to be told to move in closer... Jordan hoped that it wasn't true. She prayed that no one had been listening to Penny, as she declared herself ready to leave Black Heart by whatever means possible. Jordan wanted to send the call over the radio to have all of the agents that were fed up with life to know that there truly was another way and that it could be obtained if all was willing to stand together and fight. Regardless of the numbers, Jordan, Lane and Garrison had all vowed to fight until the bitter end, but the odds would tilt in their favor if others would join in the fight.

"What are you thinking?" Lane asked, as he laid a hand on her shoulder.

"I'm not sure, but..." Jordan tuned to the bunker. Lane jerked to attention. Nick and Penny both crouched defensively.

The sudden blast had been unmistakable. They had at last found the bunker. The door leading into the bunker had no doubt been blasted open. Garrison would be exposed to unknown quantities of the enemy forces. The room would be a spray of bullets, as Garrison lay in the cot, dead, before he even had the chance to react. Then just as Jordan's thoughts had been snatched from her head, the unmistakable sound of machine-gun-fire filled the air.

CHAPTER

44

Finally, making it to a cab, John eased into the backseat. Everything hurt. His legs were in constant burning agony. He was thankful to be away from the compound. He wanted to relax in the knowledge that he would be with Cynthia soon, but he knew that would be a mistake. No matter how many precautions he had taken, someone could be on his trail right now.

Manning the observation room the day that Garrison had brought Jordan back to The Garden to hide had taught John well how elusive a Black Heart agent could be. The thought sent a chill down John's spine, as he scrutinized the cab driver.

His bearded face was clad with sunglasses, and a low riding New York Yankees hat; A disguise? John's curiosity peaked, as the man peered into the rearview mirror several times. Why was the man looking back so much?

John decided to test the man. If he was in fact an agent, then he would not react well to John's asking him to pull over so he could get out. Satisfied with the theory, John pointed to a random bookstore.

"Right here will be fine." John said, as he gave a casual wave of his hand. The driver knit his brow and gave John a look of concern. Finally, with a shrug, the driver pulled over.

"That's fine. It'll be eleven fifty." The driver informed, as he tuned to look at John. "Although," The man waved his hand, "None of my business."

"What?" John's tone was sharper than he had intended, but he was tired. He was in no mood to be played by a spy. He hurt everywhere.

He needed a shower, but couldn't imagine taking one, unless it was cold water. But, the thought of cold water on sore and knotted muscles did not appeal.

"Well you don't have to be rude." The bearded cab driver complained. Not waiting for an answer to his earlier question, the driver continued. "Look the way I see it, you need a hospital a lot more than you need a bookstore."

"Oh." Was all John could think to say? He pointed to the rearview mirror, as if to ask for permission to view his reflection. The driver promptly turned the mirror in John's direction. John gasped. He hardly recognized himself. His face was cherry red with several tiny blisters on his cheeks and chin. The sclera of his eyes was mapped with tiny red lines. His eye lids hooded over with exhaustion and to make matters worse, he still had his black t-shirt over his head. John shook his head as he slowly removed the soaked shirt from around his head.

"I wish I could say I look worse than I feel." John offered. "Look, I need to go about thirty miles down the road. I have money. I just don't have a lot of time." John paused for a moment, as he studied the busy street; he traced the window with his index finger. When he looked back at the driver his eyes were filled with tears.

"I don't know who to trust. I hope I can trust you." John paused. He sucked in air, and winced, as the salty tears burned his cheeks on the way down his face. It was insult to injury. He was aching all over, and now here he sat in this cab bearing his soul to a man that could very well be the enemy. "I have to go to my wife. She's pregnant, and our friend's children are with her." John shook his head. He felt so hopeless. Who was he? One man not trained in the ways of battle, against a whole corporation. Jordan, Garrison, and Lane were somewhere trying to take down Tommy Hayden, as if that were not a formable enough threat; they would most likely be dealing with agents from Black Heart as well. John knew wishing he had the assistance of their well-trained minds would not make it so. He had no choice.

John thought about his escape from The Garden. It had been treacherous and there were many opposing forces, yet, with God's grace he had been triumphant. He took a deep cleansing breath. No, he wasn't his friends with years of espionage, or whatever to rely on in a crunch, but he had something better: he had the love of an omnipresent God, he had faith in his God, and he knew without a doubt that no force on earth could separate him from God's love and grace. No matter where he was, what he was faced with, it did not escape the knowledge of God.

John sat up straighter, and ran his fingers through his hair. He dusted the white particles from his clothes, and raised his head to meet the gaze of the concerned driver. He was a child of the King, and it was time he started to look and act like it.

"I need to go to Morristown, New Jersey. I have to be with my family. There are some really bad people trying to kill me, trying to kill my family and friends; I have to be there to protect them." John's eyes were filled with determination and doubt, both wrestling for center stage. His heart ached for someone to be on his side. He needed to get to Cynthia. He could only imagine how frightened she must be to have to care for someone else's children in the midst of something so awful that you doubted your ability to protect yourself.

At first, doubt colored the driver's face, but then, he scrutinized John taking in every piece of the picture that was John; the man's eyes narrowed with resolve.

"Buckle your seatbelt." The simple command seemed in some way to be a warning. Though his shoulder ached with the movement, John wasted no time complying with the driver's wishes.

"Name's Ed by the way," Ed threw over his shoulder.

John leaned forward, offering his hand. "John..." John's head slammed into the back seat. At that moment he was thankful for the warning. Had he not put on his seatbelt, John was sure he would be sliding across the backseat, as if he were surfing.

"You said thirty minutes; have you there in twenty." Ed promised, or maybe threatened as he weaved in and out of traffic. John closed his eyes, no longer able to stomach the mere misses. Tires squealed, and a horn blew. John opened his eyes just in time to see Ed almost career into the rear of a black sedan. John's body was propelled forward. His hands flew out to the sides, seeking purchase. His body abruptly stopped, as the seatbelt came to its limit and with a violent snatch, John's head was again slammed into the thankfully cushioned backseat.

By the time the cab crossed the state line, John felt like he was the sole survivor of some animated episode. His eyes felt as though they were spinning. He placed his hands on either side of his head to ward off the buzzing in his ears. He felt nauseous and disoriented. When the cab slowed at a caution light, John knew he was only a couple of miles from the cabin, he relaxed a little.

"Up here on the right is a mom and pop store; Joe's grocery. You can let me out there." John still did not know whether to trust the guy, and even if he could, arriving at the cabin in a cab, would blow any chance he had at anonymity. He had not provided the exact address to the driver. John had kept the description vague about where he would be going. The cab probably had some kind of GPS monitoring system that would allow any member of Black Heart with access to the records, insight as to where he was. As it was, he had already taken too big a risk with his family's lives.

John stepped from the cab, and thanked Ed, after handing him a one hundred dollar bill.

"Anytime," Ed called. John simply smiled, as he hurried away before Ed could start the car. He didn't want to be struck in the empty parking lot by a cab that should've had plenty of room.

Squealing tires, the cab raced away. John jumped on the curve outside the small country store.

An old basset hound with white and black splotches lay in a pile of wrinkles next to three rocking chairs made of sequoia wood. The dog twitched an ear at the squealing tires but gave no other sign that the event had disturbed his slumber. A screen door gave off a loud metallic screech, as a small bell hanging on a triangular-shaped piece of wood further announced his arrival. John sent an annoyed glare in the bell's direction. He thought having both the squeaky screen and bell was over kill.

A large plain-wood counter wrapped around the left side of the room and held an out dated register. Boiled peanuts, pickled pigs' feet and Penrose sausages flanked a glass container of steaming baked goods. John's stomach betrayed his hunger with a growl. He was starving, but he didn't have time for much. Grabbing a coke and 2 cream-filled donuts, John was almost through with the second donut before the transaction was complete.

The old man behind the counter looked more like a mad scientist than a small business owner. His unruly gray hair spiked frantically in every direction. A bald spot in the center of his head was covered in age spots. His miniscule pointy nose was barely able to maintain the silver wire rimmed reading glasses he wore. Wise brown eyes, dulling with age, peered over the top of the abused glasses that were adorned with duct-tape to keep the lens held stationary. The simple white dress shirt he wore was tucked deep into navy blue work pants that rested high on his waist, and were cinched tight with a belt causing the front of his pants to pleat awkwardly.

"Mr. Stokes." John greeted.

"John." Mr. Stokes returned the greeting in a dull hum-drum tone.

"He in the back?" John asked.

"In the back", was Mr. Stokes' simple reply. John tossed his napkin in a small white trash can, and stepped through the back door. As greasy as ever, Max stood in front of an old '67' Chevrolet Camaro. He turned, wiping his hands on an oil covered blue cloth. His black hair, feathered to the side was touching his ears. Sweat dripped off the end of an ample nose, making splatter marks on his simple black t-shirt. He wiped the oily cloth across his forehead, leaving a smear of oil in its wake. Blue eyes with brown rust stains danced with the smile that erupted across a mouth full of gleaming white teeth but just as quickly, the smile faded as shock took its place.

"John!" Max called, as he tucked the rag into the back pocket of his faded and torn jeans.

"Max! Good to see you!" John smiled, as he threw his hand around Max's neck. Max stepped away, alarm filling his face.

"Man, John, you look like you've been through a war zone." Max complained.

"Yeah I feel like it, too." John countered.

"Hey did you get that package I sent?" John asked while casting a longing glance in the direction of the cabin.

"Yeah, about that..." Max rubbed a hand through his mussed hair.

Recognition filled John's eyes.

"Oh, man, if it's not enough..." John offered.

"Hey, kill the motor, man. More like, it was too much. John I could put a down payment on a house. What are they paying you?" Max asked, as he rubbed his hand across the back of his neck and allowed a nervous laugh.

"Hey, not me," John said raising his hands in the air. "Cynthia, she's stockpiled all the money that Black Heart has given her for profiling. We've been on mission trips mostly and then keeping the kids for the Gates'." John paused to catch his breath. Everything seemed to be finally moving in slow motion. It was as though for the first time standing out behind the old store, chatting with a friend about nothing important had erased all of the events of the day. A day that he felt had lasted a millennium!

"Well, you know we've not used any of it. Besides. . . what you did. . ." John's eyes filled with tears.

Max waved a hand... "It was no more than what you would have done for me." Max smiled.

"You got that right, brother." John laughed. "Hey I need to..."John was peering off in the direction of the cabin again.

"Yeah, I know. Tell Cynthia hey for me." Max called, as John was walking away.

"Oh, John," Max interrupted.

"Yeah?" John turned quizzically, to Max, as he waited impatiently for him to continue.

"Just... I rode by the cabin earlier today."

"Was something wrong... the kids? Cynthia?" Terror blazed a trail like hot coals through John's psyche. His feet were suspended in limbo, between the cabin and Max. His right side pulling to the cabin, as his left side urged him to stay and listen, John felt completely frustrated. It was worse than climbing the ladder for what seemed hours, and after that, looking up to hundreds of feet yet to climb.

"Whoa, man! Chill out!" Max cast John a disapproving glare. "You need to do some of that singing stuff that you do to calm your nerves." Max eyed John, curiously. "They're fine John, but I drove further up the road. You know the old farm, up near the end of the road?" Max snapped his fingers, as if something had suddenly cleared up in his mind; "The old Maddox farm?" Max fit John with a quizzical, look.

"Yeah, that's the farm up the street where that man went crazy, and killed his wife and children, right?" John eyed Max. John didn't mean to rush. He felt better that Cynthia, and the children were okay, but it didn't change the fact that he desperately wanted to get to them.

"Yeah, that's the place." Max admitted.

"I know about it. Cynthia hates the place; says its pure evil." John laughed, "Almost wouldn't concede to buying the property." John rolled his eyes.

"Well, I don't know what's wrong with the place, whether it be spiritual or otherwise," Max threw his hand up and pointed in the direction of the farm, as he shook his head. "Whatever it is, the place does seem to attract an awful lot of negative attention." Max glared in the direction of the farm.

"How do you mean?" John asked, as he too, was looking in the direction of the farm.

"It's probably nothing, some hunters." Max shook his head, as if the very act could change his mind. He turned his attention back to John and smiled.

"What do you mean hunters?" John asked, as worry filled his mind and spilled over into his senses. His fingers and toes tingled with the harnessed energy that he was holding at bay. He wanted to get to Cynthia and the children now more than ever.

"Oh, just that I heard some gun fire up by that..." Max stood slack-jawed, as John ran headlong for the direction of the cabin.

45

The walls were sprayed with shrapnel, debris littered the floor, and Garrison was nowhere in sight, as far as Jordan could see. Penny filed into the room behind Jordan and in front of Nick. Lane held up the rear.

The enemy forces had not yet begun filling the room. Jordan peered over at Lane who was already acting out her thoughts. Lane ushered Nick under the stairs, in order to hide him from the enemies' prying eyes. Jordan nodded her approval, as she then grabbed Penny and moved for the hulled out portion of the wall where the hide-a-bed was to be housed. However, crazy the farmer may have eventually become, he knew how to get the most out of a small enclosed area. Jordan couldn't help, but allow a moment of simple appreciation for the deliberate use of space.

It wasn't so much that everything in the room, down to the simplest shelf though it did have a use; it was more that each thing, no matter how intricate had a multifaceted purpose. For instance the hewed out wall where the bed was housed, not only allowed the room to have more space during the wake cycle, but it was also a deep enough area that at least two adults or one adult and two children could fit. Jordan had to think according to the picture that she had seen in the newspaper clipping, that even that had been purposeful because the farmer's wife was a very petite woman and their children also were small in stature. So the space would allow him to be on one side while his wife and children took up ranks on the other side. The bed could be closed while the individuals hid in the wall, not allowing the intruder had there been one to know of their hiding place.

Jordan pressed as far into the shadows as possible. Her mind was still seized with worry about Garrison. Though he had recovered enough to exhibit traces of his former sarcastic humor, he still, in some small way seemed frail. Jordan knew she would have to put her concern aside. Wherever Garrison was, she had to believe him capable of taking care of himself. After all, it was he who had trained her.

Jordan jerked to attention, as the sound of creaky steps filled the bunker. She waited until the room was as full of as many agents as would be sent down into the depths of the bunker to give the signal to shower the enemy with bullets. Jordan waited for more of the creaking sounds to come, but there was only silence. She lifted her hand to Penny, a signal not to move and then she hesitantly peeked through the opening at the stairs. Everything was so quiet that it sent chills up her spine. The room should have been a wash of agents by now.

Jordan scanned the room again. What was she missing? She thought about the bed as they had entered. Garrison certainly was not there. But something else, the bed was covered in debris. Some of the metal pieces of the door had actually embedded themselves into the mattress at nearly the moment of impact. Had Garrison been on the bed, he would have most certainly have been impaled. So the decision to move from the bed had to come, before the impact. But, what would he have been doing or thinking. Jordan shook her head. That's not the issue, she scolded herself. Jordan looked at the bed, now, with blinding awareness she realized what it was; Garrison's guns. The guns were not on the bed.

Jordan giggled, as she moved from the small hiding space and lifted the radio to her mouth. It was now or never because in a short while there would be no one to submit to her call. Not if Garrison had anything to do with it.

"My name is Jordan Buckley-Gates." Jordan used her maiden name so that the agents listening would be aware of who was speaking to them. "I was once like you. I was abused and put through such horrible things in the battlefield of my own home that I can't begin to tell you all of it in the short window of time we have here. I was given a 'chance' by Black Heart to have their version of a better life; a corrupt life of death and destruction. I thought I could harness the hate that drove me to do Black Heart's bidding, but soon I became no more than hate's puppet.

"I no longer cared what Black Heart would have me do. I was driven by a deeper, darker, stronger, more menacing force ... I became a slave to the desire of that force. It almost cost me the life of a person who was very special to me; my husband. In a fit of rage led by hate's bloodlust, I submitted my will to that dark master. I sank the cold-steel of my six inch blade into the chest of my husband, my love." Jordan paused, as the very real possibility of Lane's death, filtered through her mind, and paralyzed her senses. She prayed for the strength to go on, when all she wanted was to fall to the floor and weep.

Lane moved behind her and pulled her hair away from her shoulder, as he tenderly kissed her cheek. Strength filled her body. She straightened, as resolve crushed the anguish threatening to topple her spirit. Jordan gripped the radio and continued.

"Maybe you weren't abused or ignored. Maybe, you had a great start in life, but couldn't see it." Jordan didn't understand why, but she spoke to Garrison now. "Maybe Black Heart reached into your circumstance and took advantage of how trapped you felt. Maybe, the prospect of having your life mapped out for you was too much and Black Heart seemed to present a freedom that you never believed you could ever hope for, much less live. Maybe, that 'freedom' in some ways made you feel unstoppable and larger than life. I know for me that is exactly what it did." Jordan admitted, as tears splashed onto her face. "Or maybe, you feel trapped by the 'powers that be'. Maybe, you've been lied to and told there is only one way out." Jordan's hand covered her heart, as the sorrow felt like a living force crushing her. She smiled, as Penny emerged from the shadows of the hewed out wall. Jordan reached out a hand to Penny. Her eyes glistened with unshed tears, as she accepted Jordan's hand of freedom.

Penny panted through her tear-soaked joy, as Jordan witnessed the doors of a thousand prisons yield to the promise of a new life... a new life that shined its glimmering promise, brightly through her niece's eyes.

"I'm here to tell you there is, but one way to leave the iron-clad prison that is Black Heart. You must renounce your loyalty to Black Heart. You have to love yourself enough to seek the one true Master that will tear down the strongholds put into place by the enemy forces." Jordan looked around the bunker, taking in the eyes of first Penny, then Nick, and finally Lane; each one of them seemed to concur with what she had said. Though each of them had their own personal reality where Black Heart was concerned, it boiled down to the same thing; they all wanted free of Black Heart's grasp.

Jordan put the radio back up to her mouth, as she finished. "Don't mortgage your future to a company that cares nothing for you, a company that demands you become exactly what you fight to rid the world of. Freedom is not free. It was paid for with a price. Christ died for the freedom that you seek. How can killing stop killing? Hate breeds hate. Join us in our retaliation against the Hippocratic campaign that is Black Heart. Help us stand and eradicate its false doctrine, its life stealing campaign, forever."

Jordan turned then, as she watched the reactions of each of the three people sharing the bunker with her. She released the radio and as it fell to the floor, shattering into black bits, she felt the time for talk was over.

46

Something had brought about a definite change inside of him. He felt alive. He felt free. He felt strong. Garrison wasn't sure exactly what it was that had filled him with such courage. He had been lying there on the cot praying for something different. He wanted to feel the things that Lane and Jordan obviously felt. The difference in Jordan was palpable. He had meant it when he had vowed to get to know a God who could bring them out of the mess that they were in with Tommy Hayden.

Garrison knew he should, by all rights be dead, but instead he was still here. The moment the rope had been cinched around his neck, it was as if some tangible part of who Garrison was had died. In his place, a new creature had risen from the ashes of fear and uncertainty filling him with desperation like he had never felt before to live. In those moments of darkness, as Garrison's soul lay bare he prayed constantly for God to intervene. In that dark place, he felt a warm light begin to filter in through the blackened canvas of his soul and all at once, his whole being became unified in one all-consuming reality, a knowing; he was not alone!

Garrison felt so giddy with the fire of life growing within him that he couldn't sit still. It was as though his feet had to move. No longer able to lie in the bed, Garrison moved to the outer wall near the door to the tunnel. He had no sooner made it to the wall than the blast had punctured the silence and sprayed the room with shrapnel. The bed where he had been laying was hammered with bits of the bunker door that had embedded into the mattress. Garrison seized the opportunity.

Grabbing the guns on the bed, he ran head long into the now open door, showering the outer limits with a spray of machine gun fire. The moment he was through the door, he took mental inventory of the bodies littering the outskirts of the shelter.

"What are they teaching these new recruits?" Garrison griped as he took in the four bodies sprawled in various positions of unmoving death. He needed to get out of plain sight. Had someone expressed the importance of that very basic war strategy, the men and women cluttering the ground may still be alive. It just didn't make sense. What was Black Heart doing? These weren't the usual battle hardened agents that filtered out of the agency's ranks. It was as though Black Heart was mass producing agents, and in so doing sacrificing the very necessary training that any agent would need in order to survive the simplest of field operations.

Garrison flinched, as his mind filled with the image of both Penny's and Nick's young faces. He moved as close to the wall as possible, hoping to be cloaked from the enemy. Kneeling down, he leaned in close and claimed the mask of one of the fallen. His heart shuddered, as he moved to the others and did the same. Each of the faces was the same. Young faces littered the ground forever, frozen in this juvenile state. None of them to ever age. This was their last day.

As he lifted away the final mask, his hand shook big doe-brown-eyes stared back unseeing. Garrison crumbled to the ground beside the young body, as the anguish he had been holding at bay burst forth and rocked his body in uncontrollable sobs. How did it come to this? How had the company, he had believed the answer to the government allowing the dark elements of society to slip through the cracks defaulted to this?

Suddenly, Garrison felt sick; he had sworn his undying loyalty to this: he had believed with all of his being that Black Heart was the answer. Though he had thought the induction process murky at best, he had fully believed that it was the basis of Black Heart's true cause that would indeed make a difference. It was what Black Heart did at the end of the day that would justify any un-seedy act between the beginning and end... but as Garrison looked down into the young face, he knew with world-shattering-realization how wrong he had been.

He pulled the small body into his arms, as he cradled the young face, no more than fifteen or sixteen years old; a face that had not yet lived and never would. An anguished cry erupted from the core of his being, as his eyes searched the starry skies for answers that may never be his.

"Garrison?" Jordan's voice was but a whisper. Her heart ached to see him coddling this child. She knelt beside him and brushed the stray strands of light brown hair back from the tan face of the young boy. Her eyes flashed to the other bodies, briefly, taking in each of the other faces. All were young, too young but the child that Garrison held seemed to be somehow younger, still. His cherub face was frozen in a mask of horror, his body littered in debris. Jordan turned her attention back to Garrison who was staring into the sky with tears streaming from his eyes. A strangled cry of why escaped his lips and remained unanswered. She had none to offer.

Life was too short and peering into the young face, though she had no way of knowing how long his life had been; she knew it was not nearly enough time for one to discover the wonders that life had to offer. Jordan remembered the shots she had heard. So that was it. Garrison believed it was by his hand that each of the young lives had tragically ended.

"Jordan, look at this." Lane's voice pierced the uneasy silence.

"Dear Lord!" Jordan gasped as she bent, and examined all of the child corpses; "There's no bullet wounds. They were all killed by the blast." Jordan turned to the tree line. She wasn't seeing the shrubbery or the trees they had dimmed, as she looked passed their green wall to the object of her intense need to retaliate.

"This ends, now!" Jordan growled, as she pulled the weapons from each of the young bodies, and closed each of their eyes.

Lane grabbed her arm holding her gently, but firmly. "Vengeance is mine, saith the Lord."

"It's not vengeance I seek, it's retaliation!" Jordan spat. She pointed to the fallen children as she, again faced Lane. "For what happened to them. They were never meant to survive this. They were on a suicide mission. I will end this! I will not allow Black Heart to continue this kind of..." Jordan's eyes filled with fierce determination, as her mind searched for the words that did not seem to be enough. So she left it unsaid. She walked to him and took his face in her hands and spoke pointedly to his heart. "This was a suicide mission." Jordan turned to Garrison then.

"Grieve them later. I need you now." Jordan said, as she started for the tree line.

"Aunt Jordan?" Penny's desperate call pulled Jordan back for the moment. Jordan turned and grabbed Penny's hands.

"Penny, I don't have time to train you in this and with all of the uncertainty…" Jordan pointed to the children littering the ground. "I can't be sure I can protect you. I need to be focused. I don't want anyone to be killed unnecessarily; least of all you. I need you to keep your eyes and ears open." Jordan looked to Nick then. "Both of you." Jordan pointed to Lane, Garrison and then herself. "The three of us will separate to cover more ground." She looked to Lane; he simply nodded his consent.

"I want you and Nick to head south of the silo. Don't veer off the path. You will eventually come to a creek; follow it east for two miles. Then cut through the forest, to the north. In about three hundred feet, you should come to a cabin. It belongs to our friends. The cabin should be empty, but that does not mean that it is. If it's not, then tell them I sent you. If it is empty, there is a key under the mat on the back patio. Go in, get something to eat and wait for us there."

Penny's eyes filled with tears. Jordan pulled her into a hug. "I need you both to be strong. You have survived this long. Watch each other's backs and do not stop until you reach the cabin. If anyone tries to stop you…" Jordan leaned in closer. "Anyone! Shoot!" Jordan let her hand fall from Penny's cheek. She, then turned back to the trees and headed straight for the place she believed central command to be.

Jordan turned back, once again. "Garrison this is a recovery mission. We will disable as many of the enemy forces as possible without lethal force but if the situation requires it…"

"I won't hesitate to kill if I have to." Garrison conceded.

Jordan nodded, as she disappeared into the tree line.

Jordan ducked behind trees and reached around using the butt of her pistol to knock out unsuspecting child-agents. Removing their belts, she tied their hands and feet behind their backs. She would make a sweep of the forest later to collect the hostages at gun point. She paled, as she thought about how easily thwarted the agents in the house and on the roof had been. It all made sense now. A few times, Jordan happened across some of Lane's or Garrison's recovery effort. She smiled at the difference in tactics used to detain the children. For example, Garrison had stuck to the belt method she used while Lane had used nature to do his bidding; a vine would be tied around the bodies of two children that were on opposite sides of a tree. She thought the method just as effective and maybe a little more comfortable for the detainee. She would have to have Lane show her the different forms of plant life and what was safe to touch human skin. She paled at the thought of tying one of the child agents up with poison ivy.

Once, Jordan walked passed a young girl whose blue eyes filled her face and emanated fear. Jordan bent to the girl who automatically retreated from what she perceived as a threat. Flopping like a fish out of water, the girl managed to put a goodly distance between herself and Jordan. Leaning in close, Jordan gave the girl a smile and nod of appreciation.

"You're safe, now." Jordan whispered, as she pushed the girl's blond hair away from her face. Big blue eyes begged to be let go. "I can't let you go, sweetie. You would just get yourself killed." Jordan searched the girl's eyes for understanding.

"Please." The girl whispered.

"I'll be back." Jordan leaned in and placed a tender kiss on the girl's head. "I promise." Jordan said, as she moved away.

The girl had nodded her understanding, as tears slipped from her eyes. Jordan hated to leave the girl tied up, she knew all too well how desperate and disorienting not having use of your hands could be. The time she had spent in the farmhouse tied up while seeing Tommy hurt her loved ones had given her all the insight on the subject she would ever need or be able to stand. Still, she could not allow empathy to color her judgment. The last thing that they needed was a bunch of scared teenagers playing army games in the woods while they tried to neutralize the enemy.

The perimeter had been scouted and all the hostages were detained waiting to be escorted to safety and to be deprogrammed as soon as possible. Along the way, two precious lives had been forfeit an unfortunate, unavoidable outcome.

Two young men, older than some of the others ambushed Jordan. She had let her guard down for a second. Underestimating the enemy, she leaned around a tree to crack one of them over the head. Instead, he had side stepped the attack and grabbed Jordan's arm; wrenching the gun from her hand while his friend circled around the tree and claimed Jordan's other arm. He twisted the arm violently behind her back. Leaning in close to her ear, he breathed seductively as if to warn her of the unwanted outcome she would face should they keep their believed upper hand.

"Well look what we have here." The young man taunted.

"Oh boy! Must be our lucky day!" The one Jordan had been about to knock out claimed.

"Or not." Jordan hissed, as she slammed the heel of her foot hard into the top of the boy's foot behind her that was twisting her arm. The boy squealed in protest and lost control of her arm. Without wasting time, she shoved her head back. Hearing a loud crunch and then a wail of complaint from her attacker, Jordan knew she had obtained her goal. The second one reached for a gun and fired a shot but Jordan moved. Unfortunately, the bullet hit the boy behind her, as he was petting his broken nose. Brain matter exploded through the air, splattering bits and pieces onto the shrubbery and foliage behind him.

Jordan could see the intent in the young man's eyes that was holding the gun. He would stop at nothing to make Jordan pay for the death of his friend. No time to waste, Jordan whirled around and kicked the boy's hand. The gun sailed through the air, landing harmlessly out of reach. Then, as her foot made an arc in front of his face she pushed up, thrusting his nose into his brain. Blood burst forth, frosting everything red in its path.

As she made her way closer to where central command was stationed, a faint glow filled the forest. The congestion of trees opened up to a clearing that held a small aluminum travel trailer. Moving up to the side of the trailer, Jordan spotted Garrison at the rear. A quick glance to the front of the trailer, told Jordan what she desperately wanted to know; Lane was well and he too had been set on taking this operation down from the top. Jordan gave a smile of approval, as she then turned to Garrison. Signaling for Garrison to move to the other side of the door, Jordan then, signaled for Lane to watch the rear of the trailer for anyone exiting that way.

Jordan held up three fingers, as she one at the time lowered each. The third finger fell, and Jordan snatched the door open. Peering inside, she was astonished! There was no one in the trailer. Immediately filled with dread, Jordan backed away from the trailer as though it were a viper about to strike. Lane screamed something that she was unable to understand and then all at once she and Garrison were being catapulted through the air.

CHAPTER

47

A dim light broke through a dip in the canvas of greenery, painting the sky a warm pinkish-purple haze. Not a cloud dotted the horizon, as John darted through the last of the thick foliage. His eyes swam with tears, as the faint glow from the kitchen light pierced the shroud of darkness, untouched by the still rising sun.

Cynthia would be in her slippers and robe, preparing breakfast for their young visitors, as they grabbed the last moments of sleep afforded them. Though, John's body ached from the abuse he had suffered the day before, he could not give into the pain. He pushed past the agony, and pressed onward to the dim light that only hinted to the brightness of their future. Soon the children lying in bed, waiting for breakfast to be prepared, would be their own.

So caught up in the moment, John had not seen the two dark figures crossing the backyard to his cabin. The closer John drew to the cabin the brighter his mood became. Pretty soon the song in his heart could no longer be denied.

"I can only imagine." John started his favorite song again. John stopped mid-verse. His eyes averted to the back of the house. At last the sun had filled the sky with enough light that John could make out two dark figures searching the mat near the back steps.

"Hey, get away from my house." John heaved the warning at the intruders.

Suddenly, the girl turned and hoisted a pistol. John froze, as his hands drifted automatically into the air.

"I'm unarmed." John called to the girl.

The girl's hand began to shake and her eyes filled with tears as she appeared to be caught in some sort of an inner turmoil.

"I live here..." John offered. His mind was scrambling for the right thing to say. It felt vital in some way that he could not make sense of.

John watched, as the boy's hand moved to the top of the gun. His hand pushed downward, as his other arm protectively pulled the girl into a tender embrace. Her shoulders sagged into a shudder of violent sobs. The back door swung open, Cynthia stood mouth agape with a dish towel in her hands.

"John?" Cynthia gasped. "What's...? Oh my God!" A shroud of darkness filled the outer edges of his vision, as Cynthia's concerned cry echoed through his mind.

Cynthia sat on the couch in front of John's supine body, caressing his brow with aloe. Penny had been pacing for nearly an hour. Cynthia tried to comfort Penny with little success but at least, for now she had halted the pitiful chant of 'I killed Aunt Jordan's friend'. Had it not been for the time spent in the slums of third world countries, trying to defuse the chaos that could erupt in less than favorable conditions, Cynthia did not know if she would have had the knowledge, let alone patience to deal with such a scene as this.

Cynthia watched Penny now, as her lower lip quivered and her shoulders sagged in utter remorse. John wasn't dead and even if he were Penny had in no way caused his death. The girl had not even been able to pull the trigger. Cynthia's heart ached for the loved ones of these child agent's fallen comrades. She could not imagine the same fate befalling their precious child. Her eyes misted, as she caressed the tiny bump beneath her heart.

The basic lifesaving skills they had been taught by The Truth served her well. She was able to check John's pulse and breathing, both seemed normal. Cynthia knew from the mission trips in those same third world countries that John had merely fainted due to fatigue. Also, the fight or flight state his parasympathetic nervous system had been in for such a prolonged period had no doubt served to exacerbate an already stressed situation; resulting in John's body shutting down for a time. Quite simply, John needed rest, and lots of it. So after bathing his burns in aloe, Cynthia covered him up with a light blanket to ward off chills.

Finally, satisfied that she had done all within her power to make John comfortable, Cynthia turned to Penny. Reaching out her hand, Cynthia pulled Penny along with her to the bathroom. As usual, the guest bathroom assaulted her sense of adventure, as the different ornamentations depicting scenes of beaches, overlooked by majestic lighthouses came into view. Cynthia only ventured into the bathroom when cleaning the area. She and John had not yet been able to move into the cabin so company had never used the bathroom. She felt a small sense of pride to finally have not only the children but now Penny enjoy the beautifully adorned room. Cynthia pushed back the shower curtain: a large myriad of a lighthouse overlooking the ocean splintered with white-capping waves, boasted proudly of Cynthia's dream getaway. She ran a warm bath and left for a short time to gather something warm for Penny to wear.

"Here's a towel and wash cloth. Take a warm bath. It'll make you feel better." Gently squeezing Penny's hand, Cynthia added. "John is only sleeping, sweetie. He's been through a lot." Cynthia placed a hand lovingly to Penny's cheek. She searched Penny's bewildered eyes.

"None of this is your fault." Cynthia caressed the girl's cheek with her thumb. "Take your time, baby girl. Come out when you are ready." Cynthia closed the door behind her. It was hard to leave Penny alone while she seemed so small. Her eyes told of pain that Cynthia had seen once before in the eyes of Jordan. That time seemed to be years past, but it still haunted Cynthia's subconscious, and from time to time would come to the forefront of her thinking.

How could a family be so dysfunctional, and where were the people who were supposed to protect children in families like that?

Cynthia had a very different reality as a child. She had been loved and cherished. She missed her family and hated that they had been lied to. She hated that she had not been able to go see her parents. To do so would only endanger them; Black Heart would not allow such a breech. She was said to be dead and though, she was now a missionary for The Truth, her status quo would remain the same, or her family would reap the consequences of such a breach of confidence.

Cynthia only had what little information she had been able to pull from Nick while trying to care for John, and sooth Penny. She did not know how Penny had come to be involved with Black Heart, but however it had come to be, Cynthia knew that the commitment would be forever; unless she could make sense of the file that John had risked his life to retrieve.

Cynthia walked disheartened back to the kitchen, as she prayed for peace in the lives of her friends. She shivered, as she thought of the far reaching hand of the bureau. She had to put the thought from her mind, as she turned to face Nick. She looked into the deep brown eyes of the young man before her. His hair was too long and fell loosely to one side. Every now and again, Cynthia would witness him flip his head casually to the side to force the unwanted obstacle away from his line of vision. He was handsome with his cloud of dark hair, and eyes that seemed to harbor scenes that would be years beyond what was reasonable for one so young to have witnessed.

"And I bet you could use some breakfast." Cynthia called to Nick, where he stood next to the fireplace, tracing the mahogany chimney while studying the painting of the hands folded in supplication.

"John bought that for me from a small shop in Honduras. The owner hand painted it. The lamps are blown glass that he etched the image into to match the painting. It's my favorite." Cynthia smiled simply at the memory of the old man's weathered face as he proudly hoisted the painting up for John's approval. She was standing next to the painting already immersed in the beauty of the lamps.

"Why?!" Nick's voice rang above the crackling fire and calming music playing on 93.3, her favorite Christian music station. John stirred a little on the couch and just as quickly fell back into his fitful slumber.

The hurt and anger filling Nick's tone almost made Cynthia want to retreat, but then she felt that familiar calm enter her spirit. It was the Holy Spirit reassuring her that all would be well.

Cynthia collapsed into a chair at the small kitchen table. She gestured to an empty chair next to hers. Long moments stretched out, as it seemed Nick would not accept her invitation. She turned to the stove for a moment, as she regarded the glowing red of the indicator lights. She had finished breakfast, and turned the burners and oven on low to keep the meal warm until the children roused. They were bound to be exhausted after the long trip. Also, sleeping in a bed that was not their own, she knew from the mission trips could make for many sleepless nights. She had been washing up some dishes when she heard the commotion out in the backyard. She was surprised that she hadn't already heard the trilling voices of the children filling the house.

Cynthia had been so lost in her thoughts that the grating of the chair on the wood floor, as Nick was sitting down, startled her.

"Sorry." Nick said flatly.

"Not at all." Cynthia smiled. "What bothers you about the painting, Nick? If you don't mind my asking." Cynthia pulled a napkin from a silver napkin holder in the middle of the table. The intricate design of musical notes always made her smile. She began folding the napkin in fours, trying to occupy her hands. Her nerves were stretched to their limit but at the moment, everyone needed her to stay calm.

Her heart sank, as the scowl from a moment ago returned to Nick's young face. He pushed a lock of his shoulder-length-brown-hair-back over his ear as his brown eyes darted to the painting once again.

"Begging; I don't like the way the hands seem to beg someone. I've never gotten anywhere begging." Nick scowled at the painting; the disgust in his eyes growing with each moment.

"Ah, supplication." Cynthia said as she too, scrutinized the painting but from a different perspective.

"What?" Nick asked obviously taken aback by the word Cynthia had used to describe something that he found so utterly repulsive.

"Supplication…" Cynthia smiled.

"Nick have you ever loved anyone?" Nick's face reddened, as his eyes drifted automatically to the bathroom door. Cynthia allowed a moment of silence to stand between them. She wasn't surprised by his silent proclamation, but felt the admission of love deserved a certain amount of reverence.

"What would you do if she were hurt? Would you be willing to die to save her life?" Cynthia cautiously laid the napkin on the table, as she allowed the question to marinate in his mind. She didn't want to rush his answer. Nick caught the corner of a placemat. His finger traced the musical notes in thought. His eyes lifted to Cynthia's, as his lower lip quivered. He fought back the tears, shimmering in his deep-brown eyes with a defiant shake of his head.

"I know you think I hesitate because I wouldn't," Clearing his throat, Nick thrust a hand through his thick-wavy-brown hair. "But I'm not like your average teenager. Neither is Lesley... Penny." Nick corrected, still having trouble with the true identity of this woman-child he had openly proclaimed to love.

Cynthia smiled at the understandable mistake, as Nick continued. "We both lived in a war-zone long before Black Heart entered our lives. So when you ask me if I would die for Penny, I think of the times that I would have gladly died just for the sake of no longer having to be me." Nick pointed a shaky finger toward the bathroom door, as he lost the battle to the tears. Cynthia's eyes followed his finger, as tears spilled onto her own face; she too lost the same battle.

"She is the only thing in my life that has ever been worth living or dying for." Nick whispered.

Cynthia dabbed the tears from her eyes, as she handed Nick a napkin.

"If there were someone with the power to grant her life, what would you be willing to do?" Cynthia strained through the tears in her throat to make her words clear.

"Beg." The word was so quiet that Cynthia would not have known Nick had spoken it, had she not read it on his lips. But, the finality that filled his eyes made the word seem as though it had been screamed from a mountain top.

"That's what that painting means to me. I would do everything in my power to protect those I love, but when it's beyond my power; I ask the One with the power." Cynthia said, as she pointed to the heavens.

48

Light loomed above the trees, casting tendrils of dancing rays that pierced the canopy, and made the burnt orange-red of the leaves come to life as if they were engulfed in flames. For a moment, it felt as though all was as it should be. Then, just as suddenly, the silence exploded into chaos. Jordan's eyes flickered several moments, not truly registering her surroundings. Then all at once, as though some unseen gate had been cast open, allowing every screaming and screeching, cacophonic abomination loose to plunder her hearing, the air exploded with sounds.

Jordan wanted to cover her ears, but try as she might, her arms would not obey. She winced, as a mind shattering pain seared through her head. Finally, emerging from the fog of confusion, Jordan realized she could not move. Her mind fragmented, as a thousand possibilities slammed into her imagination. With urgent need, she thrashed violently against the unknown trying to reclaim her freedom. Then, the unrelenting truth yielded to her awareness, it was all in her mind. Not once had she truly, moved. She had wanted to been desperate to but nothing happened. Something was around her neck.

Her eyes, still fighting for sight, through the blurry figures floating above her Jordan thrashed all the more and still nothing happened. Then, as if to push her further into the helpless ravine of lost hope, something was placed over her eyes blocking out even the blurred figures dancing in her vision above her. She was suddenly aware of how precious though distorted that tiny measure of vision had been. She could hear the muffled sounds of talking, though she could not make out what was being said. Beneath the paralyzed dark world, Jordan realized she may be at the end of her life. She may never see Lane's sweet angelic face or hold her children to her heart again. Jordan wanted to scream but nothing would come. No measure of hope swam to her consciousness; she knew there was nothing she could do. She was probably moments from being dead. Her only solace: her nephew was gone; he would no longer be able to harm her family. But, what about Black Heart...

Lane stood with tears in his eyes, as he watched the medics strap Jordan to the gurney and Velcro the neck brace into place. She was still, too still. Her eyes moved rapidly, searching always searching but other than that nothing. He had wanted to reassure her, but the medic had explained that she would be confused from the blast. It was as though all the circuits in a computer had been scrambled; that computer was her brain. The medic tried to explain it, but Lane could only register what was playing out before him. The medic placed the white gauze protectively over Jordan's eyes, but it was her reaction to the unwanted fabric that nearly dropped Lane to his knees. Her head reflexively pulled away from the fabric, and Lane knew in that moment that so many possibilities for an altered reality of what was really happening to her were probably showing their horrible lies to her subconscious mind. He could not even take solace in the movement because he knew the terror that it was based in. He could do nothing to reassure her. He could only stand by and watch helplessly as she filtered through the footage of those undesirable, possibilities and pray that she would find the truth... He prayed that somewhere down inside of her tortured psyche, she would remember what had happened and in so doing she would be able to piece together, at least in part, what she was truly experiencing.

None of it made sense. If only he would have seen the faint, flickering red light of the detonator a moment sooner. Had she not turned away from the blast to knock Garrison out of the way, they would both be dead. Lane's awareness of the detonator at all, had given them the only chance they had, but if only...

Now Garrison, having suffered only a few scrapes and bruises, thanks to Jordan landing on him, was gathering all of the teenagers at gun point with the help of the local authorities and ushering them to the jail until they could be debriefed and deprogrammed. So many hours of counseling loomed in the future of each of the teenagers. All of which, had been taken in by Black Heart, after Black Heart had killed a member of their family and insisted it had been Jordan who had committed the unforgivable atrocity.

Lane's head stayed in his hands all the way to the hospital in prayer. It wasn't a good sign that Jordan wasn't moving her lower body. They feared a neck injury and a possible brain injury as well. Lane couldn't stand not being able to talk to her, to tell her it would be alright. He wanted to hold her in his arms and protect her from whatever fears accosted her mind but every time someone so much as grazed her, she would scrunch the skin on her forehead and pull her head back away from the unwanted contact. Lane could imagine her eyes searching in a maddening race to discover what was upon her, just as they had done back at the site of the explosion. He was helpless to do a thing, and it was killing him. It was out of his hands.

Out of his hands... Lane straightened as the realism hit him. What was he thinking? It had never been in his hands. He controlled nothing. God had been was and always would be the One in control. With that, Lane eased his hand to Jordan's leg from where he sat on the long bench to the side of the gurney. His girth made it hard to not be in the way of the medic who was already holding on to the silver pole, mounted to the ceiling of the ambulance. Lane had managed to melt into the corner, and not present as much of a problem for the medic.

Now, as Lane surreptitiously laid a hand on Jordan's thigh, he glanced at the medic to be sure he had not violated some cardinal law of the medic's 'do not interfere with my patient hand book'.

The red headed medic, clad in his red and blue AMR uniform, seemed undaunted by Lane's hand on Jordan's thigh. His gloved hand assessed a bag of fluid hanging from a silver hook. With a nod, his green eyes floated to a monitor seated in a small cubicle beside the gurney. Pushing a button, the blood pressure cuff on her left arm, vibrated to life. The medic studied the numbers illuminated on the monitor, and then stood. Reaching across the small space, he opened a clear door and collected another bag of fluid and a length of plastic tubing. Turning to a row of drawers next to the chair, he occasionally sat in he claimed another IV. The medic strapped a tourniquet onto the bicep of Jordan's left arm and searched for a vein. Soon, he was busying himself with obtaining another IV.

Lane scooted forward, the tiniest of increments; he wanted to be at least, in part on his knees. It was there that he felt the closest to God. Things did not look good for Jordan. Her color was ashen. Her lips seemed a purplish-blue, though the medic had put a plastic oxygen device over her mouth and nose. The skin of her forehead remained in a scrunched position, but was starting to droop, as if she were losing the battle to the horrible thing that held her cocooned in a prison that only she was aware of. Fear slipped around Lane's heart, trying to separate him from the truth.

"You were not given a spirit of fear, my son." The words breathed across Lane's soul. Lane knew the passage of scripture, it was from, 2 Timothy 1:7; he had read it many times, while a child in the Cadotion village. It had been a great comfort and reminder that God was with him, and there was never anything he would need to fear. The nights in a village, on the edge of a river that skirted a forest, and nestled between two mountains could be a scary place for a young mind. All of the animal calls at times had seemed menacing.

"Remind me Lord." Lane whispered.

"You are more than a conqueror, my son, for I am with you always." (Romans 8:32 Isaiah 41:10) the words were like a salve to a jagged tear in his soul. Many times God had spoken to him, but this time was different. This time it felt as though, he was hanging on the edge of oblivion by the tips of his fingers waiting to fall into the deep to be consumed by the shadows that lurked beyond; shadows that filled him with fear and doubt. As he swung over the deep ravine of doubt, waiting for his world to pivot wildly with the loss of his soul mate, the still small voice of the Creator, of everything had reached down and lifted him up onto the solid ground of faith.

Things at the precinct were chaotic. Teenagers screaming their demands to be let out, or be allowed access to their attorney, filled the walls of the beige-dully-decorated-station. There were fifty one children with twelve cells available. So, the boys were divided up into groups of four, leaving the girls the remaining cell. Six girls were crammed into an eight by twelve cell; would have been seven, but Garrison had taken custody of a petite girl with blonde hair and huge blue eyes. The girl had adamantly insisted that she see Jordan. She had told Garrison over and over that Jordan had promised to come back for her. Something in the girl's eyes made Garrison feel for her. He felt that this was something that Jordan would want him to do and right now, he owed Jordan. She had saved his life. Not wanting to tip off the girl's cellmates, Garrison pulled the girl from their ranks insisting that she was being taken in for questioning. The ploy had worked; the other teenagers not in any hurry to spend time with the adults in charge of the jail, backed away from the cell doors.

The girl who had been a ball of fire back at the station, crushed as much of her minute form as possible to the passenger door. Garrison was thankful for the automatic locking system of the small brown Versa. He could only guess at the chaos that might ensue, had he physically activated the door locks to ensure her safety. Trying not to alarm the girl any further, he kept his eyes glued to the road as he drove to the hospital.

Garrison's heart skipped and stuttered in his chest as he pushed through the emergency department toward room eleven where Jordan was still being stabilized, or so that was the last update he had received. He finally managed to pull the girl's name out of her.

Kirsten, still in tow, her big blue eyes searched like a scared rabbit as she raced to keep up with Garrison's determined stride. Two nurses sat bantering about the weekend behind a curved mahogany desk. Black and white Formica gave the top of the desk a more homey appeal. The nurse with blond hair pulled back in a messy bun, wore a purple nurses' uniform, turned to acknowledge Garrison's and Kirsten's approach. The other nurse, with a black uniform, wore her brown hair in a shoulder length whimsical style that shrouded her young face and set off her blue eyes.

Garrison, in his black suit, and his CIA clearance badge, kept his stride knowing he would not be detained. Kirsten, on the other hand, fidgeted under the scrutiny of the nurse. Garrison, tucking the girl under his arm, pushed past the nurses' station. Two rooms past the desk, Garrison saw the number eleven. Again, his heart skidded into an unrecognizable rhythm. He wanted to leave. He wanted to stay, but nowhere in him did he want to see Jordan in a light that depicted her as less than the fierce, capable woman he had always known her to be. Even in the ally before she had slaughtered her attacker back when he had recruited her something about Jordan had screamed capable.

Kirsten touched the door, her eyes searched Garrison's. With a nod, he squeezed her arm lightly for assurance and then pushed the door open. He understood her fear, but he admired the bravery it took to step out when others clambered to be closest to the cell wall in order to be furthest from the police and Garrison. He tried to put the thoughts from his mind of what had possibly happened at the hands of Black Heart or the children's guardians to incite such fear of authority.

Kirsten had taken a bold step forward, insisting she be allowed to see agent, Jordan Buckley. "She promised..." Had been Kirsten's determined cry.

The hospital room was cold. As Garrison crossed the threshold a chill ran up his spine. Pulling off his coat, he detached his badge and tucked it in his pocket, and hung the coat around Kirsten's shoulders. The thin black shirt she wore had sleeves, but he doubted it would do much to ward off the chill in the room. Lane knelt in the corner, his massive six foot five form melted in a puddle of sobs in a way that made even him seem small. Garrison's eyes darted to the bed where Jordan lay. Tubes were exiting and entering her body everywhere, it seemed. Garrison's face blanched, as the blood drained from his head.

"She's just sleeping." Lane's voice interrupted the slow descent into dread that Garrison had been on.

Garrison, stunned, looked back at Jordan. Her face was bandaged covering all but her mouth and nose.

"They say it's a precautionary measure." Lane said, as he moved to Jordan's side, and claimed her hand. "The blast burned her retina. Their healing slowly, but the doctors feel it will heal more easily if she doesn't try to use her eyes." Lane caressed her hand, as he turned back to Garrison.

"Who do you have here?" Lane asked, as he pushed a lock of hair away from Jordan's face.

Garrison had never been more confused. If Jordan was going to be alright, then why was Lane crying when he entered the room? Ignoring the need for answers, Garrison turned to Kirsten.

"This is Kirsten Edwards. She was one of the child agents. She said she needs to see Jordan." Garrison said, as he placed a hand on each of Kristen's small shoulders. Kirsten pushed back into Garrison, as her head tilted up obviously enamored by Lane's bulk. Garrison rolled his eyes.

"Don't let him fool you, kid. His barks worse than his bite." Garrison smiled, and winked at Lane.

Taking the girl's hand, Lane smiled into her huge eyes and then releasing her hand, he abruptly turned and sent a bone-chilling growl in Garrison's direction. Having already slipped back into his scrutiny of Jordan's condition, Garrison jumped. Kirsten fell into a fit of laughter. Garrison turned a warning glare on Lane, and then side-stepped Kirsten, and moved closer to Jordan's side.

"She looks so..." Garrison couldn't find the words. Standing outside her room, his heart had only belied the precursor to the true battle that would wage within him, while trying not to lose control of his emotions. This was more than he could stand. His knees buckled. He tightened his grip on the bedrail, to maintain a standing position. He would be strong for her. He would not allow the anguish of seeing her so small, so vulnerable to cripple his senses. There were things he needed wanted to know.

"Her sight?" Garrison breathed. It was all he could do not to fall onto the bed and wail. It had been his doubts, his inadequacy in the field that had brought her to this. She had saved his life. She had, all but given her life to ensure that he survive the explosion. Looking at her now, in the hospital bed with tubes and bandages covering most of her body, Garrison's mind could not understand how she could be alright. In what reality did someone look like this, if all was well with them? It made no sense.

"It's hard to say. As I said before, it's a slow process. We will know more when the bandages come off, but again, the bandages are merely a precautionary measure to protect her eyes from over exertion during the healing process." Lane turned his attention back to Jordan.

"She had just fallen asleep, right before you came in. She's been awake for the better part of the day." Lane smiled at Jordan. "I think she's been worried about you."

"Me?" Garrison nearly, shouted the question.

The stern look from Lane was automatic. He immediately softened his features, as his eyes again returned to Jordan.

"Yeah, you know Jordan. Nothing is ever about her; the consummate caregiver to the very end." Lane smoothed a wrinkle out of her deep pink-cotton blanket. The blanket, like Garrison's nerve, seemed paper thin. Garrison knew the truth of what Lane was saying. It had been that protective nature that had almost cost Jordan her life. Lane cleared his throat, as the smile returned to his eyes.

"What can I do for you, Miss Kirsten?" Lane touched a hand to the chair behind where he stood, offering Kirsten a seat. She blushed, as she shook her head in refusal to his offer. Her eyes darted to Jordan's sleeping form and just as quickly fell; something in their blue depths seemed to betray her obvious disappointment that Jordan's condition would not allow her the time she needed to speak to her. It was then that Garrison had considered the possibility that the girl's desire to see Jordan may not be related entirely to the broken promise Jordan had made to return for her.

"Uh, Lane. .. How long do you think Jordan will be asleep?" Garrison asked while trying to get Lane to see the bigger need by sending the message, he could not speak aloud.

Irritation lined Lane's brow, as he started to open his mouth and then closed it again. Kirsten's downcast eyes studied Jordan, as her interlaced, fingers nervously fidgeted in front of her black shirt. Garrison casts a stern look in Lane's direction and tipped his head, indicating Kirsten to his side. A second later, Lane's features brightened as he at last caught on to what Garrison was alluding to.

"Can you give her an hour nap?" Lane's eyes seemed to be caught in a tug of war between the rest he knew Jordan desperately needed and the importance of what the girl's testimony could do for filling in the holes in the case they were trying to make against Mr. Stanton.

"No need." Jordan's voice filled with a conviction that temporarily stunned Garrison; it seemed out of place with how weak Jordan appeared.

"Lane, why don't you take Garrison to get us all something to eat? I'm starved and I'm sure Kirsten could use a bite to eat as well." Jordan's lips formed into a smile under the gauze, causing Garrison's heart to stutter. "Besides it'll give us girls time to get better acquainted and you could go check on the children while you're out." Garrison turned to Lane who seemed just as baffled by Jordan's request as he was.

"Stop standing there looking at each other like you don't know what to do; you just received your marching orders." Jordan snickered, as her hand went to her mouth and then turned to face Kirsten.

"Boys…" Jordan shook her head at Kirsten. Jordan tapped a hand on the bed next to her for Kirsten to sit down.

Kirsten collapsed to the bed in a fit of laughter. "Don't I know it?" Kirsten countered with a disgusted roll of her eyes.

Garrison looked at Lane confused.

"Don't look at me, looks like we're outnumbered. I'm going to get the food." Lane started for the door, as he tossed a look over his shoulder.

"I'd advise you to come with me before you become a prisoner of war." Lane laughed as he pulled the door open and disappeared into the hall.

Garrison was still trying to figure out how two against two would make him and Lane outnumbered, as he filtered into the hall behind Lane.

49

Folders lined the coffee table. Every piece of information available had been taken into consideration. Cynthia had poured through every remarkable and unremarkable event listed in the pages of each of the folders. As far as she could tell something in Mr. Stanton's folder like all of the others was missing. Cynthia brought all of the folders she had collected to the kitchen table because of its larger surface. Having exhausted all other methods, she decided to start focusing on the similarities in the gaps of each file. She already knew that each time there was a gap in a folder, it in some way was linked to every member of their group and Mr. Stanton. Every hole in each file was evidence lost that would connect every member to Black Heart in a significant or momentous way. The question remained who would want to make those connections disappear and why?

Cynthia plopped Mr. Stanton's file back onto the table, as she crossed to the coffee pot. It was about dinner time. She needed to get her casserole in the oven, and start getting the children washed up. She was at a standstill. She needed to have everyone involved, in the same room for questioning. Maybe that could shed some light into the dark holes of the past.

"Hey honey, you expecting company?" John's voice came from the mud room. Cynthia scrutinized his wounds. He was healing, albeit slowly. The aloe plant that Mrs. Rincon had given them was amazing. Cynthia smiled. She doubted there would even be scars to testify to the horrors John had seen that night at the compound. Though, she didn't think he would ever need such a reminder.

"No." Cynthia called, as she sat the casserole into the oven and leaned over the sink to peer out the kitchen window. Two men stepped form a brown Versa. The one on the passenger side of the car seemed to unfold, as he exited his side of the vehicle. Looking closer, the sheer bulk of the passenger was all Cynthia needed to know it was Lane.

"Amelia, Tristan!" Cynthia called.

"Should we wash up for dinner Aunt Cynfia?" Amelia's voice called from the spare bedroom, again mispronouncing Cynthia's name in that endearing way that proved that some part of her, at least, remained a child though her thinking was more often than not closer to that of an adult.

"Yeah. .. I mean no." Cynthia laughed at how excited she felt for the both of them. They had not seen their parents in nearly two days.

"Just stop what you're doing, and come out here. There's a surprise here for you both!" Cynthia chirped, as she moved from the sink to the living room. All at once, there was a calamitous sound erupting from the spare bedroom, as toys fell to the hard wood floor and tiny feet pounded against the floor.

"Daddy!" Both children chimed in unison, their eyes glowing with the surprise of seeing their father after what must have seemed an eternity to them.

"Hey guys!" Lane's massive arms lifted out, as he bent to scoop both Amelia and Tristan up into his mammoth embrace. He placed his head on each of their foreheads, and looked deep into their eyes.

"I love you." He told each of them in turn.

"Where's mommy?" Tristan's tiny toddler voice rang out.

"Mommy's a little sick right now, but we're praying she gets better and you can go see her soon. Okay buddy?" Lane said, as he pulled his son in close for a deep hug.

Tristan placed his hands on either side of his father's face, as he looked deep into his eyes. "I pway for her tay, daddy?" Tristan's eyes seemed to bounce with the laughter coming from his belly, as Lane kissed his nose and told him to be sure to do that.

Amelia waited until Tristan was back in the room playing with the toys before asking any real questions.

"Is it bad daddy?" Amelia's eyes searched Lane's.

Cynthia's breath caught, as she, too waited for the answer she was not sure even she was ready to hear. Penny moved from the couch where she and Nick had been discussing possibilities for the summer now that neither of them had to spend it doing things for the bureau. Her eyes filled with tears, as she waited near the table, tracing musical notes on the back of a chair. Lane pulled Penny into his arms, holding her to his side, he tilted her head so that she faced him and then he spoke to the heart of them both.

"Mommy;" He said to Amelia, and then turning to Penny. "Aunt Jordan is going to be fine. She has bandages over her eyes, and right now we're waiting to see if her sight has been affected, but other than that, she is fine." Lane smiled, as he looked, then at Cynthia.

"Will you take Amelia in to wash up for dinner? I need to talk to Penny for a moment." Cynthia nodded that she would, as she took Amelia by the hand. Cynthia had no way of knowing what Lane was discussing with Penny, but she had a feeling it was related to the case. She figured if Lane wanted her to know he would tell her the moment they were able to talk with the children busy in another room.

As he and Garrison drove away from the cabin back to the hospital, Lane felt bad that he had not been able to offer as much insight as Garrison had but Jordan's former life had been somewhat of a mystery to him. He could agree however, that someone had been very deliberate in their efforts to conceal any connections between all of the members of Black Heart, as pertains to Jordan. That thought made Lane feel uneasy. He needed to get back to the hospital. Even Jordan's file was missing. It just made no sense. What set Jordan apart? Other agents had gone rogue. Other agents had been filtered out to The Truth.

That line of thinking made Lane compare similarities between Jordan and Cynthia: both were married; Cynthia was expecting a baby so even that put the two women on an even playing field. What differentiated the two women? What set their time spent as agents for Black Heart apart?

Lane was becoming more frustrated by the second. He was starting to understand why Cynthia made so much money profiling for Black

Heart; it was an arduous task that just in a matter of moments had left him bewildered and yet, for all of her skills, even Cynthia had not been able to connect the dots. Maybe, he was too close to the problem. Lane looked over at Garrison who seemed just as deep in thought. Or maybe, Lane thought, he just wasn't close enough.

"What makes Jordan so special?" Lane finally blurted out.

Pulled out of his thoughts so suddenly by Lane's inquiry, Garrison knit his brow.

"What do you mean?" Garrison finally, managed.

"Just what I said, I've thought about this from every angle. Cynthia and Jordan are very similar in how they came to be missionaries for The Truth. Though I must admit, Jordan's life was completely undesirable compared to that of Cynthia. .. to most people's lives for that matter." Lane explained, as he gave an emphatic shake of his head.

"So…" Garrison said flatly.

"So, why is it that Jordan's file is the only one missing?"

"You think that Jordan's file missing, somehow implicates her as the target of a grand cover up?" Garrison's voice rose an octave as an incredulous glare colored his features.

"Well doesn't it?" Lane bantered. His hands floating up and then falling back to his lap as he too, wore an incredulous glare.

"It's not that simple, though it does make for a compelling argument." Garrison admitted while kneading his chin.

"I'd say it's more than a compelling argument." Lane fussed. "What's not that simple?" Lane adjusted his body in the seat so that he could better see Garrison's face.

"What?" Garrison's eyes seemed far away.

"You said it's not that simple, after I said I thought Jordan's file missing would somehow indicate that the cover up was in some way targeting her." Lane's eyes bore into Garrison, as he waited however, impatiently for an answer.

"Oh. Yeah. That." Garrison waved off Lane's concern with a flick of his wrist.

"Well?" Lane was starting to lose his grip on his temper. It was obvious that Garrison was miles away, immersed in his own thoughts.

"It's just a leap, don't you think? You're saying that because one file is missing that it means the person indicated in said file must be the target in a grand cover up scheme." Garrison thrust his hand out as if to say 'see'.

"So?" Lane felt like the conversation was going in circles.

"Well, think about it. How many files do you think actually go missing? This is a big company, after all. With so many staff members responsible for the files, Black Heart is unfortunately, no different than other companies. Things get misplaced." Garrison reasoned.

"That makes sense." Lane admitted. "Still, how do you explain every file being wiped clean of any evidence suggesting the individual involvement with Jordan?" Lane asked, as he turned to peer out the front window for a moment. The conversation may not be going in circles any longer, but if it was picking up momentum, or producing answers to any of his questions, Lane could not tell.

"Now that's the question you should be asking." Garrison said, as he turned into the parking lot. Garrison's declaration brought Lane up short.

Garrison hadn't meant to be so evasive with Lane, but right now he was having enough trouble connecting the dots without having to make a pit stop to bring anyone else up-to-date. He just wanted to think without interruption. He needed to collect his scattered thoughts. He understood Lane's concern with Jordan's file missing, but he couldn't allow such a common occurrence in a corporation to detain him from the real issues.

The file was missing and truth be known, it was probably missing for the same reason that all evidence of Jordan had been missing from the other files. However, a missing file offered him no evidence and right now that's exactly what he needed.

He thought of the file he had on his phone. It was limited at best, and had nothing of the events leading up to the drug bust, involving James Ruston. He needed some answer and he was beginning to believe the only chance they would have to connect all of the dots would be exactly what Cynthia had wanted to do; get everyone in the files into the same room. The problem was Tommy and James Ruston were both dead, and Mr. Stanton was obviously not going to offer any answers that would help to prove their side of the case. It would seem limited files were the best hope they had at proving Mr. Stanton's involvement.

CHAPTER

50

Silence had filled the room with a staggering discomfort for long moments after Lane and Garrison left for food. Having been trained blindfolded for weeks, Jordan was undeterred by the bandages over her eyes, but she could imagine the difficulty a teenage girl may have with being in a dim lit room with someone she had only met once and that was to tie her up; to complicate matters that someone that was probably already a source of fear was wearing gauze around her eyes. It had to be unsettling. Jordan imagined to Kirsten the bandage that was meant to protect and heal would probably look more like a mask covering the enemy's dark intentions.

"Would you look in the drawer by the bed? I think I have a comb in there." Jordan lifted her tangled hair as a discontented frown tugged at the corners of her lips.

"You don't mind, do you?" Jordan could tell by the silence it had taken a moment for Kirsten to catch on.

"Oh! Not at all!" Kirsten chimed.

Jordan felt the bed rise up a couple of inches and then the drawer was being opened; shuffling of papers filled the silence. Jordan moved slowly to the side of the bed trying to carefully move the IV and oxygen tubing so she would not pull either loose. She wanted to give Kirsten the sense that she had the upper hand. She hoped that if Kirsten could see her as being weak rather than a predator waiting to pounce that it would help the girl to relax and open up.

Patting the space on the bed behind her, Jordan exhaled contentedly. Finally, she began to feel the teeth of the comb, as it drug carefully through the gnarled tangles in her hair.

"I know you won't be able to comb it all because of the bandages but it still makes me feel better that it's been combed at all. Lane tried but boys really don't know about these things." Jordan knew from the times she had spent with Amelia, getting her to talk about her feelings, concerning her life whether it be the absence of her biological parents, her relationship with Christ, her time spent as apprentice to the medicine woman of the Cadotion tribe or just how unfair she felt their rules were—there was something disarming about two girls sitting around playing with each other's hair.

Soon, just as Jordan had thought, Kirsten was talking. At first, she talked about hair styles that celebrities wore that she liked or disliked. Then she talked about things she hated about school but eventually the conversation abandoned the superficial banter of everyday life to venture deeper as Kirsten started to talk about her time with Black Heart.

When Lane returned to the room, Jordan was laying on the bed, cradling Kirsten. The girl's face was puffy and red as though she had cried herself to sleep. Both of them seemed to be sound asleep. Lane shut the door as quietly as possible but the intrusion of the screeching door jamb sliding home was still too loud. Jordan stirred automatically, tucking Kirsten closer to her side.

"Smells good." Jordan smiled. "Love you."

"How do you do that?" Lane fussed. "Love you too."

"The same way you call upon your 'special' sense." Jordan used her middle and forefingers to put quotations around the air in front of her, as if the word was really there, though with Kirsten lying on her arm the motion lost its usual emphasis.

"I simply stop relying on what I don't have and allow what I do have to lead the way. I told you that I spent two weeks without the use of my eyes." Jordan reminded Lane, as she pushed a lock of hair away from her mouth.

"Hey, they removed one of the IV's and the oxygen is gone as well." Lane mused as he crossed the room to a chair near the window.

"Where's Garrison?" Jordan asked while laying Kirsten down and then pushing further up in the bed.

"He went for a walk." Lane smiled. "That's just unsettling, Jordan."

Jordan snorted; "Says the half-human, half-angel."

Lane ignored the remark, as he scooted closer to Jordan's side. "How do you feel?"

"Why did Garrison go for a walk?"

"You first." Lane insisted.

"Fine, I'm fine. Now you. Garrison?"

"I guess he has a lot on his mind." Lane assessed, as he caressed her hand.

"Uh oh!" Jordan griped, as she laced her fingers through his.

"You're telling me. I had to ride with him." Lane scoffed.

"He's not that bad." Kirsten's sleepy voice broke through the easy banter that Lane and Jordan was enjoying.

"Oh, no, we have a traitor in our midst!" Lane slapped a hand to his chest, as he thrust his other hand forward pretending to wield a sword.

"Kirsten combed my hair." Jordan announced, as she theatrically flipped a lock of hair over her shoulder.

"Thank God!" Lane laughed, as he rolled his eyes at Kirsten who was nearly falling off the bed in laughter.

"Hey you two! Talking about traitors!" Jordan said, as she abruptly turned and started to tickle Kirsten.

Seriousness seemed to infiltrate the air. "I guess you want me to tell Lane about Black Heart?" Kirsten's eyes misted, as she turned to face Jordan's gauze-covered face.

"Well, I was hoping you would tell them both at the same time, but..." Jordan shrugged, as a sheepish grin spread across her lips.

"It's okay." Kirsten offered.

Lane was astonished at how grown up and child like the girl could be almost, simultaneously.

"My name is Kirsten Edwards; I'm from Bloomington, Indiana. I am thirteen years old."

Lane felt the world tilt on its axis, as the gravity of Kirsten's situation weighed his heart down. Determined to allow Kristen the opportunity to do what he was certain she had only been able to do once before, with Jordan only moments, before he had entered the room, Lane held any emotional outbursts or comments until she was done telling her story.

"There was nothing about the night my family died that set it apart from any other night. I remember Chestnut and Smokey, that's our horses. Anyway, I remember them whinnying a lot. Looking back I guess it might have been a warning of the trouble that was coming." Kirsten sniffed, as her hands sought refuge in her lap. Her voice was strained when she continued. "That was the longest hour of my life." Kirsten whispered. "They were executed... my parents, I mean. I didn't know that's what it was, until I came to Black Heart to be trained." Kirsten admitted, flatly. "They were shot: one in the head, two in the chest."

Kirsten's eyes brimmed with tears and flooded over, as she looked away. "They told all of us that it was you, Jordan that had killed our families. That's why the Johnston brothers, Mike and Saith, fought so hard. Every one of the teenagers wanted to kill you. We were given your name and very indecisive orders. We were turned loose in the general proximity that you were.

"The Johnston brothers were mean, though. They would probably have tried to kill just about anyone. Heck, they probably would have killed their family had Black Heart not beat them to it." Kirsten admitted, as she laid her head affectionately against Jordan's shoulder.

Lane knew that Jordan would not allow a situation to dictate her mood, or her confidence in that decision especially, if it was the only decision afforded her. Jordan would never kill someone that she did not completely believe deserved to be killed. Even before she had come to know the Lord as her savior, Jordan had killed only those that she felt fit the profile of some larger group of deserving misfits. She had killed men and women that had crossed some unseen line between good and evil. Though, she was no longer guided by the desires of an evil being, she would still kill if need be, without second guessing the decision.

"Most of the other recruits were content to follow orders and take everything at face value, but as you know, I need to have a better understanding of the reason I'm doing what you say." Kirsten looked in Jordan's direction; though the gauze was obstructing Lane's ability to see Jordan's expression, Lane somehow knew that Jordan's eyes were dancing in agreement. Jordan had filled him in on her time with Kirsten in the woods. Kirsten had been the only captive taken by Jordan to question, or to even plead her case. All of the other child-agents had simply complied with their captors except, of course, the Johnston brothers.

"I would sneak around the compound anytime I had the opportunity. Sometimes I would only get a couple hours sleep before having to wake at five in the morning for training. I had to know what I was up against, no matter the cost.

"Most of the recruits stayed in The Garden. One day, during one of my excursions, I saw a man entering a room that somehow seemed important. I waited until he was well past the door, and then I slipped into the room behind him. I hid in a cove between three filing cabinets where I waited until the man left the room. As soon as I was alone, I rummaged through a few of the cabinets. I happened across a row of filing cabinets that were in the very back of the room. I wondered, at first why they had been separated from the other cabinets like that, but as I moved toward them, I saw a label on the wall above the cabinets. The label indicated that the files were Black Heart representatives. I immediately thought of Mr. Stanton.

"I could never understand why a company as large as Black Heart would go through so much trouble to enlist child-agents to take down a high profile agent, such as Jordan Buckley. You were the stuff of legends, Jordan." Kirsten said, as she cast an admiring glance in Jordan's direction.

"The child-agents were told of the unbelievable feats that you had accomplished while being an agent for Black Heart. They went on to tell us that you had gone rogue, and that the company was trying to detain you but that you had gone crazy and before Black Heart could stop you, you had killed our families. It sounded a little farfetched to me.

"While others were taking watered-down-self-defense courses and high-fiving each other over the impending success that their pitiful course would give them when facing master agent-Jordan Buckley, I was combing through the files."

Lane's skin prickled, as he listened to Kirsten's story unfold. He wanted to know everything yet his heart was racing with his mind toward the truth. Something big beyond all of their imaginings had happened, and as he listened he was bereft to think of one thing that a handful of agents and missionaries could do to change it; apart from praying, and he was doing plenty of that.

"As I was looking through those files, I finally came across the cabinet STU and was again reminded of Mr. Stanton." Kirsten looked at Lane then. Her eyes seemed to search through the memories of that day.

Lane could imagine the fear she must have felt. No doubt, being in an unauthorized room not knowing how or when she would be able to leave without getting caught would cause even the most witty of agents some level of distress... this was a thirteen year old child with minimal training!

"My heart skipped a beat when I found Mr. Stanton's file. I don't know, I guess I half expected finding it would not be so simple. After looking through the files, I replaced it quickly. I didn't look to see if I had put it in precisely, the right place. What I saw though was a very incomplete history on a man that I know to have done more than his file was suggesting." Kirsten stopped for a moment to acknowledge a pointed look from Lane. He was confused. Did Kirsten just say that she knew Mr. Stanton personally?

"I've already told you that I was not content to drone away in the ranks of the other zombie-child-agents. I refuse to lie to myself. I'm not CIA exactly." Kirsten rolled her eyes. "Well they want us to believe that we are, but you and I both know the truth. All of the child-agents were acceptable losses. We were never meant to survive this mission. I can't believe that I was the only one to come to that conclusion." Kirsten smiled weakly.

Lane thought she might be thinking about some of her fallen friends.

"I didn't want to die. I know it may be hard to believe after what happened to my parents but honestly that made me desire to live more. Not only that, it made me want to know the truth; why did my family, all of our families have to die? So, I started to dig. I figured I had a while to be in that room, why not make good use of the time." Kirsten stood, then her blue eyes hazing in thought as she walked to the windows and peered out for a moment.

Lane looked at Jordan. It was so hard to tell what she was thinking without access to her beautiful, green eyes. He turned his attention back to Kirsten after a moment of scrutinizing Jordan, led to nothing more than empty-frustration.

"Other than the file room which was not much help, I made myself slip into other forbidden areas of The Garden. One day, while hiding under the control desk in the observation room, I overheard a man and woman talking. At first the conversation was pretty dry: what they had planned for the weekend that sort of thing but then the man mentioned Mr. Stanton's name." Kirsten turned back to Lane. Her eyes lit with the discovery and in that moment, he saw a glimpse of the thirteen year old girl under all of the pain and loss.

"Of course, I started to listen then. I almost got caught." Kirsten laughed as she, again turned to the window. "Again, I guess I was baffled at how easy things seemed to come to me. Even though Mr. Stanton's file revealed nothing of use, it was insane how easy I was able to obtain it. That, in and of itself, made me fear that I was being baited in some way but I decided I had watched too much TV, as a kid and my imagination was getting the best of me." Kirsten returned to the bed. Her long blonde hair fell over her shoulder, as she reclaimed her place next to Jordan.

"As I listened, the man in the control room started telling the woman about the story of Mr. Stanton, you know, how he became such an old pain." Kirsten rolled her eyes, again and allowed a humorless laugh. "Anyway, it seems Mr. Stanton was in love at one time." Kirsten leaned in close, positioning her head between both Lane and Jordan. Her eyes looked first at Jordan, and then Lane as she continued, "The very agent who recruited Mr. Stanton into Black Heart.

"The woman died, and after that Mr. Stanton made Black Heart his life but not before he searched for the person who had killed his great love. Problem was, by the time he found the man that killed her, the man had already died…" Kirsten waved her hands in the air in a theatrical manner, as if to say you won't believe this, "…of natural causes." Kirsten waited a moment, as if to give both Jordan and Lane the opportunity to react to what was being said.

"The man had lived his life with his wife; a good life too. They had one child; a daughter. She was beautiful; dark-auburn hair with emerald green eyes, but she married a bum. The man was an alcoholic who tortured his wife and children but even that was not enough pay back for 'good ole Mr. Stanton." Kirsten's face showed the true level of disgust that she harbored for the man. "No, Mr. Stanton wanted it all. He wanted the seed of Cecil Schooner to pay for his sins with every generation that proceeded from that wonderful union between him and his wife, Frances."

Jordan gasped, the world tilted on its axis. This information was new. Kirsten had only filled Jordan in on so much of her time at the bureau. She had fallen asleep, and so the story had fallen short of her finding Mr. Stanton's file. She had told Jordan that she had sifted through the file, but like the other files there was holes... Jordan had not even thought that a file on Mr. Stanton would be in archives at The Garden. She had never even thought to look for his file. She had truly been impressed that this child prodigy had been intelligent enough to not only see through the holes in her captors reasoning, but had also, searched for the truth against the odds. It was that impressive feat that Jordan had been waiting to showcase like a trophy, presented with pride; it was that miraculous truth that Jordan had desperately wanted to share with Lane, but now, as she listened to all that Kirsten was saying, she could not believe it was true. Her grandfather had killed Mr. Stanton's great love; but why?

Jordan thought of all of the things that had happened since she had joined Black Heart; things that she had thought to be incidental coincidence. Now, as she thought about each thing with the new knowledge afforded her, it made sense.

Tommy was recruited into Black Heart. How had she not known? She should have been caught so many times, but wasn't. A corporation, as large and far reaching as Black Heart did not let rogue agents slip through their hands. She was being allowed to kill. She was being allowed to taint the beliefs of her dead grandfather; a Baptist minister that believed firmly in the statutes of his living Savior. Everything that had been done was in direct correlation with Mr. Stanton's one goal. He wanted to kill the man who had killed his love, but instead that man had the audacity to live a life in the arms of his loving wife while serving his Savior and being revered by a congregation of believers. Now, the only thing that Mr. Stanton had left was defiling, desecrating her grandfather's memory and then killing off every member of that bloodline.

"Where's Garrison?" Jordan's voice rose hysterically as her hands clawed frantically at the gauze covering her eyes.

"Jordan, stop!" Lane moved to her side while gently pushing Kirsten out of harm's way. "What's wrong, baby?" Lane's voice was now, as filled with alarm as Jordan's had been.

All at once, the weeks of training blindfold felt useless to Jordan. The child-agents had merely been stumbling blocks put into place to slow them down but their presence had done more whether it was intended, Jordan could not be certain, the child-agents had given all of them a false sense of control. In so doing, Jordan had been seduced by the allure. She had given into the belief that it was an easy mission, that the teenagers were poorly trained because Jordan would not have the stomach to dispatch them. That unfortunately, was not the case. They had merely been a smoke-screen, a mirage designed to hide the true enemy she would face, within and without; her pride.

Jordan's pride had once again disarmed her ability to face the enemy objectively. Now, she was sitting in a hospital bed, all but blind exactly where the enemy intended her to be. She, along with all of her loved ones and now Kirsten were easy targets; waiting to be picked off by Black Heart's elite.

CHAPTER

51

The sun was starting to set behind the trees, casting a beautiful array of purples and pinks on the horizon. Garrison wanted to walk straight into their hazy midst, and forget all that awaited him back in the real world of Jordan's hospital room. He had ventured to the park, only a few blocks from the hospital; he needed some space.

Turning his back on the painted horizon, he started dejectedly for the hospital. So, tempted had he been to fall in among all of the other people loitering at the park. The laughter of the children had for a moment closed a vale around the world of chaos that had become his existence.

Mothers running behind the toddling feet of boys and girls seemed frantic to capture their tiny escapees. What Garrison would not give for that kind of concern? The concern of a haggard mother in a blind rush to maintain a toddler seemed thousands of miles from the kind of torment that awaited his return to the hospital. He didn't know if he even had the nerve to face all of the havoc that he had caused, but there would be no such shelter of denial that he could hide away under and refuse the snares of life. This was a disaster of his own making. He would be left no other alternative but to face it and to hope that once he had, there would be some way to turn back the waves of uncertainty that his betrayals had produced.

Everything could be traced back to his failure: as an agent, a friend, a human being. .. "If only", was his only friend now: if only he had kept his training up, if only he had been brave back in the farmhouse, if only he had reacted to the threat of the bomb before Jordan had "If only"...

Not even the multi-hued horizon could brighten his sunken mood, as Garrison crossed the four-lane-highway back to the hospital.

Only a few cars crept down the highway. Traffic in Morristown, New Jersey was nothing like the busy streets of New York's Irish district where Black Heart was housed.

At first glance, the parallel-parked black SUV meant nothing to Garrison. Then, as he looked again, he could see that the young driver with premature gray staining the edge of his head around his ears and wearing a black suit was trying to cover the true source of his attention. Though the man seemed captivated by the book he was reading, Garrison could tell his real attention was more occupied by the hospital entrance. The focused intent of the man's glare did not incite thoughts of a family member or friend waiting for their loved one to exit the hospital; rather it seemed more that the man was more concerned with camouflaging the source of his true interest in the hospital. Garrison knew from his own experience, as a reader, if he were truly engrossed in a book the world around faded away especially, if it were a good book. Also, as a former agent he knew the intentions behind the man's ominous glare.

Garrison followed the man's intent glare. Scanning the general area of the front door, he could see a bench. A homeless man that seemed out of place lay haphazardly across the bench. Garrison pushed passed the front door, and disappeared into the stairwell. He exited off the second floor of the hospital, and doubled back leaping over a small brick structure. He resurfaced around the side of the hospital in front of the bench but out of the driver's line of sight. As Garrison peered around the corner, the homeless imposter was sitting in an upright position, speaking into a transmitter device on the sleeve of his shirt while making signs to the driver of the SUV.

Garrison took mental inventory of the man on the bench. His tattered clothes, stringy black hair coated in grease and filthy face all suggested that he was indeed what he was trying to portray a homeless man. As Garrison allowed his gaze to venture lower, he was able see the flaw in the man's facade of an ensemble, $500 shoes.

Garrison watched, as a blond wearing a red dress passed by the bench where the homeless man was sitting. She walked a small gray poodle that pranced happily a few feet from her. The agent on the bench hurriedly fell back into character. As he feigned a drunken stupor, one leg and arm flailed awkwardly while he groaned and wobbled in a false attempt to sit up. Finally, giving in to what would be an alcoholic's greater desired sleep, the agent flattened on the bench and didn't move.

Garrison seized the opportunity. Pulling the silenced pistol from the waist band of his black slacks, he aimed and fired. The agent would never move, again. Garrison leapt over the brick wall to the second floor entrance, once more and promptly exited the front of the hospital. He may have let Jordan down before, but it would not happen again.

Catching up to the woman walking the poodle, Garrison asked for directions to the courthouse. He hadn't really wanted the directions, just to give the driver the false assumption that he was either a pedestrian in need of assistance, or that maybe, he was a local that had passed the time of day with another local. Satisfied that the agent in the SUV was no longer watching, Garrison turned to the car and started across the street. He crossed to a tree that was adjacent to the agent. Bending down, he pretended to tie his shoe. He pointed the pistol without hesitation took the shot. The man's head slumped forward as blood and brain matter sprayed the opposite window.

Garrison lifted to his full height, as he kept walking toward the park. As he reached the park, he turned and crossed the street to a small café. Moving down an alley beside the cafe, he was able to circle around and head back to the hospital. He didn't want anyone to see him and indicate that he may have been involved in the murders of the two agents in front of the hospital.

Under the cover of the parking deck, Garrison finally allowed himself to somewhat relax. Ignoring the regular elevators, he made his way to the small service elevator that was around the corner from the public elevators. Taking a moment to check the dim-lit parking deck, Garrison could see that no one was about. He quickly struck the arrow indicating it would lead to a higher floor. The elevator door squeaked open and Garrison stepped into the safety of its hidden cove. He then, pressed the two buttons. Jordan was on the third floor, but if anyone was following him he didn't want to lead them to her.

Again, the doors squeaked open. Garrison hurriedly scanned the hall for onlookers, and then abruptly crossed to the main elevators where he finally ascended to the third floor. He felt like a child playing on the elevators. He supposed if anyone had been watching they may think him crazy, but at times, doing things in such a round-a-bout way was the only thing shrouding an agent from the prying eyes of the enemy. As Garrison exited the elevator, and headed for Jordan's room it was painfully clear that every attempt he had made at not being discovered was in vain. Jordan's voice carried into the hall, demanding that someone find Garrison. Three nurses shrouded Jordan's bed, trying to calm her. Garrison had easily slipped past the open door and into the restroom. He rushed to flush the toilet and turned the sink facets on in order to make it seem as though he was washing his hands. He exited the restroom, as if in a huff.

"What's going on? I just had to use the restroom!" Garrison lied. Lane looked thunderstruck, and then understanding colored his eyes.

"I tried to tell her, but you know how Jordan is about you." Lane shrugged.

"You were in the restroom?" The petite brunette nurse was incredulous.

"Well I sure wasn't in there relaxing with this ruckus going on, honey." Garrison rolled his eyes. "I would have been out sooner, but I just didn't feel like changing clothes. You know what I mean?" Garrison winked at the frustrated nurse.

"Well you need to know what I mean!" The nurse threatened. "Anything else upsets my patient, and I'll have you all removed!"

"That won't be necessary." Jordan interrupted. "Garrison did nothing to me. Besides, they can't babysit me every second. I just had a bad feeling that Garrison was being harmed." Jordan waved off the nurse's concerns.

"Well all I'm saying is..." The huffy nurse tried to start in again.

"I understand your concern, but I'm telling you it's unfounded." Sprigs of gauze hung loose, as Jordan's head nodded while she spoke. "Think about it. You and the other two nurses were in the room during my episode; so by your logic you will be removed, as well." Jordan's voice held no contempt. No accusation. If anything her tone was soothing, she spoke to the nurse in much the same way a mother would speak to an insubordinate child when trying to teach the child a lesson.

The nurse's mouth and eyes seemed to move independent of one another in a paradoxical fashion. Her hands smoothed the stray locks of brown hair back into the silver clip at the nape of her neck. She seemed unable to find her voice.

Garrison stifled a giggle, as the woman finally swept out of the room. The other two nurses looked briefly in Jordan's direction, and then at each other. Both women fell against each other in a fit of laughter.

"We're so sorry." The slim blond exaggerated the word sorry, as she apologized through hopeless fits of snorting. "We've just never seen bulldog... uh... Nurse Cragil at a loss for words." The plumper blond explained.

"It's okay." Lane smiled.

"That's a shame." Garrison said. "A mouth like that should stay at a loss for words." Garrison countered while casting an irritated glare at the door that Nurse Cragil had not long exited.

"Psshhh!" The thin blond snorted, as she pulled the plumper blond toward the door.

Garrison turned back to Jordan. Her hands were folded in her lap. Tufts of her auburn hair plumed from the top of the gauze that was still securely in place aside from a few jagged sprigs that floated aimlessly in the slight breeze filtering in from the vent above the bed. Jordan looked so small, her shoulders slumped.

"Are you okay?" Garrison moved to Jordan's side, and placed a hand on her shoulder.

"We need to get out of here." Jordan said, as she started to wring her hands.

"Please Jordan, you're okay. You have to stay calm..." Lane was trying to sooth.

"She's right." Garrison moved to the door, and peered out into the hall.

"Not you, too?" Lane complained, as he fluffed Jordan's pillow.

Garrison turned back to the bed. Kirsten was sitting in the chair next to the window, trying to avert her eyes. The poor girl didn't seem to know what to do with herself.

"I killed two agents out in front of the hospital." Garrison admitted flatly.

"What?" Lane's hands froze in place, no longer fluffing the pillow.

"Two agents, one was in a car the other was on a bench."

"How do you..." Lane's face was pale. His hands rushed to Jordan's shoulders. He promptly began massaging them, as though he could somehow dispense the knots in his own nerves by messaging hers.

"He knows." Jordan insisted.

"Was the man on the bench supposed to be homeless?" Jordan asked, still wringing her hands.

"Yeah, $500.00 shoes gave him away."

"You killed a homeless man because he had on $500.00 shoes?" Kirsten finally interrupted. She was standing now and pacing the floor.

"That and the transmitter on his sleeve that he was communicating with the other agent through." Garrison admitted.

"Oh." Kirsten conceded, as she plopped back into the chair.

"Did you speak to anyone? See anyone?" Jordan asked.

"I don't think so."

"You don't think? Garrison, really? This is important, you are not this far removed from the field!" Jordan was almost shrieking, as she spoke the last word.

"Honey please calm down. This stress is not good for you." Lane pleaded, as he rubbed her shoulders more vigorously.

"I'm fine, Lane. Please let me do this." Jordan pleaded softly as she tenderly stilled his hands.

"Yeah, there was a woman. She was wearing a red dress, had black sunglasses with silver sparkles. Her hair was black, and she was walking a dog. I asked her where the courthouse was. It was right after I killed the agent on the bench. I needed the cover in order to throw the agent in the car off." Garrison exhaled, as he moved back to the end of the bed. "As soon as the man stopped looking, I crossed the street, and took a knee. I pretended to tie my shoe, and took out the agent in the car." Garrison threw his hands up, and then allowed them to fall back to his side.

"That's all. There was no one else. I took every precaution to make certain I was not being followed." Garrison nodded his head, and then realizing that Jordan would not be able to see the gesture, he spoke. "That's it."

"The woman?"

"Huh?"

"The woman was an agent." Jordan insisted.

"No." Garrison shook his head. "Nothing out of place about her."

"Really?" Jordan's head cocked to the side in a defiant challenge. "Walking a dog in a red dress with heals, and I'm assuming she did have heals, and not hiking boots or tennis shoes on… that does not strike you as out of place? Don't people usually do that in shorts, or at the very least in jeans? Who in their right mind would walk a dog on concrete while wearing heals? Jordan was wringing her hands, again.

"You let your hormones call the shots!" Jordan accused.

Garrison drew back from the slanderous comment. This wasn't like Jordan, but then again, until now she hadn't been nearly blown to bits left visually impaired while sitting like a duck waiting on the enemy to come for her family and friends.

"I'm sorry. That was uncalled for." Jordan offered, as her head tilted up. The gauze over her eyes made the gesture seem more pitiful, as her unseeing eyes, no doubt searched the nothingness for forgiveness.

"No you're right, well at least, in part. The part about me being distracted is true, but I wasn't distracted because of a woman; at least not that woman." Garrison crossed the room. He hated seeing her this way. The gauze covering her burned eyes was a vicious reminder of his failure as her partner; her friend.

"I wasn't distracted by some blond in a red dress, Jordan. I was distracted by you."

"Me?" Jordan's response was so automatic that it almost seemed, as though her mouth had opened, and the word had merely fell out.

Lane shifted his weight uncomfortably. Garrison considered him for a moment. His tall, bulky form stood ready with power at her side. Garrison had never thought a man to be beautiful, but Lane did not seem to be merely a man, not exactly. His light brown hair with golden blond streaks that billowed over his shoulders was offset by a steely blue gaze that emanated love and strength in the same instant. His smooth skin seemed to be etched in the finest marble, as not a single flaw marred his visage; it was the face of an angel.

Garrison guessed it could be Lane's exquisite god-like appearance that would incite such faith in Jordan's loyalty to allow him the confidence that she had eyes only for him but it was so superficial a notion that he almost immediately dismissed it. Such patience engendered his very being. There was a kindness in his eyes that Garrison now knew emanated from the soul of a Christian. It was a patient kindness that he had witnessed that Jordan too had exhibited since becoming a Christian. It was for that very patient, kind nature that Jordan and Garrison's friendship had been able to thrive. It was the mark of a true Christian, not people who hovered in droves in churches trying to sit like judges in some preordained position of self-righteous indignation waiting for the self-appointed time in which to cast that harsh light of judgment on every life. What Lane and Jordan had was real. It was straight from a place so profoundly full of grace that it had to be a Supreme Being because Garrison had never before seen its likeness.

Garrison smiled at Lane, as he turned his attention back to Jordan. She was obviously waiting for an explanation.

"Yes you. I was distracted by the fact that I've let you down; as your trainer, your partner, but more importantly, as your friend." Garrison laid a hand over Jordan's hands to still them from the constant movement. "Look at you, Jordan. You wouldn't even be here if not for me."

"Don't go there!" Jordan warned.

"I have to because you need to know how truly sorry I am. You need to know that there is nothing that I would not do to change the choices I've made that led to you being here, instead of with your children." Garrison's voice broke, as his eyes filled with the helplessness that plagued his soul. It was his fault: every lie, every half-truth, every time he had refused to do anything more than a routine workout in the company gym, every hesitation and yes, every fear had led to this moment.

"Do you think yourself, God?" The words were dripping with acid, as Jordan's back straightened, and she snatched her hands free from his. "You think that God is so governed by your whims that he would set back, and allow things to happen to me based on your actions?"

"Jordan." Lane was holding her shoulder now, as he tried to still her anger with a touch.

"No, Lane. He needs to know. He needs to see that he is not the center of the universe. He needs to see that his life is hard because of his choices, and that yes, those choices affect others but..." Jordan waved her hands around. Garrison could see that she was frantic to make him understand.

"Your choices can be dead wrong, Garrison." Jordan's voice was softer now. She reached for his hand. He gave it to her easily. "And yes, you should ask God to help you make better choices, but you aren't the only one who allowed distractions to color the way you would normally deal with a situation. I allowed my pride to have the upper hand. I underestimated the enemy based on how easily dispatched the child agents had been. I allowed myself to be caught by two of those agents. I had to take their lives because I got cocky.

"Either one of those young men could have benefited from hearing my testimony, your testimony, or even Lane's for that matter. Instead, I was forced to kill them because I let my guard down. To make matters worse, I did not scan the trailer in the woods for bombs before entering it; a decision that was based solely on that same pride.

"Garrison, I understand how you feel. I do. But, God is not some unprepared ogre who waits for us to make mistakes so he can figure out the best way to punish us and those that we love." Jordan squeezed Garrison's hand. "Do you understand?"

"Yeah," Garrison whispered, as tears splattered unbidden across his cheeks.

Lane was brimming with pride. He, too had tears in his eyes. Garrison heard Kirsten sniff. He turned in time to see her collapse into a puddle of tears. Lane went to her automatically. Garrison had never felt so broken, and yet complete in his whole life.

Everything that Jordan had said was freeing. He had taken the blame for everything he had ever done. It was, according to his father the right thing to do, but now as he listened to Jordan, he knew that, while he was in fact responsible for his actions, God was not sitting on high, waiting to punish those that He loves, according to certain criterion breached. There was no handbook in heaven waiting for God to look through, and find the proper course of action to fit the mistake made; that was a Black Heart thing. As Garrison sat, watching the love filter from his friends onto himself and Kristen, he knew that he would never again fit that mold.

52

B uzzing, whirring, ticking, buzzing, whirring, and ticking. The sounds were maddening. Edward Stanton stared at the clock. The second hand pounded relentlessly, announcing every moment lost with a resounding: tick, tick, tick. He had sent Marshall and Denton to the hospital hours ago. There should have already, been some word on their progress.

Edward eyed the door suspiciously; there had never been so many maddening sounds coming from beyond his office. What was the staff doing? Clomp, Clomp, Clomp a pair of high-heel shoes tapped against the marble flooring. Drip, drip, drip the coffee pot, or sink, or both, who knows, carved out their pound of flesh from his already frayed nerves. Edward cradled his head in his hands. He was going to lose his mind. A shrill ringing broke into the series of noises causing Edward to push back in his chair. His arms swung out and a slight scream erupted from his throat. He eyed the intercom. He had been very clear that Sarah, his receptionist announce all of his calls before putting them through. He liked to reserve the right to decline any unwanted distractions. He had demanded all of his appointments be cancelled; even the Hayes appointment was rescheduled for Monday morning.

Victor Hayes was Black Heart's number one offender, top priority; his family had money to burn and as New York's crime boss that dirty money covered a multitude of Victor's sins... but this morning even the Hayes' case would wait.

"Hello, Mr. Stanton here." Edward squeezed his temples, as he waited for the person on the other end of the phone line to say what was on their mind. He would definitely reprimand Sarah, and then get back to the treacherous waiting.

"Good to see you haven't lost your professionalism, Stanton." The line filled with the eerie double timbre of a voice that was obviously, being disguised by some kind of electronic device.

"Who is this?" Edward demanded. It wasn't unlike Black Heart to receive threatening phone calls, but never had one made it passed the secretary.

The voice taunted. "All in due time, for now, just know it's not those two buffoons you used as watch-dogs: Marshall and Denton, is that right?"

Edward's mind raced. He couldn't breathe, Marshall and Denton? He needed time to prepare for this call, but he had none. That traitorous clock had ticked all of his moments along with his nerves, into oblivion.

"Thar's right... you think. I'll talk." The caller's menacing voice filled the line again.

In a strange way Edward was relieved for the silence granted him. Though he had been thinking all morning, it had yet to afford him one satisfactory explanation for Marshall and Denton's silence. He had further been unable to think of a plan for corking the massive hole in the sinking ship that was his life.

"I know everything." the decidedly female voice claimed. Edward wasn't sure of the gender of the caller with the voice distortion device that was being used, but after a few minutes of listening there was definitely a feminine timbre to the voice.

"I know about the child-agents. I know about the connection between you and Jordan Buckley. I know about the drug ring and gun cartel. I know about the henchman, Tommy Hayden, hired to kill Jordan, and I know that he was her nephew. I know that it played a big role in why Hayden was chosen." The voice continued to spout off an endless supply of Edward's un-seedy past atrocities. But so what? None of the things said were, at this point, anything more than hear say. All of it was knowledge that any member of Black Heart, with a level three clearance would know, but be unable to prove. Edward had personally destroyed any information linking him, and all the main players in the crime syndicate. Also, the only witness able to give damaging evidence of his personal involvement, thanks to Tommy Hayden, was now dead. Furthermore, thanks to Jordan Buckley's husband, Tommy Hayden was dead.

Edward leaned back in his black-high-back chair. His back was straighter now, as he squared his shoulders. He was feeling better all the time. He thought about the agents: Marshall and Denton, who according to the voice were now dead, as well. Edward laughed, and then covered his mouth, as he realized the sentiment had been out loud.

"Are you laughing at me, Stanton?" The caller demanded.

"Oh.... Of course not," Edward lied. He couldn't help, but see the humorous irony of the whole mess. It was as if his enemy was working for him. Edward could not have planned it better. Every key player, tying him to any illegal conduct was being killed off, one participant at a time, and with them, the evidence of their damaging testimony perished as well. Though Edward had been against the child-agent plan from the beginning, he knew that were he tied to his informant, he too would go down for the deaths of those lost... Edward hated that the children had been sacrificed. He would never have been okay with such a horrible thing, but now was not a time for looking back. He had to move forward. He had to think positively. This was his second chance. Everyone who would or could link him to any of his past sins were gone dead. It was over. Edward felt lighter, more hopeful. He had been forged in the fire, and had come out on the razor edge of freedom: he was declared innocent by fate itself who could argue with that.

"I take these types of allegations, however, misguided and false, seriously." Edward had somehow managed to strip his tone of every ounce of the humor that he felt; a feat he was proud of. Yet again, fate was making her declaration on his behalf, as she placed a hand on his shoulder, and navigated him through the unwanted distraction of a phone call.

"Before you develop a sense of humor, Stanton, you might want to turn that sixty inch flat screen in that lavish, overstated office of yours to channel nine." The voice held a certain mocking satisfaction.

Edward stiffened. Channel nine? He only knew of one thing that he would view at this hour on that channel; the action nine news at eleven. His blood turned to ice, as his eyes lifted to the large television housed on the large oak entertainment center that covered an entire wall. His attention floated cautiously to the crystal wine glasses hanging from their stems. A large crystal container with a stopper made of crystal held the fifth of brandy that Sarah had filled it with only an hour earlier.

Edward crossed the room after turning the speaker phone on. His hands trembled, as he flicked the red button on the remote. The television snapped once, and then a slender blond stood with a blue sweater outside what appeared to be the Irish Pub. All of a sudden, the screen split, and a demure brunette stood outside a small farmhouse. Ambulances and patrol cars raced in and out of the long drive in front of the reporter.

"Dozens of bodies have turned up on the grizzly scene here in Morristown, New Jersey; former residence of the Morristown Slasher, Harvey Maddox. Locals claim that the place is evil. It would seem that whatever afflicts this manner of mayhem, evil or otherwise, is still calling the shots as emergency workers and the public examiner's office share space on what seems to be a hopeless case of young lives lost…" The woman continued to vent about the dozens of bodies that had been found dead. The other reporter standing outside the pub was, all too happy to place the blame on the Head of Department of Black Heart namely, Edward Stanton.

All at once, it was as though someone had thrown back the curtains, and Edward's hiding place was revealed for the entire world to see.

"Across town, in a hospital that shall remain undisclosed, one of The Truth's own and a former agent of Black Heart is fighting for her sight as she was nearly blinded by an explosion set by one or more of Mr. Stanton's child-agents." The reporter outside the pub claimed as an image of a woman with gauze shrouding her eyes flashed briefly across the screen. Parts of the picture were blurred, making it impossible to make a positive identification, but Edward knew that the picture was of Jordan Buckley.

Edward stumbled to the crystal container of brandy. His knees felt like Jell-O holding up a mountain of cement blocks. Everything he had ever done to maintain both his and Black Heart's anonymity had been undone in a single afternoon. The two reporters seemed proud of themselves, as they shoveled mountains of lies off of the truth and into an open grave that would obviously be his final resting place; his life was over.

Edward's mind raced, as he tried to imagine who would be willing to chance such a thing, as bringing to the light a dark secret, as big as Black Heart. There were only a handful of government officials that actually knew of the Black Heart project not even the President was privy to the undercover dealings of Black Heart. Now, a business that had been underground literally for nearly thirty years was being ousted on live television.

Edward poured the Brandy into the wine glass. Some of the amber liquid sloshed onto the marble top of the massive entertainment center. His hand shook violently, as he clamored wildly to hold onto consciousness.

"So Edward, what do you think?" The voice pierced the silence with such a thunderous boom that the wine crystal and the container of brandy slipped awkwardly from his hand, and shattered onto the marble surface below. Edward reached for both of the crystal pieces a moment too late. His hand and wrist scraped heavily over several shards of crystal. Immediately, three large gashes spread wide. All three ran from his hand to his wrist. Edward could tell from years of combat experience that all three wounds would need stitches.

Edward watched, as the dark marble surface filled with his blood that mingled with the amber colored brandy and dripped to the floor. For an instant, Edward reacted with caution, as he snatched his hand free of the broken glass: maybe, it was the burn of the liquor in the open wounds, or maybe, it was basic self-preservation that made him take his hand from the cutting surface of the crystal-filled marble surface. Edward didn't know, but whatever the reason, it was short lived. Edward pushed his hand back toward the broken shards and clumsily thrust his burning flesh into the razor-sharp-jagged-edges of the broken crystal. Though the pain seemed to double with the effort, the blood loss was still, too slow for Edward's ominous desire. He reached for a larger piece of crystal and staggered to the window; his life's blood was drizzling profusely down his throbbing hand from the multiple gashes. The blood trailed over the carpet in a dotted formation, as he made his way to the window.

His life had been horribly long without his beloved, Amorous by his side. He had made Black Heart, and revenge for her death, the whole of his existence. The ache of her loss filled his every heartbeat. Edward stood near the window, peering out onto a sea of desks. People loitered the room in a frenzy of horrified faces and flailing hands that carried paperwork to boxes. Each box was being loaded onto the elevator and probably taken to another government facility where it would be destroyed, or brought further into the light of the public awareness. Tears fell down Edward's face, as he gripped the crystal shard in his mutilated hand. A lifetime of devotion to a ghost, and a secret now somehow felt hollow. Was it worth it? In an instant, Edward saw Amorous' beautiful, smiling face, she seemed to beckon him to her. So many regrets for his life, but she had never been in the midst of those regrets. He had pursued her from the very first, just as his heart pursued her now.

Edward could feel time slipping away, as his legs began to wobble, and his eyes felt heavy but still it was too long to wait. He needed to be with her, and yet, he did not know if he could go where she was. His would probably be eternal torment but it was deserved. Wherever, this journey would end, he no longer wanted to be in a world where she did not exist. Though he did not know that she would be in the world that awaited him, he knew with frightening acuity that she no longer existed in this one.

Edward could hear the voice on the phone saying something, but it sounded muffled, and meant little to him now. He gripped the tool of his exit, the crystal shard as his other hand rested on the large picture window. With a violent thrust of his hand, he speared the shard of crystal deep into his neck. First pain, and then fear, slammed into his mind, as he realized he could not breathe. In truth, he did not know that this would be a painful death. He had somehow, believed that the faithful blow would end his suffering the moment he had nicked the artery, but as he lay on the carpeted floor listening to the whirring, ticking, and mumbling that filled the room, he was reminded of a suffering he had never knew existed. He felt a profound separation from someone more important than Amorous could ever be. He felt separated from a Divine Holy Power that he had never given a second thought. He was separated, forever from God.

Kirsten stood clutching the voice distorted her shoulders shrugged pitifully as she mouthed, "he won't answer." Garrison pulled the phone from her hand, and replaced it on the cradle.

"Don't worry, you got our point across. Stanton will be running scared." Garrison placed an assuring hand on Kirsten's shoulder. "Believe me, scared people make mistakes, kid."

"I don't know, I feel something is wrong. Did you hear...?" Kirsten stopped, as she frowned, and then bit her lower lip.

"Hear what?" Lane was curious now. He had stood by and allowed Garrison his fun but this was different. If Kirsten had heard something and judging by the intense fear registering on her face she had. Then, this was now becoming all together more serious and it was time to leave the games behind them and make a real plan to figure this whole mess out.

"Well I don't know..." Kirsten admitted.

"Just relax sweetie. You're not on trial." Jordan soothed.

"She's right." Lane conceded. "But if you can think of what you may have heard that made you uncomfortable then just let us know. Okay?" Lane's voice was so calm and soothing that it surprised even him. He felt anything, but calm. His nerves were in shambles. Garrison had them playing some high-stakes gambling with one of the major players in the death game.

"Well... It almost sounded like he was... gagging." Kirsten's voice rose, as she lifted her eyes to meet Lane's.

Lane's eyes flashed with the concern that he felt.

"Okay, let's not let the imagination of one little girl get the better of us." Garrison reasoned, as he scowled at Lane.

"I'm not a little girl!" Kirsten complained with a defiant set of her jaw.

"You ain't no grown woman either, honey." Garrison's hands were on his hips, as he mockingly tapped the toe of his shoe.

"How many little girls do you know that witnessed the death of their parents have gone through some combat training and witnessed the death of her friends; all of that by thirteen and still had the wherewithal to make a phone call to the scariest person you've ever known, Mr. Garrison?" Kirsten's eyes flashed with untapped rage, her back was straight and her hands were planted firmly on her hips as she met his gaze with complete defiance. "And after all I've been through, I still have better grammar than a so-called grown man!" Kirsten spat.

"Okay..." Lane said, as he moved between Kirsten and Garrison. "She's already proved she can best you, Garrison." Lane laughed. "Let's just calm down, besides like it or not, she's right."

Garrison rolled his eyes, as he flung his hands into the air, and blew a forceful breath. Plopping into the wide-brown chair near the middle of the wall, Garrison cast a murderous glare in Lane's direction; "Not you, too!"

"I'm just saying we should at least hear her out. After all, she is the only one here with an objective opinion, remember..." Lane reminded. "Garrison it's not like the phone was on speaker. She's the only one who could hear what was happening on the other end of the line. We really have no other choice, but to take her word as fact. She heard something and it made her think the man was gagging. We need to take that seriously. This is not a game; a man's life could be at stake."

Jordan reached for the phone on the small night stand.

"What are you doing?" Garrison demanded.

"Calling the police." Jordan admitted flatly.

"Calling the police?" Garrison was moving, now. "Have you all lost your minds? Am I the only voice of reason in this room?"

"I hope not!" Kirsten sassed, as she flopped heavily into the high-back recliner near the window.

"Hey, easy kid; you'll hurt my feelings." Garrison rolled his eyes, as he, again eyed the phone. He was standing close now, waiting to see if Jordan would come to her senses.

Lane could tell that he intended to stop her if he could. "Call them." Lane nodded, forgetting that Jordan could not see the sentiment.

"We're all going to jail!" Garrison huffed, as he reached for the phone in a last desperate attempt to stop the inevitable.

"Enough!" Lane warned. "This is a man's life."

"A man?" Garrison boomed. "Edward Stanton is the underbelly of a predator! He isn't worth all of this..." Garrison didn't finish. Seeing that Lane was no longer paying attention to his childish attempts at saving his own hide, Garrison turned his heated gaze back to the door and stormed back to the chair; with a flop, he was sitting again.

Lane hated to ignore Garrison, but listening to his concepts about human life when they were so far from the teachings of Christ was grating on his nerves. Lane just did not have the patience required at the moment to get into a philosophical debate with Garrison. A phone call to the police would be the only way to ensure that Edward Stanton was not lying on the floor of his office, in a pool of his own blood. Lane did not know what it would mean for them if Stanton was dead but he could not leave things unknown. Stanton may have a lot of 'payback' coming his way for a life time of evil, but the 'payback' would be up to God. (Vengeance is mine, saith the Lord, and I will repay. Romans 12:19).

It was never too late to make a right turn off of the wrong road. Lane's parents had always taught him that. Such teaching had saved Lane from a lifetime of feeling lost. No matter what he had done he had always felt he could tell them, and they would help him seek God's guidance.

Lane listened, as Jordan explained to the police. She told them that while on the phone with Edward Stanton the line became silent and then there was a gagging sound. Jordan finally hung the phone up.

"The police were already in the building. They can't discuss the case just yet, but Stanton is on the way to the nearest trauma center." Jordan sat quietly.

Kirsten gasped and then stood. Crossing the room to Jordan, she crawled into the bed. Her arms surrounded Jordan's waist, seeking the refuge of Jordan's arms which Jordan gave freely. Kirsten was sobbing.

Garrison had seemed unmoved by the scene. His eyes rested briefly on Kirsten's quaking form but just as quickly, his attention returned to the unopened door. He seemed caught between decisions.

Lane watched him for a moment. He realized that Garrison would have to find his own way. It was not up to Lane to tell everyone how to deal with this very precarious situation. Each of them would have to work out their own salvation with fear and trembling (Philippians 2:12).

Lane turned back to Jordan. Her unseeing eyes, wrapped in gauze were cast down as if looking at Kirsten. The girl's shoulders had started to still, and she was drooping in Jordan's tender embrace. Lane smiled, as it occurred to him that she would eventually move through this time with the love of a friend. Garrison would have to work out his salvation, just as Kirsten was doing, now. Whatever, that would mean for each of them; Christ would help them through. Just as he would help all of his children that would lean on Him through whatever circumstance they were facing.

Lane watched Garrison a little longer, as he was still caught in some contemplation. His eyes seemed to seek the refuge of the door, more than the solace of truth. Lane prayed silently that Garrison would lean on the Lord for understanding. (Trust in the Lord with all your heart, lean not on your own understanding; Proverbs 3:5).

CHAPTER

53

It felt good to finally see light dancing through the few dissipating clouds. Jordan had insisted that they return to the Cadotion village where she could heal while being surrounded by the peace and tranquility of their home. As she watched the sparkling rays of sun, spill over the tents and gently kiss the skin of her children, Jordan was reminded of God's grace. She would have gladly endured blindness to be able to enjoy the love of her family. As she watched Amelia chase Tristan, gratitude for her sight filled her heart and spilled over onto her glowing face.

To never see the tan features of her beautiful daughter and both mourn her childhood and celebrate her journey into womanhood, as the chubby baby fat melted from her face and a more lean graceful creature emerged from the cocoon of youth would be too great a loss.

Jordan turned to Tristan, as his still meaty limbs flailed and scampered in an effort to escape the make-believe threat of his sister. So glorious, were the angelic features, set in the visage of her son. She watched, as his dark-auburn hair, her only physical genetic claim to Tristan, bounced whimsically on the morning breeze.

"Hey, is this seat taken?" Lane's voice broke through the reverie.

"It is now." Jordan smiled. She could feel her eyes dancing as she took in the whole sight of him. He was a glorious creature; from his massive six foot five inch frame to his smoldering blue eyes that were offset by light brown hair kissed with streaks of blond as if the sun had branded him long ago, as set apart. His chiseled countenance would have given him the allure of a formidable enemy set upon her from another time, if not for the love of God that so gently graced his features.

"You okay?" Lane's blue eyes turned to pools of concern. In an instant, the warrior before her vanished and in his place was the angel she knew and loved.

"Yeah, just thinking," Jordan smiled to reassure him.

"About what?" Lane sat next to her and laughed at Tristan's still wobbly-chubby, legs stumble away from his sister. Amelia tried to maintain the ever-menacing-monster character and keep him from harm's way in the same instant.

"Girl's got talent!" Lane laughed, as he turned back to Jordan.

"I seem to remember her father showing much the same potential, once upon a time." Jordan teased.

"Well, yeah, her mother was a handful." Lane pulled Jordan to him.

"Yeah, I guess she was." Jordan said in a flat, far away tone. Her eyes glazed over, again, as she fell back into her thoughts.

"What are you thinking about?" Lane prompted while tenderly squeezing her shoulders.

"My grandfather," Jordan confided in a lulling tone. The dreams she had been having were gone, as if the battle that they had come to warn her about was now over, and she no longer needed their constant beacon of warning. She now had a new reason for unrest.

"Your grandfather?"

"Yeah, you know, about his involvement with Mr. Stanton's great love. How did he cause her death? Why? That sort of thing." Jordan turned to Lane, then. Tears filled her eyes. Her grandfather had been the one constant in her chaotic life: beholden to his beliefs, a tower of strength and virtue; it was his guiding light that had first revealed Christ's love to Jordan. Though it had been only a glimpse that she had paid little heed to at the time, Jordan now knew it had been a seed that was planted. A seed that had grown roots, so deep that they were the bedrock of her faith in God. The harvest would be reaped many years into her future by the love of her life, Lane. Still, Jordan knew it had been her grandfather's tireless, unwavering example of faith and steadfast Christian walk that had paved the way for her, to one day, be pulled back from the unrelenting grasp of the enemy. She loved him...

she needed his memory to stay intact. She didn't know if her faith could withstand such an ominous truth being pulled from the ashes of her grandfather's seemingly spotless past.

"Some things are better left unknown, Jordan." Lane smiled.

"I know, but..."

"Everyone has a past." He soothed.

"They do." She agreed.

"Is your grandfather any less human? Any less capable of doing those things that set us apart, as sinners in need of a Savior?" Lane's gentle voice caressed the aching wound caused by the confusion of unanswered questions.

"No, he's not." Jordan admitted.

"Let it go, honey, when God deems you ready for the truth, if ever, He will reveal it to you. Until then," Lane stretched his hands wide, as if to unveil the beauty set before them. "You have all of this to occupy that beautiful mind." Lane smiled, again. "Okay?"

"Okay." Jordan returned the smile. She turned back suddenly, reminded of another concern. "How is she?"

"She's sleeping. Aniahi asked to watch over her for a few days." Lane soothed.

Kirsten had seemed well on the trip to the Cadotion village, but after seeing the beauty it had an almost opposite effect on her than what they had hoped for.

"Aniahi says she is reminded of the life she stole away." Lane captured a lock of Jordan's hair playing on the breeze and tucked it behind her ear.

"Has Mr. Stanton passed away, then?" Worry etched fine lines on Jordan's forehead, as she waited.

"No. He's still in a coma. Kirsten has prayed nonstop for him but so far, no change." Lane admitted.

"She's already lost so much because of his evil!" Jordan hissed.

"Man was not inherently evil." Lane gently reminded.

"Could you take a five minute sabbatical from being an angel?" Jordan grouched.

"You're married to me, Jordan. You should be able to answer that better than almost anyone." Lane laughed.

Jordan ignored the last comment. "Inherent or otherwise that man was... is full of plenty of evil... It's just too much! Her family, her friends and then the time she spent by his hospital bed praying and crying... when does it end? Even the law enforcement said that we were all innocent of his... well, his possible death, but still, she will not get down off that cross!" Jordan was heaving with anger. Stanton had no right to claim this much from her; no one did. Kirsten was losing ground on a battlefield that should have never been her fight.

"I'm taking her back." Lane announced flatly.

"No! Why?" Jordan whirled on Lane, and threw her hands into the air defiantly.

"Let her heal, Jordan." Lane gently pushed.

"Heal or wallow, Lane?" Jordan insisted.

"I don't believe this is a pity-party, Jordan." Lane's brows furrowed.

Jordan could tell that he was coming to the end of his endless patience, but she had had enough of the taint that Mr. Stanton had on Kirsten's young life. It had already cost her enough. It was time that she got back to the business of living.

"That's not what I meant. I mean wallow in grief, not pity." Jordan explained, as she pushed a lock of unruly hair back away from her face.

"Everyone heals differently; she asked and I said that I would take her." Lane moved to Jordan, and pulled her into his arms. "I hate this too, she needs to find her own way through this," Lane pulled her chin up, so that he could look into her eyes.

Jordan normally loved this but when they were on opposite ends of a belief system, the smoldering blue of his eyes could make it hard for her to concentrate.

"She needs to find her own way." Lane whispered.

"I know." Jordan playfully pouted, as she moved deeper into the shelter of his embrace.

"Mommy, Mommy! Watch tis." Tristan cried in his little boy voice. His mispronouncing of certain words was so enduring; at times it made it hard for Jordan to concentrate on what it was he wanted.

He threw his hands out and made a booming noise. His eyes lit with excitement, as Amelia's hands went protectively to her chest, and then she fell clumsily to the ground in front of him. Tristan bubbled with laughter.

"Oh my, you stopped that bad boy." Jordan pretended with her son, as she moved from Lane's embrace, and started for their children.

"Yeah, and her died, mommy!" Tristan celebrated, as he ran happily to Lane, and climbed into his arms.

"I'm a good angel; like daddy, mommy!" Tristan insisted, as his chubby hands clapped either side of Lane's face.

"You are?" Jordan laughed.

"Yep," Tristan bounced happily in Lane's arms.

Jordan tuned to see Amelia frowning, as if something that Tristan had said was not registering well with her. Amelia's amber eyes seemed deep in thought. Never before had Jordan felt so connected to her daughter than in this moment; for she knew with bitter certainty it was the 'like daddy' portion of Tristan's excited declaration that had brought so much unhappiness to that sweet face.

Jordan had grown up in a house filled with all of her kinsmen, everyone was blood related to her, and yet she had never once felt tied to one of them in a way that she could for a surety know that this was who she was or this was who she would be when she grew up. Even her mother, as much as Jordan had loved and cherished her had not been someone who looking back; Jordan would have wanted to pattern her life after. She would never willingly allow her children to grow up behind enemy lines because she had sold out to a false doctrine that would tell her that her only hope would be, to subject her life and the life of her children, to the ugliness of a man like her father; an ugliness that tainted the life of her brother until he became the physical and spiritual image of their father.

Now, as Jordan watched Amelia, as she tried to find her place amongst those that shared no bloodlines with her, Jordan prayed for the grace to overcome that hurdle. It would never be blood that would be the defining lines of family. Jordan was living proof that all the important traits had done nothing to protect her from those who shared its viscous quality. It was the very people in her home who shared in her bloodline that had dealt her the harshest of blows, and delivered her over to a reprobate mind, Satan, to do with as he saw fit.

Jordan refused to let something, as trivial as blood cloud the mind of her precious daughter. "But you know what?" Jordan prompted Tristan while gauging Amelia's response.

"What?" Tristan shouted, still brimming with joy that he had displayed characteristics of his father.

"We can all do anything through Christ who strengthens us! Did you know that?" Jordan asked, as she touched Tristan's cherub face. She turned to Amelia.

"Did you know that all of us, including daddy, are children of God, and that not even daddy can do anything without God?" Jordan threw out the life raft, as she prayed for her daughter to grab hold.

Amelia was listening with her whole being, now, as her eyes glistened like amber liquid in the morning sun.

"So me and you have super powers too, mama?" Amelia's timid question barely crossed the distance.

Jordan summoned all of her training, as an agent, as she leaped into the air into a summersault. She landed silently in front of Amelia, and just as suddenly, claimed her from the ground and tossed her small body high into the air. Amelia careened high above Jordan. She screamed, as her arms and legs flailed wildly in search of something that she could clutch. Abruptly, her body was safely in Jordan's arms.

"Wow! You threw sissy high, mommy!" Tristan scrambled from Lane's arms, no longer beaming over the traits that tied him to his father. His legs wobbled slightly, as he ran to Jordan.

Jordan smiled at Tristan, as he wrapped his chubby arms around her leg. Her emerald eyes searched the amber pools of Amelia's shocked eyes. "Yes, Baby!" Jordan said in a matter-a-fact fashion; "You and mama, too." Jordan smiled, as she leaned in and rubbed noses with Amelia. Jordan allowed a quick peak over her shoulder.

Lane was already walking toward them. His face was filled with pride. His eyes were so filled with unshed tears they glistened like blue diamonds.

Amelia's arms draped tightly around Jordan's neck, as she peered resolutely back; "I love you, mama!" Amelia announced proudly.

"I love you, my beautiful ray of sunshine!" Jordan searched Amelia's eyes for a moment. She needed her to really listen, now; to know that every word she was about to hear would be completely true. "You belong to me and daddy! God gave you to us, just as he gave Tristan to us..." Jordan's eyes filled with tears. Her throat tightened with the tears that had collected there, making it hard for her to continue but she cleared her throat and went on.

"One day when you are ready, I will tell you all of the mountains God moved, and all of the bridges He helped us to cross in order for you, to be our daughter." Jordan hugged Amelia to her, as she breathed the lavender smell of her hair. All at once, like an encroaching fog standing in the wait, a salty musky odor masked the smell of lavender, and was so stifling that Jordan coughed. "But right now... you need a bath!" Jordan teased.

"Him too." Lane laughed, as he pointed to Tristan who was still hugging Jordan's leg.

Jordan smiled at Lane. She knew that he had caught onto her quick change in subject, and she was thankful.

"Aniahi said she missed the children very much, while we were away." Jordan's eyes danced, as she turned to Lane, after setting their daughter down and encouraging both children to go play.

"Did she?" Lane took her cue, as he moved to her side, and watched for only a moment, as their children found several of the tribe's children playing games only a few feet away.

"She did." Jordan moved slowly into Lane's arms. "I would really like to check on our special place." Her eyes smoldered, as her hand traced the contours of his muscular arm. "It's been a while, and I wouldn't want the place to think that we have forgotten about it." Jordan cooed. Standing on her tip toes, she gently brushed her lips against his, careful not to be too forward with her intentions; she could remember, all too well what happened the last time that the two of them had given themselves over to an untapped passion. In some ways it was harder now that they had ventured into the depths of that passion... knowing what lies beneath, made the desire to cross the borders of that wonderful land all the more enticing.

"I wouldn't want the magic to be lost because we have been gone so long. I think the place needs us." Jordan breathed throatily as she abruptly pulled back and turned to the children.

Lane stood swaying in the breeze, glued to her every word. His eyes shot to her, as his lips were still puckered awaiting the promised kiss that never quite blossomed into the promise. Jordan glanced sideways, her eyes filled with light and her hand shot mockingly to her lips, as she started to laugh.

"Really?" Lane's eyebrows raised, as he moved so quickly that he seemed to blur into the shadows of the tree-covering. Jordan tried to move out of reach, but was a minute too late. He claimed her easily lifting her into the air and started purposefully to Aniahi's tent.

"Lane, put me down." Jordan whispered. "The kids, what will they think?" Jordan continued to counter his efforts, with little effect on his intent. The children started to laugh, as they ran behind him toward Aniahi's tent. Finally, reaching the healer's tent, Lane stuck his head inside.

"Hello." The healer smiled. Her English was getting so much better. She had wanted to someday go to the states, and Lane had encouraged her to listen to Amelia when she spoke the language. The two of them had made such an impact on each other's lives that it was breathtaking to watch. It was as though, Amelia had been destined to walk the same path as Aniahi.

"Hello." Lane returned the warm greeting. "I need to take Jordan to the special place to show her the magic still exists." Lane admitted.

"Lane!" Jordan admonished, with a shove to his massive arm.

"Shhh, Honey, can't you see that Aniahi and I are talking." Lane reprimanded, as if Jordan were an unruly child disrupting adults in an important conversation.

Jordan's brow furrowed, as she defiantly crossed her arms and waited for the 'adult', conversation to be over, so she could get even.

"Sorry about the interruption, as I was saying..." Lane cast an irritated glare at Jordan, and then turned back to the medicine woman. "Jordan seems to think that the magic of a place no longer exists, once the people that inhabit its borders have gone. I intend to show her that the magic of a place is not dependent of the people that are around" Lane informed.

Aniahi was smiling so big. Jordan's face filled with warmth, and her cheeks turned crimson, as she waited for the conversation about her marital magic to end.

Aniahi crossed the small tent, and took Jordan's face in her hands. "Magic already within." Aniahi smiled, as her hand fell lower to Jordan's stomach and rested there for a moment.

Jordan's face went pale, as her eyes moved to where the woman was touching her. Finally, with some effort she made her gaze go to Lane's eyes. She expected to see fear there. She expected the moment of laughter and teasing to be overcome by that fear, but instead, in the depths of his eyes was the trust that had come, since the safe birth of their son. Her body should have been torn to bits by the large Nephilim offspring of a fallen angel, growing in her womb, but instead because of the power and grace of an Almighty God, she had given birth to Tristan; without issue.

Now, as she looked deep into the depths of her husband's smoldering blue eyes, she knew that there was no change. The magic may already be within, as the medicine woman had claimed but the magic that was burning in Lane's eyes would be enough to fill any place's borders.

"Will you watch the children?" Lane asked Aniahi in her native tongue.

Jordan was sure that the woman had given her consent to the task, but she could not think past the burning desire that was clouding her ever vanishing thoughts.

C H A P T E R

54

Rays of sunlight beamed through the canopy of trees, casting a warm glow over the crystal water. The slight rippling on the liquid surface made the light seem to dance rhythmically to the beating of the distant drums. Lane's heart felt, as though it was somehow tied to those very drums, and that they were encouraging its chambers to pump. Thump, thump, thump... floated on the wind; delivering their ominous promise, but Lane couldn't allow the dreaded call to claim his attention. He was already too far beneath his wife's spell.

Lane carried Jordan to the water's edge, as he breathed in the lavender sent of her hair. He allowed his eyes to take in the long, simple, brown robes that she wore. Her auburn hair, glistened in the sunlight, as it cascaded over her shoulders, and bounced with the gentle sway of his walking. Her emerald eyes danced with untapped passion, as she took in the magical cove. It was their place, given to them by a woman of the Cadotion tribe. Though it was not truly hers to give, the secret of its existence was.

The Cadotion woman's husband had discovered the beautiful place many years before. Like Lane and Jordan, their marriage had been a budding minefield of raw passion. The woman had recognized that similarity in Lane and Jordan's marriage, and had confided its glorious anonymity to the young couple.

For all of its beauty, the Cadotion village held no secret place that a married couple could enjoy the bountiful gifts bestowed upon them in the form of intense emotion; a gift from the Creator of all. This place was, now their own.

Lane sat Jordan down. His eyes moved possessively over her body, and then stopped at her still flat abdomen. His eyes filled with tears, as his hands moved to the sides of her stomach. He gently took a knee. Untying the robe, he revealed only the sun-kissed brown of her beautiful waist. Tears streamed down his face, as he gently kissed the tiny life that had the blessing of growing beneath such a loving and passionate heart. His lips pressed gently to the flat surface that would very soon announce the life budding beneath. His eyes filled with tears, again, as his head shook slightly.

"Amazing..." He appraised in a whisper meant only for Jordan. "After all that you went through: the beating at the hands of a crazed killer, long periods with no food or water, and the blast that nearly cost you your vision; the stress, alone should have been enough to forfeit this precious life. Yet, here you are: still living, still clinging to life beneath your mother's heart." Lane kissed the place he knew that precious life to be thriving again.

"You will always know that you are loved. Never will you doubt..." Lane was holding on to her, as his hands trembled, and his lower lip started to quiver.

"Lane, what is this about? All of our children have been miracles. Amelia should have never even met us, much less have been one of our children. Yet, a bridge so vast as to connect more than two continents... it connected two worlds: light and darkness was transverse, so that we might be together.

"I was barren because of the cruelness of my father. Yet, God allowed you to cast out the demon, possessing me, and in so doing, I was healed. .. I was healed of every past scar: physical, mental, and spiritual. That bridge covered a gap, so deep and wide that I can't imagine the vast parameters that such a canyon would encompass, but it happened. God allowed us to be together, and that union resulted in the conception of Tristan." Jordan pulled his head up to face her.

"Tristan is a Nephilim, Lane... He is the offspring of the fallen angels, that alone, should have killed me, but God had other plans in mind for us, just like He has other plans now."

Jordan turned to look at the horizon. The skyline blurred with lazy blues and purples, a hint of pink streaking through the center of the glorious masterpiece connected the pastel-haze in the most artistic way; only God...

Lane, still kneeling, waited for her to finish. Jordan was like that. She had to think things through, sometimes in mid-thought, she would shift gears, and start another topic but if someone cared enough listen—and Lane did—they were able to connect the dots... Lane was sure this was one of those times. So much was said that people did not mean. Lane loved that about her. He loved that she did not waste her words. Everything that she said had meaning, and was said to accommodate a purpose... though he sometimes had to listen harder, or dig deeper in order to reach that deeper meaning.

When Jordan turned back to Lane, she looked like nothing more than an apparition come to judge his wrong doings. Her eyes shone with the weary days past. Her countenance was still the delicate flower of youth, but was somehow, older for the experiences of the last month.

"Tell me, what about this particular miracle leaves you in such an enamored state." The simple command was not lost on Lane. Though her eyes filled with the smile playing on her lips, the usual life that filled her smile seemed in some way absent. Jordan was tired. He knew, but more than that, she was tired of the worry. She wanted more than anything to relax in the moment and be able to enjoy their lives as others did. She was thankful for all that God had allowed them and for the ability to treasure life.

Being with the Cadotion villagers had enriched their lives, and the lives of their children, but at times, she longed for a place that was theirs, alone. She just wanted to breathe, to relax, and not look over her shoulder, as she navigated their children through life. It seemed that every time a doubt, a concern, or anything that called that stability into question was voiced, her dream of serenity floated further from her reach, and now, Lane was bringing those concerns into view. He was the one moving her dream further out of reach. He hated feeling that was true. He would give anything to wipe the worry from her exquisite green eyes. To take away the time that had settled unmercifully over her achingly beautiful face because of the last month but he knew that it was not in his power. Only time would erase what horrors lay beneath the surface in the aftermath of such distress. God would be with her. He would wipe away all of her tears, and Lane would somehow move past the concern that lay in the root of his soul; the belief that he had let her down.

"Not the miracle." Lane's breath came in exaggerated pulls.

"What then, honey? What is it?" Jordan's face seemed to etch even deeper in the concern that her hope was flying, still further from her reach.

Lane's heart was breaking. He had ignored all of the signs: the exhaustion, the increased appetite, with nothing more to feel the hunger... the thought nearly toppled him. He couldn't stand the idea that Jordan, and the baby had been hungry, and he had treated it as any other mission. Sometimes in the field there just wasn't enough food. You had to move on, and ignore the ache; it's not like the food or water would magically start flowing in just because some missionaries landed on the spot, though Lane had seen his share of miracles in the field. It was more likely than not, that the missionaries would be afflicted by the same issues of the people they had gone to save, at least, until provisions could arrive, or wells could be tapped into water supplies cleaned. . . But, this was no mission like he had ever been on. This was life or death from the start. This was walking behind enemy lines, and demanding they relinquish authority over an entire corporation of killers.

There were other signs that he had ignored, as well... all of which had, or should have, pointed to the obvious... she was pregnant. Smells that had never bothered her before, he had ignored it all, and allowed her to be placed in the face of danger many times over. He had allowed her to venture behind the walls of the enemy with him, as if she were some soldier for hire, and not the mother of his children... not the woman that was now carrying another life, created by their union, their love. He had vowed to protect her, but instead, had served her up to the same evil that had so many times in the past threatened to claim her very soul.

Jordan knelt down in front of him, and took his anguished face in her hands. "Please tell me what you mean. I want this behind us. I want to enjoy this life growing inside of me. I want us to be together, and for the first time not look over our shoulders." Jordan was speaking, as though she had picked the thoughts out of his head, only moments after they had sprayed their evil poison throughout his splintered psyche.

"I know..." Lane exhaled. His eyes looked straight into her soul, as he tried to collect the words. "I'm so sorry. I should have never let you go into that house. I should have protected you. Instead, I was strapped..." Lane's shoulders fell forward, as he thought about his time on the table in the farmhouse. He had been rendered helpless because he had lost focus. His hands cupped his face. He pulled back and looked at his hands. The large contours of such capable hands—they had been useless to him, no more than extensions of an un-functioning unit, his hands may, as well be the hands of a child. He had acted out in much the same way that a child would, given the same circumstance. He had lent his will to hers, he had stepped back, and allowed the adults to make the call but the adult making the call was his pregnant wife. She had already been under stress, and her only ally was a former partner with dormant skills, and a half- angel husband, acting as though he were no more than a child in her command.

"Jordan, you needed me. I promised to protect you. Instead, I allowed you to walk around like some GI-Joe while I took your flank, and waited for your command." Lane was crushed, as the words finally bubbled up and breached the surface.

"Is that what this is about?" Jordan's brows knit together, as she pulled back from him. "Always having to pet some man's ego, Are you kidding me? You have a problem with taking orders from a woman?" Jordan was brooding. Her chest heaved, as she stormed back to the tree line. She whirled back on him. "I expect this from other men, Lane, but you?" Her face was a mask of hurt and anger. Her eyes stormed with the tornado of heated emotion that she was feeling.

Lane's head was spinning. Had he said something wrong? What was this about? Jordan would be emotional, and sure, her mood swings when she was pregnant, at times were enough to give him whiplash... But, what about his comment made her think. . . Lane was on his feet. He moved with the speed of light, as he breezed in front of her and blocked her path to the woods. He would not allow the serenity of their cove to be torn apart by some misunderstanding.

"Jordan, I am not saying that I had a problem with you being my leader in the field because you are a woman. You should know better than that." Lane was irritated that she would even think that. He had, if anything, encouraged her to become better at the skills she possessed. He liked that she was capable of taking care of herself. He just did not feel that she should have to while carrying their child.

"Then you tell me, Lane why you would think it better for you, a missionary of The Truth to assume command in that situation." Jordan looked up into his eyes. Though he towered over her, Jordan never looked so magnificent than she did in that moment, as she defended her right to take control. She was a soldier. She had worked long and hard. She had withstood many a horrible circumstance that would give her the authority to take charge in the most frightening of circumstances. Lane knew that better than anyone. She was capable, but the infant growing beneath her heart was not.

Still Jordan, not fully understanding Lane's concern squared her shoulders, as she demanded the answers. "You tell me what about that screamed we need the skills of a missionary right now other than prayer." Jordan turned away from him and walked purposely back to the water's edge. "You tell me how you could have known that I was pregnant when even I didn't know, and then tell me why all of that matters now. Lane, tell me why all of that ugly has to taint every good thing about our lives. You tell me, Lane. You tell me why you can't take your own advice. Why are you the only one on this planet not in need of a Savior? Why are you the only one allowed to take control, if there is no control?"

Jordan moved to him, and placed her hands on his arms, and then moved them further up to his face. She pulled his face to hers, as she tenderly kissed each of his cheeks, and then his lips. She pulled back, and in a whisper meant only for him, she continued. "Tell me."

Lane pulled her up into his arms, and carried her out into the water. Her robes floated on the surface. He pulled her out until they were deeper still, leaving her robes to float partially on the sand and in the water. The sunlight lit the lighter tints of her hair, making it appear to be on fire. Their eyes never moved off of each other's as they ventured further into the safety of the water.

As the water lapped luxuriously against their bodies, Lane contemplated Jordan's words. Had he really stood in righteous indignation on his throne of Christianity? Had he held himself to some higher, unreachable standard while waiting for others to fail miserably because after all, they were only human? Was that even what she meant? Had she truly understood that his concerns were not just for her safety, but for the safety of their unborn child? Lane had no answers but oddly, in that lack of information, there was no confusion. He felt only contentment: God was in control, it was not his place to guide the lives of others; he was after all only human.

Soon he would leave for the states, so that Kirsten could face, and move beyond her fears. Jordan was afraid that her grandfather's past would be too much for her to bear. The fear was so paramount to who Jordan was that it made her question her faith... would her faith be strong enough to accommodate such a blow to the very foundation it had been built upon? Lane had been quick to denounce that fear, and tell her to leave it alone. Why? Did he know better than Jordan what it would take for her to move past the obstacles in her walk with Christ; she needed to draw closer to her Lord, and the only way to do that would be to walk through those things that kept her away. Leaning on God, when you feel you know better than He does, is impossible. Lane could see that, now. He had in some way—no matter how small-allowed his belief that he was the one in control and that he knew better to stand in the way of his own relationship with Christ. He had leaned on his own understanding of what he thought God wanted for far too long. . . it had almost cost him, Jordan, it had almost cost him the ability to enjoy the life of his coming son and now, it was about to taint the shores of their special place. Lane knew it was time to let what he 'knew better' take a back seat to the things that God knew better and could definitely do better!

Lane pulled back, and held Jordan's shoulders, as he searched her eyes. There in the depths of their emerald pools, he could see the truth. A fear lived behind their emerald veil that was so much deeper than any fear either of them had ever known; a fear of loss so great it could stagger the foundation of their worlds... It was a fear that mirrored his fear. They were afraid to lose each other. It was that very fear that was guiding every step that the both of them made. The fear had grown roots the first day he had come to her in front of her family home. She had been crying out for help after nearly killing her niece, Penny. Holding Jordan in his arms, seeing the fear, then that she could not face, the fear that she denied with her whole being... it was the same then, as now, but it had been left unchecked and allowed to grow. It had infiltrated places in their lives so private, and so utterly forbidden to any other entity, other than God.

Lane could see, now that Jordan had been right. His need to control everything had proven that he was in need of a Savior, a fact that he knew all along, but was operating as if it were not true. He had long ago accepted Christ into his life, but he had along the way become his own stumbling block. He had allowed his angelic side to color his judgment. He had capabilities that at times could be intoxicating, but every ability had been given as a gift from the Savior, he so desperately needed. He had forgotten that God was in control. He called the shots; nothing could or would happen to Jordan, without God allowing it to happen. (See: Job, King James Version, bible).

Instead, of believing that living that knowledge, Lane had tried to manipulate everything around her, to keep her safe from harm but that need, had not begun with the life growing under her heart; it was an innate part of him, awakened the moment God had joined their hearts. .. protecting Jordan was his job, but fear was never meant to be a part of that occupation; that need.

Lane smiled, as he pulled Jordan protectively to him. Never again, He thought. He would never again allow the enemy to contaminate such a pure part of their love with his lies. There was no need to fear. He was not in control, and that was the good news! God is in control, and always has been! He was not made with a spirit of fear! (2Timothy 1:7).

Lane threaded his fingers into her hair and gently tilted her head back to expose her long-supple neck. Bending his head, Lane trailed feather light kisses up to her ear.

"I love you." Lane breathed, as he tentatively nibbled at the lobe of her ear.

"I love you." Jordan whispered huskily, as goose bumps filled her neck and shoulders. "Are you going to tell me?" She asked softly while arching into his touch. Lane was amused at the part of her brain that was dying hard to their earlier conversation.

"I know what I can tell you." Lane teased.

"Mmhhh," Jordan moaned, as Lane pulled his hands from her hair and traced the valley between her breasts.

"This place has definitely, not lost the magic." Lane teased, as he allowed his mouth to, at last, claim the place his finger had been.

"Definitely, not," Jordan conceded with a throaty sigh.

All thought evaded Lane's mind, as they ventured deeper into the water, and the depths of their desire. Long moments passed of tender embraces, and heated touches before they returned to the village.

Jordan lay on the animal pelts used for their bed, contemplating the new life growing inside of her, and the love they had shared a few hours earlier in their special place.

"How do you think Penny is doing?" Jordan finally asked. Jordan had wanted so much for Penny to move back to the Cadotion village with them, but Penny had different plans for her future. Penny wanted to finish high school despite her family's unsatisfactory life style; Penny had high scores in school. She also intended to attend classes at the two year college in Morristown for counseling. She would then transfer to a four year school in New York.

Penny had come to terms with her new found freedom rather quickly. She did not want to waste time getting back to life. It had been a struggle before trying to maintain her GPA, with all of the negative influences around her, but now under John and Cynthia's guidance, Jordan knew she would be fine. Still, she worried... should she have insisted that Penny stay with her. Should Jordan have fought harder, was that what Penny really needed; to feel whole... did she need Jordan to keep her with her family, or had she made the best decision? Would allowing Penny to spread her wings where she felt safest to do so be the best for her?

Nick, on the other hand had seen so much ugly that he felt a slower pace was just what he needed. He now shared a tent with a young tribesman that would someday make a wonderful elder to the tribal council. Lane felt the young man's influence over Nick would be worth more than anything he or Jordan might be able to say or do.

Lane had spent long hours with Haywalo, the name translated happy hunter, teaching him English. The name suited Haywalo, though his father had been a hunter for the tribe, and had probably given Haywalo the name to direct his path to a more traditional style of hunting, the boy was a hunter no less. Haywalo seemed to soak up every word. He devoured knowledge hanging on every nuance of the new language he was learning.

The thought saddened Jordan, for American children. Had they been so pampered that they would throw away opportunities with little thought that people from other nations would gladly accept? Jordan didn't know, but her prayers were with the children of America. She hoped that kind of trivial treatment of something so precious, as to change the future of one so completely would not lead to the demise of her beloved home.

Nick planned to return to the United States with Lane when he took Kirsten back. Jordan couldn't help, but wonder what this separation had meant for his and Penny's relationship. Relationships built on such disastrous beginnings had odds mounted against their success without any other issues added.

"I think she's fine. You know John and Cynthia will take good care of her." Lane pulled Jordan into his arms. "Let's not borrow trouble from tomorrow that may never come." Lane squeezed her arm, as he lightly kissed her cheek.

"Lane?"

"What baby?"

"How many children do you think we will have?" Jordan had been thinking about this long and hard. The idea of a big family had never crossed her mind, but was fast becoming a part of her thoughts.

"I don't know, but I don't have to." Lane sighed contentedly.

"You don't have to?" Jordan's brow furrowed. Was Lane losing his mind? He doesn't have to think about the number of children they might have? How would they feed them? The Cadotion village was a small village, and there were the struggles of feeding the villagers. Adding to the numbers could not be a good thing. They were missionaries; after all, their goal was to improve the situation, to improve the status quo, so to speak... not to make matters worse.

"Nope," Lane said flatly. "It has recently occurred to me that my life is not my own. It belongs to God. Therefore, it is God's business, and He will decide what is best for my future. He hasn't steered me wrong so far." Lane's calm assurance seemed unique, given the circumstance.

Jordan realized that she had lent so much of her time to worry that she had forgotten a very important principle... God was in control! Jordan lay in Lane's arms for a while contemplating his words. God had moved mountains, and bridged continents... worlds to ensure she would have a happiness she never even knew to hope for. Soon Jordan could hear the rhythmic breathing of her family sleeping: a family she never knew she would have. Jordan rubbed her abdomen reassuring the tiny life there all would be well and in that moment she knew no matter what struggles the future may hold: Mr. Stanton, her grandfather's unknown past, Kirsten's fear, Penny's future, or a house full of children. Lane was right, God was in control, and that was all that mattered!

BLACK HEART REDEMPTION

CHAPTER

1

Morning dawned like any other: the hoots of animal calls dying on the wind, and the sound of the children's quiet whispers, as they tried not to wake their parents.

Jordan scooted closer to Lane. The chill in the air was undeniable. It was as if overnight winter was upon them.

Though she grew tired of the drums in the distance, everything felt perfect. Jordan ignored the tireless efforts of the unknown tribe; they were probably just readying themselves for the hunt. Some of the tribes, Lane had explained, were still immersed in the traditions of their forefathers. The drums were played in celebration of the impending hunt. Nothing more.

"I love you." Her voice seemed to betray her thoughts before her mind could rationalize them.

"I love you too." Lane admitted as he rolled over and pulled her body closer to his. Laughter erupted in hushed tones, from the other side of the tent.

"I think we have an audience." Jordan teased.

"You might be right, but I think I should go investigate." Lane sent out the warning.

A squeal split the air as both children fought for safety under their pallet of furs.

"No use hiding. I'll find you!" Lane moved across the tent with an exaggerated slow-gate. The menacing glare he must have held in his eyes was mirrored back in the feigned fear of Amelia's and Tristan's countenances.

Snatching the cover away, Lane roared like a beast, crazed with murderous intent. Amelia and Tristan screamed, as they ran pointedly to Jordan.

"She won't save you!" Lane carried on, weaving and bobbing as he crouched even lower. He made giant-exaggerated steps across the tent that seemed completely in place with his foreboding six-foot five stature.

Jordan choked back the laughter that was bubbling up inside of her.

"Yes she will!" Jordan hoisted the declaration. As a child stood behind each of her legs, peering out to see if their mother's assertion had made a difference in the intent of the viscous predator their father pretended to be. Giggles reigned supreme as the children hid further behind Jordan's legs, waiting for the verdict they knew would soon come: Would their father quiet his ranting? Would the savage beast he pretended to be, still under the command of their mother, or would he pursue them all?

Jordan knew too, that it could go either way. She stood ready for him to pounce. The adrenaline soaked through her veins as she stood at the helm of her feigned fort. She loved this game. It reminded her of her days with Black Heart, without the ugliness of death's dark shadow looming around every corner; calling her name.

She had been an agent for Black Heart, and like other agents, she was brought into the agency under false pretenses. Through a collective effort, Jordan, Lane, and some of their friends had been able to bring the dark dealings of Black Heart out into the light of truth.

Mr. Stanton, the Head of the Department, lay in a coma, still fighting for his life after a suicide attempt. Kirsten, one of the child-agents that Stanton had organized in an attempt to dull Jordan's senses and end her life, had been prompted by Garrison, Jordan's former partner to make a phone call. During the call, Kirsten used a voice distorter. She implied that every dark secret and every cruel deed Stanton had ever committed was known. Then Kirsten encouraged Mr. Stanton to turn to channel nine for the evening news report.

Lane had taken the story about Black Heart to a news reporter he knew well, Jerrod Fuller. Lane met Jerrod while on a mission trip in Honduras. Lane had immediately liked Jerrod. Though he was a reporter, Jerrod had always been candid in his reports of the news.

Though Jerrod had not been the actual reporter to divulge the truth on the eleven o'clock news showing, it had been his script that was read.

Jordan smiled slyly at Lane's still menacing, feigned-monster attempt. He was so into the character that it was almost believable. Amelia and Tristan alternated between giggling, and clutching the back of her legs. In moments like these, she found it easy to forget about the impending separation that they would soon endure.

It would be so easy to let her guard down, but she did not want him to see the fear and sadness that she felt. She tried to keep thoughts of his leaving, and how terribly she would miss him from belying the truth in her eyes. Theirs was a special bond, forged by God. A love that had been ordained by the Creator of life before they were born. Though the attempt was probably in vein, Jordan would make every effort to keep her anguish of his leaving from Lane's knowledge.

The serenity that she felt while nestled safely in his embrace would soon be forfeit. Lane would be headed back to the states to take Kirsten home in only a few short hours. Jordan would be left to face a world that she had only just begun to understand. In so many ways she could understand Amelia's and Tristan's need for security in the face of an imagined foe. Just as Lane loved their children, the people of the Cadotion village loved their family. Still, Jordan found herself quaking in the sight of their imagined threat. Opening up to others had never been one of her strong suits, but with Lane's ever-present example to draw upon she was able to manage.

After he was gone… Jordan couldn't finish the contemplation. She didn't want to imagine the bumbling mess she was bound to make of things in his absence.

Jordan was still lost in the revere of what ifs when Lane abruptly straightened from the menacing crouch he had adopted. Fear registered in his eyes, but only for an instant. Rocking back on his heels, Lane stared intently at the back wall of the tent. At first Jordan laughed. It seemed out of place for Lane to exhibit fear while trying to elicit fear, but just as quickly the thought passed. Jordan turned her attention to the back of the tent. She studied the furs that lined the wall: different shades of browns stood out in stark comparison to the red undertones. Some of the furs were rabbit, while other of the hides were dear…

Jordan searched with a deeper attention to detail, but still nothing about the wall, as far as she could tell would cause such a reaction. Then suddenly, as if the wall faded out of existence the sound of drums finally made it into their haven.

Jordan hadn't noticed the drums before, or more to the point she had become desensitized to their presence because they had been a part of the atmosphere for the better part of the week. Now though, as she listened, the sound of the distant drums grew, filling the air with an insistent hunger that seemed foreign and yet personal in the same moment.

"Is that the same drums that we heard from the cove two days ago?" Jordan turned her intent emerald gaze back to the rear of the tent. She half expected the material to fade, and the distant drummers to materialize.

"It's the Manerky." Lane explained calmly, though something about the ready stance he adopted seemed… Jordan studied him, while trying to fill in the word that best described what she saw. His shoulders squared as his fist tightened at his side. His beautiful blue eyes had lost the angelic kindness, and had taken on the menacing intent of an eagle, searching the prairie floor for prey. Her six-foot five, light brown hair with blond streaks, blue eyed half angel, stood glaring at the back of the tent; not a trace of love caressed his heavenly visage. He was now the intent hunter with a foe in his sights. He would track and kill the threat to his family!

A thought occurred to Jordan as she watched her husband evolve into the ready hunter. "Why do the drums sound closer?" Jordan turned her attention back to the far wall of the tent.

"Because they are." Again, Lane sounded too calm.

Jordan looked then at the golden brown face of her daughter. It had been through a brutal attack on the Cadotion tribe that Amelia had come to be adopted into their family. Her mother had died during childbirth. Her father, while protecting the Cadotion village against the onslaught of the raiders, had met with an early death as well. It had been the Manerky tribe that had been responsible for that death, and destruction. Now, as she listened to their drums filter through the air, Jordan knew that the past was upon them.

Amelia's caramel eyes peered out from her angelic face. In that moment, Jordan was helplessly aware of the onslaught of terror that would befall them. The Manerky was an opportunistic tribe that fed off the weakness of the surrounding villages.

The Cadotions, the tribe that their family now lived in, were not a warring village. Their survival had hinged on two very important components: their all-consuming love for one another, and their keen intellect. The Cadotions were experts in survival. Each member of the tribe had a specific title. The title was indicative of the abilities that each particular tribesman possessed. None of those titles would paint any of the tribesmen as an avid hunter. None of the Cadotion villagers were killers. Their survival skills were grounded in everyday living, not the victory of the hunt.

For a long time, the threat that the Manerky represented had been silenced. Several of the surrounding tribes had issued a threat: if the Manerky raided any of the surrounding villages, each member of their tribe would be annihilated; every man, woman, and child.

"But the treaty?" Jordan threw the desperate plea out, though she knew it was pointless.

"Winter approaches." Lane said simply. "Most of the surrounding tribes have moved on in search of a warmer climate." Lane studied her eyes for a moment. She knew he would shield her from the truth, if it would help, but a lie was no shield. It would leave her unprepared to deal with the horrors to come.

Jordan turned then, to their three-year-old son, Tristan. His huge blue eyes were still filled with the anticipation of the attack. She gulped back the panic that filled her throat, and threatened to cut off her life's breath. Little did her sweet boy know, there was an attack on the horizon, and it would leave his untainted existence soiled, forever in the destruction of its foreboding aftermath...